UNRAVELING THE STARS

A Starstruck Novel

BRENDA HIATT

with

BETHANY BARBER

dolphin star
PRESS

Unraveling the Stars

A Starstruck Novel

Copyright 2022 by Brenda Hiatt
Cover art by Ravven Kitsune

Dolphin Star Press

ISBN: 978-1-947205-31-4

✦

Dedication

For everyone who feels insignificant
You are far more important than you know!

THE STARSTRUCK SERIES BY BRENDA HIATT

Starstruck
Starcrossed
Starbound
Starfall

.⁺.

Fractured Jewel: A Starstruck Novella
The Girl From Mars
The Handmaid's Secret
Convergent
Yuletide Perils: A Starstruck Novella
Unraveling the Stars

Contents

1.	Open case	1
2.	Variable attraction	10
3.	Circumstantial evidence	14
4.	Opening tip off	22
5.	Electrical resistance	31
6.	Dead end	35
7.	Alternating current	43
8.	False lead	49
9.	Impedance	57
10.	Supposition	64
11.	Fast break	72
12.	Differential pressure	79
13.	Investigation	87
14.	Benefit-cost analysis	95
15.	Red herring	100
16.	Degrees of freedom	108
17.	Hypothesis	114
18.	Equilibrium	123
19.	Rebound	130
20.	Sequence of events	137
21.	Energy transfer	145
22.	Cloak-and-dagger	152
23.	Gravitational pull	161
24.	Fact pattern	169
25.	Timeout	177
26.	Destructive interference	182
27.	Alternative hypothesis	189
28.	Compensation	197
29.	Deductive reasoning	205
30.	Surface tension	215
31.	Process of elimination	220
32.	Alley-oop	227
33.	Celestial mechanics	235
34.	Elementary	243
35.	Binding energy	250
36.	Cliffhanger	258

37. Chain reaction 264

38. Narrow escape 273

39. Swish 280

40. Stress-strain curve 288

41. Denouement 292

A Brief History of Nuath 299

A Martian Glossary 303

Acknowledgments 307

About the Author 309

Open case

Deb

GLANCING at the clock on the gym wall, I frown. The Winter Formal is nearly half over, and I've barely made any progress toward getting to know my date better.

"Did you go to many dances at your old school?" I ask him as the current song ends.

Lucas, the guy I've been crushing on since the day he arrived at Jewel High three months ago, shakes his head. "Not really, no."

"This must be your first one here?" I persist, determined to draw him out at least a little.

"Um, yeah, I heard we just missed Jewel High's Homecoming." It's the longest sentence he's said to me so far.

I nod. "That's right. It was the very weekend before you all started school here. It looks like all of you have settled in pretty well by now, though?"

"I think so. My brother's definitely enjoying it here."

We both turn to look at Liam, Lucas's identical twin, who's laughing over something with my best friend, Bri, a short distance away.

"It definitely shows on the basketball court," I comment, grinning.

Bri, who goes to all the games, claims Liam's nearly as good a player as Sean O'Gara, who took Jewel to State in basketball last year.

"Yeah. It definitely does." There's an edge to Lucas's words that makes me glance up in time to see him smoothing a frown.

Before I can think how to ask him about it, the next song starts, too loud to talk over while dancing.

Is he jealous of how well his brother plays? Seems unlikely, when Lucas never even tried out for the team, or acts like he's into sports at all. Liam, on the other hand, is as big a sports nut as Bri, which is why she was more interested in him from the start. When he asked her to tonight's dance, she was at least as thrilled as I was when Lucas asked me—though maybe not as astonished.

I sneak another peek at Lucas, surreptitiously admiring his strong profile, perfectly disordered dark brown hair and gray-blue eyes. Again.

From their first day at Jewel, a month into the fall semester, I was much more drawn to Lucas than Liam, even though I met Liam first. The brothers are equally gorgeous, of course, and outgoing Liam *is* easier to talk to. But I sensed a quiet strength in shy Lucas, along with a certain vulnerability that captivated me from the moment I introduced myself in Art, the one class we have together.

Over the next three months, I tried multiple times to engage Lucas in conversation before, during, and after class but never made much headway. Since he hardly talked to anybody, I didn't take it personally—or let it keep me from obsessing over him. Honestly, though, I wasn't completely sure Lucas even knew my name until three days ago when, totally out of the blue, he invited me to this dance. Needless to say, I was over the moon!

Earlier this evening, when Bri and I were getting ready for the dance together, we couldn't stop talking about our luck in snagging the gorgeous Walsh twins as dates.

"Y'know, Deb," Bri said while smoothing her hair with a new cream she just bought, "if we play our cards right, tonight might be the start of two beautiful romances."

"Wouldn't that be wonderful?" I sighed. "Hey, can I try a little of that stuff?"

Bri handed me the jar with a shrug. The product was intended for Black hair, which Bri's sort of is, but I hoped it might also tame my blonde, flyaway frizz. It helped some.

By the time the boys picked us up for the dance at Bri's house, we both agreed that we looked the best we ever had. Even Bri's little brother

Joey, who usually teases us whenever we're primping for dates, whistled appreciatively as we were leaving.

"Do you want to get something to drink?" I ask Lucas when yet another loud, fast dance song begins.

"Oh, um, sure," he agrees.

Together, we head toward the folded-up bleachers, where a long table holds big dispensers of water and lemonade. As we cross the school gym, I notice how he has to duck to avoid hitting a few of the lowest-hanging paper snowflakes. I don't, of course. I'm probably the shortest girl in the junior class, while Lucas is one of the taller guys—taller than M's boyfriend, Rigel, if not quite as tall as Sean.

"What was your last school like?" I ask as he hands me a paper cup of lemonade. "Bigger than Jewel, I'll bet."

"A little bigger, yeah."

When he doesn't elaborate, I try again. "Where was it exactly? Somewhere in upstate New York?" I remember Liam mentioning that in Pre-Cal class once.

Lucas nods. "Between Syracuse and Utica."

"Is that where NuAgra's headquarters used to be before Jewel?"

He flashes me an uncertain look. "Um, yeah. Though it wasn't as big as the one they built here."

"So NuAgra is expanding? Does that mean they're making progress on developing those superior crops I read they're working on? That'll be good, won't it?"

He nods again. "I think so."

"Is that what your parents do out there? Work with the new plant strains? Are they, like, botanists?"

"No, engineers. They work with the, uh, mechanical systems there."

He still looks wary, though I don't know why. I'm asking perfectly normal questions.

"Engineers? That's interesting. Is that what you want to go to college for, after high school? I remember Liam saying you're in AP Calculus, so you must be really good in math."

"Er...yeah, I guess."

Because he seems so uncomfortable, I blurt out, "Sorry. I know I'm asking a lot of questions. It's not that I'm nosy, I'm just trying to break the ice."

"Ice?" His brows go up like he's totally confused...which confuses me. "What ice?"

I blink. "You know. Break the ice. Start a conversation."

"Oh. Right. Of course." He's clearly covering. "It's, um, fine."

Has he never heard that expression before? I'm suddenly reminded of another time, when I tried to flirt with him in Art class by saying, "Penny for your thoughts." He was confused then, too, so I had to explain what *that* phrase meant. Weird.

A moment later we finish our lemonade and head back to the dance floor…just in time for a slow dance. My heart speeds up as I try to hide my nervousness.

During our first two slow dances, Lucas was a perfect gentleman, his hands never straying so much as a fraction of an inch from where they rested lightly on my shoulder blades. Totally unlike my Homecoming date, who used the slow numbers to push the limits as far as I'd let him —which wasn't very far.

Like all the others, he quickly lost interest when he discovered that Bri and M's "cute little friend" wasn't as easy as he'd hoped. I'm relieved Lucas isn't like that but, okay, also a tiny bit disappointed that he hasn't even *tried*. Yet?

This time, when I put my hands on his shoulders, I move a tiny bit closer than before, though not quite touching anywhere else. Just to see…

But though a hint of a smile suggests he noticed, Lucas doesn't take advantage, again keeping me at a perfectly respectful distance through the whole song.

Darn it.

It's looking like that goodnight kiss I've dreamed about since he asked me to the dance won't happen after all. Still, I feel like Lucas and I *might* be establishing the beginnings of what might at least become a beautiful friendship. And maybe more, eventually?

⁘

A few songs later, I notice M, Molly and Bri all heading toward the ladies' room. Eager for a chance to compare notes about our evening, I politely excuse myself to Lucas to follow them. The other three girls don't see me, so they go into the restroom before I can catch up. When I push open the door a second later, I can hear Bri already talking to the others.

"—really glad Lucas followed through and asked Deb. When I told

Liam I'd only come to the dance with him if his brother went with Deb, I was terrified he'd tell me to forget it. Which would have been *awful* because I'm having a super great time with him tonight! Luckily he did talk Lucas into asking her, and the two of them seem to be having fun together. Oh! But don't either of you *dare* tell Deb I told you that! She'd be totally mortified."

M and Molly promise not to say a word as I freeze, then back up to let the door swing silently shut in front of my face. For a second I just stand there. Then, my throat suddenly tight, I turn and head for a different bathroom the next hall over.

So *that's* why Lucas has been so meticulously polite all evening! Asking me to the Winter Formal was never his idea at all, just a favor he did for his brother and Bri. I wonder how hard Liam had to work to persuade him…?

The farther restroom is blessedly empty. I linger there until I'm sure I'm not going to cry, scolding myself for being so sensitive.

After all, Bri and I *did* ask Kira to put in a good word for us with the two Walsh brothers, I remind myself. It wasn't the first time we'd begged a friend to help us snag dates, either. Plenty of girls do that all the time. How is this any different?

Somehow, though, it is. Maybe because I've never before cared so much before about whether a boy liked me or not.

Once Lucas arrived at Jewel High, Art quickly became the class I looked forward to most—because of him. We'd barely exchanged a handful of words before I started weaving all kinds of romantic fantasies. When I caught Lucas looking my way once or twice, I imagined it meant he was attracted to me, too, just too shy to do anything about it. So when he asked me to tonight's dance, I not only felt vindicated, I started believing my dreams could come true.

Now my foolish dreams feel more like a humiliating nightmare.

Tempting as it is to hide in the bathroom until the end of the dance, it's not really a viable option. Besides, I refuse to be *that* lame and cowardly! So, after a few deep breaths to steady myself, I make my way back to the gym. There, I pause outside the open double doors for one more fortifying breath before going in to rejoin my date.

"Sorry I was gone so long," I breathlessly apologize when I reach him. "I, um, got to talking." To myself, anyway.

Rather to my surprise, Lucas's gray-blue eyes show concern. "You're okay, then? Nothing's wrong?"

"Wrong?" I try for a little laugh but it sounds brittle to my ears. "Of course not. Oh, I like this song. C'mon."

Turning away from his too-perceptive gaze, I move toward the dance floor. To my relief, he follows without probing any further.

And why would he? Even if he can tell I'm upset, there's no particular reason it should matter to him. It's not like this is a *real* date, with a girl he actually wanted to be with.

.⁺⁺

By the end of the Formal half an hour later, I've mostly overcome my disappointment. I even maintain a relatively cheerful front when Lucas again avoids touching me more than absolutely necessary during the final dance, a slow one. I keep my distance, too, embarrassed now to think how close I got to him earlier. It must have made him super uncomfortable.

When the music finally stops, Lucas surprises me with a genuine-seeming smile that makes him heart-stoppingly handsome. "Thanks for coming with me tonight, Deb. It's been fun."

I smile back. "It has." And it was…until half an hour ago. "Thanks for asking me. I, um, guess we should go find Bri and your brother, huh?"

After the four of us retrieve our coats from our lockers, we head to the parking lot, Bri and Liam continuing their earlier conversation about —what else?—sports.

"It's practically a crime that you've never had a chance to attend an NBA game in person," Bri is telling him. "If my dad can score tickets to a Pacers game this season, I'll ask him to get one for you, too. For all of you, if you want," she adds, belatedly including Lucas and me.

Lucas shrugs at exactly the same time I do. "Don't go to any trouble on my account," he says.

"Or mine." I'd hate to be a third wheel all the way to Indy and back with Bri and Liam, even if I did care about pro basketball. Which I don't.

Despite that brief moment of unity, the drive home is awkward. Liam is driving, so Bri sits up front with him while Lucas and I are in back. I'm careful to stay well on my side of the seat.

When we reach Bri's house, I immediately jump out of the car so Lucas won't feel like he has to walk me to the door. Bri, on the other hand, is pretty obviously angling for a goodnight kiss, so she waits for

Liam to come around and open her door. That means Lucas has to get out of the car, too, or look rude—which he wouldn't want to do.

"It's kind of late," Bri says when we reach her front porch, "but do you guys want to come in for a few minutes?"

"Sure, if you—" Liam starts to say when his brother gives him a tiny head shake that I probably wasn't supposed to see. "Uh, actually, I guess we'd better not. Our parents will expect us back."

Bri's disappointment is embarrassingly evident. "Oh, okay. I guess we'll, um, see you after the holidays, then."

"Unless you want to come to Monday night's game?" Liam suggests. "We also have two others scheduled over the break."

I'm pretty sure I'm the only one who notices how Lucas tenses as Bri enthusiastically agrees, happy enough now that she hardly pouts at all when the boys head back to their parents' car.

"Oh, well. No goodnight kisses, but at least we'll get to see them again before school starts back up," she says as they drive off. "Did you have as much fun tonight as I did? You looked like you did. Aren't they both so dreamy?"

"Yeah, they are," I have to agree. "And yeah, I mostly did. Have a good time, I mean."

She quirks a dark eyebrow at me. "Only mostly? C'mon, you've been mooning over Lucas Walsh for three months. Didn't he live up to your expectations?"

I just shrug.

"Okay, what did he do wrong?" she presses. "You weren't expecting a marriage proposal on your first date, were you?"

At that, my intention to keep my humiliation to myself evaporates. "Hardly. Especially considering you *forced* Liam to make him ask me to the dance," I snap.

Her brown eyes go wide and startled. "How did you— I mean— It wasn't…"

"I overheard what you told M and Molly, in the bathroom," I inform her. "I came in right behind you guys but then left before you saw me. Bri, how could you?" Again, tears threaten, this time as much from anger as humiliation.

After a moment of hesitation, she frowns, her chagrin shifting to stubbornness. "Oh, come on, Deb, I did you a favor! I put my chance with Liam on the line for you! And I know you would have done the same for me. Remember last year, how you wheedled Matt into asking me to Homecoming? You nudged Gary my way, too, at the start of this year."

I want to tell her those were different, that she never cared as much about Matt or Gary as I do for Lucas. Except I'm not ready to admit how deeply I *do* care. Maybe not even to myself. So I just shrug again, instead.

"Besides," she continues, "it's not like Liam would have asked *me* if Kira hadn't put him up to it. For all we know, Lucas would've asked you anyway, because of what she said to them both. Maybe Liam was just a little quicker following through."

"Maybe," I grudgingly admit. "Still, I…wish you'd told me."

She regards me shrewdly. "Would you have enjoyed yourself as much tonight if I had?"

"That's not—" I begin hotly, then pause. "Okay, maybe not. I'd have felt like a charity case the whole dance, instead of just the last half hour. Like I do now. At least now I know why Lucas acted so…so *proper* all evening. He barely even touched me during the slow dances." My gut twists again with embarrassment at the memory.

"Yeah, well, Liam wasn't exactly forward, either," Bri admits, surprising me a little. "And not for lack of encouragement."

That makes me feel a *little* better. "You think they belong to some really strict religion or something? I mean, there's definitely *something* different about them. About all those new NuAgra folks, really." Like not knowing what "break the ice" meant.

Bri lifts a shoulder, grinning now. "If so, it just makes the new guys more of a challenge. Gorgeous as they all are, you can't say they're not worth the effort. Of course, Molly has Tristan all locked up now, and Trina was all *over* Alan tonight. That girl is *shameless*! If you're right about them all being super religious, it's no wonder he looked so uncomfortable."

We both laugh and my earlier mortification fades. A little.

"Thanks, Bri. Sorry I snapped at you."

"No, I don't blame you. I feel really bad you heard me tell the others that—I should have just kept my big mouth shut. Still friends?" She opens her arms to me.

I step in and hug her. "Best friends," I affirm. "I'd better get home, though—it's late. And cold. G'night, Bri."

"Night, Deb."

She goes inside and I crunch through the thin layer of snow to my house next door, relieved we didn't end up in a real fight. Because Bri's not just my *best* friend, she's the only really close girlfriend I have these days. M seems to have totally adopted Molly as *her* new best friend, after spending all spring and summer in Ireland with the O'Gara family.

Sure, it gets old sometimes being referred to as Bri's "cute little friend," but she and I almost always have fun hanging out together. I'd really hate to lose that.

Especially since it's looking awfully unlikely now that I'll ever be *more* than friends with Lucas Walsh.

2

Variable attraction

Lucas

"ARE YOU OUT OF YOUR MIND?" I demand as Liam drives us away from his date's house. "I can't believe you were actually hitting on the Sovereign's best *Duchas* friend. Don't you ever think ahead?"

"I didn't hit on her!" my brother protests. "I just asked if she wanted to come to some games. She almost always does anyway, and we probably won't have very big crowds while school's out for the holidays. Just doing my part to fill the bleachers."

All I can do is shake my head. "You can't really be that blind. Didn't you see the way she looked at you? The girl's got a serious crush on you."

Liam slants me a look. "Hey, your date was looking at you the exact same way all night. But of course *you're* way too principled to ever take advantage, aren't you, Mr. Play-by-all-the-rules? Not that I'm planning to. Take advantage, I mean. I happen to like Bri a lot. She's fun, and she's as much into sports as I am. Shoot, she knows way more about most Earth sports than I do, what with her dad being on the coaching staff and all."

"No wonder you were so willing to ask her to the dance when Kira suggested it last week."

"Well...yeah. I mean, Kira obviously wouldn't have said anything unless the Sovereign was on board with the idea. And after the way I screwed up during my first game of the season, I figured I kinda owed the Sovereign a favor."

I smirk. "Very selfless of you. I guess the fact you already happened to like Bri was just a bonus?"

"Okay, maybe a little self-interest was involved," he admits. "Like I said, she's a lot of fun—though thanks to you, I almost missed out. I don't get why you dragged your heels so much on inviting Debbi Andrews. You have a class with her, don't you?"

"Art, yeah. She's a pretty good artist, too. And nice enough. But we'd barely talked all semester, so it seemed awkward to suddenly ask her to a dance."

Which it was, though that wasn't the real reason I resisted asking her. The truth is, I've been fighting a weird attraction to Deb for a while now—something that will be even harder after tonight.

"If you really do like Bri," I continue quickly, "that's even more reason not to lead her on when you know nothing can come of it. You're just setting her up for disappointment."

Liam's jaw juts out as he stares through the windshield. "Why can't anything come of it?" he demands.

Since the answer is obvious, I just look at him.

"Okay, yeah, I know she's a *Duchas*," he finally says when I don't reply. "But in case you haven't noticed, there aren't exactly enough *Echtran* girls in Jewel to go around. I mean, come on. We're almost seventeen, and nobody told us we'd have to become monks once we moved to Earth. Besides, hasn't Sovereign Emileia been encouraging us all to make friends with the locals?"

"Friends, maybe. But not—"

I break off, remembering how tempted I was to respond to Deb's flirting tonight...and how I felt during that one slow dance, when she got a little closer than usual.

"Not *more* than friends, you mean," Liam finishes when I don't. "Don't you think that's a little unfair? Why are they letting us go to a *Duchas* high school at all, if we're not allowed to—" He huffs out a frustrated breath.

"Look, I get it. I do." Way more than I'm about to admit to my brother, especially right this moment. "But you know as well as I do why we can't afford to get *too* involved with any *Duchas* girls. The more comfortable we get with them, the more likely we are to let something slip that we shouldn't. Some locals are already getting suspicious."

I don't add that Liam is one reason for that. I don't have to.

"Hey, I've been doing loads better holding back during my games," he protests, his chin jutting out defensively again. "Anyway, isn't that why they let all those locals tour NuAgra last weekend, so they could see we're not doing anything nefarious out there?"

A mirthless laugh escapes me. "Yeah, and why we had to spend days hiding or disguising every little thing in the Engineering section that might have tipped them off it's not a regular Earth company. You don't want to see all that work wasted, do you?"

Liam swallows. "No. I guess not."

The Sovereign, the *Echtran* Council and especially our parents have repeatedly impressed on us the likely consequences of the *Duchas* finding out about our Martian origins before they're ready. I'm pretty sure Liam finally gets it now, but he's always tended to act on impulse before thinking things through. Partly to make up for that, I usually try to be extra careful, to the point I probably *over*think things. But if that's what it takes to keep our family, our people safe…

"Does this mean if the girls *do* come to Monday night's game, you won't sit with them?" Liam asks after a moment. "That'll look kind of rude, don't you think? After I specifically invited them and all."

"I'll see," I reply noncommittally. "If they're already sitting with a bunch of other friends, maybe it won't matter."

Which I hope they will be. I'm already way more attracted to Deb Andrews than is safe, especially after tonight.

✦

Our parents are still up when we get home.

"How was the dance?" our mother asks, clearly trying to hide her anxiety. "Did you have fun?"

"Yeah, it was great," Liam replies, grinning. "At least, *I* had a good time."

Of course, that makes Mom shift her gaze to me. "Do you mean Lucas didn't?"

"No, I had a good time, too," I assure her with a quick glare at my brother. "Deb, my date, is so bubbly it would've been hard not to. Liam's just irritated with me because I reminded him on the way home that we need to be careful not to get too…attached."

Dad gives Liam a sharp glance. "There's not really any risk of that, is there?"

"No. Not yet." Liam's looking stubborn again. "Though I don't see what would be so risky about it, as long as we stick to our cover stories. Which we both did tonight. Right?"

I nod. "I definitely did. Luckily most of the questions Deb asked me —and she asked a lot—were about the sort of things they drummed into us before we came to Jewel. But I did realize how thin those fake histories will sound if we become *close* friends with any *Duchas*."

"Yes, it is rather a fine line we're required to walk," Mom admits, her expression now more sympathetic than worried. "Even more so for you than for us, as we spend nearly all our time around other *Echtrans*. We've only encountered our *Duchas* neighbors in the most casual of settings. I'm sure at school it's much more difficult to maintain the necessary secrecy without seeming…stand-offish to your fellow students."

"You're right," Liam agrees grumpily. "It is. Especially when the Sovereign keeps warning us that acting *too* stand-offish could make them almost as suspicious as saying something we shouldn't."

Dad sighs. "We all knew coming to Earth, and especially to Jewel, would present unique challenges. What we didn't realize was that some of the trickiest ones would fall to those of you in high school. I suppose all we can ask of any of you is that you do your best. It will likely get easier as time goes on."

"Or harder," Liam mutters, scowling.

Though I don't say so, for once I'm inclined to agree with my brother.

3

Circumstantial evidence

Deb

BY THE TIME Bri calls Monday afternoon to remind me about that night's basketball game, I've just about decided not to go. I'd hate for Lucas to think I'm still pathetically pursuing him after he made it pretty clear he's not interested.

"My mom asked if I can help her with her bookkeeping over winter break," I tell Bri—truthfully. "Why don't you go without me? It's not like I'm that into basketball." I've only been to two games this season, and then only because Bri insisted and I didn't have anything better to do those nights.

"We're not only going for the game." I can practically hear her eyes rolling. "The boys *invited* us to come. That makes it almost like a second date, which is huge! You don't want Lucas to think you're standing him up, do you?"

Since Lucas rather pointedly did *not* second Liam's invitation Friday night, I seriously doubt he'll care.

"C'mon, Deb," Bri persists. "I'll feel stupid sitting by myself."

"M and Rigel will probably be there," I say, though my resolve is already starting to waver. "You can sit with them."

"M and Rigel are doing something else tonight. I already asked her. Pleeease, Deb?"

I can't hold out against Bri's pleading. Especially since I'd rather lust over Lucas from a distance than not see him at *all* for more than two weeks.

"Okay, fine. Will your dad drive us, or should I ask Maggie to drop us off?" My older sister got home from college over the weekend for her own winter break.

"Ask Maggie. That way, maybe the guys will offer us a ride home afterward."

Though I cringe inwardly at the thought of her hinting that to them, I agree and hang up. I try not to be bothered that she called M before calling me, since they *have* been friends longer, ever since kindergarten. But over the past year the two of them seem to have grown apart a little, while Bri and I hang out with each other every day.

Maggie wants to meet up with some local friends that evening, but she agrees to drop Bri and me off at the school first.

"What time do I need to pick you up?" she asks as we get out near the gym entrance.

"Deb can call you if we don't get a ride back," Bri answers before I can. "Thanks, Maggie!"

"I'll call as soon as the game's over," I assure my sister. "Thanks. And tell Mallory and Dee I said hi."

She nods and drives off. I'm a tiny bit relieved she didn't want to come to the game with us, since being around Maggie always makes me feel dumpy in comparison. She's a full six inches taller than I am, with sleek blonde hair and a perfect figure. Short as I am, it's a constant struggle to keep my weight from creeping up. Tall girls don't realize how lucky they are in that department.

Bri's the same height as my sister, but borderline skinny instead of curvy—and her hair gives her even more trouble than mine gives me. "Come on," she urges, heading for the doors. "I want to get good seats, near the action on the court."

Near Liam, in other words.

The bleachers are still more than half empty when we get inside, probably because of the holidays. Bri makes a beeline for an open spot as close as possible to the middle of the court.

Looking around, I see Kira nearby, sitting with Tristan, Molly's boyfriend. Since Sean will be playing and Molly's down front with the other cheerleaders, that makes sense. Then I spot Lucas a few rows further up, sitting with a couple of adults I assume are his parents. I hastily turn away, hoping he didn't notice me looking.

The team is already on the court warming up, dribbling balls to each other and shooting practice baskets. Bri leans forward, practically drooling, to watch Liam out on the floor. Conscious that Lucas might be watching, I nudge her.

"Don't you think you're being a little obvious?" I whisper.

She laughs. "So what? He's not even looking this way. Is Lucas here?" She cranes her neck to look behind us.

"Stop it!" I hiss. "Yes, he's sitting with his parents back there." I motion with my head without turning.

"We should go say hi, meet their parents. Want to?"

"No! Sheesh, Bri, we went on *one* date with them and Lucas had to be arm-twisted into asking me. If he's actually interested—which I don't think he is—he can come say hi to me. I'm sure he's seen us by now."

Bri turns back to me, grinning. "Yep, he has. And here he comes, oh ye of little faith."

I suck in a breath but resist the urge to look. "Really?"

Before she can answer, Lucas moves into my line of sight, stepping past a few other spectators to reach us.

"Hey, um, do you two mind if I sit with you?" He looks almost as embarrassed as I feel. I didn't *see* Bri motion him down, but…

"Of course not!" she answers, practically shoving the girl on her other side to clear a space between the two of us.

As Lucas sits down, still looking uncomfortable, my heart is hammering so loudly, I'm almost afraid he'll hear it.

"So, um, did you have a nice weekend?" he asks, looking back and forth between us.

"Kind of boring but not bad," Bri replies, while I just nod.

I'm trying to come up with something to say that won't sound stupid when whistles blow down on the court.

"Oh, they're about to start!" Bri exclaims. "Let's go wish Liam—the team, I mean—a good game." Leaving her coat, she darts from her seat and heads to the sidelines, where our team is now gathering. Lucas and I follow more slowly.

Liam grins when he sees Bri, showing no trace of his brother's discomfort. "Hey, you came!"

"Wouldn't miss it! Deb, too, and she hardly ever comes to the games." She winks at me. "She missed your first one, where you played so incredibly. I'm not sure she believed me when I told her about it, so you need to play like that again tonight to convince her."

Now Liam suddenly *does* seem uncomfortable. "I, um, I'll try." He glances at Lucas, who I notice is frowning. "I'll talk to you later, okay? I need to go hear what the coach is telling everyone." He hurries off.

The three of us go back to our seats, Bri in obvious high spirits. "Just watch how he plays, Deb. He's incredible!"

"I'm sure he is. And it's not true I didn't believe you," I tell her, irked she said that. "The day after, at school, everyone was buzzing about how well he played, especially one particular shot he made, where it apparently looked like he was flying."

Lucas clears his throat. "Yeah, um, he told me afterward it must have been pure adrenaline, he was so excited about playing in his very first game here. He was pretty sore afterward, though, so it's probably better if he doesn't push himself quite that hard again."

Bri flushes at the subtle rebuke. "Well, of course I don't want him to hurt himself! I never heard about him being sore later. But that one shot he made—" She shakes her head in remembered wonder. "That would have wowed most NBA players. I know all our fans are dying to see him do it again."

Judging by Lucas's expression, there's at least one fan who isn't— which makes sense if he really is worried Liam could injure himself. Funny, though, I don't remember Liam acting even a little bit sore in Pre-Cal the morning after that game…

With that conversation in mind, I pay more attention to the game than I normally would. Sean looks great, of course. So does Alan, the other new NuAgra transfer. But it's obvious by a few minutes into the first period that Liam's outshining them both, playing noticeably better than at the other games I attended this season. Showing off for Bri?

As the game progresses and Liam's superior play continues, everyone else on the Jewel side of the gym is as delighted as Bri is. When I sneak a few glances at Lucas, though, it's obvious *he's* not happy about it. I wonder again if maybe he's just jealous, but a glance back at his parents shows them also looking upset.

Just how badly *did* Liam injure himself in his first game? He definitely wasn't limping or anything the day after, and no one mentioned him being hurt.

Thinking back to that day, all the chatter I recall was either about Liam's incredible performance the night before, or our big football playoff game that night. Which we lost, unfortunately. Bri was almost in tears on the way home, bemoaning Rigel's first and only loss of the season.

As the first half buzzer sounds, Liam sinks an impressive three-point shot, putting Jewel well ahead. Bri again rushes down to the sidelines, well ahead of Lucas and me.

"I knew you still had it in you!" I hear Bri squeal when she reaches Liam. "You looked *fabulous* out there!"

He grins down at her. "Thanks." But then he glances over her head at his brother and me and his grin abruptly fades. "I, um, should get to the locker room. Halftime's not very long and the coaches will want to talk to us."

Bri reluctantly lets him go, but to my surprise, Lucas moves to intercept him before he can leave the court.

I watch as the two brothers talk for a moment, too quietly for me to overhear with all the crowd noise. Lucas looks almost angry in his intensity, while Liam's expression gradually changes from chagrined, to stubborn, to angry as well. Finally, with a terse nod, Liam turns his back on his brother and follows the rest of the team out of the gym.

"Huh. I wonder what that was about?" I murmur to Bri, then realize she's looking in a totally different direction.

"You mean the way Alan gave Trina the brush-off just now?" She gives me a wicked grin. "Who can blame him when she's being so clingy? *Exactly* how she acted with Rigel at the start of this year, before he got his memory back. And then with Tristan, when he first got here."

I glance toward Alan's retreating back, then at Trina, who's visibly pouting. "Um, no, I meant— Never mind."

If I describe what I saw, it would be just like Bri to come right out and ask Lucas what he said to Liam just now…and I have a feeling Lucas might not want to talk about it. Turning back, I see him climbing the bleachers to where his parents are sitting. His mother still looks worried, but his dad looks almost as angry as Lucas did a minute ago.

He and Lucas exchange a few words, then Lucas heads back our way. Maybe I'm imagining it, but I get the impression he's working hard to smooth the emotion from his face as he approaches us.

"Would you girls like anything from the concession stand?" he asks, his voice tight.

"I'll have a bottled water," I tell him, digging a couple of dollars out of my pocket. Mostly to give him the break he seems to need to compose himself. "It's the only thing we're allowed to bring into the gym."

Bri steps forward. "I'll come with you, Lucas. I want a cookie, but I'll have to eat it out in the hall. You okay saving our seats, Deb?"

So much for giving Lucas some alone time. "Sure, no problem."

As they walk off together, I'm doubly glad I didn't mention that weird exchange between Liam and Lucas, since Bri would likely have used this opportunity to ask about it—and possibly plead Liam's side of whatever the argument was. I'm sure she doesn't really want Liam to hurt himself, but she's such a huge Jewel Jaguars fan, it's possible she'd consider the risk worth it for another trip to State.

I glance up at Mr. and Mrs. Walsh before sitting back down. Their heads are together in what looks like an intense conversation. About Liam?

Bri and Lucas return just as the team comes back into the gym. Out of the corner of my eye, I see Mr. Walsh moving down the bleachers to the floor, where he has a quick word with Liam, who again looks both chastened and irritated. After a moment Liam nods, scowling, and his father heads back up.

When the game resumes, it's obvious even to me that Liam's not playing nearly as well as he did first half. Whatever Lucas and Mr. Walsh said to him over halftime, they apparently made an impression.

Bri notices, too, and she's not happy about it. "Looks like Liam's cooled off," she says with a frown. "I know hot streaks don't last forever, but he was on fire the whole first half, and now he's playing super conservatively."

"Maybe he pulled a muscle or something," I suggest, with a quick glance at Lucas.

He nods. "Yeah, he probably did. I, um, warned him that might happen, asked him if he was okay at the end of the half. He claimed he was, but it looks like he's not." Oddly, though, he seems less worried about his brother now than he did earlier.

Bri, on the other hand, looks very concerned. "Pulled a muscle? In that case he shouldn't be out there at all...but it looks like he's moving okay. Maybe he just tightened up. Hope he can shake it off!" She looks worriedly at the scoreboard, where our lead has shrunk from twenty-two points to twelve.

• • •

Jewel does win, but by just eight points—our closest game this season, according to Bri. Liam spent most of the fourth period on the bench. I kept watching him for any sign he was in pain, but he never rubbed his muscles or anything. In fact, he looked more mad than hurt. And when he stands up to congratulate his teammates at the final buzzer, there's no hint of a limp.

I notice Lucas and the Walshes all look much happier now than they did at halftime. Would they, if Liam actually sustained an injury?

As soon as the crowd starts surging onto the court, Bri goes straight to Liam. I follow her more closely this time, curious to hear what he'll say.

"Are you okay?" she anxiously asks him.

"I'm fine." His smile, clearly forced, doesn't reach his eyes. "Just... had a bad stretch there. Coach was right to bench me when I couldn't shake it off." He darts a quick frown at Lucas, then at his parents, coming up behind us.

"You did fine, son." Mr. Walsh's heartiness sounds as forced as Liam's smile. "Now, why don't you hit the showers? I think your mom has something special for you at home."

She nods, her smile also noticeably strained. "I do. I picked up one of those pies you like so much, so you could have some after your game."

For a second, Liam looks like he's going to say something rude, but then he just swallows and nods. "Thanks, Mom. I'll meet you guys outside in a few, 'kay?"

He sprints off to the showers—*definitely* no limp—and his parents move toward the exit. I notice irrelevantly that Mrs. Walsh is as short as I am, a dramatic contrast to her husband, who easily tops six feet. The twins obviously get their height from him. Mr. and Mrs. Walsh look... cute together.

That observation creates a sudden surge of longing I try to suppress as I glance up at Lucas.

"Hey, um, thanks for letting me sit with you guys," he says, as much to Bri as to me.

"Any time." Bri grins up at him, then slants a sly look my way. "You're welcome to sit with us at *all* the games if you want. Right, Deb?"

Trapped and embarrassed, all I can do is nod.

"I'll, uh, keep that in mind." Lucas now looks as uncomfortable as I am. "I'd, uh, better go catch up with my parents. Er...happy holidays."

I watch his retreating back for a moment, then turn on Bri. "Did you really have to do that?"

"What?" She looks totally confused.

"It was bad enough you pressured Liam into making Lucas ask me to the Winter Formal without *guilting* him into sitting with me at the next basketball game I go to."

Bri actually laughs, upsetting me even more. "I didn't guilt him, I just invited him."

"Right. And now he'll feel rude if he doesn't. Did you hear how reluctant he sounded?" I writhe inwardly.

"He didn't sound reluctant," she scoffs. "He was just in a hurry. It'll be fine, Deb, you'll see. Some boys just need a little more encouragement than others. Oh, I guess you'd better call Maggie since there wasn't a chance to hint for a ride with the guys."

I pull out my phone. "Unless they brought a different car, we wouldn't have fit anyway," I point out, turning away to make the call.

I'd like to believe Bri is right and things will work out with Lucas and me in spite of her meddling. Or even because of it. But I strongly suspect he's wishing right now that he'd never asked me to the dance in the first place.

4

Opening tip off

Bri

"WHAT DO you mean you're not coming tonight?" I demand when Deb calls me shortly before it'll be time to leave for the game. "The guys will expect us both to be there and you know how I hate sitting alone."

"You never actually sit alone," Deb points out—truthfully, unfortunately. "You'll probably know half the people on our side of the stands. Anyway, I've already started going over Mom's books and they're kind of a mess. She wasn't kidding about needing my help."

It's clear she's not budging this time, so I give it up. "Okay. I hope Lucas won't be too disappointed."

She gives a sour kind of laugh. "Trust me, I'm *not* worried about that. Though, um, do let me know if he asks about me, okay?"

Now I laugh. "Of course. And I bet he will. If you're really, really sure, I'd better finish getting ready. Talk later!"

Standing in front of my full-length mirror a moment later, I scrunch up my face. Is this the right outfit? This emerald green top with a little peekaboo cutout in the neckline is definitely flattering—it brings out the hazel flecks in my brown eyes and complements my pale gold complexion. But it's an away game, so shouldn't I wear one of my Jewel Jaguar shirts? Or at least the school colors? Which would Liam appreciate more?

Deciding at the last minute that supporting the team is more important than looking my cutest, I change back into the Jaguars T-shirt on my bed. It's fitted, at least, and has a nice little V-neck to it. Maybe this way it won't look like I'm trying too hard. My hair is as wild as ever, dark curls going every which way, but I'm learning to embrace it. Sometimes I wish my mom knew how to help me with it...or that I just had hair more like hers and everyone else's.

No, I tell my reflection firmly. My hair is beautiful just the way it is. I run my fingers through it, taming the mass into a slightly more ordered disarray that I hope looks fashionably windblown rather than completely out of control.

"Are you about ready, Bri?" I hear my dad call up the stairs. "We need to head out in just about ten minutes."

"Almost!" I yell in answer, applying a last touch of lip gloss.

Hurrying downstairs, I see my father waiting by the door—along with my little brother.

"Ew, he's not coming, is he?" I wrinkle my nose at twelve-year-old Joey.

"Mom said I could, since it's break and both Kyle and Davey are still out of town," he says before Dad can answer.

Dad gives me a rueful smile. "You know I've been trying to interest him in sports. Will it totally ruin your evening if he sits with you, Bri?"

Joey grins up at me and I notice again how much he's starting to look like our Dad.

They have the exact same warm, golden-brown coloring, several shades darker than my own, and almost identical smiles. I'm more a mix of my two parents, with Dad's dark, curly hair and brown eyes, but my blonde Mom's features, and skin nearly as light as hers.

I try to summon up a glower for Joey, but my heart's not in it. He's actually a fairly cool kid, as seventh-graders go, even if he's less into sports than most boys his age. "I guess not. Let's go."

I'm ridiculously excited during the forty-minute ride to Oak Hill. It's been a whole week since the last basketball game—since I last saw Liam. Way too long. To give my excitement an outlet, I chat animatedly with my dad about Oak Hill's team, our chances, our lineup, our strategies— and again about Liam's strange desire to switch positions after his first amazing game.

"I'll admit, I wasn't particularly inclined to grant his request at first," my father admits with a rueful chuckle. "But he made a compelling case, and it shows that he's thinking long-term, which is smart."

"But he was so great at forward!"

"I know. But my first duty as a coach is to consider my players and their well-being and potential futures, not just to win as many high school games as possible."

I sigh and reluctantly agree.

When we get there, there are a few other middle schoolers at the game, so Joey instantly opts to sit with them instead.

"No offense, Sis," he tells me. Like I'd mind? "If I stay here, it'll look like you're babysitting me or something. Catch you after, okay?"

"If it's okay with Dad, it's fine with me." I don't even try to hide my relief.

Dad nods, so Joey climbs up to a small group of boys his age, freeing me to look around for someone to sit with. I see Kira and Tristan sitting near center court and start to head their way, but stop when I notice that their heads are close together. It looks like they're having kind of an intense conversation. *Awkward.*

I scan the bleachers for anyone else who might be fun to sit with. Maybe Lucas? Then I notice Becky from Chorus and two other girls—I think one is named Kirsten?—huddled together in the very front row, waving enthusiastically. I glance over my shoulder, confused. Are they really waving at me? I hardly know them.

There's no one behind me and they keep smiling and waving, so I head their way. They've got great seats. And though I see the Walshes, there's no sign of Lucas in the nearly-empty visitor bleachers. It bothers me how he doesn't seem to support his brother much. At least Deb doesn't have to be disappointed she missed him.

"Hi, Bri!" Becky beams at me as I reach their little cadre front and center.

She's an alto in Chorus and I'm a soprano, so we don't interact much. And I'm not sure I've ever even spoken with her two friends, who introduce themselves as Kristina—I was close—and Deanna.

"Hi!" I respond with equal enthusiasm, figuring it's always nice to hang out with new people. "Never thought you guys were that serious about basketball—I don't think I've ever seen you in the front row before."

Deanna giggles. "Well I don't know how serious I am about *basketball*, but with so many hotties on the team, I'm surprised more girls aren't interested in front-row seats!" Becky and Kristina join in the giggling, confirming that their sudden interest springs from the same source.

I grin back, "Well, the more the merrier! I know the team really appreciates the support."

Suddenly my attention is yanked to the court, where Liam seems to be the first one out of the locker room. I'm not the only one. My companions are eying Liam, along with the other guys on the team, as they follow him onto the court. I drink in the sight of Liam after a whole week of not seeing him. Then he turns, scanning the bleachers, and a thrill runs down my spine when he almost immediately makes eye contact with me and gives me a little wave and grin. I enthusiastically return both, feeling heat rise to my cheeks. I hope I don't look too much like an idiot.

I stand up so he can come join me behind the bench if he wants, and I get another little jolt of joy when he immediately trots over, lugging a huge pack of water bottles. *Did he volunteer to bring the water out and make sure he was first out of the locker room so that he'd have a chance to talk to me briefly? Or is that an insane fantasy?*

The giggling behind me intensifies. I know we don't have much time before the coaches crack the whip to start drills, so I step forward to just behind the bench, hopefully out of earshot of my new acquaintances.

"Hey Liam!" I try to sound casual but probably fail. "Great to see you. How was your Christmas?"

He blinks as he sets the water down on the bench, like he was caught slightly off guard by the question, which seems a little odd. "Oh, um, it was great. How was yours?"

"Good! My parents got me these cool roller blades I've been lusting after for a while. Though I probably won't be able to try them out until the weather stops sucking so much."

I'm rewarded with a delicious low chuckle as he starts pulling water bottles out of the pack and goes down the row placing one under each seat on the bench. "And when is that likely to be? Please tell me it's not going to go on like this much longer!" He puts a hand to his forehead in mock drama.

"Oh my dear, sweet child." I answer in exaggerated tones of sympathy, walking with him as he sets down the water bottles. "April if we're lucky. We've got at least three more months of this crap."

"Say it isn't so! What do you *do* all winter?" he asks, still melodramatically.

I give him a sly grin. "Oh, we Indiana girls have come up with all sorts of ways to keep warm." Then, worried that might sound a little *too* suggestive, I quickly follow up with, "There's high school and pro basketball, there's the movie theater, there's pro football playoffs, there's hot apple cider, some good bands lined up to play at the Lighthouse on Saturdays…" I trail off. If he's interested, I've given him several good date options to choose from.

He's finished setting out water for his teammates now and gives me his full attention. His blue-gray eyes twinkle and he starts to say something, but right then my dad blows his whistle, calling everyone to the court to begin warmups.

Ugh, DAD!

"Sorry—talk after the game!" Liam calls over his shoulder as he lopes over to join the rest of the team.

Becky and her friends are all in a tizzy when I sit back down on the bleachers.

"Omigod, you and Liam look like you're pretty tight!" Becky exclaims.

"He took you to the Winter Formal, right?"

"Are you two 'official'?"

I hesitate, unprepared for this onslaught.

"Um, not 'officially' official, I guess," I hedge. "But I think things might be heading in that direction?"

Kristina narrows her eyes at me. "So he's still fair game for now?"

I'm too stunned by the question to do anything but stare at her.

Becky giggles nervously. "It, uh, sounds like Bri's already got a fair claim staked out."

Kristina tosses her long blonde hair over her shoulder and shrugs. "All's fair in love and war. Besides, it might be weird for him since her dad's, y'know… a coach."

Most people wouldn't have noticed that little pause. I'm pretty sure Becky and Deanna didn't. But combined with the way Kristina raked me over with her eyes, her real meaning is perfectly clear to me—that my dad is Black, not that he's the coach.

Though my stomach churns with impotent rage, mostly on my dad's behalf, I force out a too-hearty laugh. Fortunately, these girls don't know me well enough to tell the difference. I hope my cheeks aren't flaming with the suppressed anger and frustration I feel.

"Personally, I think Liam really appreciates having someone to talk to who actually *understands* basketball," I respond with a pointed look of my own. "But hey, may the best woman win!"

The momentary tension dissipates and the others begin to chatter about boys and the latest gossip. Normally I'd join in, but I'm still uncomfortable. On the surface, Kristina didn't say or do anything most people would consider really out of line. And if it were just about me, I don't think it would bother me so much. But my dad and my brother have to put up with way more of this sort of thing than I do, here in rural Indiana. It always makes me feel so furious on their behalf...and so powerless.

Finally the game starts and draws me out of my unpleasant reflections. I lean forward eagerly to watch. Dad thought it was a little strange when Liam asked if he could move from forward to guard a few weeks ago, but was happy to oblige. And Liam looks amazing out there, like he's starting to really settle into his new role as point guard—setting up plays and passing seamlessly. Oak Hill is using a zone defense, which has some effect at neutralizing our three powerhouse players, but not enough. Though the game stays relatively close, Jewel is ahead by eight points at halftime.

I jump up to shoulder my way through the cheerleaders, who are directly in front of us, to get a quick word with Liam before he heads to the locker room.

"You're having a great game so far," I tell him, grinning.

"Thanks. Having you right down front helps," he replies with an answering grin and the ghost of a wink. My breath catches. "Oops, gotta go!"

As he turns away, I see Trina sidling up to Alan. "Looking good out there Alan!" she simpers, with a little shimmy of her pompoms against him.

He just gives her a little half-smile, then follows the rest of the players off the court.

Trina turns to Nicole, rolling her eyes. "He's not playing *nearly* as well as Liam or Sean tonight. He barely looks any better than the other losers on our team."

Out of the corner of my eye, I see Alan stop mid-stride and stiffen. He starts to turn back toward the court, then he catches himself and runs off to the locker room. Alan should have been well out of earshot of Trina's nastiness, but it sure *looked* like he heard her! Her voice does have a nasal, carrying quality to it.

Serves her right, I think to myself smugly.

⁺·

The next half, I'm surprised to see Alan come out on a hot streak. He's always a solid team player and a great forward, but he's taking more shots than usual—and making most of them. Oak Hill shifts to a box-and-one defense to try and handle him, but Alan continues to light it up and Jewel ends up winning by 18 points. The visitor stands explode into wild cheering as the game ends and Trina oozes her way to Alan's side again. Cooing disingenuous nothings in his ear, no doubt.

I head toward Liam and get an instant energy boost when I see him also heading toward me.

"Great game! You did a fantastic job running the offense and making things happen out there!"

"Thanks! I feel like I'm really starting to get the hang of playing point now that I've finally accepted I'll never be tall enough to play forward in college," he says with a self-deprecating laugh.

I laugh with him. "You're plenty tall for me!" I blurt out without thinking. *Did I really just say that?* "I mean, you're plenty tall for a regular person," I cover quickly. "It's only in the world of basketball that —what, six-two?—would ever be considered 'not tall.'"

"Six-two on a good day, yeah," he says ruefully. "I guess I'm just more comfortable taking shots than handling the ball, so it's been a challenge."

"Still, it's really smart to start learning a position that might be a better fit for you at the college or even pro level, where *everybody* is crazy tall."

He shrugs. "Yeah, that's why I asked to make the switch," he says, though there's a weird hint of bitterness to his words.

"I think it makes a lot of sense. As great as you are at forward, the point guard is the biggest playmaker of the whole team. There's a lot more to the game than just putting points on the board."

He gives me a wry grin. "You sound just like your dad."

I bite my lip. "Uh-oh. Is that a good thing or a bad thing?"

"A good thing. He's a great coach."

"Hey, you're turning into a pretty amazing coach on the floor your-self. You need to be the 'general' out there and you're really stepping up and taking leadership. It's really cool to watch."

He gives me a warm smile. "Thank you. Most girls don't have the first clue about what's actually going on out there, but you— It's nice talking to someone who really gets it."

His eyes hold mine with what feels like more than just friendship and sports camaraderie. I'm starting to melt into them when I catch myself, realizing I should probably, um, say something.

"Well, um...sports mean a lot to me," I admit. "I love how every member of a team comes together to be part of something bigger than they could by themselves. It's so much more than just being athletic."

He looks both surprised and delighted. "Yes! Exactly! I feel like so many people don't understand that."

"Like Deb." I laugh. "I tried to get her to come tonight, but she claimed she had to help with her mother's accounting, instead. She mostly puts up with my sports obsession, but she *so* doesn't get it. "

"Same with my brother." He laughs, too, but it sounds like his heart isn't quite in it.

"I'm sorry—is it hard that he doesn't seem so supportive?" I ask with genuine sympathy.

Liam shrugs. "Not really. He's just into his own things. And since those aren't spectator sports, it's not like I can do much to show my support for *him*. He does come to all my home games."

Wow. Defending his brother who didn't show tonight...could he *be* any more perfect? "That's a really great point," I concede. "What's he up to tonight, anyway?"

"Working on his new pet project out at NuAgra—something to do with energy efficiency. He's always complaining that he doesn't get enough time to work on it. Oh, he did ask me to tell Deb 'hi' from him, though," he adds. "Since she's not here, could you maybe pass that along for me?"

I grin, thinking how happy Deb will be to hear that. "You bet! So... I guess I won't get to see you again until next week's game?" I hope my phrasing makes it clear I'd be happy to see him sooner...if he wants to.

"Oh. Yeah, probably." Does he sound a little regretful? Like maybe he wants to see me sooner too but doesn't dare say so? Or is that just wishful thinking?

"I can't wait," I tell him. And mean it.

By now a bunch of people around us are waiting to congratulate Liam on his great game and I realize I'm kind of monopolizing him. I move aside to make room for his adoring fans, mostly girls, trying to tamp down a flare of jealousy.

"Same here!" he replies. Again, his eyes hold mine just a little longer than is strictly friendly before turning to the gaggle of girls squawking at him.

After briefly congratulating the other players, I head out to wait for my dad, a warm, fuzzy feeling growing in the region of my stomach. Even though Liam didn't ask me on another date, there's definitely *something* there!

5

Electrical resistance

Lucas

"CRAP." I realize I've just messed up my parameter calculation *again*. "C'mon, man. Focus," I mutter to myself, glad I have the NuAgra Engineering lab to myself tonight.

I'm doing my best to keep my attention completely on my energy project, but it's been harder than I expected. My thoughts keep drifting to Liam's basketball game, which is weird since I don't even know what the Oak Hill gym looks like. Okay, maybe it's not *exactly* the game I keep thinking about…

This whole past week, Deb's face has popped into my mind at odd moments. Like while I'm recalculating—*again*—my optimum output parameters. I also keep replaying everything we said to each other at the dance. It's unsettling how much I miss her, considering I barely know the girl. And probably a very bad sign.

If I'm honest with myself, Deb's the real reason I decided at the last minute not to accompany my family to the game tonight, though it *is* true I can use the time to work on my project.

When they dropped me off, Liam promised to tell Deb hi for me tonight, even though I didn't ask him to. I wonder if he will? If he does, what will she say? Will she be disappointed I'm not there, maybe ask him what I'm doing instead?

Not that Liam can give her any details, even if he knows them, which

I doubt. This project absolutely falls into the category of things we can't let any *Duchas* know about. Maybe I should come up with a cover story in case Deb asks me about it in Art class or something...?

"Argh!" Yet again, I missed a step in the energy flow equation—a different one this time. Forcing my mind back to the task at hand, I painstakingly type everything into the holo-screen again.

Despite a few more distraction-induced errors, by the time my folks arrive to pick me up, I've come up with a formula that could increase the efficiency of a standard gravity generator by a whole quarter of a percent. In theory, anyway. Not enough to make a significant difference, even if it proves out, but it means I'm at least on the right track. Finally.

I'm just saving my work when Dad pushes open the door to the lab. "How's it going?"

I power off the last two holo-screens. "Not bad. Hopefully in a week or two I'll be ready to run some simulations. That'll give you a better idea of what I'm trying to do here. I'm obviously not going solve Nuath's energy crisis single-handedly, but maybe I can help a little bit."

"Don't sell yourself short, son." Dad claps me on the shoulder. "I've seen some of your other work. You have a knack for coming at problems from unexpected angles. It's a great quality for a Scientist, especially an Engineer."

"You think so? Thanks." I know a lot of it's genetic—everyone in the Engineering *fine* tends to be pretty good at analytical thinking. But it's cool to think I might possess something a little beyond the norm.

I follow him out to the car and climb in next to Liam in the back.

"So, how was the game?"

"We won." He shrugs. "And before you ask, no, I didn't go overboard tonight."

That was the other reason I gave my folks for not coming—so I wouldn't be tempted to get all judgmental if Liam played too well. He hates that.

"This time Alan was the one who went a little over the top," he continues. "First time I've seen him do that. I think Trina, that cheerleader he took to the dance, might have been egging him on."

"Like Bri did to you last game?" I can't suppress a smirk. "Was she disappointed you didn't go all NBA again tonight?"

He shrugs. "Maybe a little. It's not like I actually sucked. But with Alan over-performing, I felt like I had to be extra careful."

I barely hear him. I'm too busy trying to think of a totally casual way to ask about Deb that won't get me teased. Fortunately, Liam answers my question before I figure out how to ask it.

"That reminds me," he suddenly says. "You didn't have to worry about disappointing Deb Andrews tonight after all—she wasn't at the game either. Bri said she had to help her mom with something at home. Accounting? Does that make sense?"

"Oh, yeah, Deb told me at the dance she does the books for her mother's pottery business. Said her mother makes vases and things that are nice enough to sell, but is really bad when it comes to stuff like tracking her sales and expenses. I guess Deb's pretty good at math?"

Liam nods. "She is. I've got Pre-Cal and Econ with her and she gets better grades than me in both."

That startles me a little. No *Duchas* should be smarter than any *Echtran*. Not that Liam probably puts in full effort. For someone in the Engineering *fine*, he's never been very interested in math or science. Nowhere near as much as I am, for example. Given that, Liam might well do better here than he would back home. Even middling science skills, by Martian standards, should be more than enough to get by in any Earth job.

Tempted as I am to keep him talking about Deb, I don't want him to guess how interested I am.

"I'm glad I took this opportunity to work on my project," I say, deliberately changing the subject. "I haven't had nearly as much time for it over break as I thought I would. And I think I might have finally made a little bit of a breakthrough tonight." Because I've hardly said anything to my family about what I've been doing in the lab in my spare time, that gets everyone's attention.

"Really?" Mom asks. "What kind of breakthrough?"

I explain the new capacitance formula I came up with, and the potential it could have to enhance the output of the Nuath colony's base-level gravity emitters without increasing energy demand. Mom and Dad ask me a bunch of questions about how I worked out the equations, but Liam is clearly bored by the whole thing. Which irks me.

"Hey," I tell him, "if tweaking the energy flow parameters can boost the efficiency of Nuath's gravity generators by even one percent, it could extend the power supply there by decades. Especially when you consider those generators consume more than thirty percent of our power."

My brother rolls his eyes. "Don't you mean *their* power? We're

Echtrans now, not Nuathans, remember? And I, for one, am fine with that."

"Yeah, well, not everyone is. Sure, some immigration to Earth will need to continue, but if we can improve energy efficiency enough, people who really don't want to leave Nuath might be allowed to live out the rest of their lives there. And if fewer resources have to be devoted to ramping up the speed of emigration, more of our Scientists can focus on the power issue, which would probably lead to more and bigger breakthroughs. It's possible Nuath could continue to exist indefinitely with a smaller population."

"That would be wonderful," Mom agrees. "Many of our elders there are still very resistant to the idea of spending the last few decades of their lives on what they see as an alien planet."

Dad nods. "And who can blame them? Nuath is the only world they've ever known."

They fall to discussing the current political climate on Mars for the rest of the drive home...while I start thinking about Deb again.

Even though I know I shouldn't.

6

Dead end

Deb

A FEW DAYS AFTER CHRISTMAS, I'm in my room trying to sketch out a new idea I have for a painting, though I'm finding it hard to concentrate. Almost immediately after backing out of attending last night's basketball away game, I started second-guessing my decision.

What if Bri was right about Lucas being disappointed, unlikely as that seems? Did he sit with Bri anyway, even with me not there? If so, did he ask about me? I thought starting a new art project might distract me from the questions and regrets plaguing me, but so far it hasn't worked very well.

And then Bri shows up unannounced. "Hey, sorry I didn't call you last night, but it was pretty late when Dad and I got home from the game," she says, bouncing into my room and planting herself on the bed. "Not that there's much worth telling."

My sketch forgotten, I turn to face her, trying not to let my disappointment show. "So I guess Lucas didn't even ask about me?"

She shakes her head and my vacillating spirits plummet to my toes. Apparently I was right about him, much as I hoped I wasn't.

"He couldn't, since he wasn't there either," she tells me with a half grin. "And *not* because he wanted to avoid you."

I raise a skeptical brow. "How do you know that?"

"Liam told me Lucas stayed back to work on some special project or other he's doing at NuAgra. It sounded boring to me, but to each their own." She shrugs. "Though I guess you've always gone for the nerdier types, haven't you?"

I laugh, but my heart's not in it—because if Lucas had *really* wanted to see me again, wouldn't he have gone to the game? "Did Liam tell you what the project's about?"

"Something to do with energy efficiency, I think? He didn't go into any details and I wasn't really listening anyway. It's hard to concentrate when I talk to him, he's so gorgeous! Those eyes..." Her voice trails off dreamily.

Now I really do laugh. "Hey! Earth to Bri! So has he asked you out again?"

"Not yet," she grumps. "And I even threw out hints both before *and* after the game. I think he was feeling a little down, though."

"Why? Was his playing still off?"

"Not nearly as bad as during the second half last game, but nowhere near as good as he played at the start of it, either. Last night's standout was actually Alan, the new senior. He outplayed both Liam *and* Sean, scored most of our points in the second half."

She goes on to describe the whole game practically play by play so I zone out, thinking about Lucas again. Interesting that his pet project is about energy instead of agriculture, which is what NuAgra is supposedly all about. Though he did say his parents work as engineers there, not with the actual plants. Maybe I'll ask him about it when school starts back up...if I can get up the nerve to ever talk to him again.

"Were M and Rigel there?" I ask when Bri starts to wind down.

"No. But Kira and Tristan sat together again and seemed to be talking a lot to each other. Wonder if Molly and Sean are starting to get worried about that?"

I roll my eyes. "I doubt it. It's pretty obvious they're just friends. Since their parents all moved here to work at NuAgra, they probably knew each other before coming to Jewel."

"I guess." Bri lets go of what she clearly hoped might have gossip potential. "Anyway, this coming Friday is the last game before break ends. You'll come to that one, won't you? It's at home. Liam told me his brother does attend all of those."

My insides clench. "Does that mean you talked to Liam about Lucas...and me? Again? Bri!" I practically wail. "They both must think I'm the most pathetic loser in the history of ever."

"Oh, they do not. Liam specifically told me that Lucas told him to tell you hi for him last night. So there."

That helps. A little. "Or so he claims," I grumble. "It was probably Liam's idea, not Lucas's, so he'd have a good excuse to talk to *you* again."

Bri gives an exasperated huff. "When did you become such a pessimist? Usually you're the one cheering *me* up when it comes to boys."

Which is true. Bri is constantly crushing, then despairing, about some boy or other. I've talked her down countless times when she acted like some guy's loss of interest was the end of the world. I'm usually great at putting things like that into perspective. For other people, anyway. Why can't I do it for myself?

"You're right. I may as well hope for the best, huh? Worst that can happen is he never asks me out again." I say it lightly, refusing to let the depression I feel at that thought suck me down. "He's still a really inter-esting guy. Maybe now that we're sort of friends, I can get him to tell me what kind of stuff they're doing at NuAgra."

Like everyone else, I'm curious to know what could possibly be going on there that has to be kept so secret. I'd definitely like to hear more about his energy-saving project. As Treasurer of Jewel High's Earth Club, I'm way into that sort of thing.

"Maybe. Though I heard Trina ask Alan exactly that after the game and he said something about having to sign a non-disclosure agreement. It was pretty obvious he was trying to get away from her, though—she was being super clingy again—so maybe that was just an excuse."

We spend the next half hour gleefully bad-mouthing Trina, far and away the meanest girl in school. Her favorite target has always been M, since before I even got to Jewel, according to Bri. So as M's best friends, Bri and I have always come in for our share of insults from Trina, too. Fortunately, M's a lot better these days at standing up to Trina than she used to be, though that hasn't made Trina any less nasty. If anything, she's getting worse.

Before leaving, Bri extracts a reluctant promise from me to come with her to Friday's game—a promise I almost immediately regret. I'll feel like a *total* loser if Lucas shows up but doesn't sit with us.

Even if he does, I'm determined to only talk about impersonal things like his NuAgra project or Art class—nothing that could even remotely imply I have any *romantic* expectations.

Because I don't. Not realistic ones, anyway.

.*.

By Friday, I'm seriously tempted to back out of attending this game, too, I'm so worried Lucas will think I'm stalking him. He has to realize by now I care even less about basketball than he does, since I don't even have a family member playing.

"Maggie can't drive us tonight," I tell Bri when she calls that morning. "She and my mom won't be back from Kokomo in time—they're hitting the post-Christmas sales. Actually, I'd kind of like to go with them. I could use some new boots."

"Nope," she immediately responds. "I'm not letting you weasel out again—my dad can drive us. You and I can go shopping tomorrow if you want."

Unable to think of another excuse not to go, I give in. "Okay, fine. But please, *please* promise not to say anything to Lucas *or* Liam about Lucas sitting with us again. Please?"

"Why? Don't you want him to?"

"Not if *he* doesn't want to," I tell her firmly. "Promise?"

Her snort comes through loud and clear. "All right, all right, I promise. Am I at least allowed to smile at him?"

"As long as you don't make it look like an invitation."

"Fine. You can tell me on the way there exactly what facial expressions I'm allowed to use." Her voice drips sarcasm. "Come over at six, so we can head to the school as soon as my dad's ready."

I know she thinks I'm being silly, and I probably am. But I'm determined not to do anything that will screw up my chance to at least be *friends* with Lucas. Bri's attempts to help seem more likely to push him away from me than the reverse.

.*.

We're among the first to arrive for the game a few hours later, though I notice Mr. and Mrs. Walsh are already sitting in the bleachers. Cautiously scanning the gym, I spot Lucas near the edge of the court, his back to us. He's talking to two JV cheerleaders—Kira's little sister Adina, and Jana, both freshman, who also moved here because of

NuAgra. I know them both slightly from Chorus. I look away before Bri can follow my gaze and maybe break her promise.

Bri's little brother Joey, who rode here with us, runs off to find some other seventh graders to sit with, while Bri and I stake out seats near mid-court. A couple minutes later, M and Rigel enter the gym hand in hand. I wave to them and M waves back, heading our way.

"Hey, Deb, hey, Bri," she says as they join us. "I haven't seen you guys all break. How was your Christmas and New Year's?"

We all compare holidays until the team runs onto the court to start warming up, when Bri turns her full attention to Liam. I'm reminded of how M used to watch Rigel on the football field when he first got here last year—and how Bri teased her for being oblivious to everything else. Just like Bri is now.

"So did you get that new set of oil brushes you wanted?" M is asking me when Lucas finally turns around and glances up into the bleachers.

Immediately shifting my focus to M's face, I nod. "Um, yeah, I did. I can already tell they'll make a difference, too."

I barely know what I'm saying, my senses totally attuned to Lucas. From the corner of my eye, I see him take a couple steps toward us, then pause. Trying to decide whether to sit here or not? Now I regret making Bri promise not to encourage him. What if he *does* want to sit here but needs a little nudge?

"—already!" I have to replay M's last few words in my head before they make sense.

"Thanks," I belatedly respond to her compliment about the paintings I have hanging in my bedroom. "You've only seen the very best ones, though. More than twice that many are hidden under my bed. I do think I'm starting to improve, though. Art class is helping."

I'm reminded of the time in that class when Lucas said something nice about one of my sketches. With an effort, I force my attention back to M and notice how much prettier she's gotten over the past year and a half. Ditching her glasses for contacts and wearing a tiny bit more makeup—at Bri's and my urging—has helped, but it's more than that. It's almost like dating Rigel unlocked her potential somehow.

Bri elbows me in the ribs, interrupting my musing. "Lucas *is* coming this way—and I swear I had nothing to do with it!"

A moment later he's right in front of us, looking slightly embarrassed. "Um, is there room for one more?"

"Of course!" Like before, Bri scoots over to make space between us. "Have a seat."

He does, with a quick glance over at M and Rigel. M's smile strikes me as reassuring, which makes me wonder what Bri told her. Lucky for me, M tends to be a lot more discreet than Bri, so I'm less worried she'll throw out any embarrassing hints. I'm glad Lucas can't hear how my heart has suddenly sped up.

"So, how were your holidays?" I ask him before the silence gets too awkward.

"Er, fine," he replies after only the slightest hesitation. "Yours?"

I shrug, trying to look totally nonchalant. "Not bad. We didn't go anywhere, but my sister had a bunch of college friends over for New Year's Eve. That was fun, wasn't it, Bri?" I ask, mostly to stop myself from babbling.

"What?" With an obvious effort, she pulls her gaze away from the court, where Liam and the others are taking turns shooting baskets.

"Maggie's New Year's Eve party. Wasn't it fun?"

She blinks. "Oh, um, yeah, I guess…for a party with parents around."

In other words, one where no one was drinking. I'm starting to think M was right to worry about the parties Bri…okay, and I…went to during football season. There haven't been any—that we've heard about—since then. I dart a quick glance at Lucas and see him frowning.

Hurriedly, I change the subject. "So, um, Bri said you didn't come to Monday night's game, either? That you were working on some project?"

He glances over at M, then looks back at me, a flash of something like alarm in his eyes, though I don't know why. "Er, yeah. Just something I've been playing with out at NuAgra. Mostly for fun."

"What's it about?" I ask, genuinely curious. "Liam told Bri it involves saving energy?"

Now there's no mistaking the alarm in his expression. "Um, sort of, I guess? At least, I hope it will, eventually."

I smile encouragingly. "Saving energy is really important. Especially these days, what with the climate crisis and all."

"Er, yeah, I suppose so. Though this probably won't go anywhere. It's mostly just a theory I'm testing."

"Well, I hope your theory pans out, whatever it is. Who knows? Maybe you'll end up saving the world."

He gives me a sudden, penetrating look that startles me, then shifts his expression to one of studied casualness. "Hard to believe we go back to school on Monday, isn't it?" he asks, totally changing the subject.

I was about to add how impressed I am he's spending his break on something worthwhile instead of wasting time playing games online or something, but it's obvious he doesn't want to talk any more about his project. I don't push, since I can be the same way in the early stages of a new painting, and especially with the poems I sometimes write. I don't tell *anybody* about those, not even Bri.

"Yeah, this break has seemed even shorter than usual," I agree, going along with the abrupt switch in topics. "Did you get longer winter breaks at your old school?"

Lucas looks startled, then wary, but then just shakes his head. "Uh, no. Not really. About the same, I guess."

What on Earth about *that* question could have made him uncomfortable? Despite Bri's claim she had nothing to do with it, I'm starting to doubt sitting here was really his idea.

A whistle blows down on the court and like before, Bri jumps up to go talk with Liam before the game officially starts. This time she doesn't insist I come, so I don't—though Lucas follows her down to wish his brother luck. Or maybe just to get away from me for a few minutes?

"We didn't get much chance to talk at the Winter Formal," M says to me then, "but it looked like you and Bri both had a good time. Did you?"

"Oh! Um, yeah, of course." Bri must not have told her I overheard them talking in the restroom that night. "Lucas and Liam are both really nice."

Nodding, she glances down to the court. "Bri seems to really like Liam."

I look toward the court, too, where Bri's talking to him, her hand on his arm, and he's smiling down into her face. "Yeah, she does—and so far, it looks mutual."

"Yes, it does." M doesn't sound quite as pleased as I'd expect. "Though I guess it makes sense they'd hit it off, they're both so sports-crazy."

"No kidding," I say with a laugh. "It's practically all they talk about. Maybe if they become a real thing, Bri won't make *me* listen to a play-by-play analysis of every single game she sees from now on. Unlike me, Liam's actually interested in that sort of thing, so the more time she spends with him, the less I'll probably have to hear about it."

That gets a smile from M. "Probably so. If it, y'know, lasts. I'd hate to see Bri get hurt again." She's as familiar as I am with Bri's multiple ill-fated crushes. "So how about you and Lucas? Have you two found anything in common?"

"Other than art, not much yet," I admit. "He's a lot harder to draw out."

She gives me an oddly probing look. "But you like him?"

"Well, sure I do, but...I'm not sure I ever see us being more than friends."

Though M's expression is sympathetic, she doesn't try to contradict me—which must mean she agrees.

Darn it.

7

Alternating current

Lucas

AFTER WISHING my brother a good game, I retreat a few steps to watch him and Bri. What I observe worries me more than ever. Even at the Winter Formal, it was obvious the Sovereign's best *Duchas* friend was infatuated with Liam. Now, though, it looks an awful lot like that infatuation is mutual. Which can only lead to trouble.

When the coaches motion the team over for a last-minute pep talk, Bri follows me back up to our seats. I sit down next to Deb again, working hard to keep my expression neutral despite my physical reaction to her nearness. Weirdly, every time I'm around her, she seems to affect me more strongly. Something I need to fight, because that's definitely not good.

Glancing over at the Sovereign, on Deb's other side, I wonder if she guesses. I hope not. Our family's already had one warning from the *Echtran* Council, thanks to Liam. I don't want to be the cause of another one.

"How's Liam feeling tonight?" Deb asks, her smile doing something odd—but not unpleasant—to my stomach. "Bri said he still wasn't playing his best last game."

I shrug. "He says he's fine. I think he's mostly figured out how to play smarter instead of hogging the ball or overextending himself." I hope that'll hold true tonight.

"It's his first season with this team," the Sovereign—no, M—points out. "His performance is bound to be a little uneven for a while."

"Plus he switched from forward to guard a while back," Bri chimes in. "He had to learn a whole new position. Still, it's almost two months into the season. He ought to be settling into it by now. They all should."

Rigel, on M's other side speaks up. "Don't forget we've had Thanksgiving, Christmas and New Year's in there, so they've also had a lot of gaps in their schedule. Starting Monday, they'll be practicing and playing more regularly. That'll help."

"Exactly," M agrees. Then, mostly looking at me, "Try not to worry about it."

I swallow. Does she just mean Liam's basketball playing, or also the way I feel about Deb? No, no, that wouldn't make sense. She must mean Liam.

"Er, yeah," I say after too long a pause, with a respectful little bob of my head. "I'll try not to." Then I notice Deb regarding me curiously—because why would I act all deferential toward someone who's just a regular high schooler? Oops.

The game starts then, to my relief. Maybe it'll keep Deb from asking more questions. I've already come way too close to fumbling my answers. First that bit about my project—why the heck did Liam tell Bri about it, anyway? And again when she asked about school schedules. Winter breaks obviously weren't a thing in Nuath, but I shouldn't have let Deb's question rattle me like that. They drilled us on all that sort of stuff last summer, during our six weeks of Earth Orientation.

Unfortunately, there's something about Deb, I'm not sure what, that makes me want to just blurt out the truth. About everything. Which would be stupid in the extreme, not to mention dangerous. But somehow, when she looks at me with those innocent, trusting blue eyes, substituting my totally-necessary cover story for the facts suddenly feels like lying.

Then there's the way being this close to her affects me, physically and emotionally. No matter how much I remind myself she's a *Duchas*, and therefore off-limits, I just…like being near her. I enjoy looking at her, listening to her, she even smells nice. I noticed all those things the first time I met her in Art class, and even more at the Winter Formal. Things I can't recall ever noticing about anyone else, *Duchas* or not.

On Deb's other side, I hear M and Rigel whispering to Tristan. Not about me and my near-slips, I hope. I don't *think* the Sovereign was paying attention earlier.

Still, her sitting right here makes me extra nervous I'll trip up and say something I shouldn't. Not something I worried about much at all before the dance.

It suddenly occurs to me to wonder how *she's* managed to avoid any slips over the past year and more, since learning the truth about who she really is. Before all of us new *Echtrans* moved to Jewel, practically everyone she knew was a *Duchas* but M somehow kept it secret from everyone at school, including her very best friends. Not to mention her *Duchas* guardians, who also apparently had no idea until a couple of months ago.

Next time she urges us to mingle more with our *Duchas* classmates, I should ask her for advice on that. Or maybe I'll ask Rigel. He's spent his whole life pretending to be a *Duchas*, so has had more practice than anyone at Jewel High.

I try to focus on the game, but other than watching for Liam to do something he shouldn't, I can't really summon much interest. Surreptitious glances at Deb tell me she's not particularly into it, either. That makes me nervous she'll start asking questions again, ones I'll have to lie to answer—like at the dance. To prevent that, I decide to go on the offensive.

"So, have you always lived in Jewel?" I ask her.

Bri doesn't notice, clearly riveted by the action on the court.

"No," Deb replies. "I lived in Fort Wayne until the summer between fourth and fifth grade, when we moved here—right next door to Bri's family." I remember both girls mentioning that when we picked them up for the dance two weeks ago.

"Oh, no wonder you two became friends, then." Has she known Sovereign Emileia that long, too? Her very next words answer that question.

"We did—pretty much right away. And since Bri and M had already been best friends since kindergarten, once I got here all three of us started hanging out together. We did… almost everything together. It was great."

I'm surprised by the wistfulness in her voice at the end. "Was?" I ask —more quietly, since M is sitting right there. "Aren't you still friends? I've noticed you all sit together at lunch."

She shrugs, which on her is disturbingly cute. "We are." Glancing over at M, she also lowers her voice. "Though…I think Bri probably considers *me* her best friend these days."

Though she doesn't elaborate, I can guess why. Learning about Nuath and her Martian heritage, then forming that crazy *graell* bond with Rigel, must have forced the Sovereign to start distancing herself from her closest *Duchas* friends. I imagine that seemed strange from their perspective. Maybe even hurtful. Not that she exactly had a choice.

"What was Fort Wayne like?" I ask next, groping for safer territory. "It's bigger than Jewel, right?"

Her startled expression makes me realize I should have known that. They did touch on Indiana geography in our special Jewel Orientation classes, but the main focus was on how to act toward the Sovereign once we got here.

"A *lot* bigger," she affirms. "Like a quarter-million people."

I have to hide my astonishment that a place I'd never even heard of has roughly the same population as all of Nuath. I still find it hard to believe a single city—not even a very big one by Earth standards—can house that many people.

"Because of that, there was more to do there," she continues, "though the winters were a little colder, with more lake-effect snow." She hunches her shoulders with a pretend shiver and a cute little grimace.

"You don't like snow?" I'm happy to keep her talking about such a completely innocuous topic.

She smiles up at me, which does that weird thing to my stomach again. "Not nearly as much as I did when I was little. Especially since my mom won't let me drive in it yet. How about you? I'll bet you got a lot of snow in New York. Did you ski there or anything?"

"Ski?" Crap. I wrack my brain, trying to remember if they told us anything about winter sports where we supposedly came from. "I, ah—"

A big cheer goes up from the crowd, yanking my attention back to the court. Did Liam—?

"Wow, I think that's Sean's longest three-pointer so far this season!" Bri exclaims, answering me. "Glad to see he's still got it. I was starting to wonder."

Sean probably *has* had to tamp things down a lot this year to make up for Liam's early excesses. Poor guy.

Though I haven't followed Martian politics all that closely, I heard enough to realize he's had a lot to deal with. Like the huge scandal when he stepped aside as the Sovereign Emileia's presumptive Consort a week or so before we got to Jewel. Really, though, what choice did he have, considering she and Rigel have an actual *graell* bond?

Grounded in science as I am, I had a hard time believing it at first. Now, after seeing a few demonstrations and reading a research report on it, I've been forced to accept that the *graell* is more than just legend. At least in that one case.

"It's nice seeing Sean so happy these days," Deb comments then, almost like she read my mind. "I hated seeing him so sad when M and Rigel first got back together a few months ago."

"Yeah, I think Kira's a better match for him than M ever was," Bri agrees almost absently, her eyes still on the game.

They obviously wouldn't know about all the flak Sean received for his relationship with Kira Morain from our more traditionally-minded people. They consider the idea of a Royal dating someone from the Ag *fine*, like Kira, an abomination. Totally counter to our longstanding tradition of only dating within one's own *fine*.

"I think you're right." Deb's clearly more interested in this topic than the game. "Even when they were dating, M and Sean mostly just acted like good friends."

When Bri doesn't answer, Deb leans across me to whisper to her— which I don't mind nearly as much as I should.

"I always wondered what the real deal was there. Remember how gobsmacked we were when Sean asked M to last year's Winter Formal?" she asks softly.

Bri nods, her attention briefly caught. "I was even more amazed she said yes—with Rigel sitting right there!"

"Yeah, I thought sure he'd tell Sean to back off, but he didn't. So weird."

"It was," Bri agrees, turning back to the game. "But now Rigel and M are together again and everything's fine."

On Deb's other side, I see the Sovereign's head twitch slightly, but she doesn't turn, probably not wanting Bri or Deb to know she heard. I wish I could ask what exactly *did* happen last year. Back in Nuath, everyone just heard that the Sovereign—who was still a Princess then— had ended her relationship with Rigel to be with Sean. Most people assumed the *Echtran* Council made her to do it, for political reasons. But now I've gotten to know M, it's hard to imagine her agreeing when she was already bonded to—and apparently in love with—Rigel.

Even though Deb's no longer leaning across me, I'm still way too aware of her. It makes me wonder, for the first time I can remember, what it would be like to have a *graell* bond. Not that it would be remotely possible with a *Duchas* girl, of course. But then, until recently no one thought the *graell* was possible at all...

Trying not to be obvious about it, I shift a couple inches away from Deb, hoping to lessen her effect on me. I thought by now I'd be able to control it, but the reverse seems to be true. Clearly it was a mistake to give into the temptation to sit next to her again tonight.

I can't completely ignore Deb without being rude—something I don't want to do with the Sovereign right here—but I again pretend to give the game my full attention. Because the more I talk with Deb, the easier it is to forget how careful I need to be. Keeping my eyes trained on the basketball court, I try to distract myself by thinking about my NuAgra project. It doesn't work nearly as well as I'd like.

When the game finally ends, I hastily wish everyone around me a nice weekend before hurrying off to meet up with my parents. That seems much safer than accompanying Deb and Bri down the stands.

"See you at school Monday," Bri says breezily, already moving toward the court.

Deb nods, but I can't help noticing her smile seems forced. Even though it's important for her to know I'm not interested in any kind of relationship with her, the hurt in her eyes bothers me. A lot.

It makes me realize I'm doing to her exactly what I've warned Liam he's bound to do to Bri eventually.

Better sooner than later, I tell myself firmly.

If only I could make myself believe it.

8

False lead

Deb

WHEN BRI and I get off the bus Monday morning, she eagerly scans the crowd in front of the school, only turning back to me when she fails to spot Liam.

"Guess their bus isn't here yet," she says. "We can wait outside till they get here, though."

"Let's not," I reply, moving toward the building. "We don't want to look desperate."

She reluctantly falls into step beside me. "I guess you're right. Especially since Liam didn't call over the weekend like I hoped he might. Let me know if he says anything about me during first period, okay?"

"I will." Lucas is in her first-period class, but I don't ask her to return the favor.

Knowing Bri, she'd consider it a license to pester him about me, which is the *last* thing I want. It was pretty clear by the end of Friday night's basketball game that he regretted sitting with us again. His hasty goodbye when the game ended implied he couldn't get away from me fast enough.

He'd seemed willing enough to talk to me before the game started, but then he started acting more and more uncomfortable. After asking me a few questions about myself during the first half, he mostly quit talking to me. And when I tried a few times to talk to him, his responses were so brief I finally gave up.

Even so, I found myself thinking—and dreaming—about him all weekend. So much that when Liam walks into Pre-Cal a few minutes later, looking so much like his brother, I tense for a split second. I briefly pretend it's really Lucas coming toward me with that big smile, but as soon as Liam opens his mouth the illusion is ruined.

"Hey, Deb! Good weekend? That was a great game Friday night, wasn't it? What did you and Bri do afterward?"

"Um, went home. Bri's dad drove us to the game."

He nods, still grinning. "Yeah, that makes sense, what with Mr. Morrison being one of our coaches. He's really good, too. I told Bri I've learned a lot from him."

"I'm sure she was glad to hear that." I smile back, both at Liam's enthusiasm and how happy Bri will be when I relate this conversation to her. It looks like she's well on her way to that second date with Liam she's hoping for.

I can't help being a tiny bit jealous. Not about Liam, who's not my type at all, even if he's outwardly identical to Lucas. It's just...Bri's so much better at talking to boys than I am. With predictable results.

When I see her again in third-period English, I dutifully repeat every word Liam said about her.

"So he really wanted to know what I did after the game?" she whispers excitedly. "Did he look relieved I didn't have another date or anything? How did he say it? Exactly? And did he say what he did after? Do you think there was a party?"

"Even if there was, I doubt any of the newer students would have gone—they haven't so far," I point out. "Liam and Lucas probably just went home, since their parents drove them and it was past eight-thirty when the game ended."

She continues to parse what Liam's every word and expression might have meant until class starts. When the period ends, she moves on to wondering whether and how soon he'll ask her out.

"It's great he likes my dad," she says on our way to lunch after fourth period. "That's a good sign, don't you think? I know him being a teacher...and a coach...and Black...has scared off some guys from getting serious."

"Liam doesn't seem like he'd be scared off by any of that. But isn't it a little early to talk about him getting serious?"

She just grins. "Hey, it never hurts to plan ahead. Oh! There he is!"

Sure enough, Liam and Lucas are ahead of us, also headed to the cafeteria. I slow down slightly, not wanting Lucas to think I'm following him, but Bri speeds up.

"Hi, guys!" she calls out, passing a clump of other students to catch up with the twins. "How was the rest of your break?"

Liam turns instantly, his smile noticeably broader than the one he gave me this morning. "Hey, Bri! It was okay. Kinda boring. How 'bout yours?"

Meanwhile Lucas glances warily at me, still several paces back, and gives a quick nod before looking away. "I'll, uh, catch you later, okay?" he mutters to his brother and hurries on ahead.

I suspect I only heard him at all because I'm so weirdly attuned to the sound of his voice. Even though it's nearly the same as Liam's, it's also…different somehow.

"I had a pretty boring weekend, too." Bri barely notices Lucas's departure. "Hey, you want to sit with us at lunch? We can talk more about Friday's game."

He agrees without hesitation.

Now that Lucas is nearly out of sight, I catch up with them. Molly and Tristan get behind us in the lunch line, then we all head to our usual table. Sean and Kira are already sitting there, and M and Rigel show up a minute later.

"Looks like the whole gang's back together." Tristan grins around at everyone. "Hey, Liam. Great game Friday. You, too, Sean."

Bri immediately seizes that opening and soon everyone's discussing the game. Except me. My eyes are irresistibly drawn to Lucas, sitting at his usual table with most of the others who moved here from New York—Alan Dempsey, a couple of sophomores I don't really know, and two freshmen girls I know from Chorus, Jana and Adina.

When they first got here, all eight "NuAgra kids" sat together at lunch. Though some people decided it meant they were stuck up, I figured they were just nervous about being new. Sure enough, after a few weeks some branched out. Kira, of course, joined our table when she and Sean started dating. And Liam—easily the most outgoing of the bunch—often ate at the jock table to talk sports. Alan has sometimes sat there, too, but I've never seen Lucas sit anywhere else.

"Right, Deb?" Bri's voice pulls my attention back to our table.

"Er…" I dredge through my brain, trying to replay whatever she just said. "New Year's Eve, you mean?"

"Yeah. I mean, someone *must* have been throwing a party somewhere, but we didn't hear about it. Not that the one at your house was bad, of course! Maggie's friends are pretty cool."

M's watching me a little too perceptively, like she guesses why I wasn't listening. She confirms that with a secret little smile before turning to Bri. "I'm sure Trina either had a party or found one, but none of *us* would have been invited. Well, except maybe Sean or Liam. Were you?"

Both guys shake their heads.

"Didn't hear a thing." Liam shrugs. "Doubt my parents would have let me go anyway. They can be stupid strict sometimes." He slides a glance at Bri but looks away before she notices.

"They're probably just not used to small-town life yet," Rigel suggests. "They'll loosen up when they realize there's not a whole lot of trouble to get into here."

For a second, M looks like she's struggling not to laugh, but then she nods. "Rigel's right. You can't blame them for being cautious so soon after moving to a new town."

Liam snorts. "We've been here nearly four months now. But yeah, I think they might be getting a *little* better about…some things." He shoots another quick look at Bri and this time she sees it.

"Oh? What kinds of things?" She tilts her head so her long, dark curls brush his shoulder.

"They were fine with me taking you to the Winter Formal," he responds with a grin, not at all put off by her flirting. "Once they confirmed there'd be chaperones, anyway."

Sounds like my guess about their family being ultra-religious may have been right.

"Your parents aren't the only ones who are picky about that kind of thing." Bri wrinkles her nose at him. "Though there *are* ways around most rules…" She trails off suggestively.

"Yeah? I may need you to teach me some of those."

The two of them continue flirting, practically ignoring everyone else at the table. Toward the end of lunch, I notice M frowning at them a little. Rather hypocritical, considering how she and Rigel acted early on in their relationship. And still do, sometimes.

"Are you coming to tonight's game in Frankton?" Liam asks Bri when the bell rings and we all get up to dump our trays.

She dimples up at him. "You bet! Wouldn't miss it!"

"How about you, Deb?" Liam asks then, an obvious afterthought.

I shake my head. "Probably not. My mom doesn't like me going to away games on school nights."

Not completely true, especially since Frankton's so close, but it's a believable-sounding excuse. After the way Lucas acted at Friday's game, I want to gauge how he acts toward me in Art class before I commit to another one.

Fortunately, Bri doesn't contradict me. In fact, I doubt she even heard me, the way she's still looking at Liam as they walk to the tray drop together. "I, ah, guess I'll see you tonight, then," she tells him when they finally part in the hallway.

"Can't wait." He punctuates his reply with a wink before turning away.

I watch as he joins his brother to head to their fifth-period class and see Lucas whisper something that makes Liam frown and shake his head. Which makes Lucas frown. He had to notice how tight Liam and Bri looked during lunch. Does he not approve?

Any last, faint hopes I might still have been cherishing about Lucas fade even further before Bri grabs me by the arm.

"OMG, I'm *so* glad I asked Liam to sit with us! I think he really may like me! What do you think?"

"Duh." I laugh in spite of my disappointment. "Of course he does. You two were so wrapped up in each other at lunch, everyone at our table—shoot, probably the whole cafeteria—has to know he likes you."

A tiny frown forms between her dark brows. "I'm sorry, I kind of ignored you, didn't I?"

"It's fine," I assure her. "I'm used to it. You're like this every time you first get interested in a new guy. Though you two *are* especially cute together."

She's quiet for a moment, then says, "So...you think Liam is just another one of my crushes?"

I shrug. "It's too soon to tell, isn't it? I mean, I remember how over the moon you were about Gary last year. Then Matt. Then Sean when he first got here, though you two never went out. Then this year you crushed on *all* the new guys when they first got here, especially Tristan.

Not to mention just about every boy who's ever sat with you at a game or talked to you at a party."

"Okay, okay, you're right," she admits with a chagrined chuckle. "But this thing with Liam feels different. Like we have some kind of... special connection."

Just ahead of us, I see M's head twitch when Bri says that. Is she eavesdropping on us? Even as I think that, she whispers something to Molly, who half-glances back at us. Apparently so. But why? Other than getting a little judgy about Bri and me going to football after-parties, I don't remember M ever being particularly bothered by any of Bri's other fledging romances.

M *does* sometimes seem to be a little tighter with the newer students than most people at school are, though I have no idea why she should be. For now, all I can do is file it away with all the other little mysteries about the newcomers. And M.

Heading to sixth period an hour later, I start feeling nervous. Art is usually my favorite class, even before Lucas got here, but today I'm at least half dreading it. What if he acts like he doesn't even know me? I'll be mortified.

When I walk in, Lucas is already at one of the long, adjustable drawing tables. I pause near the door for a moment, dithering, then take what I hope is a calming breath before casually moving to an open spot next to him.

"Hey, Lucas," I say with feigned lightness. "Good weekend?"

He darts a quick look at me, accompanied by a *very* slight smile. "Um, not bad." Then, after a long, awkward pause, without looking at me again, "You?"

"Not bad," I echo.

As the silence stretches between us, I'm trying to get up the nerve to try again when I'm distracted by the sight of Tika Bhatta coming into the room on crutches, a cast on her leg. She's a sophomore, and even shyer than Lucas. I don't know her well, but as she awkwardly moves to the next table, I walk over to her.

"Hey, Tika, what did you do to yourself?"

She darts a quick, embarrassed glance at me from behind her sleek black hair, then looks down. "I tried to go ice skating over break and somehow broke a little bone in my foot. Doctor said no weight-bearing for three weeks."

"I'm sorry. I'm a total klutz at ice skating, so it's amazing I've never done the same thing. I can get you anything you need during class, so you don't have to navigate to the supply closet and back, okay?"

Though clearly startled, she beams at me. "Thanks, Deb! That's really nice of you."

I smile back, returning to my spot just as class starts, sparing me the effort of attempting more conversation with Lucas. While the teacher explains the elements of drawing we'll cover this semester, I sneak a few sideways peeks at him, but never once catch him looking back.

A little later, when everybody's getting paper and other supplies from the closet, most people take the opportunity to talk. Lucas never says a word to me, though, making me glad I have the excuse of helping Tika. At one point, when I ask Lucas to hand me a pencil from the cup in front of us, he does so without speaking—and without touching me.

Feeling completely frozen out, I suppress a shiver.

Before and after Chorus seventh period, then during the bus ride home, Bri can't seem to stop talking about Liam and her hopes in that direction.

"Maybe, if tonight's game doesn't go too late, we can go get a shake together at Dream Cream afterward. I'll suggest it, anyway."

"It sounds like his parents are pretty strict," I remind her. "Plus, they may only have the one car. They can't live as close to downtown as we do, since Liam rides the same bus Rigel used to." I carefully don't bring Lucas's name into it at all.

Bri doesn't seem to notice. "All the more reason you should come to the game, especially if your mom will let you borrow her car again. The roads aren't at all icy now. That way we could at least offer the guys a ride home after the game, even if it's too late to go anywhere else," she continues excitedly. "Won't you please ask if you can? Frankton's barely ten miles away—it hardly even counts as an away game."

I grope for an excuse she'll buy, then figure I might as well just be honest. "I really don't want to, Bri, sorry. Not after the way Lucas acted in Art class today. It was like he barely remembered we'd met, much less that he took me to a dance. He obviously wants to forget all about that...about me."

"Oh." Bri looks suddenly deflated. "Oh. I'm sorry, Deb, I didn't know. But maybe if—"

"Uh-uh." I cut her off. "If I go to the game and he avoids me there, too, it'll advertise to the whole world that the guy who took me to Winter Formal has already lost interest. Just—" I swallow. "Just like every other boy I've ever gone out with."

Turning away from the sympathy in her eyes, I stare out the bus window, willing myself not to cry.

"Hey," she says after a moment. "It's not like I have a great track record with guys, either. The longest I ever went out with anybody was Matt Mullins last year, and that was for what? A month? Most of the guys at this school are only interested in one thing, so once they're sure a girl won't put out, they move on."

I nod dully, trying not to fall completely into a self-pity party.

"But Liam seems different," she continues. "He didn't even *try* anything at the Formal."

"Yeah, neither did Lucas. But at least Liam still acts interested in you. Lucas almost acts...*afraid* of me."

The bus pulls up to our stop then, but as soon as we're on the sidewalk, Bri returns to the same painful subject.

"Maybe Lucas is just shy? No, hear me out! Maybe he really *does* like you, and that's what scares him, because he's afraid to do anything about it. If you're right that their parents are super religious or something, that could totally explain it."

Feeling slightly better in spite of myself, I shrug. "Maybe. But even if that *is* it, I don't see how it changes anything if he's really determined to avoid me."

"I dunno, either," she admits. "But give it time. If he really does like you, he's bound to come around eventually."

"That's a big *if*," I reply. "Maybe I won't give up completely yet, but I still don't want to come to the game tonight."

To my relief, she doesn't argue this time. "Okay. Offering the boys a ride was a long shot anyway. See you later, Deb." She continues to her house next door.

I go up my front walk, wondering if I made the right decision to stay home tonight...and how Lucas will act toward me tomorrow.

9

Impedance

Lucas

BY LUNCHTIME THURSDAY, I'm increasingly worried Liam will do or say something really stupid, if he hasn't already. I'm glad he and Bri Morrison don't have any classes together, since the way they act at lunch is bad enough—and that's when Liam knows I'm watching. I don't want to think how he'd behave if I weren't around.

Like always, I head to the table where most of us newer *Echtran* students still sit, but stop before setting down my tray.

Ugh. Trina Squires is sitting here again, trying her hardest to get Alan to respond to her flirting. Even though he resists her efforts a lot better than Liam does with Bri's, I don't relish another lunch with her at the table. Neither do any of the others, judging by their expressions.

Still standing, I look across the cafeteria to where Liam is again sitting way too close to Bri, their heads nearly touching as they talk together. What is he telling her? Hopefully nothing he shouldn't, but self-control and thinking ahead aren't exactly strengths of his.

On sudden decision, I carry my tray over to that table instead. Surely keeping my brother out of trouble is more important than avoiding Debbi Andrews? Especially now I've proved to myself I can keep my cool around her during three consecutive Art classes.

"Hey," I say to the group in general, suddenly feeling stupid. "Mind if I join you today?"

"Of course, Lucas, have a seat," the Sovereign—no, M, I remind myself *again*—says with a smile.

Deb turns to look up at me and the startled welcome in her pretty blue eyes makes me doubt this was such a good idea after all. But then she turns back around so quickly I wonder if I only imagined her expression, which was exactly what I feared. Or hoped for?

"Yo, Bro!" Liam grins a welcome from across the table. "About time you stepped out of your comfort zone."

At the same time, Molly O'Gara nudges Tristan over one spot to open up a chair. Next to Deb. Oops.

Trapped, I take the now-empty seat, flashing a quick, half-apologetic smile at Deb. Her return smile is tentative. Not surprising, considering I've practically ignored her all week. Though I keep telling myself it's for the best, I've obviously hurt her feelings in the process. Realizing that now bothers me. A lot.

"Today's Chem lab was a tricky one, don't you think?" Molly asks me from Deb's other side, breaking a silence that was getting awkward. From the corner of my eye, I see Bri give Deb a quick thumbs-up—because I'm sitting here? I'm careful to look past Deb instead of at her when I answer Molly.

"Um, yeah, kind of tricky." It's easy to still think of her as Molly, since nobody found out until recently that she's actually Princess Malena, the Sovereign's sister. "It took us two tries to get the right amount of benzene into our beaker."

That was mostly my lab partner Amber's fault. She tends to be kind of careless during the labs because she's so busy flirting with me. I remember she did the same with Liam when they were partners last semester. Objectively, I guess Amber might be considered prettier than Deb, but she doesn't attract me in the least.

Deb, on the other hand, somehow keeps getting more and more likable. She's been amazingly selfless and nice to that girl in our Art class with the crutches. And when she's at our drawing table, right next to me…

Guiltily thrusting that thought away, I take a bite of my meatloaf and listen carefully to Tristan, discussing today's Chem lab. Across from me, Liam offers Bri a cookie, then teasingly pulls it away when she reaches for it. Giggling, she grabs his wrist and brings the cookie back to her mouth to take a bite. Liam laughs and takes a bite from the other side of the cookie.

Liam notices me watching them. "What?"

"Nothing." Though I'm more worried than ever, I avert my eyes. And catch Deb looking at me.

"What?" I say, exactly like Liam just did.

"Nothing," she echoes me. "Just…surprised you suddenly decided to sit here." *After the way you've acted all week,* she doesn't say but is clearly thinking.

Willing my color not to rise, I shrug. "Like Liam said, it was time to step out of my comfort zone. Not that it's all that comfortable these days." I glance back at my usual table.

Following my gaze, Deb chuckles—a sound that sends a weird little shiver through my midsection. "Yeah, Trina has that effect on a lot of people. Poor Alan. Once she sets her sights on a guy, she's like a dog with a bone."

That draws a half-smile from me. "Pretty sure Alan can take care of himself." I hope. Even if I'm wrong, Alan's not my responsibility. Unlike Liam.

"So, everyone's coming to our game tonight, right?" Liam asks the table in general before turning a challenging look on me.

"Yeah, I'll come this time." I skipped the last one. "It's here at Jewel, right?"

Bri laughs. "Your own brother doesn't even know which are your home games? I guess I shouldn't give Deb such a hard time for not keeping track, then."

Involuntarily, I glance at Deb. Who looks embarrassed. "Not every-one's obsessed with sports," I point out, mostly for her sake.

"There are worse things to be obsessed with," Liam retorts, probably referring to my energy project.

In response, I flick a glance at Bri, then hold my brother's eye. "True," I agree.

He glares at me for a second, clearly taking my meaning, then turns to Bri. "Will you be coming early again with your dad?"

"That depends on Deb," she replies. "Think you can borrow your mom's car tonight?"

Deb looks uncomfortable. Because she doesn't want to go to the game at all? Liam told me she wasn't at the last one. Or because I said I'd be there?

"I'll ask," she tells Bri, with a noticeable lack of enthusiasm. "I'll…let you know." Her chin twitches, like she started to look my way, then changed her mind. She takes a bite of her salad instead.

That I even noticed her twitch is probably a bad sign. For the rest of lunch, I do my best to avoid thinking too much about Deb. Instead, I pay attention to how the other *Echtrans* interact with the *Duchas* at the table, trying to get a better feel for how to do that without arousing any suspicions. I also try to ignore Liam and Bri since he got so defensive before, though they continue flirting outrageously until the bell rings.

After what I consider an unnecessarily affectionate goodbye to Bri, Liam falls into step next to me on the way to fifth-period U.S. History.

"Admit it," he grumps. "The only reason you sat at our table today was to keep an eye on me."

I shrug but don't deny it. "I've told you why I think it's dangerous to get too friendly with a *Duchas*. Especially a *Duchas* girl." I'm speaking softly enough no non-Martian can hear me.

"And I told you why I think that's bunk," he whispers back fiercely. "Why don't you ask the Sovereign if *she* has a problem with it? She looked really happy when you sat at our table."

"She won't be happy if you break Bri's heart."

Liam glares at me. "You still think I'm leading Bri on? Well, I'm not. We just enjoy talking to each other, and lunch is practically the only time we can since we don't have any classes together. You make it sound like we're making out in the cafeteria."

"Okay, fine. Just…be careful, okay?"

Though Liam doesn't know it, that warning is as much to myself as to him.

I silently repeat that caution when I get to Art sixth period. After sitting with Deb at lunch today, it would look weird to revert to acting like I barely know her. At the same time, I need to make sure I don't get *too* friendly with her. Which would be dangerously easy to do.

"Hey," I say with careful casualness when I take my usual spot next to her at the big, open table. It's the first time since the holidays I've spoken to her first.

Like at lunch, she looks both surprised and cautiously pleased. "Hi. How was History?"

"It was okay," I reply, grateful for a perfectly safe topic. "You took it last year, right?"

She nods. "Not my favorite class, but not the worst. And I did learn a lot I didn't know about our country's history."

"Like what?" I can't admit that most of what I'm learning in that class is new to me. Our six weeks of Earth Orientation included only the most cursory overview of American history.

"Like all the stuff that led up to the Civil Rights Act." She shakes her head. "I had no idea. Did you know—?" She breaks off as the teacher tells us to quiet down and get out the drawings we were working on yesterday.

Just as well. Pursuing that topic would make it hard to avoid revealing how little I know about stuff most regular American high-schoolers take for granted. I give Deb what I hope looks like a regretful smile, then busy myself with pulling out my current sketch and spreading it on the table in front of me.

We don't talk again during class, but somehow the silence between us today feels comfortable instead of awkward.

Yeah, I can do this. No sweat.

At Liam's game that evening, I continue walking the fine line between casually friendly and too friendly. Though I sit with Bri and Deb, I'm careful to keep the conversation general, talking as much to the others around us as to Deb herself. The few times I do talk to her, it's about art —nothing too personal. During the game, I also spend a lot of time thinking about my energy project at NuAgra to distract myself from how nice Deb smells and the persistent pleasure of being near her. It mostly works. I'm more confident than ever that being friends with Deb won't be so hard after all.

Over halftime, the whole group of us go to the concession stand. We all talk comfortably about the game while we drink our sodas and eat our candy out in the hallway. Bri dominates the conversation, knowl-edgeably dissecting every play of the first half, which makes it easy to avoid saying much to Deb or anyone else.

Jewel ends up winning again—hard to avoid with three *Echtrans* on the team. Our guys *are* doing a decent job of holding back, but I'm still surprised the *Echtran* Council allows them—us—to play sports at all. Maybe the fact that Sean O'Gara's mother is on the Council has some-thing to do with it?

Afterward, while we're all congratulating the players, Bri pulls Deb aside to whisper urgently to her. Deb looks skeptical, but then shrugs and nods. Grinning, Bri hurries back to Liam as the worst crush of fans starts to disperse.

"It's not all that late," Bri says to him. "Would you guys like to go get a shake at Dream Cream or something? Deb's got her mom's car tonight, so she can drive us."

Liam looks like he's about to agree, so I speak first. "Sorry, we'd better not. Our parents are waiting for us over there, and they're pretty strict about us not being out late on school nights."

For a second I think Liam's going to contradict me, since I totally made up that last bit, but he contents himself with a quick glare before nodding.

"Yeah, sorry. Besides, I can't very well go anywhere public before showering. I'd stink up the place. But let's do something together soon for sure, okay?"

At that, Bri's obvious disappointment vanishes, replaced by a smile. "Definitely! Okay, see you tomorrow at school. Um, g'night."

She sways forward slightly, her face tipping up like she expects Liam to kiss her or something. Fortunately, even he has enough sense not to do anything *that* stupid, especially with our parents watching.

"Right," he says, taking a step back. "See you tomorrow."

I nod a quick goodbye to Deb—and Bri—then hurry Liam away. He doesn't say anything as we join our parents, but his expression makes me wonder if he was tempted to give Bri the kiss she seemed to be angling for. I don't ask.

✦

I sit at Deb's table again at lunch the next day, but not right next to her. I considered not sitting here at all, but after last night it seems more necessary than ever to keep Liam out of trouble.

"So, your mom is a nurse?" he's asking Bri as I sit down next to him, across from Deb and down a little.

Bri nods. "She works nights a lot. It's why she never comes to the games. Both your parents work at NuAgra, right? What do they do there, exactly?"

I tense, but Liam gives a safe answer. "They're both Engineers, so engineering-type stuff. Does your mom like being a nurse?"

To my relief, Bri doesn't seem to notice his deflection.

"She really does, though I know it can be stressful for her sometimes. From what she says, the hospital is almost always understaffed and most of the equipment is old. Maybe that'll change now that Jewel's economy is improving…thanks to NuAgra."

"Hey, glad to do our part." Liam says it lightly, but his glance at M shows he realizes that's dangerous ground. Good.

"So," Liam continues to Bri, "after the game last night we talked about getting together and one of the guys mentioned there's a good band playing at the Lighthouse Cafe tomorrow night. Want to go?"

I stare at him in disbelief, though I manage to keep my mouth from dropping open. Is he nuts?

"Sure, that sounds great!" Bri instantly responds, flashing a grin across at Deb.

"It…does," I force myself to say. "Why don't we all go?" That's got to be a lot safer than letting the two of them go out together alone. "What do you say, everyone?" I look around the table, trying not to let my panic show.

M and Molly both shake their heads.

"I can't," Molly says. "There's a cheerleading thing, and then I, ah, promised my mum I'd help her with something afterward."

"And I have a project to finish up," M says. She and Molly exchange a glance and I suddenly remember the *Echtran* Council has a meeting every Saturday night, which they both have to attend. Duh. Neither Rigel nor Tristan volunteer to go without their girlfriends, and Kira has a basketball game, so Sean's out, too.

Crap.

Swallowing, I look at Deb. "Just us four, then?"

She hesitates like she's not sure I mean it. Then she says, "Okay, yeah, if you— I mean— It sounds fun."

I smile like I agree with her, though I feel more like strangling my brother. "Yeah, I'm sure it will be."

Maybe…*too* much fun?

10

Supposition

Deb

"I WAS RIGHT! I WAS RIGHT!" Bri squeals on our way to fifth period, once the Walsh brothers are out of earshot. "About both of them—though I swear for a second I thought you were going to say *no* when Lucas asked you, too."

I look at her uncertainly. "Should I have? So you and Liam could be alone?"

"No, silly, it's fine. There's no being alone at the Lighthouse anyway, not on a Saturday night. If you two weren't coming, other people would probably sit at our table anyway, maybe people I don't like as much. Sure, dinner and a movie would be more, um, intimate. But for a second date, I'll totally take it."

"Yeah. Me, too."

I force more heartiness into my voice than I feel, since I suspect Lucas only asked me to keep Liam and Bri from having a solo date. He's probably never been to the Lighthouse, so he wouldn't know how crowded it usually is on Saturdays.

In Art class I tentatively bring up the subject, hoping to get a better gauge of his feelings. "Do you happen to know what band is playing at the Lighthouse Saturday?" I ask him as we're getting out our drawing materials. "I haven't looked at their schedule lately."

Lucas shakes his head. "No idea. I'll ask Liam. Why?"

"Oh, um, I was just curious. Have you ever been to the Lighthouse on a Saturday?"

"No, I've only ever seen it from the outside. What's it like?"

Yep, I was right. "It's pretty much the only teen-friendly hotspot in Jewel unless you count Dream Cream. So it's usually crowded in the evenings, especially when there's a popular band. That means the service will probably be slow, but the food is great. Their onion rings are to die for, though I don't dare eat a whole order by myself."

"To— Are they dangerous?" He looks confused.

"Uh, no. Just fattening. Haven't you ever had onion rings?"

The wariness I've noticed several times before is back in his eyes. "I, ah, guess not. So 'to die for' means good?"

Seriously? "Er, yes. Really good. Tell you what, we'll split an order tomorrow night and you can form your own opinion. I'm sure if you don't like them, Bri and Liam will bat cleanup."

"Bat—?" For a second he looks confused again, but quickly recovers. "Yeah. Okay. Sure."

Averting his eyes, he starts lining up his pencils and charcoal sticks with unnecessary precision, a clear signal he doesn't want to talk anymore. With an inward sigh, I take the hint, more certain than ever that he didn't really want to ask me out. Also that there's something seriously off about him...and maybe all the NuAgra people.

But what?

On the bus that afternoon, I share my observations with Bri.

"All these newer kids supposedly attended a big public high school back in New York, but some things they say—that Lucas says, anyway— make me wonder. Does Liam ever act like he's never heard some really common expressions before?"

Her brows go up. "What do you mean?"

"Okay. Like at the dance, I said something to Lucas about breaking the ice. You know, to make conversation. He seemed to think I was refer-ring to actual ice. And did you notice *none* of the newer people except Tristan, who came here from Denver, knew the motions to 'Y.M.C.A.'?"

Bri just shrugs. "So what? It's a super old song. They probably stopped playing it at dances back East decades ago. A little Midwestern town like Jewel is bound to be pretty backward in comparison."

"Yeah, maybe so. But there's other stuff. Just today, in Art class,

Lucas acted like he'd never even *heard* of onion rings, asked me if they're *dangerous*. I was like, 'What? No! Just fattening.' And it obviously weirded him out when I suggested splitting an order at the Lighthouse tomorrow. I'm telling you, there's something distinctly weird about him —about most of these NuAgra kids. And every time I ask Lucas anything about where they lived before, he gets nervous and clams up. What has Liam told you?"

"Not much, I guess," she admits, "but I don't ask nearly as many questions as you do. Liam's asked *me* plenty of questions. About myself and about Jewel's previous sports seasons and just sports in general. We always have fun talking."

I regard her thoughtfully for a moment, my gears turning. "When he asks you about sports, is it sometimes stuff you think he should already know? That most guys his age would?"

Again, she shrugs. "Maybe. Sometimes. But I get the impression they didn't play many of the same sports back in New York—except basketball, of course."

"Even that. Has he talked about what schools they played against, stuff like that?"

"Not really, no. But again, I haven't asked."

By now, I'm getting frustrated. "Why don't you? I'm really curious what he'll tell you."

Bri rolls her eyes. "Like you care what schools they used to play? Seriously? I am *not* going to ruin my second date with Liam by asking a bunch of questions he might not want to answer. Did you ever think you being so inquisitive might be why Lucas backed off before?"

"I didn't—" But now that I think of it, it did kind of seem like that. "Okay, maybe. Still, if there really is something strange going on with Liam and Lucas and all the other NuAgra folks, don't you want to know what it is?"

"Not enough to risk what seems like a really promising relationship," she tells me. "Keep digging if you want, and let me know if you find anything out. But don't blame me if you end up pushing Lucas away—again—in the process."

⁺
⁺⁺

Possible weirdness aside, I can't keep my hopes from bubbling up once I'm at Bri's house the next evening getting ready for our second double date with the Walsh boys.

"That color is perfect on you, Deb," Bri tells me, touching the shoulder of my soft blue cashmere top. "It makes your eyes look even bluer. Is my hair okay?"

She's fastened back the front part with a gold butterfly-shaped clip to keep her wild curls at least partly under control.

"Yeah, pulling it away from your face like that emphasizes your cheekbones, gives you kind of a cool, exotic look." I glance over her outfit—a sleek, purple sweater dress that makes the most of her tall, slender figure—and experience a pang of envy. "You look really great. Liam won't know what hit him."

Bri laughs delightedly. "Here's hoping! And you look totally adorable. Very cuddle-worthy."

Probably the most I can hope for, since I'll never be as elegant as Bri. Not that I expect Lucas to try to cuddle me, much as I'd like that.

We're just putting the finishing touches on our makeup when Bri's mom calls up the stairs that our dates just drove up. Bri and I exchange a last excited glance and hurry downstairs, grabbing our coats off the hooks in the front hall just as the doorbell rings.

"Hi, guys!" Bri greets them, flinging the door wide. "I'd ask you in, but we should probably head out right away if we want to snag a decent table. The Lighthouse always fills up fast on Saturdays, especially when the Epic Embers are playing. They're really good." Over her shoulder, she calls out, "Mom, Dad, we're leaving!"

Her mother pokes her head around the corner. "All right, have fun. But be careful on the roads—this rain is supposed to turn to sleet later."

"I will, Mrs. Morrison, don't worry," Liam tells her.

We all hurry through the thin, icy rain to get into the car for the short drive to Diamond Street. Despite my earlier doubts, I can't stifle a thrill of anticipation when I slide into the back seat next to Lucas, even though he hasn't said a word to me yet.

"Sucky weather," I comment, just for something to say.

"Er, yeah," he agrees. But that's it.

I sigh inwardly as Bri and Liam, up front, fill the silence with chatter of their own.

"Hey, at least it's not snowing," she tells Liam cheerfully. "Though I guess that wouldn't bother you, coming from upstate New York. You probably got tons of snow there, didn't you?"

Liam nods, though I'm glad to see he keeps his eyes on the road. "More than three times as much as Jewel gets, according to the internet. Not that I ever drove in it myself. Got my license over the summer, then we moved here. Doubt I'll have a problem, though."

"Guess that's true for Lucas, too?" Bri glances back at us.

"Er, yeah," he replies, exactly like before, and again falls silent. My expectations for the evening, already low, fall further.

Fortunately, it only takes five minutes to get to the Lighthouse Cafe. Unfortunately, all the street parking nearby is already full. Liam has to park more than two blocks away, in front of Glitterby's, which closed at six.

"At least the rain's mostly stopped," Liam says cheerfully as he gets out.

Just like he did after the dance, he goes around to open Bri's door for her. And like I did then, I get out before Lucas feels obliged to do the same.

"Are you going to watch the Colts play Denver in the playoffs tomorrow?" Bri asks Liam as we walk briskly through the cold. "I think their chances are good to go all the way this year!"

"That would be cool," Liam replies. "And yeah, I plan to watch it. Maybe—?" He glances back at Lucas.

Which makes me glance at him, too, in time to see the tiny frown he gives his brother.

"We could watch it together?" Bri finishes eagerly, not having noticed their exchange.

"Um, yeah, maybe?" Liam sounds slightly less enthusiastic now. Warned off by Lucas again? Why?

I'm dying to ask, but don't quite dare. Instead, I say, "Are you having as much trouble drawing hands in Art as I am? Though the teacher did say that's one of the hardest things to get right."

Lucas shoots me a startled look and *again* replies, "Er, yeah." Then he actually elaborates. "I probably should be practicing at home, like she told us to, but I, um, haven't had time yet."

"I *have* been practicing at home, and I still can't make the fingers look real. I'm not sure drawing people will ever be my strong suit. I think I'm more into impressionism and interesting use of color."

Apparently deciding art is a safe topic, Lucas responds with his opinion of how color was used by Matisse, one of the artists we're supposed to be studying, by which time we've reached the Lighthouse.

"Ugh, it's already pretty crowded," Bri comments when we go in. "But that table in the corner looks empty—and relatively private." She slants a flirty glance up at Liam.

"Uh, how about that one?" Lucas suggests, pointing to a more brightly lit table near the stage instead.

Bri shrugs. "Okay, sure. It'll be hard to talk once the band starts, but at least we'll be right by the dance floor."

We make our way to the table Lucas indicated at the edge of the Lighthouse's minuscule dance floor, roughly the size of three missing tables. Liam pulls out a chair for Bri and, rather to my surprise, Lucas does the same for me before I can sit down. My murmured thanks is rewarded by a small smile. Maybe there's hope for this evening after all?

Bri and Liam again carry the bulk of the conversation, dissecting the Indiana Pacers' season so far, until a server shows up with some menus to take our drink orders. I get my usual diet cola, while Lucas sticks to water. Bri orders root beer like always and Liam does the same, rather obviously because she did. Which is cute.

"Have you guys thought any about what colleges you're interested in?" I ask as we open our menus, hoping to steer the talk away from sports. "Lucas, you mentioned maybe studying engineering? What branch? Chemical? Petroleum? You're interested in energy, right?"

He nods cautiously. "Mechanical engineering could play into that, too."

"Especially for new technologies, like solar and wind." I can't suppress my own enthusiasm now. "I've thought about going into environmental engineering myself, since I really want to do my part to save the planet." Then, realizing I'm starting to babble, I look over at Bri. "You still want to study sports medicine, right, Bri? How about you, Liam?"

Seemingly caught off-guard, he blinks. "I'm hoping for a basketball scholarship but I'll probably study engineering, too…if I can't get into the NBA."

"I bet you will, though." Bri looks up at him admiringly. "You're really, really good, bordering on amazing when you're on form."

Lucas clears his throat. "So, what does everyone want to eat? Deb, you mentioned onion rings?"

"Let's get an order for the table," I suggest. "The servings here are huge." I'll probably get a dinner salad for my meal, to make up for them.

When the server comes back with our drinks, Lucas orders a burger and Liam again copies Bri by asking for fish and chips. I dutifully order my salad, dressing on the side, trying not to be resentful about how carefully I have to watch my calories compared to the rest of them. I happen to be looking at Liam when he takes his first sip of root beer and there's no mistaking his surprise.

"Wow, this is really good! Root beer, I mean. What...what brand is it?"

Bri apparently sees nothing odd about his reaction. "A&W, I think. And yeah, it is good." Grinning at him, she takes a big sip of her own. "Free refills, too."

"Nice." Liam takes another long pull at his straw.

We all continue discussing college options until our food arrives. When Lucas picks up his first-ever onion ring, cautiously crunching into it, I watch for his reaction. His brows go up and he nods approvingly to me.

"You were right. These *are* to die for."

Is he really poking fun at himself for his earlier ignorance? I beam back my own approval. "Told you."

Our gazes tangle together for a second and my heart speeds up at the little something extra I see in his eyes. He takes what sounds like a slightly shaky breath, then blinks and looks away, ending our brief moment of connection.

The band starts then, making conversation more difficult, but I feel like Lucas and I may have just made a tiny bit of progress.

As soon as they finish their meals, Bri and Liam hit the packed little dance floor. Lucas looks at me questioningly and I shrug.

"Only if you want to," I have to practically shout.

"Awfully crowded," he shouts back, so we stay put.

After that, Bri and Liam dance almost every song, only coming back to the table for occasional sips of root beer. Lucas and I eventually dance together a few times, too—always fast songs. When the band starts another slow one shortly after their second break, I notice him tensing. Again.

"I, ah, I'm going to hit the ladies' room." I get up, sparing Lucas the awkwardness of asking me to dance...or not.

I turn to ask Bri if she wants to come, too, but Liam is already tugging her back onto the dance floor. As I make my way around the tightly-packed dancers, I notice Bri and Liam are pressed together as tightly as most of the other couples. Not at all like the way they—and Lucas and I—danced at the Winter Formal. Not that I'm surprised, after the way they've been flirting all week, and especially tonight.

Glancing back at Lucas, I see he's watching them, too…and doesn't look happy. Maybe being that close to a girl really is against their religion? For Bri's sake, I hope not.

11

Fast break

Bri

LIAM PUTS his arms around me as the soulful strains of the Epic Embers' indie-folk arrangement of "Can't Help Falling in Love" wash over us. Swaying with him to the music, I lean my head against his chest, feeling deliriously happy. *This* is exactly how I imagined dancing with him at the Winter Formal. I almost can't believe it's finally happening!

Over Liam's shoulder, I see Deb getting up from our table. Lucas's expression is almost… relieved? But then he looks over at us and scowls. When he notices I'm looking at him, he quickly averts his eyes. It's at least the third time tonight that's happened. What's his problem? Maybe Liam knows? I decide to just ask.

"Your brother, um…doesn't seem too happy. About us, I mean," I say tentatively.

Liam frowns and rotates us around so he can look past me at his brother and I watch his face as he glares for a moment—he must have caught Lucas glaring at *us* again—then suddenly sticks his tongue out.

Startled, I laugh. "What was that about?"

"Lucas is such a prude. I swear, sometimes he's as bad as our parents," he tells me, shaking his head. "My theory is he's mostly jealous because he won't let himself have any fun."

Maybe it's true that Lucas is just jealous. Or maybe… An unpleasantly familiar thought occurs to me, but I push it aside, not wanting to go there right now.

"So your parents really *are* giant prudes?" I say instead. "I, uh… kinda wondered."

He laughs at that—a rich, hearty sound, but one tinged with bitterness. "Yeah, they kind of are. But don't worry. *I'm* definitely not, and I don't care what *they* think. Any of them." His arms tighten around me and I respond with a contented sigh.

"Did you mean what you said about getting together tomorrow to watch the playoff game?" he asks me a few moments later.

I look up at him eagerly. "Of course! If you want to?"

"You bet I do. It's a date, then." Smiling, he holds my gaze and I get lost in his gorgeous blue-gray eyes.

The words, "some things are meant to be," crooned by the lead singer, strike me as amazingly appropriate right now. I feel a weird flutter start somewhere deep in my stomach that slowly rises and settles in the vicinity of my heart. Soaking in the feeling of Liam pressed up against me, I wonder if he can feel the way my heart is pounding. Or is that his heartbeat I feel? It almost feels like our hearts are beating together, in perfect sync.

This moment feels so *right,* so *perfect* and so *different* from anything I've ever felt before. It's dizzying. As the song comes back to the refrain, it hits me in a blinding flash, with absolute certainty, that I *am* falling in love with Liam. And that there's absolutely nothing I can do about it.

All the crushes I've had before seem almost laughable in comparison to the enormity of what I now feel for Liam. In fact, it's a little terrifying. What if Liam doesn't feel the same? But even as I think that, he gives me another little squeeze that dispels my brief fear. Whether he's as far gone as I am or not, I willingly give myself up to the beauty of this perfect moment.

Too soon, the song is over. We head back to the table hand in hand and I notice Deb isn't back yet. Maybe she's in the bathroom? Still overwhelmed by the vastness of my emotional revelation, I excuse myself, hoping to catch her in there. I need to tell her!

I'm just getting in line when she comes out of the ladies' room. The moment she reaches me, I grab her arm and pull her off to the side.

"Oh, Deb, I'm having the best, *best* time tonight! You are, too, aren't you? Please say you are."

"Yeah, I'm having a way better time than I expected," she tells me—truthfully, I think. "I don't know if Lucas and I will ever be a 'thing,' but at least we're getting to be friends. Which is fine." Before I can tell if she means that, she grins and adds, "You and Liam looked awfully cozy out there on the dance floor just now."

"Omigod Deb, it's so amazing!" I breathe. "I think…" Leaning close, I whisper in her ear, "I think I'm falling in love with him."

Deb's wry, skeptical smile is one I've seen before. Because, yeah, I probably am the girl who's cried *love* one too many times. I open my mouth to explain how this is different, that it's really, truly real this time, but realize I don't have the words. Besides, I don't want to make her jealous when things clearly aren't going as well between her and Lucas. Closing my mouth, I just shrug.

"C'mon. Let's go back to the table. I don't really have to go to the bathroom anyway, I just wanted to talk to you."

She laughs and we head back together. As we approach the table, Lucas and Liam appear to be having a pretty intense conversation, though I can't hear anything over the music. Liam sees us first and nudges Lucas, who quickly straightens to greet Deb with an obviously-forced smile.

"Sorry I was gone so long," she says, glancing between the two boys. "There was a line. Is, um, everything okay?"

"Everything's fine," Liam replies a little too quickly, flashing what's almost a glare at his brother. "In fact, we're having a great time. Aren't we, Lucas?"

Lucas nods, his smile becoming slightly more natural. "I hope you girls are, too?"

"Definitely." I smile at Liam. "I'm not sure I've ever been happier."

There's nothing the least bit forced about Liam's grin at that. "Really? That's awesome. Me, too."

I dart a quick look at Lucas, who hurriedly smooths a frown. "Yeah. Good to know," he says, but with a noticeable lack of enthusiasm. The next song starts then, a fast one, and he turns to Deb. "You, uh, want to dance?"

⁺.⁺

"It's getting kind of late," Lucas comments when the band finishes their final set of the evening. We've been at the Lighthouse Cafe for over three hours now and the crowd is starting to thin a little. "How about I go pay, so we can head out soon?"

Liam sighs loudly and gives me a look of mock anguish that makes me giggle, then reluctantly nods. "Yeah, okay. You have enough cash?"

I feel my pulse quicken, realizing this is a moment of truth. Is this a date? It sure *feels* like a date! Though we should probably at least *offer* to pay…

"We can totally pay our share," Deb says before I can volunteer, but Liam shakes his head.

"Nah, we'll cover it. Right, Lucas?" He winks at me and I let out a breath I didn't realize I was holding.

It's official. This is *definitely* a date!

"Sure," Lucas responds with a shrug. "Least we can do, after you introduced us to the life-changing experience of onion rings." With a quick, impersonal smile at all of us, he gets up and heads toward the cash register.

Giddy from such an amazing evening, I laugh and playfully squeeze Liam's arm. "Glad we could play a part in expanding your horizons! Had you seriously never tried onion rings before?"

He gives me an easy grin. "Nope. Saw them on menus but always thought, 'ew, why?' Now I know better."

"You have to give things a try before you write them off." I try to sound cute and flirty, but worry I might sound more like a ditz. "How else can you find out what you really like?" I'm talking about more than just onion rings now—and I get the feeling Liam is on my wavelength. He often is, lately.

"Definitely." There's an intensity to the word, to the way he holds my gaze, that takes my breath away.

Suddenly, he seems to remember that Deb is at the table with us, though she's dutifully pretending to be interested in the band packing up their instruments onstage. She really is a grade-A friend.

Turning to her, Liam says, "Hey, why don't Bri and I go get the car and bring it closer? We can meet you and Lucas out front."

Thrilled at the prospect of a few minutes alone with him on the dark street, I give Deb a significant look, which she's more than perceptive enough to interpret correctly.

"Oh, um, sure. I'll wait here and tell Lucas when he gets back."

Thank you! I mouth to her silently as Liam helps me into my coat— such a gentleman!

We make our way past the long line at the register, where I notice Lucas has been waylaid by Trina, who's talking determinedly.

"Should we let your brother know—?" I start to ask.

Liam shakes his head. "Nah, he looks busy. Come on."

A moment later, we open the door and are greeted by a blast of cold air, along with the unmistakable sting of sleet on my cheeks. So much for the romantic stroll down Diamond Street I was looking forward to!

"Ugh, the rain really did turn into sleet! We'd better— Uh…Liam?"

He's frozen in his tracks, staring into the night like he can't believe his eyes, wincing at the sleet on his face. It's a few seconds before he manages to close his mouth and answer.

"Yeah, yeah…sorry. This is wild! Guess we'd better get to the car as quick as we can, huh?" He grins then and grabs my hand.

Giggling together, we dash down the sidewalk and I forget all about that odd moment. Two-plus blocks later, we reach his parents' car and he fumbles with the keys.

An extra-strong gust of frigid wind hits me, driving more icy sleet into my face, and I shriek with something between giddy delight and genuine shock. "Hurry!" I laughingly tell him.

"Believe me, I'm trying!" he responds with an answering laugh.

Finally, he manages to push the button to unlock the doors—then he actually escorts me around to the passenger side and opens my door before rushing back through the sleet to the driver's side and getting in himself. *My God, could he be any more perfect?*

He thumps down into the front seat and we slam our doors shut in perfect unison, flushed and laughing and wet and cold. Running through the sleet with Liam has made me feel even *more* alive and awake than I have all evening, which I didn't think was possible.

"That was actually kind of fun!" I exclaim as I fasten my seatbelt. Turning back to Liam, I see him looking at me with an open longing that catches me off guard.

"You…um…you look amazing tonight. Have I told you that yet?" he asks, his voice suddenly thick, his eyes holding mine.

My heart starts to pound in a way that has nothing to do with our recent sprint down Diamond Street. "Yeah, I…I'm sure the sleet did wonders for my hair," I respond with a nervous chuckle. What am I even saying?

"You're so vibrant. I love the way you laugh, the way you can make anything fun—even turn something like crappy weather into an adventure." He reaches over and brushes aside one of the damp curls plastered to my face, then gently traces the curve of my cheek.

Suddenly, I'm not cold at all. In fact, my winter coat feels much too hot. When did he start leaning toward me like that? When did I start leaning toward *him?* A strange mixture of exhilaration and panic flutters in my belly. Is this really happening? Is this the right moment? What if I do something to screw it up?

But then, mid-worry, one of us closes the remaining distance between us—maybe him? Maybe me? Maybe both of us at once?—and his lips are on mine and I can't hold a single thought in my head anymore.

Kissing Liam feels so dizzyingly *right*. It's like we've somehow dissolved into one person and I don't even know who I am anymore. I'm only aware of Liam, Liam, *Liam*—the essence of him, bright and golden, strong and heady. Even though it's not, it feels like my first-ever kiss. Because never before have I experienced anything anywhere close to this.

Several ecstatic minutes pass before it occurs to me that Deb and Lucas might be waiting for us by now. Sensing a change, Liam pulls back slightly to look at me, longing still clear in his eyes. I'm tempted to just lean back in, but force myself to speak.

"Um, shouldn't we—?"

He blinks like he's only now realizing where we are. Like I just did. "Oh. Right." With a slightly embarrassed smile that only makes him more gorgeous, he starts the car.

A spot just a few spaces from the Lighthouse is open now, so Liam pulls into it and puts the car back in park. "Good, they're not out here yet," he comments. Then he turns to me, a question in his eyes.

"I, ah, guess we'll just have to wait for them." I swallow, unable to look away from him.

"Guess so," he whispers, leaning toward me.

An instant later, I'm again melting in a swirl of sensation and emotion. I lose all sense of time and space, my whole world narrowing to this moment, this place, this perfect person.

When the driver's side door is suddenly ripped open, the rude intrusion of the rest of the world into our private nirvana is so jarring that I gasp. Our shining connection abruptly severed, I'm genuinely confused for a moment about where I am and what's happening.

"What—?" I hear Lucas roar, glaring at his brother, at *me* with a look of such...fury? terror? disgust? that the golden warmth suffusing me is abruptly replaced by an icy splash of instinctive shame at being caught making out with his brother.

12

Differential pressure

Lucas

I GROAN when I see the long line for the register, though I should have expected it now that the music has ended. Twice earlier, I hinted to Liam that we should leave, but he obviously didn't want to cut his date with Bri any shorter than necessary. Also not surprising, but definitely worrisome.

As I take my place at the end of the line, my thoughts drift back to Deb, almost against my will. Once tonight, when our hands accidentally brushed, I imagined I felt a tingle like I would from an *Echtran* girl. Which is impossible. Worse, all evening I've had to fight the temptation to touch that fuzzy blue sweater she's wearing—the same blue as her eyes—to see if it's as soft as it looks. Who knew an Earth girl could seem so…huggable?

To distract myself from that dangerous line of thought, I firmly turn my mind to my power-saving project. Maybe if I tweak the energy in-flow rate by the same percentage as the out-flow, it could—

"Oh, hey, Liam! Or is it Lucas?" It's Trina, the cheerleader who went to the Winter Formal with Alan Dempsey. "I don't suppose you've seen Alan here tonight?"

"Lucas. And no, sorry."

She heaves an exaggerated sigh of disappointment. "We talked about maybe meeting up here tonight, but my cheerleading meeting went later than I thought. I wanted to apologize, so he wouldn't think I stood him up. Are you sure he wasn't here earlier?"

"Uh, I don't think so, but I wasn't exactly looking for him." I glance off to the side, hoping she'll move on. Trina's voice has a whiny, nasal quality I always find irritating. Totally different from Deb's voice, which is simultaneously calming and stimulating. I sometimes—

"So tell me, Luke, what does Alan say about me?" Trina asks then, instead of leaving.

Reluctantly, I turn back to her. "Um, I haven't noticed."

She frowns. "But you two know each other pretty well, don't you? You must get lots of chances to talk out at NuAgra."

"We, uh, work in different areas there, so not really."

I've nearly reached the cashier now, but Trina waves the person behind me ahead, waiting for my answer. I glance back toward the table where I left the others, since I've been gone a while now, but there are people in the way. All I can see is the sleeve of Deb's blue sweater.

"He must at least mention me sometimes?" Trina persists.

"I haven't really paid much attention, sorry." Craning my neck, I finally get a good view of our table. Deb is sitting there alone. Crap! Where have Liam and Bri disappeared to?

"Thanks anyway," Trina says sourly. "If Alan couldn't make it here tonight either, I won't feel guilty for not meeting him." She flounces off.

Relieved, I hand the cashier our meal check. I brought plenty of cash, since they told us during Orientation that the boys usually pay when they take girls out. Unlike Nuath, where each person's individual credit balance is automatically debited.

As our order is rung up, I do a visual sweep of the dwindling number of patrons still here. No Liam. No Bri.

The cashier seems to take a ridiculously long time making change— no wonder the line moved so slowly—but finally I'm free to head back to the table. Deb stands up when she sees me coming and puts on her coat.

"Where are Bri and Liam?" I ask when I reach her, trying to disguise my uneasiness by putting on my own coat.

"Liam went to get the car, so we wouldn't have to walk as far in the cold. Bri went with him. He left the tip first, so you wouldn't have to." Deb nods toward a five-dollar bill on the table. "Bri and I offered to cover it, but he wouldn't let us."

So the two of them are alone together outside. Definitely not good. "Um, how long ago did they leave?"

"Right after you went to pay. They didn't say anything to you on their way out?"

"Er, no." My sense of foreboding intensifies. Because that probably means Liam didn't want me to see them leaving. "I, ah, guess we'd better go find them."

I try to keep all trace of panic from my voice, but Deb's curious look makes me think I wasn't completely successful.

So does her soothing tone when she says, "I'm sure they're just outside."

Right now, though, I'm less concerned about what Deb thinks is going on inside my head than what's happening between Liam and Bri. The way they've behaved all week at lunch was bad enough, but tonight they took it up another notch. Especially during those slow dances. I'd like to *think* my brother is smart enough to keep things from going any further, but....

I quicken my pace until Deb is practically trotting to keep up. Pushing open the outer door, we're greeted by a blast of cold air accompanied by what seem to be tiny ice pellets. I nearly exclaim aloud but stop myself in time.

"Ugh, Bri's mom was right," Deb says. "It's sleeting. Hopefully the roads aren't too bad yet."

I've heard of sleet, but this is the first time I've experienced it. Which I obviously can't say. Instead, I start walking toward where we parked, squinting through the freezing onslaught for our car.

"There they are," Deb says before I locate it, pointing. "Oh. Oops."

The look that accompanies her words is half embarrassed, half amused. But when I look where she's pointing, I feel the exact opposite of amused. *That idiot!*

Our parents' car is now parked at the curb a few spaces away. Through the sleet I see Liam and Bri in the front seat, straining toward each other over the center console. Their arms wrapped around each other, they're kissing like there's no tomorrow. Which there might not be for Liam, once I'm done with him.

Forgetting about Deb for a moment, I stride forward and yank open the driver's side door. "What—?" I start to demand when Bri's startled gasp brings me at least partially to my senses.

"You, uh, took longer than we expected," she stammers, clearly embarrassed.

Liam, damn him, actually grins at me, his face flushed despite the cold, his expression dazed. "Yeah, we had to pass the time somehow. You know how it is."

I glare at him. "No. I don't."

I'm about to launch into a full-scale rant, then realize I can't do that in front of the girls, or the other now-interested *Duchas* on the sidewalk. Instead, I force myself to take a deep breath and shrug.

"Never mind. But we should get out of this sleet and go. You girls need to be home soon anyway, don't you?"

Deb's watching me a little too closely, puzzlement furrowing her brow. "Neither of our parents are super strict on weekends," she replies, "but they might worry now that it's sleeting. Plus, the roads could start getting bad soon."

"Why don't you drive?" Liam suggests, getting out of the car. "You're better than I am on slick roads."

Total fiction, but because he still looks a little disoriented, I agree—then immediately regret it when he and Bri move to the back seat. I almost insist he sit up front with me but realize in time how odd that would sound.

Thankfully the drive to Bri's house is short enough that I don't feel a need to make conversation. I'm still struggling to keep my temper under control and don't want to make Deb even more curious—or suspicious. The two in back have no such inhibitions.

"We're still on to watch the game tomorrow, right?" Liam asks Bri. Glancing in the rear-view mirror, I see he has his arm around her shoulders.

She smiles, her eyes positively shining, and nods. "Give me a call at some point and we'll decide whose house. You still have my number?"

"Are you kidding? No way I'd lose that. Precious as gold."

She giggles.

I pull up in front of her house a moment later and we all get out, Liam and Bri now holding hands. I flick a quick, sideways glance at Deb, afraid she'll expect the same, but she again just appears slightly amused, watching the other two.

The sleet is still pretty bad, so we all say a quick goodbye at the front door. Then, after a defiant look my way, Liam leans in and gives Bri one last kiss that she eagerly returns. Now Deb *does* look embarrassed.

"Let's go before the streets get worse," I snap at my brother.

With an audible sigh, he nods. "See you tomorrow," he says to Bri, then accompanies me to the car. Like I did after the Winter Formal, I wait till we're out of sight of the girls' houses to unload on him.

"You. Are. An. Idiot," I say through clenched teeth. "I honestly thought you had more sense than that. Obviously, I was wrong. Do you have any idea what you've done?"

"Had the best evening of my entire life?" he responds, looking startled but not the least bit guilty. "What's it to you, anyway?"

"She's a *Duchas*," I grind out. "Or did you somehow forget that?"

I'm watching the road now but hear him huff out a breath. "Of course I didn't, but I don't see why it should matter to you if it doesn't matter to me. And it doesn't."

"It should," I tell him. "How far do you plan to let this...thing with Bri go?"

"As far as she'll let it. I've never wanted to be with a girl nearly as much as I want to be with her. If she makes me happy and I make her happy, where's the harm?"

I take a steadying breath as I turn onto the county road that leads out of town. "The harm is the risk you're taking—for all of us. The tighter you two get, the greater the chance she'll figure things out. Hell, I can tell Deb is already wondering, just from me screwing up an idiom or two. And we're nowhere near as close as you and Bri are suddenly getting. It's not safe, Liam. Not for any of us."

"I know you think I'm stupid, but—"

"Not stupid," I interrupt. "Just short-sighted."

Even without looking at him, I can tell he's glaring at me now. "Am I? Maybe you're the one who's being short-sighted. The Sovereign herself has said that the eventual plan is to integrate peacefully with the *Duchas* and even let them know the truth about us someday, once they're ready for that kind of info. That has to start somewhere, doesn't it?"

I glance sharply at him. "Did you tell her something tonight you shouldn't have?"

"No. But I was tempted to. I honestly think she'd be okay with it."

"That is *not* your call to make."

He grumbles but doesn't reply. I don't say anything else to him until we get home. I'm busy crafting an argument he'll listen to.

"Will you agree to cool it with Bri?" I finally ask as I pull into our garage. "Or do I need to bring Mom and Dad into this?"

Clearly outraged, he opens his mouth to retort, then suddenly shrugs. "Sure. Go ahead. In fact, I'll do it myself. I bet they'll be on my side." He slams out of the car and heads into the house.

I follow more slowly, marshaling my thoughts, since I obviously underestimated the level of Liam's infatuation with the *Duchas* girl. Sure, I've fantasized a few times about kissing Deb, mostly when dropping off to sleep. But that's miles away from the path my brother seems determined to pursue.

"—tell Lucas he's full of it, okay?" Liam is saying when I walk into the kitchen, where our parents are sitting at the little drop-leaf table in the breakfast nook. They both look at me in puzzlement.

"What is he talking about?" our mother asks me, concern in her eyes. "Did something happen tonight that…shouldn't have?"

I frown at my brother. "You might say that. Liam—"

"I kissed Bri, okay?" He glares around at all of us defiantly. "What's wrong with that? It's what guys do when they take a girl out on a date."

"You make it sound like you gave her a peck on the cheek good night." My voice is heavy with sarcasm. "Tell them what you and Bri were doing when Deb and I came out of the Lighthouse."

His glare is just for me, now. "Okay, so I kissed her kind of a lot. It was nice. *She's* nice. I…I think I might be in love with her."

Mom's eyes go wide and Dad's eyebrows almost disappear into his hairline.

"What?" He says it louder than even I expect. "Don't be ridiculous, Liam. That girl is a *Duchas*! We only agreed to let you take her to that formal dance because you insisted Sovereign Emileia wanted you to. Was that even true?"

Liam shrugs, not meeting Dad's eye. "Like I told Lucas, Kira wouldn't have suggested it if the Sovereign weren't okay with it. And Bri *is* her best friend, not counting Molly, er, Princess Malena, her sister. M and Bri and Deb have all been super close friends for years, since way before M found out who she really is. I'm sure she wanted them to have dates to the dance."

"*Echtran* dates?" Mom's frowning now, too.

Swallowing visibly, Liam shrugs again. "Maybe. Why not? She's always saying we should mingle more with the *Duchas* students at school."

"Making out goes a little beyond mingling," I point out.

"Your brother is right," Dad tells Liam. "For you to become that involved with a *Duchas* puts us all at risk of discovery. Being chosen for Jewel was a tremendous honor. Fewer than ten percent of those who requested to live here were selected. The *Echtran* Council—and the Sovereign—have placed a great deal of trust in those of us who were allowed to come here. We can't allow you to betray that trust, Liam."

"Betray—? What do you mean? I haven't betrayed anything! Is it a crime to fall in love?"

Our mother stands up and puts a hand on Liam's shoulder. "Sweetheart, you barely know this girl. What you feel for her may seem like love right now, but you're young, at an age where hormones frequently supersede reason. I'm terribly sorry you've become so attached to Bri, but for all our sakes, you need to break things off."

"Yes," Dad agrees. "Immediately. I'd like your promise that you'll do your best to avoid her going forward. You don't have any classes together, do you?"

Liam stares at them both in outrage and I feel the first twinges of regret for my part in bringing things to this point. Maybe if I hadn't come down so hard on him…

"No, but we've been sitting together at lunch. And we agreed to watch the Colts game together tomorrow, either here or at her house. What am I supposed to tell her?"

"Nothing." Dad's tone is uncompromising. "That will be far safer than any sort of explanation you might try to make."

Mom nods, her hand still on my brother's shoulder. "I'm sorry, Liam. But the sooner you make it clear you can't pursue this, ah, friendship, the sooner she can get over her disappointment and move on. You want her to be happy, don't you?"

Still rebellious, Liam glares at her. "*I'm* making her happy! How is that a bad thing?"

"Liam," Dad snaps, "this is not open for debate. You will break things off with this *Duchas* girl, or we'll be forced to take you out of school and leave Jewel entirely, for the safety of our people. We'll move back to Bailerealta, or to Dun Cloch or another all-*Echtran* community until you've matured enough to behave more responsibly. Of course, there's no guarantee we'd be allowed to return to Jewel even then, given how many of our people are clamoring to live here."

Liam stares at him, stricken. "Move away? You…you wouldn't. Would you?"

"Only if you give us no other choice, dear," Mom tells him gently.

"We can't risk you violating the Secrecy Statute. Perhaps by morning, you'll be able to consider things a bit more rationally."

Dad regards Liam narrowly for a moment. "In the meantime, I think you'd better give me your phone."

"My phone?" The outrage is back. "Why?"

"If the girl doesn't hear from you tomorrow, she may take the hint," Dad replies. "That should make it easier to avoid her at school on Monday."

"Yeah?" Liam sounds belligerent again. "And what am I supposed to tell her when she wants to know why I stood her up? Won't that be just as dangerous as staying friends with her?"

With a sad little smile, Mom shakes her head. "I doubt it. *Duchas* boys and girls your age fall in and out of so-called love very quickly, according to all I've read. No doubt she's observed that herself. Once Bri realizes you are avoiding her, I imagine she will wish to avoid you as well."

Flushing, Liam closes his eyes. "Yeah. Yeah, she probably will. In fact, she'll probably hate me. Do I really have to do this?" Opening his eyes, he looks from Mom to Dad and back, pleadingly.

"I'm afraid so, Son." Dad's voice is gentle now, too. "We really are sorry."

"Not as sorry as I am," Liam says bitterly, then looks at me. "What about Lucas? Does he have to dump Deb, too?"

Caught off-guard, I open my mouth to protest, then close it again. "We, ah, haven't reached a point where it would be like dumping," I say after a moment. "But yeah, I should probably avoid her, too, even in the one class we have together. Otherwise, she's bound to ask me what's going on with you and Bri and I'd...rather not have to lie to her."

A weight settles in the pit of my stomach as I say it. I know it's for the best, but it sure doesn't feel that way.

13

Investigation

Deb

THE BOYS' car isn't even out of sight yet when Bri turns to me, her face practically glowing.

"Oh, Deb, oh, Deb, oh, Deb!" she breathes, then seizes both of my hands in hers and whirls me around on her front walk, heedless of the sleet pelting us. "What an amazing evening! I don't think I've ever been so happy in my entire life! Liam is absolutely *perfect.*"

Laughing, I stop her spinning after the second rotation, since the sidewalk's getting a little slippery. "And a good kisser, too?"

Bri's smile gets even bigger, her eyes now gazing off into the distance. "*So* good! It's like...like our lips were made for each other. Honestly, I felt like I was in absolute heaven when he kissed me. No boy has *ever* made me feel that way before. Oh, Deb, I really, truly think I'm in love with him. Like, for real."

Because she clearly means it, this time I'm careful to keep all trace of skepticism or amusement off my face. "That's...wonderful, Bri."

"It *is.* It's amazing." Her expression becomes dreamy. "I can't wait to see him again tomorrow." Belatedly, she focuses on me. "Maybe you and Lucas can watch the game with us? You two seemed to hit it off really well tonight, too, talking about art and saving the planet and all."

"We did." I smile, too, remembering. "Turns out we have more in common than I thought. Which, um, includes not being into sports. So probably not, for the game tomorrow. Anyway, won't you and Liam want to be alone?"

She shrugs. "Either my parents or his will be around, so we really won't be. So it's totally fine if you guys want to be there, too."

"Lucas didn't say anything about it. I doubt he's any more interested in the playoffs than I am." In fact, judging by his disgusted expression when Bri and Liam reconfirmed their plans a few minutes ago, it's the very last thing he wants to do.

"I should get home," I say then. "With this weather, my mom will be worrying."

Bri looks startled. "Aren't you sleeping over? We can have fun talking over our evening together."

"We can talk tomorrow. I'm really tired." I fake a yawn. Fortunately, she lets it drop.

"Okay, get some sleep," she says. "But come over right after breakfast, okay? So we can compare more notes."

"I will. See you tomorrow."

Once home, I hurry through washing my face and brushing my teeth so I can get into bed—not to sleep, but so I can relive my own wonderful evening without hearing Bri go on and on about how much *more* wonderful hers was. I may not be as over-the-top euphoric as Bri, but tonight's date was successful enough to give me hope Lucas and I *might* possibly become more than friends. Eventually.

Really, the only off-note was Lucas's puzzling overreaction to catching Bri and Liam making out. While I was a little embarrassed, Lucas seemed positively angry, though he tried not to show it. I'm not sure Bri noticed, so I didn't want to mention it while she was so deliriously happy.

Cautiously optimistic as I am about Lucas and me now, I'm also more certain than ever that something very strange is going on with the Walsh brothers.

✦

My lingering doubts about Lucas don't keep me from having at least one amazing dream about him—one that involves the two of us kissing the way Bri and Liam did. When I wake up Sunday morning, I laze in bed for several extra minutes, still enjoying the dream-memory of Lucas's arms around me, his lips on mine.

"Good morning, sleepyhead," Mom greets me when I finally make it downstairs to the kitchen. She's already started making French toast, our Sunday morning tradition. "How was your date last night? Sorry I conked out before you got home."

"That's okay." I get the maple syrup out of the fridge and put it in the microwave to warm up. "My date was fun."

Eager as I am to go to Bri's house to talk over last night, I don't rush through breakfast. Now that Maggie's back at college, it's just Mom and me and I know she cherishes these rare moments of togetherness. Not that I share very much when she asks for details about my evening.

"Yeah, I'd say last night was even better than the formal," I reply to her prodding. "I think Bri and Liam might actually be on the verge of getting serious."

"Already? This was only their second date, wasn't it?" At my nod, Mom leans forward over her plate. "So, what about you and Lucas?"

Carefully keeping my expression neutral, I shrug. "Too soon to say. He's a lot shyer than his brother, but we did talk more last night than at the dance."

After three slices of French toast, I finally feel like I can leave without being rude. "Bri wanted me to come over first thing, since I didn't spend the night there," I say, taking my plate to the sink.

"Are you sure you don't want another piece? I made plenty." Mom waves at the stack still on the serving plate.

"Better not." I pat my hips with a rueful smile. "It freezes and microwaves well, though. Handy for school mornings."

Half an hour later, I ring Bri's doorbell.

Flinging the door open, Bri drags me inside, then upstairs to her room, where she shuts the door. "*Now* we can really talk! Were your dreams as awesome as mine were?" She heaves a romantic sigh that makes me laugh.

"Maybe not *as* awesome, but…yeah. I definitely had some good dreams. Looks like you're still flying as high as you were last night."

She nods happily. "I can't help it. Liam and I just…click so well. He's not at all like other jocks I've gone out with, doesn't brag on himself or anything. He actually asks me about *me* and pays attention when I answer."

"Lucas does that, too. In fact, I have trouble getting him to tell me much at all about himself. Is that true for Liam, too?"

"A little, I guess, but it's honestly kind of refreshing. He does talk about school stuff, classes he's in, what he likes and doesn't like. Oh! And you hurried home last night before I remembered to tell you, but he also told me when we were dancing that he thinks Lucas really likes you."

My heart skips a beat. "Really?"

"Really! He says you're the first girl Lucas has ever even asked out—that where they lived before, they only ever went out in groups. And that Lucas has *never* acted interested in anyone in particular…until now."

Elated, I try to tamp down my hopes before they get *too* high. "Is that true for Liam, too? Did he mention if he ever had a girlfriend before they moved here?"

"I didn't have the nerve to ask directly, but he definitely made it *sound* like not. And he *did* say he was having the best time he could ever remember. Also while we were dancing." She smiles dreamily.

"You two *did* dance kind of a lot," I point out with a laugh.

Though last night I sometimes wished Lucas liked dancing more, I also enjoyed just sitting at the table with him, picking at what was left of the onion rings and doing our best to talk over the music. Once, when we both reached for an onion ring at the same time, our hands accidentally touched and he didn't exactly flinch away. Instead, he gave me a look that made me catch my breath. That touch—and look—featured largely in one of last night's dreams, I now recall….

Bri and I spend an enjoyable hour dissecting every moment of last night's date and indulging in increasingly unlikely fantasies about what the future might hold. When I finally, regretfully, go home to finish my homework, my optimism about Lucas is higher than it's ever been before.

"I'll let you know if Liam says anything about you and Lucas joining us this afternoon for the game," Bri promises as I'm leaving.

By now, I'm half hoping that'll happen—whether Lucas and I actually watch the game or not.

⁜

When I get a call from Bri just after four o'clock, my spirits soar, my heart leaping into my throat. Maybe Lucas—

"Hey, Deb." Bri's voice is so strained, it instantly squelches my excitement. "You don't happen to have Lucas's number, do you? Or his email?"

"Um, no. Why?"

"Well, the game starts in half an hour and Liam still hasn't called. Do you...do you think he changed his mind?"

Remembering the way he looked at Bri last night when they said good-bye, I can't imagine that. "No way. But maybe his parents put the kibosh on it or something? He and Lucas have both said they're really strict."

"Wouldn't he at least tell me if that was it?"

He definitely *should* have... "Did you try texting him?"

"Finally, a few minutes ago. When he didn't answer, I even tried calling but it went straight to voicemail."

"Huh. That is weird. Maybe he lost his phone, or it ran out of juice. Or he could be hung up doing something and lost track of the time."

"Maybe, but he seemed awfully excited about this game when we talked about it last night. Also about...about watching it together." Her voice quavers on the last few words, like she's holding back tears.

Abruptly, I ask, "Do you want me to come over? I can always leave the moment Liam shows up."

"Would you? If you're here, I won't have to explain to my parents why I'm so distracted. You don't even have to watch the game if you don't want. You can bring homework or your sketch pad or something."

"I'll do that. See you in a few minutes."

Five minutes later, I ring her doorbell, sketch pad tucked under my arm. Bri leads me past the living room, where her parents and little brother are already ensconced in front of the big screen TV with a bowl of popcorn, to the kitchen, which has a much smaller TV.

"I told them we'd watch the game in here so you can draw or do homework and we can talk without disturbing them," she explains. "I already made extra popcorn for us. And no, he still hasn't called." She says it off-handedly, but I can tell she's a lot more upset than she lets on.

Since I can't think of anything to say that might help, I just set out my sketch pad and pencils on the kitchen table while she pours us both root beer—diet for me.

The game starts and Bri seems to be watching it. But only a couple of minutes pass before she suddenly blurts out, "What if Liam was in an accident? Or maybe Lucas or one of their parents? Then he probably wouldn't think to call."

"Um, I guess that's possible," I concede, careful not to let any trace of skepticism—or pity—show.

"He might even be in the hospital," she continues worriedly. "What if he's asking for me and his family doesn't know how to contact me? Maybe his phone got destroyed or something."

I hesitate, then say, "Should we try calling Kira to see if she's heard anything?"

Bri considers for a moment, then shakes her head. "No. Not...not yet. I don't want to scare anybody when... Well, when maybe that's not it." She glances toward the living room, though we can't see her parents from here.

In other words, when Liam might have just gotten cold feet about getting serious—especially if his parents gave him a hard time.

As the game progresses, Bri gets more and more despondent while I get more and more angry. How *dare* Liam behave like he did last night, dancing, flirting and even making out with Bri, then not even call her today when he promised he would? Maybe he's just another jerk jock after all.

Or maybe Lucas is the one responsible. He seemed awfully upset when we caught them kissing. Maybe he told their parents and they grounded Liam and took away his phone? Which would mean Liam's mostly blameless and Lucas is the jerk.

Either way, Bri and I are better off without them.

Somehow, coming to that conclusion doesn't make me feel any better.

I stay all the way to the end of the game, for Bri's sake. When the Colts win, she pretends to join in her parents' jubilation, but it's obvious her heart isn't in it. Tomorrow, I vow, I'm going to get to the bottom of this and make Liam or Lucas, or both, sorry they messed with my best friend's happiness.

✦

Bri is quieter than usual on the bus the next morning, clearly still upset about Liam, though she never mentions him until we get to school.

"At least we don't have any classes together," she comments dully as we're getting off the bus. "That'll make things a little less awkward if...if the only reason he never called was because he didn't want to."

I don't reply. I'm busy planning what I'll say to Liam in Pre-Cal first period.

He's already in the classroom when I get there, well before the bell rings—and shows zero sign of any injury. Jerk. Squaring my shoulders, I move purposefully his way, determined to read him the riot act before class starts.

Turning, he spots me. Instead of avoiding me like I expect, he comes straight over to me, anguish on his face. The same anguish is in his voice when he speaks before I can.

"Deb, will you please tell Bri how sorry I am? I don't even want to imagine what she must think of me right now."

I stare at him in disbelief. "Me? You need to tell her yourself, Liam. Why did you stand her up like that?"

"I...I can't tell you, except that I'm really, *really* sorry. I swear I didn't want to. And I *would* tell Bri myself, but—" Glancing over my shoulder, he breaks off, then hurries to his desk and sits down.

Puzzled, I look behind me, where M, Rigel, Molly and Tristan have just walked in, all apparently continuing some conversation they started on the way here. Since *they* couldn't have spooked Liam into silence, I peer past them to the hallway. Did Lucas go by and send Liam some kind of nonverbal warning? Possible, though I don't see him now. Hmm.

All through class, I keep trying to catch Liam's eye again, hoping to get more out of him, but now he's careful not to look my way. And when the bell rings, he's out the door before I can even stand up. Coward.

Because I know she'll ask, I tell Bri in third-period English what Liam said to me. I expect her to be as angry as I am, but instead she makes excuses for him—again.

"Maybe the reason he couldn't tell you has something to do with his brother and he didn't want to make you mad at Lucas?" she suggests. "Lucas was pretty obviously avoiding me in first period, so I didn't have the guts to ask what happened yesterday."

"Maybe," I concede, though I can't imagine Lucas alone could have kept Liam from even *calling* Bri yesterday. I intend to ask him during lunch, if he and Liam sit with us again. Except I'm guessing they won't.

My guess turns out to be right. When Bri and I get to the cafeteria, the Walsh brothers are already sitting at the NuAgra table with their backs to *our* usual table. I repeatedly glance their way while Bri and I are in the lunch line and notice Bri doing the same, though neither of us comment on it.

Watching them out of the corner of my eye as we walk past on our way to our own table, I see Liam half turn, like he might call out to Bri. Then Lucas whispers something and he turns back around—but not before I see the scowl on Liam's face. Looks like Bri was right that Lucas was involved...and still is.

Everybody at our table has to notice the Walsh brothers' defection, so I'm surprised when no one comments on it. Then I remember M and Molly had both Chem and Lit class with them earlier, so they might already know what's going on. Bri doesn't ask—because she's afraid of what the answer will be?—so I wait till she goes over to talk to a couple of other girls from Chorus to do it myself.

"Do you guys have any idea what's going on with Liam?" I whisper. "He was supposed to get together with Bri yesterday but he stood her up, no explanation."

"Really?" M looks over her shoulder at the NuAgra table. "I thought the plan was for you and Bri to go to the Lighthouse with him and Lucas Saturday night?" She doesn't *act* like she knows anything.

"We did," I confirm. "And Bri and Liam had a really great time together, so much that they made plans to watch an NFL game together yesterday. But then he never called or showed. She was...pretty upset. Then this morning, in Pre-Cal, Liam asked *me* to tell her he's sorry. I really thought better of him than that."

M frowns. "That does seem odd. But...maybe it's for the best? If he doesn't want to get serious with her, better for him to decide now than later, right?"

I'm surprised she's not more indignant. "Well, yeah, I guess. But you didn't see them together Saturday night. He sure didn't act *then* like he didn't want to get serious." I'm about to tell her about them making out in the car when I see Bri coming back. "Anyway," I quickly add, "I thought maybe you'd heard something."

"Er, no, sorry. If I do, I'll let you know."

But I have no intention of waiting for that. I mean to pry the truth—the whole truth—out of Lucas during Art class. Whether he wants to talk to me or not.

14

Benefit-cost analysis

Lucas

"I *HATE* THIS!" Liam whispers fiercely as we leave the cafeteria for fifth period. "You don't have any idea how much I hate this. Seeing Bri but not being able to talk to her, even to tell her I'm sorry. It's torture."

"I told you not to look at her," I remind him, wishing I could let him know how much I regret promising our parents I'd enforce their edict at school. How much I regret making a big deal about them kissing in the first place.

He glares at me. "I didn't, not really, but it hardly mattered. I knew she was right there, just a couple tables away. I could *feel* her there, all through lunch."

"Don't be ridiculous. It's not like *Duchas* have *brath*. You just imagined that."

"No, I didn't," he insists. "Maybe she doesn't exactly have *brath*, but she has *something*—like her own *Duchas* version of it. Something I can sense when she's nearby, anyway."

I just shake my head, afraid to admit I've occasionally imagined something similar with Deb—though only when she's right next to me, never from that far away. There's no way it can be real, though.

"Look, I know this is hard right now." I try for a soothing tone. "But it'll get easier as the week goes on. Soon she'll start flirting with other guys and you'll be off the hook."

Liam stares at me in disbelief. "You think that will make it *easier*? You've never been in love, so how would you know?"

I open my mouth to tell him—again—that he can't possibly be in love with a girl he's only gone out with twice, no matter how well she kisses, but then I close it without saying anything. Because he's right. I don't know. And I'm secretly terrified of finding out.

Sixth period, I purposely get to Art class just as the bell rings. Deb is already at our usual drawing table. She looks my way when I walk in, but I don't join her. Instead, I go to a table as far away from Deb as possible and near the door, acutely aware of her eyes following me.

During class, I do my best not to glance in Deb's direction, but somehow I still do. More than once. Once, when I accidentally catch her eye, the combination of confusion and condemnation in her expression makes me squirm with guilt.

I immediately look away, glad I'm all the way across the room. Being around Deb tends to make me say things I shouldn't and I don't want to be tempted into giving her an explanation—maybe even the true one.

When class ends, I'm out the door and gone before she can even gather up her supplies. I know I'm only delaying the inevitable. She's bound to corner me and demand answers sooner or later. But not today.

✦

Liam is still morose that evening. Over dinner, our parents take turns trying to cheer him up, reminding him of all the things he likes about Earth, about Jewel, but he just glares at them.

"Everything I've liked most, I'm not allowed to do. Can't play my best at basketball, so I won't be getting any scholarships or a shot at the NBA after college. Can't get too chummy with any of the *Duchas* guys on the team or in my classes. And the one girl I really want to be with, that I *love*, I'm forbidden to even talk to. Maybe we *should* move to Dun Cloch. At least I could be myself there."

Mom and Dad exchange a glance. "If you really think—" she begins, tentatively.

"No!" There's a touch of panic in his voice. "At least here I can *see* Bri, even if I can't get close to her. It's frustrating, but better than nothing." Shoving away his plate, he storms away from the table, his dinner practically untouched.

Figuring he has to be starving since he usually eats twice what I do, I bring a big slab of Mom's cherry pie to his room an hour or so later.

"Hey, figured you might want some of this. It's really good."

I get the same glare he gave our parents. "Is that supposed to be a peace offering? No thanks. It's obvious you're on *their* side."

"Not…completely," I tell him, setting down the pie on his desk. "I do agree it's risky to get too involved with a *Duchas* girl, but I didn't expect them to make you stay away from Bri entirely. I don't much like not being able to talk to Deb, either. It *is* safer this way, though, don't you think?"

"No. I don't. All we're doing is convincing both of them we're humongous jerks. Not quite the impression the Sovereign told us to create." Then he perks up slightly. "I'll bet Bri told her I stood her up yesterday. You think M might get mad enough on her behalf that she'll take my side against Mom and Dad?"

I doubt it. Rather than crush Liam's hopes, though, I say, "The Sovereign must know the risks better than anyone. But you're probably right that she doesn't want the locals to hate us, either. So maybe?"

Grabbing the plate of pie, he takes an enormous bite, then another. "That would be great," he says around a mouthful of pie. "Do you really think she might?"

I take my time answering, to give him time to polish off his pie. "It's, um, probably more likely she'll persuade Bri to move on. Being Royal and all, she probably has that 'push' thing a lot of them have."

For a second, I think Liam is going to throw his empty plate at me. Then his shoulders slump. "Yeah. You're probably right. And I guess I *should* want that, if it'll make Bri get over me quicker. No point both of us being miserable." He hands me the plate. "Thanks for the pie."

Since he clearly wants to be alone, I take the hint. Carrying the plate back to the kitchen, I wish more than ever things hadn't come to this. Partly because I'm missing Deb a lot, too. Maybe not as much as Liam misses Bri, but still.

With a heavy sigh, I put the plate in the sterilizer and head to my own room. Once there, I try to erase the persistent image of Deb's accusing blue eyes by immersing myself in homework, trying to get a few days ahead in all my dumb classes. Anything to avoid thinking too much about what Liam is going through because of me. Or about Deb.

✦

97

"Deb wouldn't even look at me in first period," Liam complains when we both get to Chemistry class the following day. "Not that I blame her. For all she knows, ignoring Bri was my idea."

I worried that Bri might demand an explanation during Econ yesterday or today, but she hasn't spoken to me at all. Not even when she was right behind me when we were leaving class this morning. I'd like to think that means she's already decided to give up and move on, but if Deb's giving Liam the cold shoulder, too, probably not.

Still not trusting myself to keep my mouth shut, I again arrive slightly late to Art class that afternoon. There's no spot near the door this time, but apparently Deb's decided to freeze me out, too, since she doesn't so much as glance my way when I walk past her. Which is fine. Safer, anyway.

Or so I think.

When the bell rings at the end of sixth period, this time she's one of the first out of the room. She must have gathered up her supplies ahead of time. I hang back for several seconds to make sure she's well on her way to her next class before I step into the hallway. Except there she is, waiting just outside the door. She immediately gets right in my face.

"Okay, what's going on?" she demands.

"What…what do you mean?"

She gives me a *don't be an idiot* look. "You know what I mean. Liam and Bri were supposed to get together Sunday and he totally stood her up, didn't even call. And now you're both avoiding her. Why?"

"Liam, um, decided they aren't such a great fit after all." Even as I say it, I know she won't buy it.

She doesn't.

"I don't believe that for a second. He looked really upset in Pre-Cal yesterday, when he asked me to apologize to Bri for him. And when I told him he needs to do that himself, he said he can't. Only the way he said it, it sounded more like he's not *allowed* to. Was this your idea? Or your parents'? What are they threatening him with?"

Yikes. I knew she was observant, and smart, but I didn't expect her to come this close to the truth so quickly. When I hesitate, groping for a reasonable-sounding excuse, she continues.

"Do all you NuAgra people belong to some kind of super-conservative religion or something? Is that why your parents are so strict? Is there some rule that you're not supposed to get too friendly with people outside it? Because that's how it looks from here—like you're all part of some weird cult or secret order no one else is allowed to know about, and Bri was getting a little too close."

Worse and worse! "No, it's…it's nothing like that." Except it sort of is.

"Then what? The only other thing I can figure is it has to do with Bri's dad being Black. That's not it, is it?"

Desperate, I take the out she's offering.

"Er, yeah. Yeah, it's that."

Deb gasps, a look of mingled horror and disgust on her face. *Not* the reaction I expected. "Seriously? You're *admitting* your family is racist?"

Crap! What have I walked into? Something bad, obviously. But if I backtrack now, I could end up on even more dangerous ground.

"I, uh, I guess so?"

Deb just stares at me, slowly shaking her head, disappointment now added to the disgust in her eyes. I hate it, but what can I do?

"I thought better of you, Lucas. Of all of you. Obviously I was wrong." With that, she turns her back on me and walks away.

I stand there, watching her go, fighting an incredibly powerful urge to run after her and tell her the truth—the whole truth. Anything to erase that disappointed, betrayed expression from her face. But I can't. With a sick suspicion that I just made things way worse than Liam ever could have, I head to the school office. I still have to sign out before catching the van to NuAgra for my seventh-period work-study program.

"What's wrong with you?" Liam asks when I join him, Kira and Alan out front a couple of minutes later.

"I…nothing." I can't very well explain without letting on to the others what happened Saturday night—or just now. Especially when I'm still squirming inside from the way Deb reacted to my excuse.

To my relief, the van pulls up before Liam can ask more questions.

15

Red herring

Deb

I'M LATE TO CHORUS, but that's fine, since I'd rather not talk to anybody right now—especially Bri. I work really hard to keep my expression neutral as I pass her, not wanting her to guess how upset I am. Fortunately, today is all about casting solos for the spring show choir competition show, which has Bri too distracted to do more than glance at me.

Normally, Bri's right up there with Molly as one of our best singers/dancers, but yesterday, for obvious reasons, she was way off her usual form. Today she's focusing a little better, plus the director takes into account how she's performed in the past, so she still gets one of the front line spots and a solo. I'm assigned to the back row, like always. Not that I mind. I'm only in Chorus at all because Bri dragged me into it freshman year and I just stuck around. I'm an okay singer and a not-terrible dancer, but I'll never be star material.

When Bri shoots a curious look my way once or twice during class, I pretend not to notice. No way I'm going to tell her what Lucas said, it's so awful.

During the bus ride home, though, my resolve starts to waver.

"I saw Liam in the hall on my way to Chorus," she informs me.

"Oh?" I say cautiously. "Did he talk to you?"

She shakes her head. "He kind of looked like he wanted to, though.

His expression...I think maybe he really does still like me, Deb. Yesterday he asked you to tell me he was sorry, right?"

"Yes, but I told him he needed to apologize to you himself—which he hasn't."

"Maybe...maybe he's afraid to? If it's true his family belongs to some super-conservative church, they might have decided letting him go on dates was a bad idea after all. If he was raised in that religion, it would be pretty hard for him to go against it. Remember how he and Lucas sort of kept their distance at the Winter Formal? And how Liam, um, didn't Saturday night? Maybe he started feeling guilty afterward...or maybe Lucas told their parents about us making out. Or both. So...it could be he's having to cool it for a while. But maybe after a week or two, he and I can at least be friends again," she finishes wistfully. "I really miss talking to him."

If what Lucas said is true, I doubt a week or two will make a difference. "I don't know, Bri. If they're as conservative or whatever as all that, maybe you two aren't such a great fit after all."

"But we are!" she protests. "We're a *perfect* fit. Saturday night, he and I...we just *clicked*. And I know it wasn't only on my side. He felt it, too. I think maybe he just panicked about it later. But the way he looked at me this afternoon..."

Frowning, I shake my head. "Honestly, Bri, I think you're better off without him."

"Why would you say that?" she demands. "Wait. Did...did Lucas finally talk to you about it in Art class?" She looks half hopeful, half fearful.

Though I hate to dash the hopeful part, I reluctantly nod. "Not till after, and not willingly. I had to ambush him and force it out of him, though now I wish I hadn't. Anyway, from what he told me, you should definitely count yourself lucky Liam has backed off."

Frowning, she studies my face like she's trying to read my mind. Like she's trying to decide whether to probe deeper or not. Unfortunately, curiosity gets the better of her. "Okay, what did he say? Is it..." She hesitates. "Is it because I'm biracial?"

I can't bring myself to answer, but my expression must be all the confirmation she needs. My heart hurts as I watch Bri close her eyes, pressing her lips tight together like she's fighting not to cry.

"I'm sorry, Bri. But if Liam's willing to go along with whatever rules his stupid, narrow-minded family is putting on him, he's not worth getting upset over. No boy is, but especially not one who'd let his bigoted family tell him who he can date."

Swallowing visibly, she nods. "No, I know. You're right," she says, a quaver in her voice. "It's not like there's anything I can do about it anyway...or like this hasn't happened before. I just... I really thought Liam was different. Coming from back East and all, I thought he'd be more open-minded than most of the other boys here. Saturday night—" She swallows again. "—it really seemed like he was."

"I know. And I think *he* probably is. I definitely got the impression it's more about his parents. And...and maybe Lucas. Or maybe it's all the NuAgra people. You've seen how they stick together and how they'll never talk about what's going on out there. Honestly, it's like they're all part of some secret society or cult or something."

I suddenly remember the look of panic on Lucas's face when I suggested exactly that. Was my guess close enough to the truth to worry him? Come to think of it, he didn't admit Bri being biracial was the reason until after I directly asked. Almost like that was a *less* terrible reason to keep Liam away from her. Which doesn't make sense, unless their cult is into something seriously illegal, like drug running or human sacrifice.

"C'mon, Deb. You know as well as I do that people don't have to be in a cult to be racist," Bri bitterly reminds me. "Besides, the NuAgra folks can't *all* be bad, or M and Molly wouldn't be friends with so many of them." Her sorrowful resignation seems so unlike the Bri I know, always ready to march into battle on a friend's behalf, that I'm suddenly even angrier at the people who caused it.

"Maybe they wouldn't be, if they knew how prejudiced some of them are. That's seriously not okay. I think we should tell them."

She manages a half smile. "Yeah. I guess." But it's obvious *she* won't.

Because I can't completely know how Bri feels, I stop pushing. I just keep fuming silently for the rest of the bus ride home.

.*.

Needing an outlet for my fury on Bri's behalf, I call M as soon as I get home. "Hey," I say when she answers. "Can we talk?"

"Sure. What's wrong, Deb? You sound upset."

"Yeah, I am. It's about Bri. And Liam."

There's a pause at the other end. "What about them? Did something else happen?"

"Not *between* them, but… Would it be okay if I come over to tell you about it?"

I'd rather not have this discussion over the phone. I want to be able to gauge her expression when I bring up my suspicions about the NuAgra people, in case she accidentally gives something away.

"Oh, um, sure, I guess. My aunt shouldn't be home for another hour or so."

"Great. I'll be right over. See you in a few."

I drop my backpack, take the dog out back to do her business, then jump on my bike for the five-minute ride to M's house. She comes out on her front porch as I pull up, looking both curious and concerned.

"Come on in and I'll get us a snack," she says as I lean my bike against the big tree in her front yard.

I follow her into the house and through to the kitchen, where she pours us both glasses of milk and sets out a plate of her aunt's cookies—Mrs. Truitt is always baking.

"So what's up?" she asks, sitting down at the kitchen table.

I sit down across from her and take a sip of milk, marshaling my thoughts. "You've seen how Liam's avoiding Bri at school, right? After he went out with her Saturday, then stood her up on Sunday?"

She nods, her eyes now slightly wary.

"Well, I finally got a chance to confront Lucas about it today, and he admitted it's because Bri's biracial."

As I hoped, M looks every bit as shocked as I was. "*What?* No way! Are you sure? Lucas didn't actually *say* that, did he?"

"Basically. I asked him directly if that was the reason, and he said it was. Can you believe it?"

"I…" M slowly shakes her head. "No. I really can't. I never got the impression he or Liam cared at all about that."

"Neither did I! I mean, what the hell? You saw how Liam flirted with her all last week before asking her out. Plus, her dad is one of the basketball coaches, so it's not like he just suddenly found out he's Black. Liam even told me how much he likes Mr. Morrison, what a good coach he is. Do you think it's their parents? Could the Walshes be so bigoted they'd threaten to ground Liam if he didn't dump Bri?"

M frowns. "I don't think so. They'd met Mr. Morrison before Liam took Bri to the formal. And when I've talked with the Walshes myself, they've seemed really nice."

"They probably are…to you. Anyway, I'm not sure it's just them. Have you noticed there's not a single person of color working at NuAgra? Maybe the whole company is racist."

"No, I'm positive that's not true," M protests, almost too quickly. "Whatever reason Liam had for backing off, I honestly don't believe it could have anything to do with that."

I stare at M in disbelief. "How can you defend them?" I demand, suddenly pissed at her, too. "Didn't you hear me? Lucas came right out and told me it did! Why would he say that if it's not true? Unless…the real reason is something even worse?"

Her brows go up. "Worse? Like what?"

"I don't know, exactly. But when I confronted Lucas today, I first asked if his family is in some kind of secret society that doesn't allow outsiders. He…sort of flinched before denying it. So then I asked if it was about the race thing and he admitted it was. Do you think they might all be involved in something so awful, even illegal, that they'd rather be considered racists than let the truth come out?"

M's expression is definitely guarded now. "That…sounds like a pretty big stretch."

"Does it? You can't deny there's something awfully strange about those NuAgra people. You know I'm not the only one saying so. There've been rumors going around since they got here. Except for that one tour before the holidays, they've never even allowed visitors inside. What are they hiding?"

"Trade secrets, according to Tristan and Kira," she replies—again, just a little too quickly. "Apparently, corporate espionage is a real thing when it comes to cutting-edge technology like NuAgra is doing—that's why they all had to sign nondisclosure agreements. Anyway, I went on that tour last month, with my aunt and uncle, and to me it looked like exactly what they say it is—a big agricultural research company."

I regard her doubtfully. "Isn't it possible they have some other, hidden agenda, too? What if the whole farming thing is really just a front for something more…sinister?"

M laughs, but I think it sounds a little forced. "Sinister? C'mon, Deb, really? I know you read a lot of mysteries and thrillers, but this is Jewel, Indiana."

"Which definitely has its share of narrow-minded bigots." I revert to my original argument. "There are at least a couple of those white-supremacist militia groups in Indiana."

"Maybe so," she admits, "but none of the NuAgra people are from around here. The company started in Ireland, with its American head-quarters in New York. That's what it said in the newspaper. They only moved it to Jewel when they decided to expand last year—probably because farmland is cheaper here. On that tour, they told us about all the new plant strains and farming technologies they're developing that will cut way down on pollution and waste, pull excess carbon out of the atmosphere, maybe even end world hunger. You've always been a big one for saving the planet, right? So you should be completely on board with what they're trying to accomplish."

She leans toward me, looking and sounding so earnest, it's like she's *willing* me to believe her. I almost do. I want to. I really do. Maybe she *is* right about NuAgra's mission? Even so—

I shake my head slightly. "If that's all they're doing, why would Lucas tell me what he did? And why would Liam suddenly go from making out with Bri Saturday night to totally ignoring her this week?"

"Making out?" She stares at me, clearly startled. "Whoa. You didn't tell me *that* part before!"

"I, uh, wasn't sure Bri would want me to, especially with the way Liam's acting now. But...yeah. They left the Lighthouse ahead of Lucas and me to go get the car and when we joined them outside, they were, like, *seriously* kissing. It was totally obvious Lucas wasn't happy about it, though he didn't say much in front of us. I'm guessing when they got home, he told their parents and they went ballistic. And poor Bri. I've seen her bummed after breakups before, but never like this. It...kind of reminds me of how messed up *you* were the first time you and Rigel broke up."

M blinks. "Bri's not feeling sick, is she?"

"She hasn't said so. It's hard to tell, though, she's trying so hard to pretend she's okay. Especially at lunch, when Liam might be looking. Sick or not, I've never seen her this broken up over a guy before, not even Gary. I tried to convince her she's better off without him after what Lucas said, but..." I shake my head sadly.

"You didn't actually *tell* her Lucas said it was because of her race, did you?"

"I wasn't going to, but when she asked, I couldn't exactly deny it. I expected her to get mad, like I did, but she mostly just got...sad. Which made me even madder. That's why I wanted to talk to you. You've made friends with some of the NuAgra kids, and Molly and Sean are dating two of them. I thought you should know what they're really like. The Walshes, at least, and maybe all of them."

She shakes her head emphatically. "Sorry, I still can't believe that. Are you *sure* you didn't misunderstand what Lucas said?"

"Yes. I'm sure." I start getting pissed again. "I even repeated it back to him, asked if he really meant his family is racist and he said yes. Trust me, I was floored, too. But I *definitely* didn't misunderstand him."

She frowns, still looking skeptical. "It just...seems so out of character."

"Not if NuAgra is part of some racist cult."

"It's not! No way. There has to be some other explanation."

"How can you possibly take their side about something like this?" I flare, infuriated by her continued defense of them. "I thought you'd be every bit as outraged as I am, considering what a good friend Bri has been to you. To both of us. You know she has. C'mon, if she hadn't gotten in Rigel's face last year when he was being a jerk to you, you and he might never even have ended up together! Not to mention all the work she did to get you on this year's Homecoming Court."

M opens her mouth, closes it, then nods. "You're right. In elementary school, she's the only one who used to stand up to Trina when she bullied me. She also gave me a lot of great pep talks over the years. I do owe Bri a lot." She falls silent for a moment. "Maybe...maybe Sean knows what's really going on. He sees Liam every day at practice, and Kira knew the Walshes before they moved here. I guess I could—"

She breaks off at the sound of tires on gravel outside.

"Oops!" M jumps to her feet. "Aunt Theresa's home already, and she'll want to know why my chores aren't done. If I, uh, find out anything, I'll let you know, okay?" Is it my imagination, or does M actually look relieved her aunt is home early?

"Oh, um, okay. Guess I'll head back."

I smile a greeting at Mrs. Truitt as she comes in, then go out and get on my bike, re-running my whole conversation with M in my head as I slowly pedal home.

Why on Earth would she keep defending the Walshes after I told her Lucas directly confirmed his family is racist? She was also really quick to insist NuAgra isn't up to anything it shouldn't be. Again, why? Just because she's close friends with Molly and Sean, and they're dating Tristan and Kira, whose parents work there?

The more I think about the way M reacted to everything I said, the more convinced I am that she knows a lot more about what's really going on at NuAgra than she's letting on.

16

Degrees of freedom

Lucas

"SEE? I WAS RIGHT." Liam scowls at our parents, then me, when we talk to him briefly right before his basketball game starts. "Bri's not here—first game she's missed all season. I wonder what she told her father? I can't believe you thought me dumping her would be *best* for her!"

"Perhaps not in the short term," Mom admits, exchanging a glance with Dad. "But surely it's better for her to suffer a temporary disappointment now rather than waiting until the two of you became even closer… friends. You must realize how much harder that would be for you both."

Liam starts to say something else, then turns away with a snort. Mom watches him for a moment, worry creasing her brow. Shaking her head, she lets out a little sigh. "I wish it hadn't had to come to this."

Dad shrugs, heading up into the visitor bleachers. "It's his own fault, Eilis. He should have known better than to become romantically involved with a *Duchas*."

"True, but it hardly seems fair to the girl," she says.

I privately agree—and not just about Bri. All afternoon and evening I've been haunted by the look on Deb's face when I stupidly agreed to the reason she suggested for Liam's change of heart. I seriously considered making some excuse not to come to tonight's game, mostly to avoid having to explain what I did to Liam, but then I thought there might be a chance to undo the damage I apparently caused with Deb earlier. Looks like not.

The game is just about to start when M—the Sovereign—climbs up to where we're sitting and joins my family on the bench. Before I can even make a guess as to why, she turns to me.

"Lucas," she whispers, "did you *really* tell Deb the reason Liam's avoiding Bri now is because her dad is Black? Because that's…seriously not okay."

My parents look at her, then at me, in surprise.

"You didn't tell us that," Mom says.

"I, uh, I kind of panicked," I admit. "Deb cornered me today and demanded answers. She's, um, pretty mad on Bri's behalf. When I didn't explain right away, she started making guesses I thought were a little too accurate about our family and all the secrecy around NuAgra. So when she asked if it was the race thing instead, I figured that was safer and went with it. She…got a lot more upset than I expected."

M stares at me. "Upset? She's downright furious, and with good reason. Honestly, that was about the *worst* thing you could have told her, Lucas—and you absolutely can't let it stand. Coming from Nuath so recently, maybe none of you realize how big a deal race and racism is on Earth, especially in the United States, but you might want to read up on its history. Trust me, the very last thing we need is for a rumor to spread that NuAgra is a front for some kind of white supremacist organization. That would seriously undermine our ultimate goal of peacefully inte-grating into Earth society, not to mention going directly counter to NuAgra's progressive messaging. We need to persuade the locals that what NuAgra is doing will benefit Jewel and eventually all of Earth, not —" She breaks off with a frown, shaking her head.

"What should we do?" Dad looks alarmed now.

"First, Lucas needs to somehow convince Deb she misunderstood what he meant."

I cringe. "That won't be easy. I mean, she directly asked me if that was the reason Liam suddenly cooled it with Bri and I said it was."

She frowns for a moment, thinking. "Okay, then, tell her what you just told me," she finally suggests. "Say you panicked because you were afraid you might violate your nondisclosure agreement with NuAgra. Explain that they're really strict on enforcing secrecy because they're paranoid about protecting trade secrets to prevent corporate espionage.

That's what Kyna told those *Duchas* conspiracy nuts who got too nosy during the NuAgra tour last month."

"That...could work." I feel a sudden glimmer of hope I might possibly be able to stop Deb from hating me after all. "I can try, anyway."

Both of my parents still look worried.

"But what about Liam and the *Duchas* girl, Bri?" Mom asks M. "We were afraid if he became too involved with her, he might find it impossible to avoid telling her things about our people that he clearly mustn't."

Dad nods. "Yes, we're well aware of the trust you and the Council have placed in our family by allowing us to settle in Jewel. Rather than risk Liam accidentally breaching secrecy, we thought it safest for him to completely avoid the girl from now on. We, ah, warned him that if he refused, we would feel obliged to leave Jewel entirely rather than imperil our people's safety."

"I assume he wasn't too happy with that ultimatum?" M asks. We all shake our heads. "I noticed he's been really down these past two days at school. So has Bri. He can't have told her anything he shouldn't, or Bri would definitely have said something to me—or at least to Deb. So making them both miserable simply as a precaution seems pretty...harsh."

My parents and I all exchange guilty looks at the implied rebuke from our Sovereign.

"How do *you* do it?" I blurt out. It's an impertinent question, but I really need to know. "Is it true you actually kept the secret from your *Duchas* guardians for an entire year?"

"I did, though it got a little dicey sometimes. But let's face it, even if someone happens to notice a few...anomalies, they're hardly going to jump to the conclusion that a person they've known for years is from another *planet*. In fact, my aunt took a ton of convincing when we finally told her the whole truth about me." She laughs. "I wish you could have seen her face."

Reassured that she wasn't offended by my question, I ask another—one that matters even more to me. "So you think it really might be possible to be, um, close friends with a *Duchas* without risking...everything?"

"I'm still good friends with Bri and Deb," she points out. "We may not be quite as close as we were before I learned the truth, but we still spend a lot of time together. It's been almost a year and a half now, and I've never gotten even the slightest sense they suspect, well, you know. I think as long as you and Liam are solid with your background stories—and maybe explain that some things at NuAgra simply have to stay secret—you can safely go out with *Duchas* girls without them randomly guessing you're from Mars."

M suddenly grins. "It's funny now when I remember it, but I basically called Rigel a liar to his face when he first told me he was a Martian and accused him of making fun of me." She stands up. "Seriously, I think you'll both be fine."

A huge sense of relief spreads through me, even bigger than I expect. "Thanks."

"Yes, Excellency, thank you," Mom whispers. "I'm sure Liam will be very, very happy to hear this."

So am I. Assuming my idiocy hasn't already damaged both potential relationships beyond repair.

✦

When the Sovereign goes back to her seat, I start watching the game. Liam looks terrible out there, the worst I've ever seen him play. Worse than any of the *Duchas* on either team. Twice before halftime the coaches pull him out to talk to him, not that it helps. Even so, I don't notice Bri's father ragging on Liam especially hard. Maybe Bri didn't tell him how Liam's been ignoring her at school?

There are too many people around during halftime to let him know what the Sovereign said, so I'm not surprised when his second half is no better than his first. The coaches still put him back in a few times, probably hoping he'll shake off his slump, but there's no sign of that.

There are definitely no worries tonight that Liam's playing will raise any *Duchas* suspicions. It's only thanks to Alan and Sean playing just barely good enough that Jewel squeaks out a four-point win.

Once the game's over, Liam is clearly eager to escape the fans and the rest of the team as quickly as possible. Our family heads to the car as soon as he can get away, not even waiting for him to shower.

"Well, that sucked," he remarks as we cross the parking lot. "I might as well make the Council happy and quit the team after all."

Mom puts a hand on his shoulder. "I'm sorry, dear. But we, ah, have some news that I believe will cheer you up."

Liam glowers at her. "I doubt it. I saw M talking to you at the start of the game and I guess you told her why you're making me stay away from Bri. Is she going to give me a commendation for going along with your rules?"

"Uh, not exactly," I tell him. "I didn't want to say anything earlier, but...Deb kind of got in my face after Art class today. She wanted to know why you were ignoring Bri after the two of you hit it off so well Saturday night. Because she caught me off guard, I, ah, sort of gave her the impression it had to do with Bri being biracial."

He stops cold and rounds on me. "You did *what*?" he yells. "How could you possibly—?"

"In the car, both of you," Dad interrupts, glancing around nervously. "We should continue this discussion away from prying ears."

With a last, poisonous glare at me, Liam takes the last few strides to our car and slams himself into the rear seat. I follow more slowly to join him there as our parents get in front.

"Okay," Liam snarls at me as Dad starts the car. "Tell me *exactly* what you told Deb—and why you would ever make up something like that."

"Look, I know I screwed up." I throw up both hands. "The Sovereign was absolutely clear about that. Deb was asking a lot of questions and making guesses I thought were getting too close to the truth and I...panicked." I relate exactly what she said about our parents threatening Liam if he didn't stay away from Bri and us being part of some super-secret group. "Then she asked if it was about race instead and that seemed safer than her other guesses, so I...went with it. I didn't realize how much it would upset her."

Liam rolls his eyes. "Upset *her*? Imagine what Bri must be thinking! No wonder she didn't want to come to the game tonight. Crap, do you think she told Coach Morrison?"

"I...I don't know. Probably not? Did he act like she did?"

He thinks for a moment. "No, not really. I sure hope she didn't. But Lucas you've got to fix this!"

"I know. Deb apparently told the Sovereign what I said—that's why M was talking to us at the game. She says it would be really, really bad for the *Duchas* to believe our family, or maybe all the NuAgra people, are racist. I, ah, didn't think that far ahead, or realize what a huge, awful deal that might be. I'm sorry, Liam. I'll do my absolute best to undo whatever damage I've done."

"You'd better. We *can't* let Bri think that's what's going on. She must already deal with so much crap like that. I want do all I can to *protect* her from it, not make it worse! Hell, I'll tell her that myself—if I'm allowed to?" He looks to our parents, up front.

They exchange a glance, then Mom nods. "The Sovereign seems to think our ultimatum was a bit...harsh. She believes it's very unlikely any *Duchas* would guess the full truth about us, even if some things strike them as odd. Particularly if we're able to give them a plausible explanation for why some measure of secrecy about NuAgra is necessary. That was her recommendation. You'll still need to be careful, of course."

"Then I really am allowed to talk to Bri again?" For the first time all day, Liam looks happy. "That's great!" Then his face falls. "That is, if she'll *let* me talk to her. She might not." He darts an angry glance my way.

"I'll explain to Deb tomorrow," I promise. "I'll tell her how strict NuAgra is about secrecy and that I only agreed it was the race thing because I panicked. Which she might have noticed. Deb is...awfully observant. But M seems positive no one will automatically assume we're from Mars just because we have to keep some secrets. She knows from experience how unbelievable that would seem to most *Duchas*."

Liam's expression lightens again. "Yeah, now that you put it that way, I guess it would."

To encourage him—and myself—further, I relate what M told us about how her *Duchas* guardians reacted when they were told the truth, and how she herself reacted when Rigel first tried to tell her.

"If she's right that the truth is about the last thing anyone would randomly suspect, keeping it secret should be a lot easier than we thought," I conclude.

Unfortunately, what *won't* be easy is convincing Deb I'm not a total jerk.

17

Hypothesis

Deb

THAT EVENING, spurred by my new suspicions about NuAgra and M, I spend what should be homework time doing online research about cults. What I learn is alarming enough that I worry all through dinner, then call Bri. I remember Sean and Molly mentioning an away basketball game tonight, but under the circumstances, I kind of doubt Bri went.

Sure enough, there's no crowd noise when she answers her phone.

"Hey, are you home?" I ask.

"Yeah. I told my dad I wasn't feeling great. He didn't ask for details, probably thinks I have my period."

I smile, glad my mom's not weird about that stuff like most dads seem to be. "Okay if I come over?"

"Oh, sure. If you want." I'm not insulted by the lack of enthusiasm in her voice. She's been acting depressed since Sunday evening.

Mom's busy in her basement pottery studio throwing a new vase, so when I poke my head in to say I'm going over to Bri's, she just nods. A couple minutes later, I ring Bri's doorbell.

"Hey, Deb," she greets me, still in that listless tone. "What's up?"

"I, uh, thought maybe we could talk."

With a dull nod, she goes to the kitchen to get us each a root beer, then leads me upstairs to her room.

"What did you want to talk about?" she asks, closing the door. "The same thing as on the bus?"

"Not…exactly." We sit down opposite each other on her bed, cross-legged. "I went over to M's this afternoon."

She quirks an eyebrow at me. "Why? To tell her what you told me?"

"Originally, yeah. I was still really pissed about it when I got home and needed to vent. But when I told her the reason Liam backed off was…what you guessed, she flat out refused to believe it. She *insisted* it had to be something else."

Bri gives me a sad little smile. "M always tends to believe the best of people. Kind of like you do. Did she say what else she thought it could be?"

"Something to do with all the secrecy surrounding NuAgra—which she *claims* is only to protect against corporate espionage. Though why they'd consider either of us a threat, I don't know. It's not like we'd even know how to sell agricultural secrets to anyone. Though if what they're *actually* doing is unethical or even illegal, I guess that *could* get them all in trouble if outsiders like us found out about it."

"So…what? You think something nefarious is going on at NuAgra, and M knows or suspects it but won't tell us? That's pretty far-fetched, Deb."

"M said the same thing when I suggested that. But what if she's been brainwashed?"

Bri stares doubtfully at me across her black and gold Jaguar bedspread. "Brainwashed?"

I nod. "She spends kind of a lot of time with the newcomers these days. Tristan and Kira, at least, because of Molly and Sean. What if she's somehow been sucked into whatever they're doing out there? If it really is something bad, she could be in actual danger—in which case it's our duty as her friends to help her."

Bri's clearly not convinced. "I dunno, Deb."

"Just hear me out. We've both talked about how much M has changed over the past year or so. Not just her looks, but how she used to do everything with us but now mostly hangs out with Molly and Sean and Tristan and Kira."

"And Rigel." Bri gives me a patient look. "He's obviously the real reason she started spending less time with us, starting when they first got together at the start of sophomore year. Sure, it bothered me a lot at the time. I guess I was jealous. But…it's really not surprising. A lot of girls neglect their friends when they get their first boyfriend."

True. Bri's even done it to me a couple of times during one of her short-lived romances. "Still, that only explains Rigel," I say. "What about the others?"

"Well, Molly and Sean did move in right around the corner from her, so it only made sense they'd become friends," Bri points out. "Just like you and I did when you moved into the house next door. And they're dating Tristan and Kira now, so of course M and Rigel hang with them, too."

"Which is exactly how she could have gotten lured into whatever's going on at NuAgra," I persist. "You've heard some of the rumors about that place, right?"

She chuckles. "You mean all that crazy stuff about building high-tech weapons or doing weird experiments on people? You don't believe any of that, do you? Besides, even if it was true, what does it have to do with M?"

"Suppose NuAgra's just a front for some bizarre cult and she's been…indoctrinated? I did some Googling and several of the signs are there. Especially how M has pulled away from longtime friends like us to be with a whole new group of people."

I pull out my phone, click to one of the articles I found earlier and hand it to Bri. "There's other stuff, too. See? Those nondisclosure agreements everyone at NuAgra has to sign, swearing them to secrecy, and the way they mostly keep to themselves. Also, you can't deny there's something a little…off about most of the new people, even Lucas and Liam. I've mentioned how they sometimes don't seem to understand things they should, like 'break the ice' and onion rings. As though they came here from a whole different culture or something."

As Bri reads off my phone, her expression gradually changes from skeptical to concerned. At least my new theory is temporarily distracting her from being so sad about Liam.

"Think about it," I continue when she hands back my phone. "NuAgra moved their headquarters to Jewel way last September but they haven't hired *anyone* local. Like, at all."

"Unless you count Rigel's dad."

I stare at her. "What? When? I didn't know that."

"A month or so ago, I heard Pete Warner and Nate Villiers discussing the NuAgra rumors during Spanish class. They even talked about going out there to spy on the place and try to get answers. But then Rigel told them he'd been inside with his dad, who apparently set up their computer systems. He said it looks just like what they say it is, with greenhouses and labs to study seeds and stuff. M went on their tour last month and said the same thing."

"Of course they had to make it *look* that way. If they—" I begin, then break off as another puzzle piece suddenly clicks into place—an important one.

Bri looks at me questioningly.

"That's…really interesting about them hiring Rigel's dad," I say slowly, my mental gears turning. "Y'know, the Stuarts are also pretty new to Jewel—and the O'Garas are even newer. What if they *all* have some connection to NuAgra? No, hear me out! They could have been sent here a year ahead of the main group to…to scout Jewel out, then lay some groundwork before moving the whole organization here."

Bri starts to laugh. "Jeez, Deb, you make it sound like some kind of alien invasion. Don't you think you're getting a little—" But then *she* breaks off.

"Come to think of it," she continues, "Pete and Nate said almost exactly the same thing, about the O'Garas being some kind of advance guard. I thought they were just being paranoid, but along with all this other stuff—" she nods at my phone— "it would almost make sense. Except…why would M be part of it? *She's* not new to Jewel. I've known her since kindergarten."

"Maybe they needed someone on the inside, a regular Jewel resident," I suggest, still thinking hard. "Someone to help them fit in here and divert suspicion."

At that, Bri shakes her head. "No. I can't imagine M going along with anything illegal or dangerous."

"Unless they somehow convinced her what they're doing is really okay, or even for the greater good, somehow. That's what this says cults usually do. And M totally fits the profile for the kind of person they tend to recruit."

I reopen my phone screen to prove my point. "This says people without close friends or family ties are more likely to join cults, so they're often targeted. M's an orphan, and we were pretty much her only friends when Rigel's family first moved here. You can't deny it was kind of odd how Rigel made a point of talking to M at lunch his very first day here, even though Trina was all over him. I mean, M's a wonderful person and all, but…why?"

"Love at first sight?" Bri suggests. "It happens."

"In books, maybe. You and I were every bit as stunned as M was, you know we were."

She shrugs. "Maybe a little. But then we gave her that epic makeover—which totally worked. It was only afterward that Rigel started *really* paying attention to her."

Technically true, though I now doubt our makeover had anything to do with it. "I still think the way he singled her out right from the start was strange. He'd only been here about a week when he first kissed her—and we *know* that was M's very first kiss. She was so over the moon, he probably could have convinced her of anything after that."

"They did get really involved really quickly," Bri concedes. "They were practically inseparable and M was distracted all the time. We razzed her about it. Then a couple weeks later, they suddenly broke up, with no warning at all. That *was* weird."

"It was," I agree, remembering. "Neither of us could believe Rigel could possibly prefer Trina, of *all* people—though fortunately that didn't last long. Remember what a mess M was? Not just emotionally, either. She actually got sick."

Bri nods. "Rigel acted kind of sick, too. Even his football playing sucked for a couple of games, to the point we actually *lost* the second one."

"Was that the one where Trina kissed him, right in front of M's face? I swear, that girl is *so mean!*" I shake my head in disgust.

"She is. But she must be an awful kisser," Bri adds with a wicked grin. "Not only did Rigel's playing get even worse after she did that, he dumped Trina the very next week and went back to M."

I grin, too, remembering. "Yeah, Trina went ballistic when she saw them together but Rigel shut her right down. I swear, it was a thing of beauty!"

We both chuckle.

"And after that, Rigel finished out the season just fine," Bri recalls, "though that one loss kept us from going to the playoffs."

"You know, M never did tell us what led to that breakup," I say thoughtfully. "Even though we kept asking her. Maybe if it had to do with Rigel and his parents being part of a cult, she wasn't *allowed* to tell us the real reasons. The same way she can't tell us the truth about NuAgra and all the new people now."

Bri sucks in a breath. "So Liam and Lucas probably aren't allowed to talk about it, either. That would explain why they made Liam back off when we started getting too friendly. I'm starting to think you may actually be on to something!"

Her eyes glisten with hope, but only for a moment. "It's still an awfully wild theory, Deb," she says with a sigh. "Sure, I'd *rather* believe Liam was forced to dump me because of some top-secret NuAgra plot than because his family is prejudiced, but...isn't that what Lucas implied?"

He did more than imply, unfortunately. "Yeah, but if M's right, maybe he only said that to cover up something else. Something...worse."

"You keep hinting at that, but worse how, exactly?" Bri demands. "What do you actually think they're doing?"

"I don't know," I admit. "But when I suggested to M that NuAgra might be a front for some kind of illegal activity, she was awfully quick to deny it. *Too* quick. Like she knows something she's not allowed to tell."

When Bri still looks skeptical, I bring up the O'Garas again, and how they also glommed onto M as soon as they moved here, just a couple months after Rigel's family. "It might make sense that she and Molly became friends right away, but why would Sean immediately start coming on to M when she was obviously with Rigel? Didn't you tell me Sean and Rigel nearly got into a fight over her once?"

"Yeah, in the school courtyard," Bri confirms. "Matt saw them out there. He said they looked pretty tense, but M and Molly stopped them before they actually fought."

I think about that for a moment. "Doesn't that strike you as odd? I don't think M ever even flirted with Sean. Then, out of the blue, he asked her to the Winter Formal. And she said yes! With Rigel sitting right there at the lunch table!" I shake my head in remembered disbelief. "We all nearly died of shock."

"And Rigel's face!" Bri recalls. "He looked as stunned as everybody else for like ten whole seconds and then...just went along with it. It was *so weird!*"

"What if..." I pause, my gears turning again. "What if some bizarre cult rule decreed M *had* to be with Sean instead of Rigel? Like maybe

Sean outranked him or something, so she and Rigel had to go along with it, whether they liked it or not?"

Bri blinks at me. "You know, it almost did seem like that. Even though they all mostly still acted like friends, it was pretty obvious Rigel wasn't really over M, the way he and Sean kept taking little digs at each other."

"I never thought she was completely over Rigel, either," I tell her. "The way they still looked at each other when Sean wasn't watching…"

"I thought the same thing," Bri says. "I mean, she and Sean did sometimes hold hands in the hallways, but I never once saw them kissing. They weren't at *all* like she and Rigel used to be—and are again now. I asked M more than once what the deal was, but she was always really vague about it. You really think somebody *made* M break up with Rigel to date Sean? Ew. That's…kinda creepy."

"Totally creepy," I agree. "But it *would* explain how they all acted toward each other after winter break. Then they all went off to Ireland together. Supposedly they all got some study abroad scholarship, but now I wonder."

Bri's brows go up. "You think that was related, too?"

"Well, NuAgra *is* an Irish company—M reminded me of that today. Seems like an awfully big coincidence."

"I'd forgotten that." Bri looks worried now, too. "If you're right and M's been brainwashed, they had the whole spring and summer to do it."

I nod. "That's what I was just thinking. You know, M never did tell us exactly what happened in Ireland."

"We didn't push too hard for details, though," Bri reminds me. "Rigel still had amnesia from that accident they were in there, and M nearly died. That's what we heard, anyway. So it made sense she wouldn't want to talk about it."

"Even though they both came back without a scratch. Whatever happened in Ireland," I say, "it obviously changed things between M and Sean. They definitely weren't still dating, even before Rigel got his memory back. What if—"

My phone dings, interrupting me. "Oops," I say, glancing at it. "It's my mom, reminding me it's after ten on a school night. She must have finished up in her studio and noticed the time. I'd better go. We can talk more about this tomorrow."

"For sure. See you in the morning!"

I head home, relieved I convinced Bri to take my theory seriously.

Together, surely we can figure out some way to help M? It was also great to see Bri acting more like her usual perky self than she has since Sunday.

I hope it lasts.

I hurry to the bus stop the next morning, eager to brainstorm ideas with Bri for getting M out of the NuAgra cult or whatever it is. Before going to bed, I made a list of all the anomalies we discussed, along with a couple others I thought of. When I see her coming, I pull it out of my backpack—but then I notice her expression.

"What's wrong?" I ask, my list momentarily forgotten. She looks nearly as down as she did yesterday.

"I thought a lot about your new theory last night." The shadows I hoped I'd dispelled are back in her eyes. "It was…pretty elaborate. And I admit some of the weird stuff we remembered sort of fit. But—don't be mad, okay?—are you sure you didn't concoct it just to make me feel better? And, um, so you wouldn't have to hate Lucas?"

"No! I—" I start to protest, then stop. *Am* I sure those weren't my real motivations? "Didn't you agree all those anomalies we talked about couldn't just be coincidence?" I brandish my list. "What about—"

The bus pulls up just then, so I wait till we've boarded and found a seat before continuing.

"Look, I made a list." I hand it to her. "There's way too much here that—"

"No, I know." She takes the list but doesn't look at it. "I agree something strange is going on with M. That doesn't mean some NuAgra conspiracy is the only reason Liam dumped me. Cults can be racist, too, you know."

Unfortunately, I can't deny that. I was the one who suggested to M that NuAgra might be part of a white supremacist group. "Okay, I guess that's true, but—"

"Even if it's not," Bri continues, "what difference does it make, if Liam won't ever talk to me again?"

"Maybe none," I admit. "But if M's been lured into something dangerous, we still need to get her out. Which means we need to figure out what NuAgra's really doing, and how M ties into it."

The bus trundles past two or three barren cornfields before Bri nods. "Okay, I'll help with that part…for M."

She falls quiet again until we're nearly to the school, then adds, "But until we know for sure my race *isn't* the reason Liam dumped me, I think we should assume it was. And like you said yesterday, if he's willing to give me up because of that, he's not worth suffering over. Good riddance." She draws a shaky breath. "Remind me of that if I start to weaken, okay?"

"I will," I promise. "It's absolutely up to Liam and Lucas to make the first move. Nothing short of an abject apology and a *really* believable alternate explanation can ever make Liam deserve you after the way he's acted. Until then, I say we totally ignore them both."

Bri gives a sour laugh. "That should be pretty easy, since Liam hasn't even *looked* at me since—" She breaks off, staring ahead as the bus pulls up to the school. "Wait. Isn't that—?"

I follow her gaze and see both Liam and Lucas standing on the sidewalk, watching our bus like they're waiting for someone. Us?

18

Equilibrium

Lucas

AS THE BUS carrying Deb and Bri pulls to a stop at the curb, I fight a crazy urge to run away. "Are you sure—?"

"You stay put," Liam snaps. "This is your fault, so it's totally on you to make sure neither Bri *or* Deb believe what you said yesterday for a second longer than necessary."

Swallowing, I nod. Because he's right.

When we got home last night, I pulled out my U.S. History textbook, remembering what the Sovereign said before the game. After reading the chapter on the Civil Rights movement Deb mentioned last week, I flipped back to the parts about slavery and the Civil War. Then, since our textbook sort of glossed over the details, I went online for more info on the history and current state of race relations in the U.S.

What I learned shocked me. I'd thought it was similar to the way a lot of Martians feel about inter-*fine* dating, but I was seriously wrong. No wonder the Sovereign insisted we can't let people believe what I stupidly told Deb. Now that I understand how horribly I screwed up, I'm more determined than ever to fix things…if I can.

I swallow again as Deb and Bri make their way off of the bus. They've definitely seen us, judging by the way they keep darting glances our way. But then they exchange a look and angle off toward the school building, apparently having decided to ignore us—not that I can blame them.

Squaring my shoulders, I stride forward to intercept them.

"Hey, um, can we talk for a minute?"

I hate how my voice comes out higher than it should. Liam, I notice, is hanging back, forcing me to take point. Which is fair.

They stop, but hesitate for a long moment before Deb finally turns to face me. "About what?"

"I, um…about what I told you yesterday. I never should have said what I did."

"I asked for the truth." Her blue eyes are as cold as I've ever seen them, sending a little shiver down my back. "Don't apologize for giving it to me."

Bri hovers uncertainly a couple yards away, the same way Liam's keeping his distance, underscoring that I have to make things right with Deb before anything else can happen.

"What I told you *wasn't* the truth, though." I pack all the sincerity I can into my words. "This whole, um, thing with Liam staying away from Bri didn't have anything to do with…with what I said. I completely made that up."

"Why?" she demands. "What on Earth could *possibly* make you say something like that if it's not true?"

My rehearsed speech flies right out of my head as I look down into her cute—but currently hostile—face. I desperately try to remember exactly what the Sovereign said last night.

"I…I panicked. You were asking questions I wasn't allowed to answer, so when you suggested a different explanation, I, um, took it."

"Weren't *allowed* to answer?" She looks skeptical but a tiny bit less angry—a good sign.

Taking a deep breath, I nod. "That's right. Maybe you've heard that we all had to sign nondisclosure agreements to do our work studies at NuAgra? So did everyone else who works there. And they're not kidding around. They're so strict that if I—or Liam—were to tell someone who doesn't work there too much about their research, not only would we get booted from the work-study program, our parents could be fired."

Her brows go up in obvious surprise. "Fired? Seriously?"

"Seriously. NuAgra is unbelievably paranoid about corporate espionage. It's apparently not that uncommon with cutting-edge technology companies, since whichever company can get the new tech to market first reaps all the profits."

One brow comes back down while the other stays up. "Have you been talking to M?"

"Huh?" Crap. Did I accidentally—?

"Never mind." She gives a little shake of her head. "What does all this have to do with Liam dumping Bri after the way they—you know—Saturday night?"

Fortunately, I remember this part of my speech. "I—and my parents —were worried if she and Liam got too involved, he might be tempted to tell her things he shouldn't. Especially since Liam sort of tends to do and say things before he thinks." I dart a quick, apologetic glance at my brother. "They—we—thought it would be safer if—"

The warning bell rings, cutting me off.

"If he was grounded from talking to her at all?" Deb finishes for me, glancing at the crowd of students now streaming past us to the school.

"Er, yeah," I admit.

At that, Liam finally comes forward. "Only now they finally realize how ridiculous they're being."

Bri takes a cautious step forward, too. "Does that mean—?"

"That we can hang out together again, yeah," Liam eagerly confirms. "That is, if…if you still want to?"

By now, we're almost the only students still outside, so I say, "We should probably get to class if we don't want to get in trouble. Can we talk some more at lunch?" I'm mostly asking Deb, anxiously watching her expression for some sign of relenting.

To my relief, she nods. "I guess so. If you're sure—"

"I am." I infuse the two words with conviction, desperate for her to believe me.

She seems to, at least partly, because she walks alongside me as we all hurry toward the school. Bri and Liam are walking ahead of us. Not exactly together, but exchanging frequent, questioning looks at each other. It's a start, at least.

Bri's in my first-period Econ class, so after class I try to do a little more damage control.

"I guess you heard everything I told Deb earlier?" I ask her.

She nods. "Liam also insisted it's true. That your parents—?"

"And me," I reply to her implied question. "We all came down kind of hard on him, yeah. He, um, didn't take it very well. Ranted all day Sunday when they wouldn't let him even call you. Dad took away his phone to make sure he couldn't. I don't blame you for being mad. Neither does Liam. He felt really awful about it."

"Good," she says with a return of some of her former spunkiness. "Because he—all of you—made me feel awful, too. And I still don't understand why—"

We only have a minute, so I interrupt her. "I know. We'll try to explain better over lunch. Please don't stay mad at Liam, though. If you want to hate me, that's fine. I deserve it. But my brother...really likes you. A lot."

She sucks in an audible breath. "I— Okay. Lunch. Thanks, Lucas." Bri hurries off to her next class then and I head to mine, thinking. And hoping. About things I probably shouldn't.

⁀⁺

"Deb's talking to me again," Liam tells me with a grin when we both get to Chemistry third period. "I wasn't sure she bought it when you tried to explain before school, but she's at least not acting like she hates me now. A pretty good sign, I think."

I can't help smiling at the dramatic change from his black depression of the past few days. "Glad to hear it. I talked a little more with Bri after first period, too, and I think she mostly forgives you now. Maybe not me, but I'm okay with that."

"You don't think I'll need to grovel, then?"

"I don't know. Maybe a little? I think she was pretty hurt."

He winces. "Yeah. I could tell. It nearly killed me. I'm totally willing to do some groveling if that's what it takes to get her back."

"It really means that much to you?" I regret asking as soon as the words are out of my mouth, not sure I want to hear the answer.

Liam gives me a look, then nods. "You wouldn't know, since you've never been in love, but...yeah. Totally."

I give a quick nod and head to my lab table. That's what I was afraid of.

• • •

At lunch, instead of sitting at Deb and Bri's usual table, I suggest the four of us sit at an empty one in the corner. I know Deb's going to want more of an explanation than I gave her before school this morning, and I'd rather not do that in front of other *Echtrans*—especially the Sovereign.

Sure enough, the moment we all sit down with our trays, Deb asks, "So, what changed? What convinced your parents—and you—to loosen up?"

"Liam, mostly." I absolutely can't mention M's involvement. "He wore them down, made them see how much they'd overreacted. I, um, helped some, too," I add, hoping to earn a smile from her. "I never expected them to come down that hard on him."

"Then why did you rat him out?" No smile.

I'm grateful when Liam comes to my rescue.

"He didn't. I did. I was still on a high when we got home Saturday night, I'd had such a great time." He smiles over at Bri, who manages an uncertain smile in return.

"That's true, though I, um, did threaten to say something to them," I feel obliged to admit. "Mostly so Liam would stop and think about the consequences of violating our NDAs. But he was so sure our parents would take his side, he—"

"I kinda bragged about how great our date was," he finishes, with another soppy smile at Bri. "They, er, sort of went ballistic."

Her return smile is again reserved. Yep, it looks like Liam will have to do some groveling.

"I think they panicked, too," I say. "The need for absolute secrecy has been impressed on them so many times, they're almost as paranoid as the people in charge at NuAgra."

Deb looks puzzled. "Is what they're doing out there that dangerous?"

"Dangerous? No! Not at all." I can tell from her expression I was a little too emphatic, though what I said is perfectly true. "Just...really, really cutting-edge. Did either of you go on that tour they had before the holidays?"

Both girls shake their heads, so I trot out the rest of the speech I prepared last night.

"Well, if you had, you'd have seen the greenhouses and some of the labs, things you'd expect from an agricultural development company, and I'm sure they talked about some of the progress we're making. But not the actual techniques we're using. As far as I know, no one else has discovered those yet, and NuAgra wants to keep it that way until they have them patented and ready to market."

"So, it's just those techniques you're not allowed to talk about?" Deb still doesn't look completely convinced.

"Right," Liam replies before I can. "So why my parents worried I, of all people, might give away trade secrets, I don't know. I don't even understand most of it. It's not like I could tell anyone the kinds of details that would ever help a competitor." He shakes his head in disgust. "Like Lucas said, they *way* overreacted. It took a couple days, but we finally managed to convince them of that."

Deb pins me with her disconcertingly perceptive blue eyes. "Then why did you panic yesterday? It's not like I was asking for NuAgra secrets, just an explanation for why Liam started avoiding Bri all of a sudden."

True. I actually panicked because I was afraid she'd somehow guess we're all from Mars, but of course I can't say that. "I...I overreacted, too. When you started speculating about us being part of something secret, I immediately thought of NuAgra. I wasn't sure I was allowed to admit they even *have* secrets. Afterward, I realized how stupid that was, because a lot of people already know we had to sign nondisclosure agreements."

"Which we wouldn't have to do if there weren't secrets, duh." Liam glares at me for making the rift between him and Bri even worse. "It's obviously no big deal for people to know there *are* secrets. Nearly everyone at school already knows that. We just can't tell you what those secrets are, that's all. So, um, don't ask, okay?"

"We won't," Bri agrees. "Right, Deb?"

An anxious two seconds pass before Deb nods. "As long as you promise NuAgra's not doing anything really dangerous—or illegal—we'll try not to ask too many questions. It's not like either of us would know who to give trade secrets to anyway, or would understand those cutting-edge processes, even if you tried to explain them."

"Thanks," Liam and I exclaim together. I think I'm as relieved as he is.

"And yes," I add, "I swear to you that NuAgra isn't doing anything dangerous or illegal, or even unethical. If all their research pans out, what they're doing should eventually benefit not just Jewel or the

United States, but the whole world. But until then, it has to stay really secret."

Deb finally, finally smiles at me and I feel it right in my gut—in a good way.

"I guess that's good enough," she says.

Overtaken by a sudden surge of optimism, I surprise myself by saying, "In that case, do you girls want to do something together this weekend? Let us make up for what jerks we've been?"

Both girls also look surprised—but not as surprised as Liam does.

"That's a great idea!" he exclaims. "What do you say, Bri?"

The girls look at each other, hesitating. Making us sweat. On purpose? If so, I deserve it, though Liam really doesn't.

"Sure," Deb finally says, and Bri nods. "What did you have in mind?"

Amazingly, an idea pops into my head. "How about Donner's Farm? Have either of you been there?"

Deb's eyebrows go up. "Yes, but not for years."

"Same here." Bri still sounds cautious, too. "My parents and I used to pick apples there. Not in January, obviously."

"This time of year, they have homemade hot cider and stuff, and the grounds are still worth seeing. They even have a maze," Liam offers. "It's not far from our house, so we've been a few times."

I nod. "What do you say we meet there Saturday afternoon, right after lunch? We can explore for a while, then stop into their little shop for cider and a snack afterward to warm up."

After exchanging another glance, both girls shrug. "Sounds fun," Bri admits, though rather guardedly. Deb doesn't object.

"Great," I say. "It's settled, then."

We all turn our attention to our lunches then, since we only have a few minutes left until the bell. Shoveling down my food, I fervently hope the Sovereign was right that our secret will be easier to keep than we thought. Because the idea of spending quality time with Deb makes me happier than I've felt since landing on Earth last summer.

19

Rebound

Bri

"WHAT THE BOYS told us almost seems to confirm our suspicions, don't you think?" Deb whispers to me on the bus the next morning. "I mean, it's a relief to know they're not actually prejudiced, but it's hard to believe their parents would be worried they might get *fired* if their sons get too friendly with the locals."

"That does seem crazy," I agree. "Unless something weird really is going on out at NuAgra. There's still that whole list of weird stuff about M we came up with the other night."

Deb nods. "Though those mostly had to do with her and Rigel, and maybe the O'Garas, and how they might be connected with the other new folks."

"Lucas sounded absolutely positive when he swore NuAgra's not up to anything shady," I remind her—and myself. "He's in a way better position to know than we are, right?"

"That's true," Deb concedes. "Maybe I really have been reading too many thrillers lately…though it's weird how much of his explanation was almost word for word what M said to me yesterday afternoon."

That *is* a little odd. Or is it?

"M went on that tour, right?" I say. "They probably told her the same thing then that the boys told us today. You know, that the technology NuAgra's developing is super cutting-edge, and because of that a lot of it has to stay under wraps for now. If all that's true, it makes total sense she and the boys would say the exact same thing."

"Yeah, I guess that's a good point," Deb admits.

As our bus turns into the drive in front of the school, I'm almost afraid to look and see if Liam is waiting out front for me again. But I do…and there he is! A rush of joy and adrenaline shoots through me at the sight of him before it's tainted by squicky, lingering feelings of doubt and betrayal from the past few days.

"I guess they were serious about wanting to spend time with us again," Deb comments as we stand up to get off the bus.

"I guess so. I wish I knew what was really going on with them, though. I…don't think I could deal with Liam going totally cold on me again." I have to will the lump out of my throat at the thought.

Like yesterday, Lucas is there, too. For a long moment after Deb and I get off the bus, the four of us just stare at each other awkwardly. I want to move closer to Liam, maybe even give him a hug, but I can't bring myself to be the one to make the first move. He looks uncertain, too. Is he feeling the same way? Or is he having second thoughts?

"Good morning, ladies!" Lucas's heartiness sounds slightly forced to me.

"Morning," Deb answers with a reserved smile.

Liam turns to me then and offers me his arm, his eyebrows raised in a hopeful, pleading expression. I'm torn between wanting to laugh and hug him, or coldly refusing his arm because of what he put me through. I hate not knowing how to act around him now, when we were so friendly last week—and especially Saturday night.

After a moment's hesitation, I accept the peace offering of his proffered arm, slipping my hand through the crook of his elbow with a tentative smile. His look of relief almost undoes me, but I still don't dare completely relax with him. Not just yet.

"Are you coming to the game tonight?" he asks with what sounds like a genuine note of vulnerability in his voice, as we head toward the school.

"Probably?" I'm not willing to fully commit, but I don't want to torture him, either. "Sorry I couldn't make it on Tuesday. How did it go?"

He gives me a look, and I realize I already know the answer.

"Your dad didn't tell you? That was nice of him." He snorts in disgust. "I was a total disaster. Probably should have spent the whole game on the bench, but the coaches seemed to think I'd be able to shake it off and pull it together. They were wrong."

I can't help but empathize, considering how crappy *I* felt on Tuesday. "I'm sorry to hear that. Why, um…why do you think you had such an off night?" I stammer out, not wanting to assume it had anything to do with me.

Liam stops walking and gives me an incredulous look. "Are you kidding? Because I was a mess, Bri! I couldn't stand it, not being able to talk to you, not being able to even explain to you what was going on. I was in agony!"

Agony? I feel bad for him, but at the same time, a small, awful part of me is glad he experienced at least a measure of the same misery I went through. That part abruptly wins out as a thin, narrow streak of anger surges through me.

"Agony? Let me tell *you* about agony!" I hear myself saying, barely controlled fury flaring around the edges of my voice.

I see alarm spark in his eyes, but before I can let him have it, we're saved by the bell. I close my eyes, half annoyed and half grateful for the interruption. I was on the verge of saying something I'd probably regret later, so maybe it's for the best.

"Can we talk at lunch, please?" I look up to see him staring into my eyes, desperately pleading. "Just us? I know there's nothing I can say to make up for what you went through, but I have to try."

I don't trust my voice right now with the complicated swirl of emotions welling up inside me, so I just nod.

He responds with one of his heart-stopping smiles, relief written all over his face. "Thank you. I'll see you then!"

And then he's gone, rushing off to his first-period class. I blink, then realize I need to do the same. As I head to Econ, I wonder what he could possibly want to tell me at lunch.

I'm about to enter the cafeteria later when Liam catches up to me. Leaning close, he whispers, "Where can we go to be alone?"

Swallowing down my thrill of excitement at his words, I force my brain to work, reminding myself that I'm still upset with him. "Um, I guess we could go to the media center? The courtyard is a good option when the weather is nice, but pretty much out this time of year."

He gives me another one of his infectious grins. "The sun's shining. I don't mind the cold if you don't? It'll be more private than the media center."

"Um, okay." Despite myself, I can't help returning his smile. "But won't we need our coats?"

"Good point. Let's go." We turn around and head to our lockers, which we discover aren't all that far from each other.

He jogs up to me with his coat over his arm as I'm pulling mine out of my locker. "Want to head back to the cafeteria and get our lunches first?"

My stomach is already tying itself into knots. At the thought of food, it gives an uncomfortable lurch. "I'm not actually hungry, but you should go ahead."

"Yeah, I'm not so hungry either. Let's just go." He takes my coat and holds it up for me, just like he did when we left the Lighthouse Saturday. Right before we…

I'm sure I'm blushing as I put one arm, then the other into my puffy coat. Then he offers me his arm like he did this morning and I take it, my ears still burning.

When we step out into the courtyard, I'm surprised by how pleasant it is out here. Completely sheltered from the wind, the midday sunshine is trapped, creating an illusion of warmth. But because it's January, it's completely deserted. I turn to Liam expectantly. This was *his* idea, after all.

"So…what did you want to tell me?"

He takes a deep breath and closes his eyes. "Mostly that I'm sorry. I know it's too little too late, and it doesn't undo any of what you had to go through. But please believe me, I am so, *so* sorry for what we…for what *I* put you through. If it's any consolation, I was absolutely miserable, too."

Some of my earlier anger flares back to life. "Yeah? So why didn't you *do* anything about it? At least to tell me what was going on? Almost anything would have been better than the way you just completely ignored me after—"

"After the most amazing night of my life? I know. You must have thought I was the worst kind of jerk imaginable. But you have to believe me—my parents not only took my phone away, they threatened to yank me out of school completely if I so much as talked to you."

I blink. "Wow, I knew your your parents were strict, but that is *super* harsh. So they had your phone this whole time, not just Sunday?"

"Yes! They only gave it back to me after the game Tuesday night, even though I begged for it earlier." He holds my gaze with his, willing me to believe him. "If I'd had *any* way to contact you without them knowing, I absolutely would have."

"Like here at school? Why not then? It's not like they could keep tabs on you here, but you still avoided me like the plague." I don't even bother to hide the hurt in my voice.

Liam mashes his lips together in what looks like anguish. "I know. I wish I had. That's what I really can't forgive myself for. Even though Lucas took their side and agreed to 'keep an eye on me' at school and report back to them."

"Seriously?" Maybe Lucas is the one I should be maddest at.

"Seriously," he confirms. "My parents insisted they might get fired and we'd have to move away if anyone at NuAgra thought you knew things you weren't supposed to. That scared me enough I...went along with it. I figured staying here where I could at least *see* you, even if you hated me, was better than leaving Jewel and never seeing you again at all. I wasn't willing to risk that. Now, though... I wish I'd come straight to you Monday morning and at least told you how horribly, horribly sorry I was for standing you up on Sunday."

The tight knot that's been wound around my heart since Sunday afternoon finally starts to ease a little bit. "I wish you had, too," I whisper, swallowing the lump in my throat. I am *not* going to cry in front of him, no matter what!

"I know I can't undo what happened," Liam says, "and I won't blame you if you don't want to forgive me. But thank you for at least giving me this chance to apologize. I don't know if I even deserved that much."

He looks so distraught, so disgusted with himself, that I desperately want to fling my arms around him and reassure him that everything is okay, that I forgive him. But something still holds me back.

"I'm sorry, I just..." I shake my head. "See, when your brother told Deb what...what the reason was you were avoiding me, it was way too easy to believe. So I'm still having a hard time accepting that's not at least *part* of what's going on. It's...happened to me before."

There's a definite trace of bitterness in my voice. I vividly remember how Gary Chambers, the guy I'd crushed on my whole freshman and half my sophomore year, finally asked me out, then lost interest after introducing me to his parents. I can't know for *sure* that was why, but they acted really surprised to learn Coach Morrison is my dad. Then Gary started ignoring me the very next day, which makes me think it probably was.

"Bri…?"

Blinking away a bit of excess moisture in my eyes—maybe from the cold?—I look up to find Liam looking at me, his expression unexpectedly tender.

"Even if my parents were prejudiced like that, it would never change the way I feel about you. At all. You're the best thing that's ever happened to me. Anyway, your dad is an amazing coach. You wouldn't be the sports-obsessed nut you are if he wasn't your dad. So of course I'm happy Coach Morrison is your dad. He's part of you, and I like everything about you *exactly* the way you are. Nothing my parents or anyone else says could change that. And Bri, I swear I'll never, ever willingly do anything to hurt you, ever again."

At that, I lose control. I simultaneously laugh and sob, the tears that were threatening finally spilling over. Liam opens his arms and I fall into him, wrapping my arms around him and taking strength from his warm embrace. Still sniffling, I brush away my tears to gaze up at him.

"Could you possibly be any more perfect?" I ask with a shaky laugh, which he echoes. "How did you know exactly what I needed to hear?"

"Was that the right thing then? Thank goodness!" He looks massively relieved, and like he's on the verge of tears himself. How can I not forgive him? The knot around my heart finally dissolves the rest of the way and the euphoria I usually feel when I'm this close to Liam floods through me.

Holding me close, something in his expression shifts. The look in his blue-gray eyes suddenly makes me feel very warm despite the January air.

"Would it be all right…" His voice is husky. "I mean…may I…"

Feeling pretty sure I know what he's asking permission for, I answer by closing the distance between our lips myself. Suddenly, nothing else in the world matters except this moment, bathed in golden sunlight and wrapped in the golden warmth of Liam's embrace.

The amazing feeling of his lips on mine swirls and rises around me, making me dizzy, though I can still *sort* of feel my feet planted firmly on the concrete. Time loses all meaning. When we finally break apart, Liam's dazed expression probably mirrors my own.

"Wow. I, ah, guess Saturday night wasn't a fluke after all." I manage a little chuckle, still flushed with wonder.

"No. It definitely wasn't!" He gives himself a little shake, like he's trying to clear his head and return to reality.

I get it—I feel like I need to do the same.

Then he blinks. "What time is it? Is there time to grab some lunch? I'm starving!"

I laugh and check my phone. "We've still got ten minutes till the bell. So probably, if we hurry." I suddenly realize I'm hungry, too, now that the serpent that had taken up residence in my stomach has been banished.

Liam gives me a last, quick kiss that sends tingles all the way down to my fingertips and shoots me an impish grin. "Guess we'd better hurry, then!"

We race back to the cafeteria hand in hand, both of us laughing now. And why not? This week has gone from being the worst of my life to the best!

20

Sequence of events

Deb

BY FRIDAY AFTERNOON, I'm cautiously optimistic that Bri and I are mostly back to where we were with Liam and Lucas before everything fell apart after Saturday night.

After the boys explained and apologized on Wednesday, Lucas started sitting next to me in Art again. Bri told me that she and Liam worked out their remaining issues over lunch Thursday, though their blissful expressions when they got to our table five minutes before the bell made that pretty obvious. Then, when we went to that night's basketball game, Lucas acted more like he was "with" me than he ever had before. Bri even commented on it afterward.

"Just last week, you seemed positive Lucas didn't like you," she said on the way home. "You sure can't claim that now! M noticed, too—she mentioned it when we were both getting sodas at halftime."

"Did she seem upset at all?"

"What? No! Why would she be?"

I just shrugged. She'd definitely looked a little concerned last week when Bri and Liam were flirting so much at lunch, but I haven't really noticed that this week.

Friday, Liam and Lucas both sit at our usual lunch table, chatting easily with M, Rigel and the others. And in Art class, Lucas is even more talkative than the day before, though we mostly just discuss art

137

and our current projects. I feel like we've picked up where we left off Saturday night, before things got so tense outside the Lighthouse. It's…nice.

On the bus home that day, Bri is brimming with excitement about tomorrow's date at Donner's Farm, despite the gray drizzle outside.

"After last night's game, Liam talked about us watching Sunday's playoff game together, too," she gushes. "He's going to ask his parents if we can both come over to their house for it."

"Really? Does Lucas know that?"

Like me, Bri has to be remembering what happened the last time she and Liam were going to watch a pro football game together, but she just shrugs, apparently not worried at all about a repeat. "He didn't say, but he'll obviously tell him. Even if you and Lucas don't care much about the actual game, it'll be another chance for the two of you to hang out together."

The thought of sitting next to Lucas for three whole hours—maybe with his arm around me?—sends a little thrill through me. Still…

"Let's see how tomorrow goes first, okay?" I suggest. After the way Lucas has gone from cool to warm to icy cold, then back to warm, I don't dare assume too much. Especially since I still suspect more may be going on at NuAgra than anyone's telling us.

⁺_⁺

Later that evening, the drizzle becomes a steady rain, followed by a hard freeze after midnight. Saturday morning, I look out my window and groan when I see everything within sight encased in ice.

"So much for our date," I mutter to myself. No way Mom will let me drive in this.

With a sigh, I pull on my old jeans and sweater instead of the newer clothes I'd planned to wear today.

After dispiritedly eating a breakfast of cold cereal, I'm about to call Bri so we can commiserate and consider alternate plans, when I get a text from her.

Dad just got back from the hardware store and he says the roads are fine! I was so scared we'd have to cancel but it looks like our date is a go!

My mother confirms Bri's news when she gets home from the grocery store half an hour later.

"I suppose because the ground was still fairly warm from the past few days, the ice only formed on trees. And power lines. One was down two streets over. We're lucky we didn't lose electricity."

Not long after that, Bri shows up at my door. "Liam texted and confirmed we're still on for this afternoon," she says, bouncing inside. "Let's plan what we'll wear and stuff!"

I readily agree, my spirits bubbling back up. We spend the next hour and more on our outfits and makeup, going for pretty-but-super-casual, which seems fitting for a rustic setting like Donner's Farm.

The all-organic farm and plant nursery has been a Jewel fixture since well before Bri and I were born. It's run by a couple of aging hippies who have added to the grounds over the years to make it a local attraction, particularly in summer and fall. Now there's a produce stand and store, and in season you can also pick your own berries and fruit. I'm eager to visit it again.

At one o'clock, I pull into the gravel lot next to the produce stand, currently closed for winter. The Walsh brothers are already waiting in front of the little country store at the back of the lot. As Bri and I get out of my mom's car, they come over to us.

"Hey," Liam greets us with a big smile. "We just checked inside and they're fine with us wandering around the grounds for a while before we go in and get cider and stuff. You girls warm enough?"

We both nod. It's at least twenty degrees colder today than it was yesterday, but Bri and I dressed with that in mind, wearing thick sweaters under our winter coats.

"Let's go!" Bri dimples up at Liam and he takes her gloved hand in his.

Lucas hasn't spoken yet. He looks a little awkward, maybe wondering if I expect him to hold my hand, too. I smile at him, then follow Liam and Bri. Half second later he falls into step beside me, the awkwardness gone.

In front of us, Bri is already chattering away about the Colts' chances in tomorrow's game, prompted by eager questions from Liam.

"You've been here before, right?" Lucas asks me as we walk.

"Yes, but it's been a while. I guess you come more often, with it so close?"

He nods. "Our mom bought produce here when the stand was still open last fall and got to know the Donners a little. Then Liam talked me into picking apples with him so Mom could make pies. He was bummed we missed cherry season—his favorite kind of pie."

"You said they still have a maze?"

"Yeah, just past the pear orchard. It's not big enough to get lost in, but still kind of cool."

I grin. "I loved that maze when I was ten. Got my mom to bring me here a bunch of times, until I learned every path by heart."

We continue walking and chatting about nothing in particular, several paces behind Bri and Liam, who are now shoulder to shoulder, their heads close together. I'm happy to see Lucas doesn't seem to have a problem with that. So far.

Following the gravel paths past big beds of what will be strawberries in a few months, we make our way toward the orchards beyond. When we get close, we all stop and stare, marveling.

Every single tree is still encased in ice, glittering in the sunshine like something out of a fairy tale. It's beautiful.

"Wow," Bri breathes. "Toto, I don't think we're in Kansas anymore!"

I chuckle, but to my surprise, both boys look totally confused.

"Kansas?" Liam echoes. "Why—?"

Bri grins up at him. "I feel like Dorothy when she first stepped out of her house in Oz," she explains.

His expression doesn't clear. Neither does Lucas's. If anything, they look more baffled than before.

"Haven't either of you ever seen 'The Wizard of Oz'?" I ask.

They both shake their heads.

Bri and I stare at them in amazement.

"Really?" she says. "I didn't think any kid could grow up in America without seeing it at least once. Not that it matters, of course," she adds when the boys exchange a worried glance. "I guess your parents didn't let you watch a lot of TV?"

"Um, no," Lucas confirms, looking slightly relieved. "They were really strict about screen time and what we were allowed to watch."

Liam nods vigorously. "Yeah, they were. Still are, but not as bad as when we were younger. So, um, walk some more?"

We continue wandering, the odd moment forgotten. Bri and Liam take a path leading off to the right while Lucas and I take another going left. If I remember correctly, both paths will link back up on the other side of the orchard.

"It really is pretty," I comment after several seconds of silence, gazing up at the twigs and branches shimmering in the sun. "Not very good for the trees, of course. I hope they don't lose too many branches."

"Yeah, me, too," Lucas agrees. "Oh, the maze is over that way. Unless you'd rather just enjoy the ice show?" He's staring around at the trees, too, his expression awed. "This would be cool to try to paint, don't you think?"

I nod. "Now I wish I'd brought my sketch pad along. It would be hard to capture that iridescence, though."

He agrees and we continue slowly on, both of us marveling at the unusual beauty created by the ice.

Gradually, I become aware of how alone we are. Bri and Liam are completely out of sight, though I can still hear their voices in the distance. Fortunately, Lucas doesn't seem particularly concerned by that, unlike last Saturday at the Lighthouse. I glance up at him to confirm that and discover he's looking down at me, his expression as soft as I've ever seen it.

"I'm, uh, glad we can still be…friends," he says, his voice slightly husky.

Caught in his gorgeous blue-gray gaze, I nod. "Me, too." It comes out almost like a sigh. "I— That is—"

I barely notice a crackling sound above us as I grope for words, mesmerized by the look in Lucas's eyes. Then the crackling suddenly gives way to a loud *snap*. I finally look up…just in time to see an enormous branch plummeting straight at my face.

Before I can duck or even scream, an arm flashes in front of my terrified eyes and the ice-covered branch rockets away to crash into a nearby tree. At the same instant, another arm wraps around my shoulders, yanking me in the opposite direction. Everything happened so quickly, it's a moment before it completely sinks in.

Gasping in a shuddering breath, I turn to Lucas to find him staring at me, his face an intense combination of terror and dawning relief.

"What—? How—?" I start to ask when he abruptly pulls me against him, then amazes me even further by cutting off my questions with a kiss.

And what a kiss!

For several long, incredible seconds, I feel like I'm melting right into him, my lips perfectly conforming to his. As the kiss goes on, remarkable sensations unlike anything I've ever felt before spread all through my body until I half expect to levitate off the ground from pure euphoria.

When Lucas finally pulls away, I feel dazed. Disoriented. Exhilarated.

Gradually, my ability to focus returns and I see him gazing down at me with such tenderness, it steals my breath all over again.

"Are you okay?" he asks urgently. "You're not—?" He sweeps me with a quick, worried glance.

"I'm not hurt, no." I'm startled by how…normal my voice sounds. "But okay? I'm—" I break off, not sure what to say. *I may never be okay again? Or maybe, I feel more okay than I ever have in my life?*

I know I should ask him how he kept that branch from hitting me— what he did shouldn't have been possible—but at the moment, I can't seem to form any coherent thought except *please kiss me again!*

As though reading my mind, he lowers his lips to mine, much more slowly this time, letting us both savor a delicious moment of anticipation before we're kissing again.

If anything, this second kiss is even better, unmarred by my sudden scare. It lasts longer, too, though still not nearly long enough. As before, I'm infused with an intense feeling of well-being, as though I was never fully alive before this moment. Maybe I wasn't.

All too soon, I hear voices and footsteps approaching. So does Lucas, because he finally—reluctantly?—releases me. He gazes down at me with an expression of tenderness and longing that makes my heart expand with delight before he looks toward the sounds.

"Hey, guys," he calls, his voice slightly hoarse. Clearing his throat, he tries again. "We're over here!"

A few seconds later, Bri and Liam appear on the path ahead, still hand-in-hand. From the way Bri's glowing, much like she did last Saturday night, I strongly suspect they've been kissing, too.

"Hey," Liam says. "We, er, waited a few minutes where the paths join up, but when you two didn't show, we thought… Is, uh, anything wrong?" A slight frown creases his brow as he looks from his brother to me and back.

"Not now," Lucas replies with admirable nonchalance. "But a couple minutes ago we almost got clubbed by that branch over there."

He points and I notice for the first time that the branch is now a good twenty feet away. Did Lucas really knock it that far? I look questioningly at him, but he's still facing the others.

"Gave us a bit of a scare, so we, uh, needed to catch our breath before joining you. Didn't want to worry you. Though I guess we did anyway. Sorry."

Bri looks worriedly at me. "You're both okay, though?"

I nod. "We're fine." *So* much more than fine! "Though after an ice storm like that, I don't know if the trees will be. That was a really big branch that broke."

We all turn to look at it again and I realize that was an understatement. The thing is huge, nearly eight inches across—the size of some of the tree trunks.

"Wow," Bri says. "Good thing it wasn't directly over you, huh?"

Lucas nods, so I do, too. Even though it *was* directly over us. Over *me*.

Which he knows as well as I do.

"So, you guys still want to do the maze?" Liam asks.

We do, so we all go back the way he and Bri just came. The path soon leads us to what looks like a solid wall of holly bushes until we reach the narrow entrance.

"Huh. It seemed a lot bigger when I was nine or ten," Bri comments. "We can still do our best to get lost in it, though." She slants a suggestive glance up at Liam, who grins back.

We follow the two of them through the gap, but when they turn right, Lucas again turns left. Which is fine with me, both for the chance to finally ask him what happened back there, and to kiss some more. Since the latter is bound to make me forget all about the former, I ask my question first.

"So," I murmur once I'm fairly sure Bri and Liam are out of earshot. "Care to tell me what exactly you did to keep me from being pulverized by that branch?"

Shrugging, he takes my hand. Even through my glove, it feels amazing. Then he catches my gaze with his, distracting me further. "Pure adrenaline, I think," he replies.

Mesmerized by his eyes all over again, it takes me a second to recall what I just asked him. With an effort—it takes a surprising amount—I force my attention back to my question and his answer.

"I know adrenaline can sometimes allow people to do incredible things, but…*that* incredible?"

He shrugs again. "What else could it be? I was so scared that branch would smash into you, I just…reacted. Didn't even have time to think about it. I, uh, was pretty surprised, too, when I realized what I'd done. Really glad I did, though." The smile that accompanies those last words speeds up my heart.

"So am I. Even if I don't quite understand how."

Leaning close, his eyes darken and then we're kissing again. It's heaven on Earth.

At least fifteen minutes pass before we make any effort to find Bri and Liam. Hand in hand, we wander through the maze until we finally discover them sitting on the little bench in its center. Because they hear us coming, we don't actually catch them kissing, though it's pretty obvious from their expressions that's what they've been doing. Not that I'm one to judge.

"There you are!" Bri exclaims as we join them. "Guess I'd better not ask what *you* two have been up to," she adds with a sly grin.

I feel myself flushing but don't confirm—or deny—her assumption. There's an awkward moment of silence as we all look at each other, then Liam jumps to his feet.

"I'm ready for some hot cider and apple crullers," he announces. "How about you guys?"

The four of us make our way out of the maze and back to the shop by the parking lot, though none of us hurry. I can't speak for the others, but I'm savoring the moment—and the incredible memory of what it felt like to be thoroughly kissed by Lucas.

As we eat our crullers and drink our cider at one of the four tables in the tiny shop, I can tell by the looks Bri keeps shooting my way that she can barely wait to ask me about the progress of my relationship with Lucas. She'll be delighted when I tell her, though not nearly as delighted as I am.

I suspect my niggling doubts will return once I'm well away from Lucas's intoxicating presence, but for now I'm as happy as I can ever remember.

21

Energy transfer

Lucas

WHEN THE BIZARRE cuckoo clock behind the shop's counter strikes three o'clock, I regretfully suggest we should head home. These past two hours have been the best I can ever remember spending, but we can't very well stay here all day. Unfortunately.

"Yeah." Deb sounds regretful, too. "Mom might need her car back." She glances through the windows toward the parking lot. "Speaking of cars, I don't see yours. Did you guys walk?"

Liam and I nod.

"It's only like a quarter of a mile from our house," he says. "Took us maybe five minutes."

"We can drop you if you don't want to walk back," Bri offers. "Right, Deb?"

"Of course."

She smiles over at me and yet another warm tingle skitters through my body, though not as intensely as when we were kissing.

"Actually," I say, smiling back, "I think the walk might do me good." Not to mention the fact that Liam and I didn't exactly tell our parents we were meeting the girls when we left for our walk.

"Er, same here," Liam agrees, then says the quiet part out loud. "Today's been awesome, but our folks don't need to guess *how* awesome." He winks at Bri, who giggles.

An adorable, tiny frown creases Deb's brow. "If you're sure?"

Again, we both nod.

I take our empty cider cups to the counter and buy a dozen more crullers to take home as a cover story for us being here. We all thank Mrs. Donner, then troop outside to Deb's mom's car.

Feeling suddenly awkward, I try to work up the nerve to give Deb one last kiss goodbye. Then Liam takes the initiative with Bri, making it a whole lot easier. The moment the two of them aren't paying any attention to us, I tug Deb closer. She doesn't resist at all.

"I had a great time today," she murmurs against my lips after a wonderful, lingering kiss. "Thanks for suggesting it."

"So did I," I whisper back. "Thanks for coming."

One more nice, long kiss for good measure, then I reluctantly straighten. "Ready, Liam?"

With an audible sigh, he pulls away from Bri and nods. "Ready as I'll ever be, I guess. See you both tomorrow night to watch the game?" he asks the girls as they get into the car.

"Absolutely," Bri enthusiastically agrees.

"I still need to ask my mom, but probably." Deb's smile warms me to my core.

Having tomorrow to look forward to makes parting for today easier. Not easy, but easier.

Deb starts the car and Liam and I turn toward home.

"Looked like you and Deb had a really good time together today," he comments. Just like I knew he would.

"We did." No point denying it.

He gives me a long, sideways look. "So do you finally get why I want to be with Bri so much?"

"I… Yeah. Yeah, I guess I do." I frown over at him. "I was already sorry for siding with Mom and Dad last Saturday, but—"

"But now you understand where I was coming from," he finishes.

I nod.

We walk in silence for a minute or two, then he says, "Bri told me she thinks you and Deb look really cute together. She's right. The two of you kind of remind me of Mom and Dad."

That stops me in my tracks for an instant because the exact same thought flitted through my mind earlier. Not that Deb and I could ever—

"Do you think you're in love with her?" Liam asks then, startling me even more.

I start walking again. "Little soon for that, don't you think?" I reply, not looking at him—because his question makes me realize, with sudden, deep certainty, that I am.

He shrugs, grinning. "Who's to say? I fell in love with Bri even quicker. And before you ask again, yeah. I'm sure."

I give him a sharp look. "Have you told her?"

"Not yet," he admits. "I don't know if she's ready to hear it. Don't want it to sound like just a line, you know? Especially after what we put her through this week. I need to wait for the right moment. But I'll tell her."

My brother sounds so positive, so confident, I'm a little envious. I'd like to feel that same certainty. Except it would make breaking up with Deb even worse. Which, after the stunt I pulled today, could happen sooner rather than later.

Kissing Deb distracted her—distracted both of us—from dwelling on it right away. But I know at some point, maybe as soon as tomorrow, she'll want to know exactly how I kept that branch from smashing her. My adrenaline excuse seemed to satisfy her today, but I doubt she'll buy it once she's had time to think things through.

What else could I have done, though? Allow her to be injured, maybe even killed? My insides grow cold at the very thought.

"Guess I'd better ask Mom and Dad about the girls coming over for the game tomorrow night, huh?" Liam says when our house is in sight.

"You mean you didn't already? Back there, you said—"

My brother looks uncomfortable. "Yeah, I know. I was going to ask them last night, but then Dad made another comment about how careful I need to be now I'm, er, talking with Bri again."

Both of our parents made a point of cautioning him again on the way home from Thursday night's game. Probably because of the way Bri and Liam behaved toward each other when she ran down to congratulate him afterward. They didn't actually kiss, but nobody watching would assume they were just "friends."

"How about I ask them, instead?" I offer. "They might be less suspicious if it comes from me. And more likely to agree." Anything to increase the odds I can spend more time with Deb tomorrow.

"Hey, that's a great idea! You can even tell them this will help convince the girls what you told Deb on Tuesday wasn't true. I bet that'll work."

Our plan gets a little dicier when we get home and discover Mom is already suspicious.

"Where have you boys been all this time?" she demands the moment we walk in. "Did you walk all the way to downtown Jewel and back? I didn't expect you to be gone nearly this long."

I hold up my paper bag of crullers as both explanation and peace offering. "We stopped in at Donner's Farm for a while. I thought some of their apple crullers would be good with breakfast tomorrow."

Taking the bag, she peeks inside and sniffs appreciatively. Then frowns again. "It can't have taken you more than two hours to buy these. Where else did you go?"

"Um, nowhere."

Even as I say it, I wonder if I should have claimed we did—especially when she turns on Liam, her eyes narrowed.

"You met that *Duchas* girl, Bri, didn't you?"

His chin comes up. "Yeah, I did. So what? Her friend Deb was there, too. We were outside the whole time, except at the end when we went into the shop for cider and these crullers. They're really good, by the way. Try one."

"Don't try to distract me, young man," Mom snaps. "We've warned you against stringing her along. I'm certain Sovereign Emileia wouldn't approve of you doing so, either."

"I'm not!" he exclaims, clearly stung. "I really, really like Bri. How many times do I have to tell you that?"

Their raised voices bring Dad from the back of the house.

"What's going on?" he asks, looking from Mom to Liam and back.

She turns to him. "Your son just had a…a tryst with that *Duchas* girl without telling us. After we expressly warned him—"

"Oh, Eilis, calm down," he tells her, making her blink. "You know as well as I do that there are no unattached *Echtran* girls their age living in Jewel right now. Certainly no Engineering girls. And the Sovereign herself said she doesn't consider an *Echtran* boy dating a *Duchas* girl to present any significant risk of revealing our true origins. Surely some leeway—"

"The Sovereign may not be the best judge about such matters." Mom prims up her lips. "Quite a few of our people still question her wisdom in continuing her relationship with Rigel Stuart, for example."

Dad shakes his head. "You read the reports. Our own Scientists confirmed the two of them share a true *graell* bond, so it seems she has little choice. If not for their bond, we might all have been killed, or as good as, by those Grentl aliens, according to that bulletin from the Council. Personally, I think her expressed goal of giving all *fines* increased representation in Martian politics is admirable. Isn't it what we've hoped for most of our lives?"

"I suppose," Mom reluctantly agrees. "But equality, even intermingling, among our own people is one thing—and a far cry from attempting the same with a *Duchas*."

"Don't say it like that!" Liam glares at her. "Maybe Lucas wasn't so far off when he told Deb our family's racist. *You* sure seem to be, at least if the races happen to be *Duchas* versus *Echtran*."

His words bring her up short. "Liam! I am not—" She looks helplessly at Dad, who shrugs.

"Boy has a point, Eilis. If our people plan to truly integrate into Earth society, we'll eventually have to stop drawing such hard distinctions between us and the *Duchas*. In their last broadcast, the Sovereign and Princess Malena talked about working toward a day when we can all openly be who we are, here on Earth."

"Eventually, perhaps." Mom still looks stubborn. "But not today. Even the Sovereign has made it clear the *Duchas* aren't ready to learn the truth about us yet, and may not be for many years. Likely decades. Until that time, the risk—"

"Is minimal, from what she told us the other night," Dad cuts in. "When we petitioned to settle in Jewel, it was with the understanding that our boys would be attending a *Duchas* school, socializing with *Duchas* students, and eventually making friends with them."

Liam nods vigorously. "Exactly! It's not like I'm going to suddenly blurt out to Bri I'm from Mars, no matter how much I—" He breaks off, apparently realizing he was about to say too much.

"How much you want to?" Mom prods. "Or how much you...care about her?"

He lifts a shoulder. "I like her a whole lot, Mom, but I'm not stupid. Shoot, even if I *did* tell her I'm Martian—which I won't!—she probably wouldn't believe me. Isn't that what the Sovereign said?"

"He's right, Eilis." Dad puts a hand on her shoulder, his voice soothing now. "Still—" He turns to look at Liam. "I do agree with your mother that you can't let things go too far with Bri. It's one thing to be friends with her, even to go on dates—in public—but becoming seriously involved, romantically—" He shakes his head. "I can't imagine that ending in anything but unhappiness. For both of you."

"I—" Liam swallows. "I hope you're wrong. But you *are* okay with us dating, right?"

"Casually," Mom stresses.

I've stayed quiet this whole time but decide that's my cue.

"Tomorrow night is the final NFL playoff game before the Super Bowl," I say. "Bri and Liam both really want to watch it, and we thought maybe having Bri and Deb over to watch it here would finally convince Deb our family's…normal. Not racist, at least. What do you think?"

Our parents are both clearly startled.

"This game will be on television?" Dad asks.

Liam rolls his eyes. "Dad. No actual American man would *ever* ask a question like that. I guess it's a good thing you don't have to interact with *Duchas* regularly, like we do. The Super Bowl is like the biggest sporting event of the year in America. And since practically everyone in Jewel roots for the Indianapolis Colts, them making the final playoffs this year is huge. If you're really that out of touch, I'd say there's a bigger risk of *you* outing us as Martians than there is of *me* slipping up."

Dad flushes slightly. "I've been meaning to learn more about Earth sports, but we've been so busy at NuAgra lately—"

"Don't worry." Liam sounds positively patronizing now. "Deb and Lucas aren't very into sports either, so it'll seem totally normal if Bri and I explain stuff about football while the game's on. If you pay attention, you'll probably learn a lot tomorrow."

Dad looks at Mom. "That…should be all right, don't you think? For the two girls to come here to see this game with the boys? Particularly if you and I are in the room the entire time?"

She thinks for a moment, then nods. "I suppose so. As long as it's perfectly clear to Bri—and to you, Liam—that this is a *casual* gathering, not some sort of romantic date. What time is this game?"

"Kickoff is just before seven," Liam replies. "Hey, how about we invite them to eat here, too, since it'll be right around dinnertime? We can have all-American, game-watching type food, just like a *Duchas* family would!"

"But…I have no idea what that would be," Mom glances nervously at Dad.

Liam grins. "Don't worry, I do. I'll make a list right now, then Lucas and I can go to the grocery store for everything we'll need. It'll be fun, Mom, you'll see. And it'll go a long way toward convincing them there's nothing weird about us."

Not only do our parents both agree then, Dad actually looks a little excited at the prospect.

I follow Liam to the kitchen to see what we already have and make our list. Privately, though, I doubt an all-American, football party spread of food will be enough to keep Deb from remembering how I rescued her today—or from eventually demanding answers.

22

Cloak-and-dagger

Deb

BRI CHATTERS happily all the way home from Donner's Farm, clearly on cloud nine after her afternoon with Liam.

"I'm so glad we did this! Could today have been any more perfect? Even the cold just made things more romantic, don't you think? And all that glittery ice was so gorgeous..."

Though I don't contribute a lot to the conversation, I smile and nod a lot, floating along on at least cloud eight as I relive that last kiss from Lucas. Today really was a perfect date, way better than last weekend at the Lighthouse. And not just because Lucas kissed me for the first time. Though he *is* the most amazing kisser—and most amazing guy—I've ever met.

Even before that incredible first kiss, I felt like he and I had reached a new level of understanding. Now, I'm *almost* completely confident he won't suddenly go all cold on me again. The way he looked at me when we were alone, and again when he said goodbye...

Bri comes inside briefly so we can spend a few more minutes squee-ing, though all I tell my mom is that we had a "nice afternoon." I don't start drifting back to Earth until after Bri's gone home and I'm alone in my room. Only then, as the euphoria from Lucas's intoxicating effect gradually wears off, do I recall the *extraordinary* way he knocked away

152

that huge branch before it hit me. He claimed it was just adrenaline, but...was it? Really?

"M and Bri are right," I mutter aloud to myself. "I have too darned much imagination for my own good."

Shaking my head to dispel the suspicions trying to buzz their way back into my brain, I go down to the kitchen for a diet root beer. Once there, I realize I'm starving. I shouldn't be, after two apple crullers, but I grab half a dozen carrot sticks and a handful of cashews to take back upstairs. I *did* do kind of a lot of walking today.

I'm at my desk, munching and trying to focus on my Pre-Cal homework instead of spinning new theories, when my phone rings. It's Bri.

"Liam just called," she says excitedly. "He asked if we can be there by six-thirty for the game tomorrow, that they'll have enough food to count as dinner. Did you check with your mom yet?"

"Oops, no, I'll go do that. But first I should tell you what really happened when that big branch nearly hit me today."

She laughs. "Not necessary. Liam might not have figured it out, but it was pretty obvious to me you two were making out. Did you really think I'd be upset about that?"

"No, that would be pretty hypocritical," I admit. "And yeah, we were. But I was talking about—" I break off, not sure how to describe what Lucas did.

Oblivious, Bri continues. "It was great how well you two hit it off—again. Not surprising, I guess, considering how much you guys have in common. How did the two of us get so lucky, Deb? Remember what losers we used to be?"

"Definitely. Before last year, M was our only other real friend. Nobody else wanted anything to do with us."

"Exactly. Who would have predicted then that *we* would be going out with the two hottest guys in school?" She sighs dreamily. "Anyway, go tell your mom about tomorrow. If she won't let you take her car, I can ask my dad to drop us."

I agree and hang up without mentioning Lucas's almost superhuman feat to her. Maybe it was just adrenaline, like he said? Curious now, I flip open my laptop and start scouring the internet for a reasonable explanation for how he was able to deflect a branch that probably weighed more than me.

To my surprise and relief, some descriptions of "hysterical strength" sort of fit. Apparently some of those urban legends about moms lifting cars to save babies really are based on fact, though documented instances are rare. Most have only happened in life-and-death situations, where the threat was to the person themselves or to someone else they cared about.

For obvious reasons, the phenomenon hasn't been very thoroughly studied, since it would be pretty unethical to risk someone's life to find out if they can call on normally-untapped resources. Even so, I learn enough to quiet my suspicions…for the moment.

After that, I go downstairs and ask Mom about going to the Walshes' to watch the playoff game tomorrow night. She's fine with it, though her knowing smile tells me she's well aware my eagerness has nothing to do with football.

"You really like this boy, don't you?"

Shrugging, I nod. "Yeah, I do. He's…different from the other boys at school. More interesting. Smarter." *Better looking.* "We seem to get along really well, too."

"That's nice. Just don't let him distract you from school *too* much, okay?" She reaches over and ruffles my hair.

Grinning, I push her hand away. "I won't."

After helping with dinner prep, I head back upstairs to attempt more homework. But despite my best efforts, it's not long before I start thinking about Lucas again—and just *how* different he is.

Abandoning my open Pre-Cal book, I rummage in my backpack and pull out the list of "oddities" I wrote down Tuesday night. Reading it back over revives my suspicion that something strange really is going on with the NuAgra folks, and that the Stuarts and O'Garas are connected to it.

And that M knows a lot more about it than she's telling.

I dither for a moment, biting my lip, then grab my phone and call M before I can change my mind.

"Hey, Deb, what's up?" she answers on the second ring. "Oh! You and Bri had another date with Liam and Lucas today, didn't you? How did that go?"

"Really great," I admit, momentarily distracted. "Better than I think either Bri or I expected. But there was one kind of weird thing that happened, and I wondered if—"

She interrupts. "Um, Deb, can we talk later, maybe tomorrow? I'm practically on my way out the door right now."

"Oh, sorry. Date with Rigel?"

"With Molly, actually—though not a date, obviously. Anyway, I'm already running late, so I need to go. Later?"

"Sure." Frowning, I hang up.

I hadn't really thought about it before, but now it strikes me as odd how often M and Molly are busy on Saturday evenings—with something *other* than dates. I wonder…? It's only a couple minutes to M's by car, so if I hurry, and I'm lucky, I *might* be able to find out why.

I hurry downstairs. "Mom, can I borrow the car again? I won't be gone long."

Startled, she looks up from the casserole she's putting in the oven. "Where are you going?"

"Just over to M's."

"Will you be back for dinner? It'll be ready in less than an hour."

"Definitely. Thanks, mom!"

Grabbing the keys off their hook by the door, I rush out to the car. I'm on Opal, almost to M's street, when I spot her up ahead. I slow down, then stop four houses away to watch as she, Molly and Mrs O'Gara all get into the O'Garas' maroon van.

A minute later, the van backs out of the driveway and heads away from me toward Diamond Street. I don't think they saw me but to be safe, I wait a few seconds before following them.

I expect them to turn left on Diamond Street, toward town, but instead they turn right. I keep following. For nearly a mile, I assume they're headed to the school. But then the van turns south, onto a country road. Toward NuAgra?

It's dark, but M still might recognize my mom's car if she looks back, so I let them pull farther ahead. I'd really rather not have to explain why I'm following her, especially since I'm not a hundred percent sure myself. Feeling very cloak-and-daggery, I slow down to let another car pass me, then speed back up to keep the van's taillights in sight.

We continue on for almost another five miles before Mrs. O'Garas turns onto another, smaller country road. There are two cars between us now, which seems a little strange. Other than a lot of empty farm land, I don't know of anything but NuAgra out in this direction…and it's not exactly normal working hours.

Glancing at my rear-view mirror, I see more headlights in the distance. Are they going to NuAgra, too? Spotting a graveled side road just ahead, I turn onto it rather than risk being identified way out here, in the middle of nowhere.

Executing as quick a U-turn as I dare, I kill my own headlights and creep almost back to the main road, where I stop to watch as another car, then another, go past. *Something* must be going on at NuAgra tonight. Or maybe every Saturday night?

I stay where I am for another ten minutes, but no other cars come along. Finally, since I told my mom I wouldn't be long, I turn my headlights back on and pull onto the road—but not toward home. Not yet.

Soon, the long, ten-foot-tall fence around NuAgra comes into view. Ahead in the distance, I see a brightly lit entrance. I slow, with a half-formed idea of turning in for a closer look, but when I get close I realize that not only is there a sturdy looking gate—closed—but some kind of gatehouse. A *manned* gatehouse!

Speeding up slightly, I continue on past. I'm uncomfortably aware of the guard watching me, though I doubt he can see who's inside the car. Hoping there's some way to get home other than turning around, I drive until I'm well out of sight of the gate, then pull over to check my phone's GPS.

To my relief, it shows another road up ahead that will get me back to Jewel, though not as directly. Panning out, I also confirm there's absolutely no other place in this direction M and Molly might have gone.

Driving back by the slightly longer route, I think over what I just discovered…and what it might mean.

⁘

"You seem awfully preoccupied today," Mom comments as we're finishing our French toast the next morning. "Still thinking about yesterday's date with Lucas?"

I grin self-consciously, since I'd just been reliving an incredible dream I had last night—that definitely did involve Lucas.

"I really do like him," I admit. "He seems to be as interested in saving the planet as I am, and he's into art, too. He's also not the least bit obsessed with sports, like most boys seem to be. That makes for much more interesting conversations."

Not to mention more time for kissing….

"And it's his brother that Bri is so interested in?"

"His twin, Liam. Right."

She frowns. "But isn't that the boy who stood her up last weekend, when you went over to her house to supposedly watch a football game?"

"Yes, but apparently it was a big misunderstanding. They've made up now. They had a really good time together at Donner's Farm yesterday. She gushed about it all the way home." I pause. "Speaking of Bri, can I run over there for a little while after I clear the table?"

"To compare more notes about yesterday?" she asks with a knowing smile.

I smile back. "Exactly." Just not the kind of notes Mom thinks.

After texting to make sure Bri's home, I go over. She drags me upstairs before I even suggest going to her room to talk.

"So, Liam called again a few minutes ago," she tells me as soon as the door's closed. "Just to talk, mostly, but also to ask what kinds of party snacks you and I like, because they're planning quite a spread. That *must* mean his parents are okay now with the idea of us dating! You and Lucas, too."

"I sure hope so."

Before I can bring up the reason I came over, she goes off into a litany of all the reasons Liam is so perfect for her. Her high spirits are infectious, momentarily distracting me with a memory of how amazing Lucas made me feel yesterday. When she finally pauses for breath, I abruptly remember why I'm here.

"I, um, did something last night I wanted to tell you about," I say before she can start back up.

"Ooh, something with Lucas?" she guesses excitedly.

"No, with M. Well, not *with* her, but about her."

She looks confused.

"You know how M and Molly always seem to have something going on Saturday nights? Like, *every* Saturday night?" I ask her.

Her expression clears slightly. "Now that you mention it, I guess they do. Not with their boyfriends, either. At the start of the school year, before Tristan even got here, M spent the night at the O'Garas' practically every Saturday—I remember Trina gave Molly a hard time about it."

"Right. And last weekend, when Lucas tried to get up a crowd for the Lighthouse, they both claimed they had plans but were kind of vague about them. Well…last night, I think I found out where they've been going. NuAgra."

Bri blinks at me. "Really?"

I nod. "I called M after dinner. She didn't have time to talk then because she was about to meet Molly, but she didn't say where. That made me curious enough to snoop."

I describe driving over in time to see her getting into the O'Garas' van, then following it almost to NuAgra. "I don't know if you've been out there recently—I hadn't—but the place has some serious security. A guard at the gate and everything."

"The boys did tell us they're pretty serious about keeping their secrets," Bri reminds me. "But M and the O'Garas went in?"

"They must have. I drove on past to make sure, but there's nothing else out that way. There were four other cars behind them, so I assume they went in, too—on a Saturday night. When I talked to M about NuAgra a few days ago, she made it sound like the only time she'd ever been inside was on that tour last month, but obviously not."

Bri shakes her head, frowning. "It's not like M to lie. Why would she, unless she's doing something she knows would either upset or worry us? Did you see who was in the other cars?"

"No. It was dark, plus I wasn't close enough. And by the time I drove past the gate myself, they were all out of sight of the road."

"But not the Walshes' car?"

"I don't think so—not the one we've seen, anyway."

She looks even more relieved by that than I was. "Then maybe Liam and Lucas aren't involved in whatever's going on out there. Not directly, anyway."

"Maybe not," I agree, hoping that's true. "It looks like I was right about M, though. I think the O'Garas—and maybe Rigel's family?—must have lured her into something she's not telling us about."

"It sure sounds that way." Bri looks worried now. "But what can we do about it?"

I've been wondering that ever since last night. "I'm not sure. It would help if we knew what they're telling her—or doing to her. Then we'd have a better idea of whether she's really in trouble or not."

"Lucas swore to us that NuAgra's not doing anything illegal or dangerous," Bri reminds me.

"I know. But if NuAgra really is some kind of cult, and M's been brainwashed to believe in what they're doing, it only makes sense that Liam and Lucas would believe in it, too. Which means even if they *are* up to something sinister, the boys weren't exactly lying to us, just repeating what they were told."

Bri thinks about that for a moment. "Still, let's not confront her today, okay? Just in case…I mean…I don't want anything to ruin tonight."

"You mean in case the guys, or maybe their parents, are in on whatever it is?"

Bri lifts a shoulder, looking slightly embarrassed. "We don't have any reason to think M's in any *immediate* danger, do we? Tomorrow, at school, you can ask where she had to rush off to last night and see what she says. It's totally possible she'll have a perfectly reasonable explanation for why she went to NuAgra."

I can't help hoping Bri's right, for all our sakes…though I doubt it.

"And if she doesn't?"

"If she flat out lies about it—which I can't believe she will—we'll know she really is covering something up. Then we can work on figuring out what."

I agree to that and Bri goes back to talking about Liam and how perfect he is. Again, I come close to telling Bri about that weirdness with Lucas and the big tree branch, but again I don't. Not yet. Not until I get a chance to ask Lucas himself about it, when I'm not distracted by his kisses. Maybe tonight?

Late that afternoon, Bri calls to say the guys have offered to pick us up and bring us home, so I should be at her house before six.

I relay the slight change in plans to my mom, who frowns. "What time does this game start?" She's no more into pro football than I am.

"Around seven, I think? That's what Liam said, but they're turning it into a kind of watch party, with food and stuff, so they want us there early."

"It sounds like this will run rather late for a school night. Maybe you girls can leave at halftime? Unless the game is really close—I imagine it will be hard to drag Bri away in that case."

No kidding. And not just because of the game. "I'll, uh, ask Bri and the guys if that'll be okay," I tell her. "I can call you at halftime with an update. Right now, though, I'd better get ready."

As I run back up to my room, excitement bubbles up in me at the thought of seeing Lucas again in less than an hour. I miss him a whole lot more than seems reasonable, considering it's only been a day since we were together.

23

Gravitational pull

Lucas

"CAN'T YOU DRIVE ANY FASTER?" Liam complains when we're halfway to the girls' houses. "It feels like ages since I've seen Bri."

"You were with her barely twenty-four hours ago," I remind him. "Besides, if I get stopped for speeding, it'll take a whole lot longer to get there."

Still, I inch the car's speed up by a couple miles an hour. Because I know exactly how he feels. All day I've felt almost like a piece of me is missing...and that piece is Debbi Andrews. It's crazy, but I can't seem to reason it away. The dreams I had about her last night didn't help. They've been teasing at me ever since I woke up.

I need to play it cool, though, I remind myself. Just because Deb let me kiss her yesterday doesn't mean she will today. By now, she's had time to really think about what I did to that big branch—something no "normal" human should have been able to do. I'm sure she also noticed how I avoided telling Bri and Liam about it. For all I know, she might be afraid of me now.

After an interminable five minutes that feel more like five hours, I turn onto Bri and Deb's street. Liam is leaning forward against the dashboard, peering eagerly through the windshield like that'll somehow help.

161

"We're going to be early," I point out. "They probably won't even be ready yet."

The words aren't out of my mouth before I see Deb up ahead, standing on Bri's front step about to ring the doorbell. At the sight of her, all my nerves snap to attention. Swallowing, I pull into Bri's driveway as her front door opens.

"Oh, they're here already!" I hear Bri exclaim. Deb turns and looks straight at me—which makes my insides go all jumpy.

Bri reaches behind her to grab a coat, calling out something to her parents. A moment later, both girls are coming toward us. We get out of the car to greet them and I suddenly regret my deal with Liam to drive now in return for him driving later, when we take the girls home. It means I'll have to wait that much longer before—

"Sorry, I know we're a little early," Liam is saying, both of Bri's hands already in his. "Are you ready?"

She nods, practically sparkling up at him. Clearly, Bri's not having any second thoughts.

I smile down at Deb, half afraid of what I'll see in her eyes. "We, uh, neither of us wanted to wait," I tell her. Not what I'd planned to say.

Her answering smile sends a wash of relief flooding through me. "I'm glad," is her simple reply.

Unable to resist a second longer, I lean down for a kiss, which she unhesitatingly returns. Pressing my lips to hers, I feel my missing piece click into place, making me whole again. It's all I can do not to pull her against me and deepen the kiss right here and now. But there are a lot of windows facing this way and I have no idea who's looking out of them. So, after an incredible few seconds, I reluctantly release her.

"Guess we should go." My voice sounds husky in my ears.

Opening the passenger door for her, I see Liam has not only pulled Bri into the back seat, he's already making out with her. Firmly telling myself that the delay—and anticipation—will only make the trip back here after the game sweeter, I hurry around to the driver's side and slide behind the wheel.

I back out of Bri's driveway and head to our house, carefully *not* looking in the rear-view mirror. Instead, I glance over at Deb and notice her cheeks are pinker than usual...and her left hand is lying on the seat next to her, palm up. An invitation?

After only a moment's hesitation, I reach over and take it, reveling in the way her small fingers thread themselves through mine. Like our hands were made to hold each other. *Everything* about Deb seems like she was specifically designed with me in mind. I wonder if she thinks that about me? Maybe someday I'll ask…

Trying to ignore the faint sounds from behind me that make me wish it was us back there instead, I turn on the radio and clear my throat.

"So, uh, did you sleep okay last night?" It's a stupid thing to ask, but nothing better comes to mind.

"I did, actually." Her voice sends a shiver through me—the good kind. "You?"

Remembering my dreams, I can't suppress a smile. "I did, too. Better than usual."

Glancing over, I see her smiling, too. For a split second we share a look that's nearly as intimate as another kiss. I wonder if her dreams were along the same lines as mine. I hope so.

It's weird how *not* worried I am about getting involved with a *Duchas* girl now, after all the dire warnings I gave Liam. But honestly, I can't imagine ever liking another girl, *Duchas* or *Echtran*, as much as I like Deb. No matter what our parents think. Which reminds me…

"I, uh, should probably warn you both that our parents, especially our mom, is, er, sort of a prude. So we should probably all, um, cool it a little in front of her." Now I do glance into the back, to make sure Bri and Liam heard me.

"No worries." Bri grins at me in the mirror. "We'll behave ourselves. Won't we?" she asks Liam playfully.

My brother gives an exaggerated sigh. "It won't be easy, but yeah. We'd better."

"Speaking of parents," Deb says, "my mom asked if we can maybe not stay till the end of the game, since it's a school night?"

Predictably, Liam and Bri protest that idea. "What if it's a close game?" Bri asks.

"I told her I'd call her at halftime and let her know," Deb replies, which apparently contents the two in the back enough to go back to kissing.

We pass Donner's Farm a moment later and I squeeze Deb's hand, reminded of our awesome day here yesterday. She squeezes back and something in my chest warms and expands. Oh, yeah. I'll be more than happy to take the girls home early. For *our* turn in the back seat.

A couple minutes later, we reach our house. It's a single-level built out of tan bricks, something the *Duchas* apparently call a "ranch home," though I'm not sure why.

"Here we are." I pull into the garage and put the car in park, then turn to Deb. "One last kiss before we go in?" I whisper.

In response, she leans toward me. Because Mom could open the door any second, I have to keep it quick, but it helps fortify me for the hours that will pass before I get another chance.

A moment later, I hear footsteps approaching, making me grateful for my enhanced Martian senses. Liam's too wrapped up in Bri to notice so I clear my throat loudly and nod toward the house. By the time our mother opens the door from the kitchen, we're all out of the car, Liam and me on one side, the girls on the other.

Even so, Mom sweeps a quick, penetrating gaze over the four of us before belatedly donning a smile. "Welcome, girls. Won't you come in?"

Dad's waiting in the kitchen. His smile is a lot more genuine than Mom's. "Glad you could both come. As you can see, the boys have put together quite a football feast." He waves an arm toward the food arrayed on the kitchen island. "Help yourselves."

"Thanks for taking the pizza rolls out of the oven, Mom," Liam says, urging Bri forward. "I wanted them to still be warm."

"It smells and looks amazing." Bri smiles up at him in a way that makes our mother's eyebrows rise. I hope those two don't ruin things for all of us.

At least Deb took my warning about Mom to heart. She's careful not to touch me as we approach the assortment of chips, dips, chicken wings, mini eggrolls and everything else Liam insisted was necessary for a proper football-watching party.

Liam and Bri fill plates to overflowing before continuing on to the living room, where he and I earlier set out TV trays so everyone could eat while watching the game. I put about half as much food on my plate as Liam did and Deb takes less than half of what I do—mostly carrot and celery sticks, with a little dip.

"Is that really all you want?" I ask as we pick up cups of lemonade from the counter next to the refrigerator on our way to follow the others.

She gives a cute little half shrug. "For now. I'll probably get a little more later."

"You sure don't eat much, Deb," Liam comments when we join him and Bri on the couch. Fortunately, it's long enough to accommodate all four of us without sitting *too* close together.

Deb shoots an uncertain glance my way. "I, uh, kind of have to watch my weight. One downside of being so short."

"You're right, it is," Mom unexpectedly agrees, perching on the edge of the chair nearest Deb and me. "It's a curse none of you towering males ever need to worry about."

She and Deb share a smile—a real one—and some of my tension recedes. It would be great for the two of them to get along.

"It's really nice of you to have us over," Bri tells our parents then. "Have you become Colts fans since moving to Indiana?"

"To an extent," Dad replies after a brief pause. "Though I'm afraid none of us except Liam have ever watched much football."

Deb laughs. "That's okay. You won't find many people more into sports than Bri and Liam are. I'm more interested in things that actually matter, like the work NuAgra is apparently doing. It must be exciting to be involved in something that could eventually solve world hunger."

"Where...did you hear that?" Mom shoots an alarmed glance my way.

"From M," Deb replies. "She went on that tour last month."

"M?" Dad echoes, brows raised. "Do you mean the—ah, Miss Truitt?"

Sheesh, and they're worried about Liam arousing *Duchas* suspicions?

"You've met her, then?" If Deb notices my parents' sudden awkwardness, she doesn't let on. "She's in Pre-Cal with Liam and me, and has a couple of other classes with both him and Lucas. Chemistry, right?" she asks me.

"Right. She and Rigel went out of their way to be helpful our first few days at Jewel High." I force an extra-casual tone to emphasize how normal that would seem, so my parents will relax.

Fortunately, Dad takes my cue. "Oh, ah, yes. The boys introduced us to her at one of Liam's basketball games." He goes on to ask the girls a few questions about their classes at school, which keeps the conversation safely away from taboo topics until the game starts.

At that point, Liam and Bri take over most of the talking, commenting on every play and the various football players involved. I'm impressed by how well Liam carries his end, considering he never attended a single football game before moving to Jewel.

After a little while, Mom and Dad start drifting in and out of the room to do other things, though I notice the four of us are almost never left completely alone. Mom, in particular, checks often to see if anyone needs more food or drink—or so she says.

I pretend to focus on the game whenever she comes through, though with Deb just a few inches away it can't hold my attention. My senses seem totally attuned to her nearness, making me long to touch her, kiss her. Of course, the more I think about it, the more frustrated I am that I can't. Not here. Not yet.

Liam must feel the same, so I try to keep almost as close an eye on him as Mom does. What I see isn't particularly reassuring.

He and Bri started out sitting a few inches apart, same as Deb and me, but they keep shifting closer as the game progresses. Their eyes *seem* to be riveted to the action on the TV screen, but every time one of them reaches for food or reacts to something in the game, they almost can't help touching. The next time Mom comes into the room, I can tell she's noticed.

"So, um, why are they moving the ball backward?" I ask, mostly to remind Liam and Bri they're not alone.

"Another holding call against the Colts," Bri replies with obvious disgust.

"Yeah, they're *never* going to get any points on the board at this rate," Liam chimes in.

Their responses seem to reassure Mom that they really are paying attention to the game. Way better than I am, anyway.

There's a dicey moment partway into the second quarter when the Colts finally get a touchdown. Bri and Liam both go a little nuts and for a second I'm afraid he'll actually kiss her—just as their yelling brings both Mom and Dad hurrying back into the room.

I quickly pretend more excitement than I feel and pull Liam and both girls into a quick group hug. So softly the *Duchas* girls can't hear me, I whisper to Liam, "Careful! Or you'll screw this up for both of us."

Fortunately, that's enough warning to keep him from doing anything too stupid in front of Mom for the rest of the quarter.

When the game breaks for halftime and goes to a commercial, I turn to Deb. "This is when you promised to call your mom, right?" I don't know if I can stand another hour-plus of this torture. Being so close to Deb without touching her is killing me.

"Oh, right." She pulls out her phone.

"Wait, we're not leaving now, are we?" Bri protests. "The Colts are only down by ten. They can totally turn things around in the second half. We don't want to miss a comeback!"

Deb makes her call. "Hi, Mom, yeah, it's halftime, but Bri really wants to stay longer."

I clearly hear her mother's voice on the other end, reminding Deb that her school night curfew is ten o'clock.

"All right," Deb replies. "If the Colts fall further behind, we'll come home. Okay, Bri?"

Bri reluctantly nods. Liam appears torn, not wanting to cut short his time with Bri—especially knowing he won't get the back seat again—but also aware he has to keep his distance while our parents are around.

Fortunately for my sanity, by halfway through the third quarter the Patriots have doubled their lead and even Bri is willing to leave. Dad retrieves the girls' coats while they thank Mom again for her hospitality.

"It was our pleasure," she assures them. "It's nice to see our boys making friends here in Jewel." I notice her slight hesitation before the word *friends* but hope the girls didn't. Then, with a quick glance at Liam, she says, "Would it make your parents more comfortable for my husband to drive you home?"

What?

"C'mon, Mom." I fight to keep panic out of my voice. "You know Liam's a perfectly good driver."

As I hoped, she relaxes slightly. "Yes, yes, of course. Both of you are. Liam will be driving, then?"

Could she *be* any more obvious?

"Yeah, Lucas drove earlier, so it's my turn," he confirms with a noticeable lack of enthusiasm.

Mom relaxes even more. "All right, then. Mind you boys come straight home, though. Debbi's mother is quite right that it's already late for a school night."

Dad comes in with the coats and Liam and I help our girls into them. Then we all head out to the car. Mom watches as Liam and Bri get into the front, clearly reassured by the middle console between them. Deb and I get into the back and conspicuously buckle our seatbelts, also well separated. The girls wave a last goodbye and Liam puts the car in reverse.

The moment we're completely out of sight of the house, Liam pulls onto the shoulder.

"Just for a sec, okay? Um, unless you're willing to drive the rest of the way?" he asks me hopefully.

"Nope, we had a deal." I throw an arm around Deb's shoulders.

With a *well, I tried* shrug, he turns to Bri. "One for the road?" he asks, grinning. She responds by leaning toward him.

Rather than watch, I pull Deb closer and she willingly obliges. I barely notice when Liam pulls back onto the road a couple minutes later.

24

Fact pattern

Deb

WRAPPED in Lucas's arms with his lips on mine, the drive back home is pure heaven. Normally I'd be super embarrassed making out like this with Bri and Liam in the same car, but being with Lucas feels so very right, the only emotion I'm aware of is joy.

Besides, all the way to the Walshes' house they did the exact same thing. Apparently the brothers made a deal ahead of time, and now it's our turn in the back seat. It would be a shame to waste it.

"Mmm," Lucas murmurs as the car turns onto our street. "I'll bet my dreams tonight will be even better than the ones I had last night."

A giggle escapes me. "You, too?" And then we're kissing again, storing up even more dream material.

All too soon, Liam pulls into Bri's driveway.

"Nobody's looking yet, are they?" he whispers to Bri. She glances at her house, then mine, and shakes her head.

Which gives us all time for a last minute or two of goodnight kissing before leaving the cozy warmth of the car. Though I'm still plenty warm from Lucas's kisses, he puts an arm around me as we step out into the frigid air.

"How about I walk you to your door for a change?"

"Sure." I smile up at him, pleased at the idea of a few moments of relative privacy. "'Night, Bri."

"'Night, Deb." She's looking at Liam, not me, but I don't care.

Slowly, Lucas and I traverse the thirty yards or so to my house, our arms around each other.

"Did you have a good time tonight?" he asks as we walk.

"I did—in spite of the game." I laugh. "I, um, especially enjoyed the ride home."

He smiles down at me, the warmth in his gaze making my heart do funny things. "Same here. Maybe we can get together one night this week...someplace my parents aren't."

I swallow, both at the thought of being truly alone with him and at the implication in his words.

"They're really that opposed to you and Liam dating?"

"To us getting really serious, anyway. They, um, think we're too young for that. I told you they're prudes."

Are we serious? The question is on the tip of my tongue but we reach my door before I work up the nerve to ask it.

"I'd invite you in, but your mom seemed pretty adamant about you both getting back right away," I say instead.

He looks as regretful as I feel. "Yeah. Maybe next time, when it's not so late?"

That's twice in a one-minute walk he's mentioned a next time! "Let's plan on it." My voice sounds breathless to my own ears.

"Deal." An unspoken question in his eyes, he slowly lowers his lips to mine. I answer by going up on my toes for his kiss, one more I can look forward to dreaming about tonight.

I'm still smiling when I go inside. Mom, coming upstairs from her studio just then, notices.

"Looks like you had a pretty good time for someone not into pro sports," she comments with a twinkle in her eye.

I shrug, my face warming despite my best efforts. "Lucas is... I probably wouldn't care what I was watching as long as it's with him."

"Bri and his brother and their parents were there, too, right?" Mom's not normally the suspicious type, but my face must have given me away.

"Of course," I reassure her. "But, um, he did kiss me goodnight just now." She doesn't need to know about all the kisses that preceded this last one.

She nods, the twinkle back in her eye. "Ah. That would explain why you're glowing like that. Just...be careful, Deb, okay? You seem to be falling pretty hard for this boy and I'd hate to see you get hurt."

"So would I." The idea of Lucas suddenly reverting to the way he acted a week ago chills me. "But he seems to really like me, too. More than any other boy I've ever gone out with."

"And you, ah, trust his motives?"

I laugh at her studied casualness. "Yes, Mom. He's nothing like all the boys who are only after one thing. At the Winter Formal, Lucas barely touched me, even during the slow dances. He was the same at the Lighthouse last weekend."

"Good. There's nothing wrong with taking things slowly. You have your whole life ahead of you, you know."

"I know, Mom," I say dryly, rolling my eyes.

Now she's the one who laughs. "Sorry. I can't help feeling a bit protective of my remaining chick now that Maggie's flown the coop. I'll try not to cramp your style...*too* much."

Chuckling and shaking my head, I go up to my room. Two seconds later, Bri calls.

"This time, I *know* you had just as good an evening as I did," she exclaims before I can even say hi. "Bummer about the game, though."

"Oh, was there a game tonight?" I grin even though she can't see me.

She gives a snort of disgust. "Not a very good one."

"I take it we didn't miss a comeback after all?"

"No, it's still going downhill. The third quarter just ended and it's 38-7. But enough about the game."

I gasp loudly for her benefit. "Who are you, and what have you done with my friend Bri?"

"Okay, okay," she says, laughing now. "But come on, dish! Is Lucas as good a kisser as Liam is?"

"It's not like I can directly compare them, you know. He's absolutely amazing, though, yeah. Far and away the best ever. At least in my limited experience. And he wants to go out again sometime this week!"

"Oooh, so does Liam!"

We spend a few minutes congratulating each other on our amazing luck, but when I start to comment on how the Walshes never left us alone with the guys during the game, Bri cuts me off.

"Sorry, my folks are yelling downstairs. If the Colts are about to score again, I don't want to miss it. Talk tomorrow, okay?"

"Okay." But she's already gone.

Now that I've talked out my first rush of euphoria with Bri, other thoughts finally find room in my brain. It's only then I realize I had a perfect opportunity to ask Lucas about yesterday's incident with the branch, while he was walking me to the door. Oops.

I promise myself I'll ask him tomorrow, even though the explanation somehow doesn't seem to matter as much now.

Now that I'm head over heels in love with him.

At the periphery of my vision, a forest seemingly grown from diamonds shimmers and sparkles, but I'm only dimly aware of the beauty surrounding me. My whole attention is given to something much more glorious—Lucas, his lips on mine, his arms tenderly cradling me as we snuggle together on a grass-green brocaded quilt spread out on the forest floor.

"You're amazing," Lucas murmurs against my lips. "You know that, don't you?"

"So are you," I whisper back, my whole heart behind the words. "More amazing than anyone I've ever known."

His arms tighten around me, the look in his eyes stopping my breath. "Deb, I know we haven't been together long, but I think I—"

My soul seems to expand inside me as I prepare to tell him that I love him, too. But before he can actually say the word, the scene around us abruptly changes.

Darkens.

Confused, I look around and notice that the diamond trees have stopped sparkling. Then I realize they're no longer trees at all. They're people, coming at us from all sides, their expressions angry, outraged. Some of them seem to be holding weapons I don't recognize.

"What—?" I start to ask, but Lucas immediately shushes me

"No. Don't say anything," he whispers urgently. "You'll only make it worse."

I want to ask what he's talking about, but already he's turning to face them.

"I'm sorry," he calls out. "I couldn't help it."

Now I finally start discerning faces in the crowd. I see all the other new NuAgra students, as well as the Walshes and a lot of others I don't recognize. Then M pushes her way through them to the front, looking angrier than I've ever seen her—at us!

"You know the rules," she tells Lucas.

To my dismay, he nods. "You're right. I'm sorry." Releasing me, he gets up and walks toward M and the others. Then, just before he reaches them, he turns back to look at me, anguish in his perfect, blue-gray eyes. "I'm sorry, Deb. So sorry."

Countless hands reach out to draw him into their circle. Scrambling to my feet, I try to go after him, to protest, but I can't seem to move or make any sound. All I can do is watch, horrified, as all the people around me, including Lucas, become insubstantial, as though made of smoke, quickly dissipating.

A moment later, I'm alone in the dark, frightened and bereft.

.⁺.

I wake with a start, my heart pounding.

Gradually the dream recedes, along with the fear. I close my eyes again, desperately trying to recapture the earlier, wonderful part of the dream, the part where I was still kissing Lucas. But before I can completely push away the weird, scary ending, my alarm rings.

Rubbing my eyes in an attempt to erase those final, unsettling images, I get out of bed. "It was just a dream," I tell myself firmly.

I repeat those words to myself several times as I get ready for school. By the time I go downstairs for breakfast, I finally believe them, though I haven't quite shaken the feelings the dream evoked, both good and bad. Worse, my earlier suspicions, temporarily lulled by spending so much time with Lucas this weekend, come back stronger than ever.

When Bri joins me at our bus stop, I try to put some of what's worrying me into words. "So, um, last night before the game, did you notice how Mr. and Mrs. Walsh acted when I mentioned M?"

Bri's all smiles this morning, despite the Colts losing, but at that, her brows go up. "Not really. They just said they'd met her, right?"

"After Lucas reminded them. But right before that, they seemed almost...alarmed. Startled, at least, that I'd brought her up. Since M was actually *at* NuAgra Saturday night, we were obviously right that she's involved with it somehow. Their reaction seemed to confirm that. I just wish I knew why."

"Then you're still planning to ask her about it at school today?" She sounds worried now.

"I thought we agreed I should?"

She hesitates. "We did. It's just... What if she tells us something we're not supposed to know? Liam told me his parents actually threatened to move away from Jewel if he didn't stay away from me before. If they think we know too much, they might actually do it."

The thought of Lucas leaving, for good, sends a chill of dread through me, too. But— "That would be on M, wouldn't it? All I'm going to do is ask where she went, to see if she'll lie or admit it was NuAgra."

"She'll only lie if she really is connected with something she shouldn't be," Bri admits heavily. "Maybe even something dangerous. Yeah, I guess we need to find out. I just hope…"

"I know. Me, too."

The bus pulls up then, so we leave off our conversation until we're seated and on our way to the school.

"I did notice how the Walshes never left the four of us completely alone the whole time we were at their house," Bri says after a moment. "And the way Mrs. Walsh told the boys to come straight home. She seems awfully protective of them—like she's worried we're going to corrupt her sons."

Despite my concerns, that makes me giggle. "Are we?" I ask.

"That's my plan," Bri replies, grinning. "Though it would help if any of us had our own cars."

"True. Ah, well, we'll just have to be creative. And maybe mother-protectiveness really is all that's going on," I say with more hope than certainty. "Lucas did tell me last night that their parents think they're too young to get 'serious.'"

Bri gives me a sharp look. "Does that mean he admitted you guys *are* serious now?"

"No," I confess. "And I didn't have the guts to ask. But it seemed like he was implying it?"

"Things are feeling pretty serious with Liam, too," she admits, no longer laughing. "But I thought that the weekend before, and then… You don't think they'll suddenly start avoiding us at school again, do you?"

"I sure hope not." Then, because she looks so worried, I add, "If they do, I'll just get in Lucas's face again—and you should do the same to Liam. Why should they get to call all the shots in our relationships?"

That gets a smile from her. "Good point."

Even so, I can't help feeling a little on edge as we approach the school a few minutes later. From Bri's expression, she's anxious, too.

Then she sits up straighter, pointing. "Look! There they are, waiting for us."

Sure enough, Liam and Lucas are at the curb, watching our bus pull up. Leaning forward, I try to decipher Lucas's expression in case they have bad news again, but he looks more eager than worried. I relax.

Even better, the moment we're off the bus, he moves to my side and takes my hand.

"Hey," he says, smiling. "I missed you."

I can almost swear I get a little tingle from his touch, but it's probably just because being close to him always sends such a thrill through me.

"Same here." We start walking toward the building, Bri and Liam right behind us. "Bummer we don't have more classes together."

"Yeah. Liam and I actually talked about switching places for first period but decided it would be risky since we didn't plan ahead."

That makes me chuckle. "Have you guys pulled that trick a lot in the past?"

"Not a lot, and not recently, but a few times. Definitely not since getting to...Jewel."

His hesitation makes me wonder if he almost said something else.

"It's funny," I say as we go into the school. "Your first day here, when you showed up in Art class, I did think you were Liam for a split second, before I noticed you were wearing different clothes. But now...I can't even imagine mixing you up. It's hard to believe anyone could."

"I think I'll take that as a compliment." He smiles down at me.

"Good. Because it was." We're in the atrium now, and his locker is unfortunately in the opposite direction from mine. "I, uh, guess I'll see you at lunch?"

"Count on it," he says, then leans in to give me a quick kiss that I eagerly return, heedless of whoever might be watching.

My head is so full of Lucas, I drift to my locker, barely conscious of putting my coat inside or the walk to Pre-Cal. Just outside the door, I see Liam and Bri saying their own goodbyes until lunch. Then, with a quick grin at me, Bri takes off for Econ at a run.

I'm still smiling as I walk into the classroom, but when I see M and Molly, I suddenly remember I was going to ask them about Saturday night. My desk is next to M's, but the bell rings before I get there.

All through class, I mentally rehearse different ways to phrase my question. When the period ends, I almost chicken out before finally turning to M as we're all packing up our books.

"So, M," I say as nonchalantly as I can, "what was it you were rushing off to do Saturday night when I called? You didn't say."

She looks startled, then wary. "Oh, ah, Molly and I—" She hesitates, like she's groping for words. Immediately, Molly speaks up.

"I wanted to shop for shoes at that new outlet mall near Kokomo, and M offered to help," she tells me. "I didn't find anything I liked, though."

M nods. "Molly's really picky. I thought at least a couple of pairs she tried on were pretty cute. What was it you wanted to talk about when you called? I meant to call you back yesterday to ask but forgot."

Even though I half expected it, I'm still a bit shaken by how *casually* she and Molly just lied to my face. "Oh, um, nothing super important. I was just going to tell you Liam and Lucas invited Bri and me over to their house to watch last night's playoff game."

"Really?" She seems surprised. "How did that go?"

"Fine. I mean, the Colts lost, but the Walshes were really nice and all. I guess I was wrong about them," I add, since Liam's already left the room.

Though M smiles, a tiny frown remains between her eyebrows. "I was sure you were. I'm glad you all had a good time."

I head to second period then, wondering more than ever what could be going on with M—and whether Lucas and Liam are involved in it or not.

25

Timeout

Bri

I'M ABOUT to go into my third-period English classroom when Deb comes hurrying up. Even before she speaks, my heart sinks at the worry I see written all over her face.

"So, I talked to M at the end of Pre-Cal," she whispers.

I suck in a breath. "Did you ask her about Saturday night?"

"Yep. And she and Molly both claimed they went to the new outlet mall—which is totally not true. That mall is nowhere near NuAgra."

Sighing heavily, I close my eyes against my disappointment. I was *so* hoping M would have some reasonable explanation. "Crap. I guess you were right, then. She really has been drawn into something she doesn't want us to know about."

"I'd rather be wrong," Deb admits. She probably doesn't want to rock the boat with Lucas any more than I do with Liam. "It's still possible she's not in any actual danger."

True, but M is my oldest friend, so I don't dare assume that. "We won't know whether she is or not until we find out what's going on," I say. "Any idea how we can do that?"

Deb starts to say something, but the second bell rings, so we both have to duck into the classroom to take our seats. I can't focus at all on whatever it is we're supposed to be doing in class, but thankfully the teacher doesn't notice or call on me.

My thoughts chase each other around and around, leading me nowhere.

What on *Earth* could M be doing out at NuAgra on Saturday nights? It would have to be really bad, or secret, or both, for her to flat-out lie about it to Deb. Does Liam know? Can I ask him without freaking him out? Probably not. Besides, even if he *does* know something, I'm sure he wouldn't be allowed to tell me.

But what if M's in actual danger? What if they all are?

I'm afraid if I really start digging into this hornet's nest, I'll lose Liam for good—a terrifying thought that makes my hands and feet go cold and my stomach drop all the way down to my toes. Still, tempting as it is to just ignore all this weirdness, I can't do that. M is my best friend and she has to come first.

There's also the strong possibility that if M's in danger, Liam is, too. I'd rather risk him breaking up with me than let him get hurt or arrested because of whatever NuAgra's doing. If it really is a dangerous cult, then Deb and I have to at least *try* to save both M and the boys. And maybe all the other NuAgra kids, too.

By the time I get to lunch, my stomach is in knots. Even the usual flutter I get when I see Liam coming toward me is overshadowed by all the other anxiety I'm feeling. Only after he takes my hands in his and gives me a quick kiss do I feel some of the tension in my gut drain away.

He doesn't seem bothered or worried at all, just happy to see me. Maybe I'm overreacting?

"Missed you," he says, with a warmth that dispels most of the remaining chill I've been feeling since English.

"Same!" I respond with only slightly forced enthusiasm. Hopefully he can't tell my return smile is a little strained.

We go through the cafeteria line together and take our trays to our usual table. M, Rigel, Molly, Tristan, Kira and Sean are already there. Lucas and Deb join us a moment later. During lunch, everyone talks and laughs and flirts and acts totally… normal. It's surreal. As I look at each of them in turn, I find it almost impossible to believe everyone at this table except Deb and me could be involved in some big, shady conspiracy.

"You okay?" Liam whispers, interrupting my thoughts and sending a delicious shiver down my spine at the nearness of his lips to my ear. "You seem a little out of it today."

"Yeah, sorry. Just, um, tired I guess. I stayed up late last night watching the rest of that disaster of a game." It's true, even if it's not the whole truth.

Liam gives me a look like he knows that's not the only reason. He opens his mouth and I think he's about to push, but instead he shakes his head with a rueful laugh. "Yeah, it was pretty awful. My parents already had the TV off when we got home. I turned it back on, but they made us go to bed before it ended. Even with the Colts so far behind, it was hard to walk away."

I groan, allowing some of my bigger frustration to come out under cover of talking about the game. "Yeah, sort of like watching a train wreck. Thank goodness my dad is just as obsessed as I am—he and I both stayed up to watch to the bitter end, so at least I didn't have to suffer alone."

He looks into my eyes with something that seems to go way beyond sports camaraderie. "I hope you don't ever have to suffer, Bri. Especially not alone."

I don't think I'm imagining a deeper meaning behind his words than just sympathy about my football team losing. I swallow hard, losing myself in his gaze.

"Me either," I whisper, allowing myself to be a little vulnerable.

Can he tell how conflicted I feel? Does he suspect that Deb and I have figured out something weird is going on at NuAgra? Does he know where M fits into it?

"I wish you could tell me—" I break off, swallowing again.

He closes his eyes and leans his forehead against mine. "I wish I could, too."

Closing my eyes, too, I lean into him, taking comfort from his touch, this moment of intimacy, even if we can't tell each other everything we're thinking and feeling.

A sudden burst of laughter from the others in response to some quip of Molly's startles us apart. Catching each other's eyes, we chuckle ourselves, then pretend to laugh with the others even though we weren't paying attention.

For the last few minutes of lunch, I'm mostly able to go with the flow and pretend everything is normal. As we're leaving the cafeteria, Liam and I agree to meet briefly in the atrium after sixth period before he heads out to NuAgra, which helps my mood even more.

When the twins head off to fifth period, I catch up with Deb on the way to our Government class.

"So...you're absolutely *positive* M went out to NuAgra Saturday night?" I whisper to her. "You said you didn't actually see the O'Garas' van turn in. Is it at all possible she and Molly didn't actually lie about where they'd gone and we're just misinterpreting things?"

"Like I said, I'd *rather* be wrong," Deb tells me, "but that outlet mall is north of Jewel, the exact opposite direction from NuAgra. So...yeah. I'm positive." Her voice sounds hollow, like she's just as bummed and conflicted about all this as I am.

Though that's the answer I expected, I stifle a sigh. "So what do we do? Should we tell her we know she lied, see if she'll maybe spill the truth?"

"We may have to at some point, but maybe not until we have more reason to believe she's in actual danger?" It sounds like she's also trying to rationalize leaving well enough alone. "First, why don't we see how much more info we can get on our own? Maybe if we confront her with all the things we *do* know, she'll be less likely to fudge about the rest."

"Maybe," I agree. "Do you still have that list we started?"

Deb nods, a little frown between her brows. "I've even added a couple things to it. We can keep doing that if we pay attention and keep gathering evidence. The more we know, the better equipped we'll be to deal with...whatever it is."

"Good idea." It's not much of a plan, but at least it doesn't involve permanently alienating anybody...yet. For now, I'll take it.

Even so, when I meet Liam in the atrium after sixth period to say goodbye till tomorrow, I can't resist digging just a *tiny* bit.

"What is it you guys do out there for these work-study programs you're getting credit for?" I ask as innocently as I can.

Immediately, his expression becomes guarded. Just like I was afraid of.

"Um, in Lucas's and my case, engineering stuff, since that's what our parents do. It's, uh, sort of like an engineering internship, I guess you could say."

He's clearly uncomfortable, so I don't push. Much. "Oh, um, that sounds interesting. Maybe you can tell me more about it sometime?"

"Er, maybe. Probably not much, though." His blue-gray eyes plead with me to understand.

I decide to let it drop so I can enjoy these last few seconds with him.

Smiling up at him, I nod and he responds by giving me a quick kiss that goes a long way toward buoying my spirits again.

But then Alan Dempsey clears his throat loudly from the far side of the atrium. "Hey, Liam," he calls out when we reluctantly part. "The van's going to leave in a minute. You'd better hurry."

"Oops. Right." With a quick nod to Alan and an apologetic glance at me, Liam rushes off, leaving me to hoof it to Chorus while wondering—again—what's *really* going on out at NuAgra.

26

Destructive interference

Lucas

FIFTH-PERIOD HISTORY SEEMS to last forever, I'm so eager to see Deb again. When the bell finally rings, I head to Art class at top speed, barely keeping myself from running. She gets there at the same time I do.

"Hey," I greet her before we go into the room. My greeting seems ridiculously lame compared to the feelings surging through me the instant our hands touch. I thought I imagined the tingle I felt when we first touched by accident at the Lighthouse more than a week ago, but now it's become too strong to ignore—even if I can't explain it.

"Hey," Deb echoes, smiling up at me with that look that practically forces me to kiss her.

Even though I make it really quick, this kiss rocks me to my toes just as profoundly as all the previous ones. The effect is surely bound to fade eventually, but there's no sign of that yet.

Hand in hand, we go to our drawing table. Out of the corner of my eye, I see heads turning our way as other students take note of our clasped hands. I belatedly count myself fortunate that I'm the only *Echtran* in here, so any gossip is unlikely to reach my parents. I know I'd hear about it from Mom if it did.

I'm amazed by how different Art class feels today compared to Friday, before things ramped up between Deb and me over the weekend. Now, while we work on our separate projects, we continually sneak little glances and smiles at each other, enjoying being next to each other.

Today I also pay closer attention to Deb's drawing than I did last week, noticing how effectively she uses color and light. She has a real gift. I frown critically at my own effort, which is nowhere near as good as hers.

"Do you think you can give me some pointers sometime?" I whisper partway through class. "Show me how you get that aura effect?"

Her eyes light up. "Really? Of course. When?" She sounds both surprised and pleased.

"After school tomorrow?" I suggest. "I only have to go to NuAgra three times a week for work-study credit. I've just been going every day because it's more interesting than spending seventh period doing homework in the media center. By myself, anyway."

She responds to my grin with one of her own. "Let's plan on it."

Turning back to my drawing, I realize this will be a perfect way to spend time with Deb without Mom knowing about it. Maybe we should make it a regular Tuesday-Thursday "date."

When I suggest that as class ends, Deb's quick to agree.

"The Earth Club won't start meeting after school again until March, to gear up for Earth Day, so my afternoons are mostly free. Spending time with— I mean on art, seems like a great way to fill that time."

We pack up our stuff and head out to the hallway, again holding hands. But then I have to leave her to catch the van to NuAgra.

"I'll see you tomorrow," I say, more reluctant than ever to part from her.

She nods, her eyes reflecting exactly what I'm feeling.

After a quick glance around, I lean down for one last kiss to fortify me. A real one this time, but still not nearly as long as I'd like. Straightening, I brush a finger across her cheek in a farewell caress before forcing myself to head to the front office to sign myself out.

I'm the last of the work-study group to get outside but the van's not here yet, so it doesn't matter. As I join the other four—Tristan's here for a change—I notice a definite tension between Liam and Alan.

"—why it's any of your business?" Liam is saying.

Alan scowls. "Because it puts us all at risk. Which you'd know if you ever stopped to think."

"What's going on?" I ask.

Alan turns his frown on me. "I just saw your brother kissing a *Duchas* girl, that's what. Maybe you can talk some sense into him, explain why that's not okay."

I glance at Kira and Tristan. Neither looks as upset as Alan, their expressions a mix of concern and amusement.

"What Liam does is his business," I tell Alan. "As long as he's careful to stick to his *Duchas* background story, where's the risk?"

"And what if he forgets and doesn't stick to it?" Alan counters. "Sean and I told him over and over how careful we need to be during basketball games, and look how long that took to sink in."

"You're one to talk," Liam protests. "What about our second game over winter break, where Sean and I had to cover for you?"

The van pulls up then. They shut up while we all pile in, but as soon as we're underway, Alan responds, though more quietly.

"That's why I know just how risky that sort of thing can be. I let Trina's flattery get to me and it made me…kind of stupid for a while. No more, though. I never should have taken her to that dance. At least I came to my senses before I did anything worse than show off on the court. Looks like you're already *way* past that if you're going around kissing *Duchas* girls."

"*One* girl," Liam tells him. "One. You make it sound like I'm turning into some kind of player, keeping a bunch of them on the string."

Alan snorts. "Maybe that would be safer. Then you'd be less likely to get so involved with just one that you forget to keep your mouth shut about the stuff that matters."

"Look," I say to Alan. "The Sovereign herself said it's okay for us to go out with *Duchas* girls, as long as we're careful. She pointed out—and she's right—that even if we do make some dumb little slip, they'd never guess the real truth. She told us how hard it was for Rigel to convince her of it, even after she'd noticed all kinds of odd things."

"I still don't like it."

Liam glares at Alan. "Nobody asked you to like it. Doesn't mean you need to keep harping on it."

Alan looks over at Kira and Tristan, clearly hoping for support. When he doesn't get it, he turns away with another snort and doesn't say another word the whole rest of the way to NuAgra.

Once there, Liam and I head to the Engineering lab, like always, to see what boring busywork they've assigned us this week.

Last week I was told to recheck the connections on a new piece of hydroponics equipment, which was nearly pointless since it had been constructed by a team of fully trained Engineers, including my dad. Hours of mind-numbing work only yielded one slightly loose spot that probably would have held for years before becoming a problem.

Today Mom asks me to come with her to Greenhouse Four, while Liam is assigned to Head Engineer Greely and his team to help adjust the power conduits from the solar panels on the roof.

Walking back through the main reception hall with my mother, I marvel again at the huge amount of energy Earth has available from the sun—and what a tiny percentage of it they've harnessed. Too bad that's not an option for Nuath, a mile underground and nearly twice as far from the sun. Solar power on Mars could never come close to meeting the colony's needs. Not even if we risked putting photovoltaic collectors on the surface, where they might be spotted by *Duchas* satellites or rovers.

"The Ags in Greenhouse Four are having trouble with their pumpkins and other gourds getting too heavy for their support structures," Mom tells me. "They've asked if we can find a way to shore things up without impeding nutrient flow. Someone from Maintenance already tried unsuccessfully, so they called us."

I nod. People in the Maintenance *fine* are great at fixing existing systems when they break down, but not so much when it comes to designing something new. That usually falls to us Engineers. This project is obviously low priority, but it sounds marginally more interesting than what I was doing last week.

NuAgra is huge and the greenhouses are back behind the main buildings, so it's a fair walk to Greenhouse Four. It's been a while since I was last inside a greenhouse, and I don't think I've ever been in this particular one. When we step inside, I'm momentarily startled by how warm, green and humid it is. A vivid contrast to the gray Indiana winter outside.

One end of the greenhouse is completely devoted to vine-growing plants like squash, and as we approach it's easy to spot the problem. Several pumpkins—which I'd never seen before coming to Earth—have grown to twice the size of a basketball. They must weigh well over ten pounds each. Not only are they threatening to overbalance the whole, long hydroponics platform, they're also crowding out everything else nearby.

"We'll need to build separate supporting structures for these," Mom tells the Ag in charge of gourds once she's looked things over. "Cages suspended from the roof may be easiest, and would interfere least with your operations."

"I trust you to know best," the man tells her. "What supplies will you need?"

While he punches her list into his tablet, I look around for Alan or Kira but don't see either one. They must be working in other greenhouses today.

After a few minutes, Mom turns to me. "You may as well go back to the Engineering lab while I finish here. I doubt we'll have everything we need for this project before tomorrow—longer, if some of it has to be bought locally."

"Oh, okay. I'll see you back there."

I head out. With luck, I can use the rest of today's shift to work on my side project. I didn't get much time for it last week and there are a couple of new simulations I'd like to run, to test another idea I came up with.

Since no one suggests I do anything else when I get back to the lab, I go to the console where my data is stored. Soon, I'm immersed in energy flow equations. The first two simulations I create don't improve output at all, unfortunately. I'm about to attempt a third when Mom comes back.

"Where's your brother?" she raps out, striding over to me.

I blink. She looks really upset for some reason. "Um, I'm not sure. Maybe up on the roof? They were doing something with the solar panels, I think. Why?"

"I've just heard something I'd like him to explain."

"What did you hear?" I ask, though I have a sinking feeling I know.

Grimacing, she lowers her voice. "I hope it's only gossip, but apparently there's a story circulating in the greenhouses that Liam was seen kissing a *Duchas* girl at school. Bri, I presume."

Thanks a lot, Alan.

"I guess it's possible he gave her a quick kiss goodbye before leaving school today, but I'm sure it was no more than that." Good thing Alan didn't see me kissing Deb right around the same time.

"No more?" She sounds incredulous. "I thought your father and I made it clear that he would only be allowed to remain friends with the girl on the condition he not become *romantically* involved with her."

"Um, I think maybe it was already a little too late for that. And I don't remember you putting it exactly that way."

Arching a brow, she pins me with a steely gray glare. "Perhaps not in those precise words, but I'm sure he understood what we meant. I take it you already knew about this?"

"Er…that he and Bri really like each other, yeah. I haven't seen them actually kissing at school, though." Which is technically true. I've only actually *seen* them kiss in the car and outdoors. I doubt he could resist also kissing her inside the building, though, any more than I have with Deb.

"This can't continue." There's no compromise in my mother's tone.

Unfortunately, Liam picks that exact moment to return to the Engineering lab. Mom immediately pounces.

"Is it true?" she demands in a fierce whisper.

"What?" Liam asks, already looking both guilty and defiant.

Mom's eyes narrow. "You know what. It needs to stop, Liam. I won't have you and that girl making our family the subject of gossip. We'd likely be ostracized by the *Echtran* community if word got around. In fact, I wouldn't be surprised if the Council itself got involved—again."

She's obviously referring to the way they came down on Liam—all of us, really—after his first basketball game at Jewel High.

"Just last week, you said I could spend time with Bri again," Liam protests. "Are you going back on that now?"

"There's a difference between spending time and…what you've apparently been doing with her in public."

He rolls his eyes. "Sheesh, you make it sound like we were having sex in the middle of the cafeteria or something! It was just a kiss. Anyway, can we talk about this later? I need to catch the van back to school for basketball practice."

I shut down my work station. "I'm going to head back, too. I can get started on my homework in the media center and catch the late bus home. Oh, that reminds me," I add, "I won't be out here tomorrow. There's a school project I want to work on." That "project" being Deb.

"You're well ahead on your hours here, so that should be fine," Mom says. Then, to Liam, "We'll speak more about *your* activities this evening."

Alan, Tristan and Kira are already in the reception hall near the front doors when Liam and I get there. Alan avoids looking our way. I can guess why.

As soon as we're all back in the van, Liam lets him have it. "Real nice, Alan, to blab all over the greenhouses that you saw me kiss Bri today. Remind me to do you a return favor sometime."

Though his chin goes up defensively, Alan looks distinctly uncomfortable at being called out.

"I didn't 'blab all over the greenhouses,'" he says. "I only mentioned it to my hydroponics team."

"Who apparently told everyone they saw, who told everyone else—including my mother, who was in Greenhouse Four for something Engineering-related. Now she's blaming *me* for the gossip *you* started."

Lifting a shoulder, Alan looks away. "I wouldn't have had anything to start if you hadn't—"

"Come off it, Alan," Kira startles me by saying. "It was a jerk move and you know it. The least you can do is apologize."

He glowers at her, a flush creeping up his neck. "Look. You dating outside your *fine* is one thing, but this is…totally different."

"Is it?" she asks. "Hasn't the Sovereign said all along we'll need to eventually integrate with the *Duchas*? Liam dating Bri seems like a good start."

Alan huffs out a disgusted breath before finally turning to Liam. "Fine. Sorry. Though it still seems risky to me."

"Let me worry about my own risks, okay?" Liam says, not at all appeased by what was barely an apology. "And maybe mind your own business from now on."

The rest of the ride passes in chilly silence.

As we near the school I lean forward, thinking maybe I'll have time to catch Deb for one more quick kiss before she gets on her bus. Alan and Mom be damned. But when we get there, the last buses are leaving.

Why didn't I suggest meeting after school *today* instead of tomorrow? Then I wouldn't have to wait so long to… Ah, well.

With a sigh, I head to the media center to do homework, just like I told Mom I would. The "good son," like always. Though this time not by choice.

27

Alternative hypothesis

Deb

TUESDAY MORNING, Bri and I aren't nearly as anxious on the way to school...but we still exchange a relieved grin when we again see the boys waiting for us by the curb. Today we both took the precaution of sitting as close to the front of the bus as possible, so we could get off that much quicker.

The moment the bus stops, we're both out of our seats—across the aisle from each other in the second row. Bri manages to be the very first one down the steps and I'm right behind her. To my delight, I see Lucas practically shouldering his way through the people on the sidewalk to get to me.

"Good morning," I greet him, reveling in the first touch of his hand on mine.

"It is now," he replies, grinning, then leans down to give me the kiss I've been eagerly anticipating since I woke up this morning. Then, after a blissful two seconds, "Sleep well?"

I nod. "Great dreams, too. You?"

"Same." His expression says more than the single word. "We still on for the media center after school?" he asks as we head to the building, hand in hand.

Lucas's hand feels so...*right* holding mine.

"Definitely. Unless you have to be at NuAgra after all?"

For a half-second I feel his hand tense around mine. "No, I told my mom I wouldn't be there and she was fine with it. Most of the others only go two or three times a week."

Like yesterday, we part in the atrium, where I notice Lucas carefully glances around before giving me another quick kiss. Then he joins Liam to go to their lockers. Bri's locker is that way, too, so Liam still has her by the hand.

I catch up to Liam again on my way to Pre-Cal. "Bri's not walking you to class today?" I tease.

He shakes his head. "It made her late to Econ yesterday, so we had to say our goodbyes sooner." From his woeful expression, you'd think Bri was leaving town for a month.

"Just till lunch," I remind him, amused. Lucas and I aren't nearly that pathetic. I don't think. "You'll—" I break off when he suddenly turns to glare at Alan Dempsey, who just passed us—and who glares back. "What was that about?"

Liam turns back to me with a scowl. "Alan's big mouth, that's what. He spotted me kissing Bri goodbye yesterday and blabbed about it all over NuAgra. My mom got wind of it and, well, let's just say she wasn't happy. Don't tell Bri that, okay?"

"Okay."

As I continue on to class, I think about that. Why would Alan care enough about Liam and Bri to bother carrying tales? And is that why Lucas looked around the atrium before kissing me? To make sure Alan wasn't around? Maybe NuAgra actually has some rule against dating— or kissing—outsiders?

I don't ask Liam any more questions, but I wonder again if they all belong to some religion—or cult?—Bri and I should know about before we accidentally violate any other taboos.

When Lucas and I are together in the lunch line later, I attempt to discreetly probe for more info.

"Liam told me Alan got him into hot water with your mom yester- day. She's really that opposed to you guys, um, dating?"

Lucas darts an almost panicked look at me, then nods, his panic receding as quickly as it appeared. "Er, yeah, she kind of is. Mostly, though, she really hates gossip—at least about us. Alan was a real jerk to start rumors about something that's none of his business." He shoots a poisonous look toward the NuAgra table, where Alan's already seated.

"She didn't get mad at you, though?" I persist.

"Um, no. Not yet, anyway." Only because Alan didn't see *us* kissing?

The smile Lucas slants down at me suggests he won't care if his mother does get mad. I hope that's true, but I see a trace of worry lurking in his eyes.

Despite Lucas's distracting nearness during lunch, I try to watch M more closely than usual. I notice Bri doing the same, showing she's still convinced M knows more about NuAgra than she's told us, and might even be in trouble. At some point, we'll need to come up with a plan to do something about it.

In Art class later, I also realize I still haven't asked Lucas about that incident with the branch on Saturday. I meant to yesterday, but somehow never got around to it. Now, I feel conflicted all over again. Everything's going so well between us right now that I hate to risk messing things up. Even being next to him like this, without talking or touching, feels awfully good.

Between that and anticipation of our "date" this afternoon, it's hard for me to concentrate on my drawing. Judging by the number of times he has to rub out mistakes in his own drawing, Lucas is nearly as preoccupied as I am.

My distraction is even more noticeable when I'm supposed to be rehearsing the show choir routine in Chorus. Instead of paying attention, I keep trying to think up lame excuses to get out of class early, imagining Lucas in the media center, waiting for me.

"Left foot first," Ms. Thurmond calls out in a singsong voice to the whole choir, but looking down at my feet and then surreptitiously around me, I realize I'm the one she's really talking to.

During a quick break, I complain to Bri. "Nobody's looking at our feet anyway, right? Especially in the back row. Who cares what foot we start on?" I whisper.

She gives me a knowing look. "I know exactly where your mind is, but come on, we really need to get this routine down." By "we," she means me, since Bri's already solid with the choreography.

She was openly envious when I told her why I wouldn't be on the bus today, since she won't see Liam again until his game this evening. His mom insisted he not only go to NuAgra today, but stay there until his parents take him home. I guess Lucas and I are lucky she apparently doesn't know—yet—how close he and I have become. The fact that she almost certainly wouldn't approve bothers me, though.

The instant Chorus ends, I practically race to the media center.

Lucas has staked out a small table near the windows, well away from the school librarian or any other students. Fortunately, not many are here today. That'll change as we get closer to exam time.

"Hey," I greet him, trying to play it cool despite my accelerated heart rate. "I see you're ready for your first lesson." I nod toward the drawing materials he has spread out in front of him.

"The first of many, I hope." His answering smile warms me to my toes.

I sit down and scoot my chair a little closer to his. Making out in the media center is a guaranteed ticket to detention, so we have to settle for sitting shoulder to shoulder. Even that much contact is heavenly. It takes an effort to recall why we're supposedly here.

Leaning closer, I look at what he's done so far. "Okay, see how the shadow from this tree is at a slightly different angle from this other one?" I point. "Part of creating the illusion of light is to imagine a fixed source of it, even if it's not in the frame, and staying consistent with that."

We continue talking about art for the next half hour or so, Lucas carefully following my suggestions. Then, because I promised myself I would, I finally risk ruining the mood by asking the question that's nagged at me off and on since Saturday afternoon.

"So, um, what you did to keep that branch from smashing me at Donner's Farm," I whisper, as casually as I can. "How did you *really* do that? The more I think about it, the more incredible it seems."

As I feared, he immediately tenses up. "Adrenaline surge, like I said. I, uh, can't explain it any other way."

"Can't? Or won't?" The words are out before I can stop them.

Now his expression becomes shuttered. "Does it matter? Please, Deb, just let it drop. You weren't hurt, and I'm incredibly grateful for that. Aren't you?"

"Of course! I just... Sorry. You did say there were certain things you're not allowed to talk about, so I shouldn't ask."

Still looking acutely uncomfortable, he manages a stiff smile. "Thanks. So, um, back to my drawing. Do you think I should just start over from scratch at this point?"

As he speaks, he turns his head to look down at his art project, which gives me a chance to compose my own expression before he can notice my shock.

I take one deep, silent breath, then go back to talking about art, though it's harder than ever now to keep my mind on the subject. Because whether he realizes it or not, Lucas just confirmed to me that the incredible strength and speed he demonstrated on Saturday really *is* connected to NuAgra and its secrets.

Which is downright scary.

On the late bus home, I text Bri. *Are you home?*

She replies with a thumbs-up.

We need to talk ASAP! Come over in ten minutes, okay?

When she asks why, I tell her I'll explain in person. Without knowing what kind of surveillance NuAgra's people might have, I don't dare put my latest theory into a text.

Bri's waiting for me at the bus stop when I get there. "So what is it?" she demands the second I reach her. "Did Lucas tell you the real reason his folks don't like Liam and me dating?"

"Not directly, but— Come on, we can talk at my house." I'd rather not risk her little brother eavesdropping while I share my theory.

I unlock the front door and let her get us snacks from the kitchen while I take the dog out. Five minutes later, we're up in my room with glasses of milk and a plate of Oreos. She knows I'm trying to avoid sweets, but I don't complain. I can use the sugar boost right now.

"So. You know how Lucas and I had a sort-of date in the media center?"

"Supposedly so you could tutor him on art stuff, yeah. So what really happened? More making out?"

I scoff. "With Ms. Gunderson watching? Hardly. But I did get him talking—a little."

"About?" she prompts, clearly impatient.

"First I need to tell you what happened at Donner's Farm on Saturday—besides making out, I mean. Remember that big branch that nearly hit us? You saw it."

She nods. "It wasn't really all that close, though."

"That's just it. It was. It broke off *directly* over us—over me. I heard it crack and looked up and it was coming right at my head…and then it wasn't. Somehow, Lucas batted it aside before it could hit me. Before I could even duck. He reacted so fast, knocked it so far…it shouldn't have been possible. Not for a normal human."

Bri blinks at me. "Wait, what are you saying? That he has, like, super-powers or something?"

"I don't know. I tried to make him explain right then, but, um, that's when he kissed me for the first time. I...kind of forgot to ask after that, then never really had a chance later. Until today."

"What did he say?" A cookie hangs suspended from her fingers, forgotten. "Did he admit he *does* have superpowers?"

"No, but he *did* basically admit that what he was able to do is somehow linked to NuAgra, to the stuff we're not supposed to know about. Bri, I don't think plants are the only thing they're experimenting on out there."

Now she looks as alarmed as I've been for the past hour. "You think the rumors are true, then? They're doing things to people, too? That's... scary stuff, Deb."

"I know. But it would explain a lot. Like—who are Jewel High's very best athletes?"

"In football, Rigel. Duh," she promptly replies. "In basketball, it was totally Sean last year. He took us to State. This year Liam and Alan are nearly as good as he is." She pauses, wide-eyed, as it sinks in. "Kira's also far and away the best player on the girl's team," she continues more slowly. "And Molly's our best cheerleader. The most athletic, anyway, plus excellent in show choir. And Tristan used to play quarterback at his old school in Denver, so he's probably really good, too! Omigod, Deb, you're right! Every single one of them moved here over the past year and a half. How did I not make that connection before?"

I shrug. "I think we both sort of did. I'm sure a lot of people have, but chalked it up to Jewel being such a backwater that almost anyone coming from somewhere bigger would be better than our local athletes."

"And of course I didn't want to look any of those gift horses in the mouth," Bri admits, shaking her head. "I was just happy they turned around our lame sports program. Not to mention the guys all being really good-looking."

I definitely can't dispute that. "So are the girls—and their parents, come to think of it. Remember last year when we first saw the Stuarts, we thought they looked like movie stars? And the others aren't far off."

She nods, looking both thoughtful and worried. "What do you think it means?"

"I don't know, exactly, but there's no way it's just coincidence. Maybe they're being exposed to weird radiation, or being injected with some special serum, or maybe it's pills. *Something* that changes them. Makes them faster, stronger, maybe even smarter. What if…" I pause, almost afraid to put my thought into words. "What if NuAgra is creating all these super-humans so they can take over the country? Or even the world?"

Bri stares at me for a horrified moment, then fiercely shakes her head. "No! I don't believe that. I can't. Liam is a really good guy, Deb, I know he is. He wouldn't be part of anything like that."

I don't want to believe Lucas would, either, but— "Remember the first basketball game we went to over break, where Liam played amazingly well the first half and a whole lot worse the second half?"

She nods.

"Maybe you didn't notice," I continue, "but I saw him and Lucas arguing at the start of halftime. Then, just before the second half started, Mr. Walsh also talked to Liam. Both times, Liam looked kind of pissed, but also like he agreed with them. Lucas *claimed* they were all worried Liam would hurt himself, but maybe…maybe he's not *allowed* to play quite that well?"

"Allowed?" Bri sucks in a breath. "You mean…because it would be too obvious?"

"Exactly. If whatever they're doing to the NuAgra kids is supposed to be super secret, it totally makes sense that the Walshes would've warned Liam to cool it."

Bri falls quiet for a long moment. "I *guess* you could be right," she finally admits. "Do you think M knows about this?"

"She must know more than she's told us, or she wouldn't have lied about where she went Saturday night. Hm. I wonder if she's being given the same thing the others are?"

"What do you mean?" Bri looks startled.

I pick up my backpack and pull out the list I made last week. "I mean all the ways M has changed since Rigel got here. Before that, she was at least as ordinary as we are. Glasses, pimples…she used to complain about it all the time."

"True. Though that makeover we gave her—"

"It's way more than just makeup, you know it is. After she started spending time with Rigel, her skin miraculously cleared up, her hair started looking better and she even stopped wearing glasses. She *said* she got contacts, but do we actually know that? Getting together with Rigel definitely changed her…mostly for the better."

Frowning, Bri stares at me, obviously thinking hard. "If that's true," she says slowly, "I think it was mutual. Way last year, we noticed how much better Rigel played when he and M were getting along. This year, too. His playing ramped way up when they got back together this past September."

I realize she's right. "Of course, he did get his memory back right around then," I point out. "That probably helped."

"I guess. But think about how they both got sick during their first breakup. Oh, and when M was grounded from spending time with Rigel later that semester, then Rigel left town for a whole week for Thanksgiving right after. M was so sick then, she actually stayed home from school the day before Thanksgiving. Pretty sure that was the first time M *ever* missed school. From kindergarten on, she always got perfect attendance awards."

Now my gears are turning again. "Yes! I remember she still looked like death warmed over the Monday morning after Thanksgiving, on the bus. But Rigel was waiting for her when we got to school. Then, just a few minutes later in first period, M was totally healthy again. So if she's really getting something from Rigel—or his parents?—maybe *not* getting it makes her sick."

"Like...drug addiction withdrawal?" Bri looks really alarmed now. "Omigod, it *was* almost like that!"

The more I think about all this, the scarier it seems. "If we're right, the same thing is probably true for *all* the NuAgra kids."

Bri's eyes go wide with horror. "You mean whatever makes them... super...is something they can't stop taking? Or else? Holy crap! If that's true, if Liam and Lucas are also addicted, no wonder they won't tell us anything! Deb, we've *got* to do something!"

28

Compensation

Lucas

ON THE WAY to Wednesday night's basketball game, I can hardly contain my impatience—which has nothing at all to do with the actual game. What I'm looking forward to is seeing Deb. Sitting next to her for a solid hour and a half. Talking to her.

It's weird, but when I'm not with her, I feel all wrong, somehow. Like a little piece of me is missing and I'm only complete when she's right next to me. Which makes the way she acted at school today worry me. A lot.

Though she didn't actually avoid me—she even kissed me back when she got off the bus—I sensed a reserve in her I hadn't noticed before. Because of the way I deflected yesterday when she asked me how I kept that branch from hitting her? Maybe.

Thinking back over that conversation now, I suspect my evasion did more harm than good. As sharp as Deb is, she'd have noticed how uncomfortable I was. She might even have deduced that the reason I asked her to drop it had something to do with NuAgra and its secrets. Crap.

What *is* it about Deb that makes me say things I totally shouldn't? *Love,* whispers a tiny voice in the back of my brain.

"Remember, Liam," Mom says as we approach the school, "nothing that will cause talk. I mean it. Quite a few people from Jewel's *Echtran* community will likely be at this game."

Liam rolls his eyes. "I *know*, Mom. You've told me that at least ten times already today. You do realize it will also cause talk if I'm rude to Bri in front of everyone, right? Didn't M warn us against exactly that?"

"You needn't be rude to the girl," she snaps. "But you don't need to be overly encouraging, either. She needs to understand that things simply can't go any further between the two of you. Perhaps then she'll turn her attention to other boys. *Duchas* boys."

He tenses beside me in the back seat and for a second I think he's going to start yelling. But after a couple of deep breaths, he manages to rein in his temper—barely.

"You really don't get it, do you, Mom?" he says through clenched teeth. "I don't *want* Bri to go out with other guys. Like it or not, I love her."

Even from behind, I can see Mom flinch at the word.

"But…" Liam pauses to take another steadying breath. "I'll try, really try, not to do anything that'll cause more gossip. Especially in front of other *Echtrans*. Okay?"

After a moment, she nods—reluctantly, I think. "Very well. See that you don't. Or tomorrow I'll start making inquiries about available homes in Dun Cloch."

Liam and I exchange a worried—more like scared—look.

The first time Mom made that threat, before I'd ever even kissed Deb, I didn't like the idea of never seeing her again. Now that thought is enough to turn my blood to ice.

The girls enter the gym just a moment after we do, before Liam can join the team in the locker room. When he and Bri approach each other just inside the gym doors, Mom watches them like a hawk. Liam sends her a quick glare, then greets Bri with a big smile but no kiss. I take advantage of Mom's distraction to move to Deb's side.

"Glad you could come," I whisper. "Mom's still pissed about that gossip, so Liam's having to cool it some tonight. We probably should, too."

Though she looks a little disappointed—I am, too!—she nods. "Yeah, you're probably right. Can we still sit together?"

"Definitely." We have at every other game we've both attended, so Mom shouldn't see anything suspicious about that. I hope. I'm still shaken by her renewed threat to move our whole family away from Jewel.

Liam hurries off to the locker room then, so the rest of us go up into the stands. My parents go to sit with another *Echtran* couple they're friends with, while Bri leads us over to where Tristan and Kira are already sitting. We exchange greetings, then M and Rigel join our group as the team comes back out for warmup drills. We all talk about school until a whistle blows out on the court.

Like she always does, Bri immediately races down to wish Liam a good game. Even from here, it's obvious she wants to give him a kiss, too, but he whispers something to her and she backs off with a frown as he follows the team off the court.

Still frowning, Bri makes her way back up to us and sits down between M and me with a thump.

"Seriously?" she grumbles, turning her frown on me. "Your mom's so uptight I can't even give Liam a quick kiss for *luck* without getting him in trouble?"

I shrug, carefully not looking at M. "Probably safest not to, while she's watching. You don't want him grounded again, do you?"

"Hmph. No. But it's not fair."

I'm acutely aware that M is hearing our exchange. I wonder what she thinks? Should I ask her to intervene with our parents again? It definitely made a difference before, but that was about us being *friends* with the girls to help undo the damage from my stupid lie to Deb. Nothing was said about actual romantic relationships.

The game starts, and I do try to pay at least some attention, but I'm much more interested in Deb, sitting right next to me. During the game, we talk about art and the state of Earth's environment but mostly I'm dying to kiss her. Which I don't dare do with my mother just a few rows behind us. Maybe there'll be a chance at halftime, or after the game…?

"I swear, I get so frustrated sometimes," Deb says. For a second, I think she also means being careful because of my mom. Then she continues, "We humans are so incredibly short-sighted when it comes to taking care of our planet—and it's the only one we have! The people who could make a difference act like short-term profits are more important than long-term survivability. Did your old school have anything like our Earth Club?"

"Um, I don't think so?" I say, caught off guard. Again. "Or, um, maybe I just never knew about it. I wasn't into much extracurricular stuff."

The more I have to lie to Deb, the less I like it. I'm suddenly seized by a crazy desire to tell her what my old school was *really* like. That instead of an Earth Club, we had entire Earth Studies classes to learn about the history and culture of her planet. I feel sure she'd be more fascinated than repulsed if she knew the whole truth about me. Not that I'm likely to ever find out.

But how cool would it be? I could show her vids of where we lived in Nuath—the city of Monaru, the school Liam and I attended, the zipper trains we took to get from town to town. Even better would be if I could actually *take* her there, let her see it for herself.

Before I know it, the whistle blows for halftime. Again, Bri's eager to snag a moment with Liam before he goes to the locker room.

"You guys coming?" she asks Deb and me as she stands up. "I'm gonna get a snack, too."

Deb glances at me and I'm about to agree when Rigel leans over from M's other side.

"Hey, Lucas, can I ask you something about today's Chem lab?"

"Oh, uh, sure. You girls go on," I tell Deb, realizing this might be a chance to get M's opinion of my mother's attitude. "I can catch up."

As soon as they leave, M turns to me. "I'm really the one who wanted to talk to you. I just got Rigel to say that so you'd stay for a minute. I heard what Bri said at the start of the game. Would your parents really punish Liam if she gave him a kiss for luck?"

"Our mom might," I admit. "He kissed Bri goodbye yesterday at school and it caused some gossip out at NuAgra. Word got back to Mom and she kind of freaked."

M frowns. "But I thought she'd agreed they could go out together?"

"She did. Grudgingly. But I think this has as much to do with gossip as anything else. She hates the idea of people judging our family because of it, worries no one will want to associate with us. She even threatened—again—to move us away from Jewel if Liam causes more talk."

"You don't want to leave any more than he does, do you?"

I shake my head.

"Because of Deb? You like her, don't you?"

"Er, yeah. Yeah, I do." Huge understatement!

She studies me for a long moment, then her eyebrows suddenly go up. "Oh. Oh! Well, um, that's nice. I, ah, think she really likes you, too." I get the feeling she almost said something else, then changed her mind.

"We, uh, seem to have a lot in common," I explain, though it's much more than that. "I didn't expect that with a, well, you know."

She nods, a tiny frown creasing her forehead. Like maybe she's not happy to hear that? I hope that's not it. Because even if the Sovereign herself tells me to back off, I don't think I can. Not now.

"Do you think your parents will mind if I come by your house after the game to talk to them?" she asks then. "Maybe I can get them to lighten up a little more. On Liam and Bri, I mean."

"No, I'm sure they'll be honored," I assure her, pleased. Anything she persuades my parents to allow for Liam will likely benefit me, too.

M looks amused, almost like she knows what I'm thinking. "Here's hoping. But now you'd better hurry if you're going to catch up with Deb and Bri before halftime's over."

When I step into the hallway outside the gym a minute later, I see the girls already coming back from the concession stand. They have their heads together, whispering, both of them looking concerned.

"Is something wrong?"

They immediately stop whispering to look up with a start, then greet me with guilty, artificial-looking smiles.

"No, no," Bri assures me a little too quickly. "Just…worrying about a test we both have in English tomorrow morning."

Deb nods. "Neither of us have studied much for it."

Though they clearly made that story up on the spot, I don't challenge them.

"Oh, well, good luck. I hope coming to the game tonight won't hurt your grades."

They both thank me, still looking uncomfortable. As we go back to our seats, I nearly ask Deb again what's wrong, but don't. Since I'm keeping a really big secret from her, she's entitled to keep at least one of her own.

During the second half, I notice Deb is paying more attention to the game than usual. I also notice her occasionally exchanging a significant look with Bri, but they don't seem connected to anything special Liam's doing on the court. Maybe it's something to do with Molly or one of the other cheerleaders, instead? Some girl thing I wouldn't know about? Probably.

Again, I don't ask.

When the game ends—Jewel wins, but again not by *too* much—we all go down to the court to congratulate our team. It's obvious Bri and Liam want to do a whole lot more than touch hands and smile at each other but don't dare, not with Mom right there.

I don't dare kiss Deb good night, either. Maybe if M's talk with our parents goes well that won't be true next time? I can hope.

⁘

"So, um, I think the Sovereign might be stopping by our house this evening," I tell our parents on the ride home after the game. "She asked if that would be okay and I told her it would."

Mom glances back at me, clearly startled. "Of course you couldn't have refused! Did she say why?"

"Er, not exactly." I glance at Liam and see him looking curious but hopeful. I try to give him a tiny nod of encouragement without tipping off Mom. "Guess we'll know soon."

We've only been home a few minutes when the doorbell rings. Mom sweeps the living room with a quick, critical look, then opens the door.

"Excellency! How nice of you to call. Lucas said you might. Please, come in."

M and Rigel both step inside and I realize he probably drove her here, since I don't think she has a car of her own. Plus, he's her Bodyguard. Mom ushers them both into the living room, where they sit side by side on the couch while my parents perch on chairs facing them, looking nervous. Liam and I remain standing.

"Thank you, Mrs. Walsh," M says. "I know it's getting late for a school night, so I won't stay long. I, ah, wanted to check back on the issue we discussed last week."

Mom sucks in an audible breath. "Then you…you heard the gossip that's been circulating at NuAgra this week? I assure you, I've spoken with Liam about it."

"Gossip?" M frowns. "No, I haven't heard any gossip. What about?"

From Mom's expression, she wishes she hadn't mentioned it, but she's stuck now. "Er, about Liam and the *Duchas* girl, Bri. Apparently, they were seen, ah, kissing at school, by another *Echtran* student. Perhaps it would be safest after all if we leave Jewel for somewhere like Dun Cloch if—"

"It was just a quick kiss goodbye," Liam protests, looking scared.

He's about to say more, but Mom silences him with a shake of her head before turning anxiously back to the Sovereign.

"I've tried to impress upon him how inappropriate—" she begins.

"Please, Mrs. Walsh," M interrupts. "I think you're worrying far more than is necessary. Goodness knows, Rigel and I have come in for more than our share of gossip, but we haven't let it stand in the way of the work we've been able to accomplish. Nor have we let it undermine our relationship, which is stronger than ever."

Mom's face goes pink. "Yes, but—" she pauses, clearly struggling for the right words. "I, ah, know some of our people have criticized your... choice, Excellency, but an *Echtran* outside your *fine* is hardly on the same level as attempting some sort of romance with a *Duchas*."

"Some of our people would disagree," M replies with a small smile. "They believe a Sovereign has no right to indulge personal feelings on such matters, that my position requires sacrifices I have no intention of making. Your family is fortunate in that no one is likely to hold any of you to such unreasonable standards. If you've read any of my articles or watched my broadcasts, you know we all need to work harder at befriending our *Duchas* brethren. As more and more of our people immigrate to Earth, as they must, it will become even more important. My hope is that one day we will no longer have to conceal our origins at all, but in the meantime, we need to be establishing trust and rapport with the *Duchas*, one person or family at a time."

"See, Eilis?" Dad says. "I told you that you were overreacting. Maybe Liam's little romance with this girl will actually turn out to be a good thing for the Sovereign's long-range goals."

Mom gets her stubborn look. "I still don't like it. I'm sorry, Excellency."

Then Rigel speaks up for the first time. "It's not easy to be the subject of gossip, Mrs. Walsh. Believe me, I know. My parents and I have had to deal with a lot of it—and worse. They don't like it, either. But persuading our people to accept the changes to tradition that will be necessary for our long-term future here is worth a few short-term aggravations. Like gossip."

"I...I suppose," Mom concedes. "Still—"

M holds up a hand. "Honestly, Mrs. Walsh, I think insisting on stricter rules for Liam than most *Duchas* parents would impose is more likely to arouse suspicion than trusting his judgment. I'm sure he doesn't want to see Bri hurt any more than I do."

Beside me, Liam nods vigorously. "She's right. I'd never do *anything* to hurt Bri, or get her in trouble. Anyway, the teachers at school take a pretty dim view of PDA."

"PDA?" Dad echoes, brows raised.

"Public displays of affection," Rigel explains with a small smile. "Pretty much anything beyond holding hands in the halls. They'll look the other way for the occasional quick kiss, especially outside the building, but more than that is likely to get a reprimand."

M nods. "Cormac has even warned *us* a couple of times, since it would look weird if the Vice Principal gave us special treatment. If someone actually spread gossip because of a quick goodbye kiss, I'd say that someone was looking to cause trouble." She looks over at Liam and me. "Let me guess. Alan?"

"How did you know?" I ask, astonished.

"Simple deduction. It had to be someone who's at school and NuAgra, and Alan tends to be both self-righteous and a little petty. Ask Molly or Tristan about it sometime." Then, turning back to our parents, "Please don't let a bit of gossip drive you away from your home here. Bailerealta and Dun Cloch are already at capacity and we expect nearly twice as many Nuathans to arrive during the next launch window. It's therefore vital that our people integrate themselves into *Duchas* communities. Jewel is sort of a test case, as it has the highest concentration of *Echtrans* for its size."

Dad gives Mom an I-told-you-so look and she manages a small smile. "I, ah, see your point, Excellency."

"Good." M stands. "And now, we should go before it gets any later."

My parents immediately stand up, too.

"Thank you, Excellency," Dad says as they accompany her and Rigel to the door. "I'm sure you've put my wife's mind at ease. Again."

He glances at Mom, who nods—a little reluctantly.

"Yes, thank you, Excellency," she says. "We all appreciate you taking such an interest in our family."

M gives Liam and me an almost imperceptible wink. "Of course. Your sons are good friends of mine, so it's nice to see them getting to know my best *Duchas* friends. Please, try not to worry. Good night."

29

Deductive reasoning

Deb

"WHAT WE FOUND out tonight clinches it, if it wasn't already clinched," I tell Bri on the way home from the game. "This thing's gone way further than we thought if even nearby schools' best athletes are connected to NuAgra."

Just before the game, Bri noticed Liam chatting with Alexandria's best player. When she asked him about it at halftime, Liam told us he'd met the guy, Eric, at a couple of NuAgra family functions because his parents work there, too.

"You're going to call M's Taekwondo school tomorrow, right?" We came up with that idea on the way to the game earlier.

"Right," Bri confirms. "I'll pretend I'm interested in taking classes and say M recommended it. If she's become some kind of super athlete since Rigel got here, maybe her teacher will mention it."

I figure the odds of that are low, but every data point might help us figure out what to do—and what to say to M if we decide to confront her.

"I also think we should stake out NuAgra Saturday evening," I say then. "If we go out there early, we should be able to find some vantage point to watch the front gate without being seen."

Bri hesitates a moment before answering. "You, um, do realize there's another basketball game Saturday night, right?"

I glance over at her, one eyebrow raised. "Don't you think this is more important?"

"I guess so. It's just—"

"You hate to miss any of Liam's games. I know."

When she still doesn't answer right away, I say, "Look, if it matters that much to you, I'll do the NuAgra stakeout by myself. Maybe I can get a video with my phone or something."

"No. No, you're right." She lets out an audible breath. "M matters way more than any basketball game—or even romance. We'll both go. If we have solid proof, M won't be able to deny she's involved with NuAgra. Maybe then it'll be easier to convince her to get out of whatever they've sucked her into. If she still can."

Another glance at Bri shows her lips pressed together in a determined line but her expression is anguished—an anguish I share. It's totally likely our snooping will permanently alienate Liam and Lucas. But we've both agreed M's safety has to come first...no matter how in love we are.

Our resolve—mine, anyway—is put to the test when we get to school the next morning, where the boys are again waiting for us at the curb.

"Hey, missed you," Lucas says, leaning down for our morning kiss.

Just like yesterday, the uncertainty and tension that built up inside me during our hours apart begins to fade the moment he touches me. I keep thinking I'll get used to kissing him, that it won't feel quite so special after a while, but so far it's been exactly the opposite.

"I missed you, too," I say when he straightens, smiling up at him.

He examines my face. "Is something wrong? You seem a little tense."

"I was," I admit, though the feeling of well-being I always get from his touch has crowded out most of my worry for the moment. "Not now, though."

Grinning, he throws an arm around my shoulders for the short walk to the building. "Yeah, I always feel better when I'm with you, too."

I grin back. "Nice to know it's mutual." Maybe that will help keep Lucas from breaking up with me if Bri and I confront M and it goes badly.

Almost as though he senses our time together could be limited, Lucas holds my hand a little tighter once we're inside the school and gives me a more lingering goodbye kiss in the atrium when we part—

without even looking around first. Liam gets to Pre-Cal just as the bell rings, and in English Bri tells me that's because he walked her to first period for a change.

"I swear, his kisses just keep getting better and better." There's a wistful edge to her sigh. "I really hope—"

"Yeah. Me, too."

At lunch, both guys still behave more affectionately than usual. Lucas even steals a couple of quick kisses right at the table, apparently not caring that Alan is facing our way.

"So, we were thinking," Liam says at one point. "How about another double date at Donner's Farm Saturday? Though it can't go too late, since I have a game that night."

Bri and I eagerly agree. She's as aware as I am it could be our last chance to be with our guys before everything blows up in our faces. Which I hope it won't.

While we eat, I try to keep a close eye on how M interacts with the newer students, but I keep getting distracted by Lucas's gorgeousness and the wonderful thrill I get from his voice and touch. Not till I'm carrying my tray to the drop do I realize I ate way more than usual, including the two chocolate chip cookies I usually offer to the boys. Oops.

So I'm even more surprised when Bri looks me over on the way to fifth period and says, "Have you lost weight? You're looking great these days."

I blink. "I doubt it, the way I've been eating lately. But you know, you're looking really good lately, too. Your skin is the clearest I've ever seen it."

She shrugs, grinning. "I guess being in love agrees with both of us."

"I guess so." But then a more sinister explanation occurs to me. "You...you don't think *we're* starting to be affected by whatever's changing the NuAgra kids and M, do you?"

"What? No!" Bri exclaims. Then, after a pause, "Do you?"

I shrug. "If they're slipping us some special serum, they're being awfully sneaky about it. Or maybe just being around them does it? In which case—"

"In which case, the only way to rescue M would be to get her completely away from Rigel...and you know *that's* never going to happen."

That certainty is reinforced during Government class, watching the way M and Rigel look at each other and make excuses to touch as often as they can without the teacher noticing. If my latest wild theory is right, this will be even tougher than we thought.

Lucas's attentiveness continues in Art, where he's even more complimentary than usual about my work. "Are we good for another tutoring session in the media center today?" he asks at the end of class.

"No," I tell him with a sharp pang of regret. "We have to stay after in Chorus today. The first big show choir competition is coming up in a few weeks and the director's insisting we need extra rehearsal time."

"Oh. Bummer." His disappointment is evident but he quickly rallies. "See you tomorrow morning, then. Bye, Deb." He leans down to give me a super-sweet parting kiss that I wholeheartedly return.

⁎

Just before dinnertime that evening, Bri calls.

"I just got off the phone with M's Taekwondo teacher," she tells me, her voice quivering with suppressed excitement—or maybe tears? "He practically begged me to convince her to enter their next tournament, said she's become their very best sparrer over the past year. He went on and on about how much she's improved since her first few months there."

Whoa! "In other words, since Rigel got here," I say.

"Yeah," Bri agrees heavily. "So M really must be getting whatever they're giving the other NuAgra kids."

"Which means it'll be that much harder to convince her to stop taking it," I worry. "It probably makes her feel great."

I hear Bri sigh. "I know. But we absolutely have to try. We have tons of proof now that they're doing *something* to her, along with all the others. I'm not sure we even need to do that stakeout Saturday."

"We can't very well stage an intervention at school anyway," I point out, "so I think we still should. The more evidence we can lay in front of her, the better. We should also do some research on the best way to extricate someone from a cult before we confront her, so we don't accidentally make things worse."

⁎

"I don't know if I can take much more of this," Bri says while we're waiting for the bus Friday morning. "I barely slept last night, worrying about M and the guys and all the things that could go wrong…or if it's already too late. And Liam was so sweet yesterday. All this plotting behind his back feels wrong."

"It should only be for another couple of days," I try to reassure her, though I know exactly how she feels. "Anyway, it's not like the guys are exactly being upfront with us, either. They've told us flat out they're keeping secrets, and we know for sure now it's about more than cutting-edge farming techniques."

Bri presses her lips together. "I know. It's just…I don't know what I'll do if Liam dumps me again. It was bad enough last time, but now…."

The bus arriving spares me from replying, but the thought of losing Lucas twists my insides, too. I never even imagined feeling this strongly about a boy, like we were designed for each other. Like I just might die if he breaks up with me or leaves.

"Let's just enjoy the heck out of being with them today, and especially tomorrow at Donner's Farm," I suggest once we're sitting down. "Then we'll at least have more wonderful memories to look back on if… if the worst happens."

Bri swallows, then nods. "You're right. No point borrowing trouble before it happens. M has to come first."

Unfortunately, the boys greet us with bad news when we get off the bus.

"We can't go to Donner Farm tomorrow after all," Liam says, clearly upset. "Mom has decided to repaint the living room and we have to stay home and help. She thinks it'll be a 'fun family project.'" He makes air quotes, his expression sour.

I look at Lucas, who shrugs and nods unhappily. "There's no changing Mom's mind when she gets like this. Tonight's out, too. We're supposed to move furniture and put down tarps so we can get an early start tomorrow."

But then he leans in for a kiss and suddenly the day gets a little brighter in spite of my disappointment.

"At least there's the game tomorrow night," Liam comments as we all walk toward the building. "Not that Bri and I will get nearly as much time together there as you two will."

Bri flicks a startled glance my way. "Um, yeah, about that—"

"We can't go," I blurt out before she can waver. "We, er, promised a friend, way last semester, that we'd go to her birthday party and….it's tomorrow night."

Even though I totally made that up, Bri nods. "Er, yeah. What Deb said. We're really, really sorry."

The brothers both look crestfallen. And slightly suspicious?

"Oh. Well. I guess if you promised." Liam looks from Bri to me and back. "What about Sunday?"

"Sure!" Bri says before I can stop her. "Let's meet at Dream Cream Sunday afternoon. Around four?"

Both boys agree to that, so I reluctantly do, too. Though as I remind Bri in English class later, we have zero idea where things will stand by Sunday afternoon.

"By then, M might have told the others we're onto the whole NuAgra scheme and the guys will be forced to break up with us," I quietly point out.

"But if we're right, they're in as much danger as M is," she whispers back. "What if the government finds out what they're doing? Everyone connected with the company could be hauled in for questioning. Or even arrested!"

I swallow, remembering some of the thrillers I've read. "Or maybe they'd just be spirited away, never to be seen again…along with anyone else who knows the truth."

Bri looks as scared as I am by that idea.

⁘

By lunchtime, Bri and I are both stressing to the max, eaten up with worry about the guys, about M, and now about ourselves. We're obviously not hiding it well, either. Lucas keeps darting curious looks at me, and when Liam starts pestering Bri about tomorrow's game, she suddenly snaps.

"Are you *sure* you can't get out of that party?" he wheedles her. "Maybe just tell your friend you forgot?"

She frowns at him, possibly the first time I've seen her do that. "No, Liam, I can't. I promised. Stop trying to guilt me."

He blinks. "What? What's wrong?"

"I'm just…trying to figure things out." She jumps to her feet. "And you're *not* helping!"

Bursting into tears, she rushes out of the cafeteria, leaving everyone at the table stunned and confused. Except me. I understand all too well.

When we get to Art class, Lucas tentatively brings it up. "Is Bri okay? Do you know what's going on with her?"

"She's, um, going through some stuff right now," I reply evasively. "We...kind of both are."

He stares at me for a long moment, clearly worried. "Because of us?"

"Only partly." Which is true. "But I think—I hope—everything will work out okay."

Lucas keeps watching me, like he's trying to read my thoughts. I hope *that's* not one of his superpowers!

Finally, he says, "I hope so, too." But he still looks worried.

We don't talk much more during class, but when the bell rings, Lucas puts his hand over mine on the table. "I'm really going to miss you this weekend, Deb. Sunday afternoon seems like a long way off."

Relief that I haven't completely alienated him spreads through me, only slightly tempered by caution.

"It does. I wish— But hey, we'll survive. Right?"

That finally gets a smile. "Right."

His parting kiss is the sweetest yet, though not nearly as long as I'd like, since that would get us both in trouble. Somewhat reassured, I head to seventh-period Chorus.

"Did you find a pair of binoculars?" I ask Bri when she meets me in my driveway early Saturday evening.

Because M and the O'Garas left for NuAgra around a quarter to seven last Saturday, we decided it would be safest to drive out there a little after six.

"Yep, right here." She holds up something smaller than the palm of my hand. "I know they're tiny, but they're pretty powerful. Mom and Dad got them for camping trips."

I unlock the car doors. "Cool. I've got my mom's birding binoculars. I was going to borrow her digital camera, too—it has a good zoom lens

—but the battery's dead and there wasn't time to recharge it by the time I thought of it."

"A camera would probably be more likely to get us arrested for corporate spying anyway," Bri points out. "You realize that's a risk, right?"

"Don't know why it should be." I try to sound more confident than I feel. "It's not like we plan to actually break into the NuAgra grounds. We'll just hang out on top of that old gas station where we'll have a good view of their front gate."

Bri relaxes slightly. "You're sure it's still there?"

I nod. "I drove out there this morning while you were shopping with your mom. It's been closed for nearly twenty years, so it's kind of rickety, but I think we can get up there."

"Okay, let's go!" Now she sounds excited.

So am I. It'll be like a stakeout from one of my crime thrillers—though even if NuAgra *is* doing something illegal, I doubt they'll shoot at us or anything. I hope.

It's not quite six-thirty when we reach the narrow, rutted entrance to the abandoned store and gas station. It's on the other side of the county road running past NuAgra, maybe five hundred yards from the main gate. A lot closer than where I pulled off last weekend.

I drive the car around to the far side of the building, where it's out of sight of the road, before parking.

"Are you sure about this?" Bri asks, eyeing the decrepit building. "How are we supposed to get up there without breaking our necks?"

"I saw a bunch of old crates around back," I tell her. "We can stack them to climb up."

That proves harder than I expect. Only a few plastic ones are big enough and intact enough to hold our weight. The wooden ones are falling apart. After fifteen minutes of hauling them into place and muscling them on top of each other, we've built a rough structure that lets us clamber onto the flat roof.

I check my phone. "Twenty till seven," I say. "Now we wait."

We find a semi-comfortable spot along the side nearest NuAgra, where we can just barely see the main entrance. Lying on our stomachs, we take out our binoculars and focus them on the gate.

"You were right, there is a guard," Bri comments. "Is it the same one you saw last week?"

"I think so? I didn't get a good look, though. I didn't want to make him suspicious."

Fifteen minutes creep by. We brought snacks, but we're both too nervous to eat. It's cold, too. While we were messing with the crates, my winter coat seemed way too warm, but now I'm glad I wore it.

Bri shifts restlessly, clearly getting bored. "Are you sure—?"

"Shh!" I hiss, even though there's no way the guard can hear us. "Look!" I point back the way we came, where a set of headlights approaches.

We watch as a car I don't recognize pulls up to the gatehouse. The driver—there's just one person in the car—speaks with the guard, then the big gate opens and the car drives through. Immediately, the gate closes again.

"Wow, they really do take their security seriously," Bri observes. "That gate, a guard, barbed wire all along the top of the fence, and what look like cameras every twenty or thirty yards. Sure hope they don't spot us here."

"Me, too." I noticed the barbed wire this morning, but not the cameras. Yikes. We're already lying down, but we flatten ourselves further.

Less than a minute passes before another set of headlights draws near. This car has two people in it, but neither looks familiar, at least from here. When they reach the gate, the same thing happens as before —the guard looks into the car, there's a brief conversation, then he lets them pass, closing the gate behind them.

It's nearly five minutes before we see more cars coming, three more.

"That makes the same number I saw last Saturday. I'll bet one is the O'Garas' van," I murmur to Bri.

Sure enough, as the vehicles get close enough to identify, the second one turns out to be the same maroon van I followed last week. Again, Mrs. O is driving, with M in the passenger seat and Molly in the back. I quickly train my binoculars on the car in front of them and I'm almost sure it's Rigel's dad, in what looks like the Stuarts' SUV. The third car is nearly past us before I can get a good look, but—

"Is that Mr. Cormac, the Vice Principal?" Bri sounds as astonished as I am.

"It sure looks like him! Pretty sure that's his car, too. I've seen him getting into it after school."

"Weird."

"Yeah," I agree, shifting my binoculars back to the gate, where Mr. Stuart is now turning in.

Like the drivers of the last two cars, he speaks briefly with the guard before proceeding. Mrs. O'Gara pulls up next. This time, the guard takes a step back when she stops, straightens up like he's coming to attention, then bows deeply before motioning her to continue to the NuAgra complex.

"What was *that*?" Bri gasps. "Did you see that?"

"I did! That was as weird as Mr. Cormac being here." Even as I say that, our school's Vice Principal pulls up to the gatehouse and is waved through to follow the others. No bowing.

Slowly, I lower my binoculars to stare at Bri.

She stares back, wide-eyed. "Just yesterday, we were wondering who's in charge of this NuAgra cult or conspiracy or whatever it is," she says. "Looks like Mrs. O'Gara is some high-ranking bigwig, at least. Maybe even their supreme leader. We were right about Rigel's family, too."

I chew my lip. "It's like every friend of M's other than us is involved with NuAgra. I knew rescuing her wouldn't be easy, but if they have their hooks into her this deeply, it might be completely impossible."

"It won't be impossible," Bri stubbornly insists. "It can't be. I'm not letting them assimilate M without a fight. I say we go to her house tomorrow and simply refuse to leave until she hears us out."

I can think of several possible flaws in that plan, but I don't mention them. Because what choice do we have?

30

Surface tension

Lucas

"WOW, I know the Council told Liam to hold back on the court, but I don't think they meant he has to play *this* badly," Rigel comments during the second half of Saturday night's basketball game. "Or is he still upset about Bri blowing up at him at lunch yesterday?"

"Probably some," I admit. "Though he said she apologized later."

Unlike Liam, I haven't made any *Duchas* friends except Deb and Bri, so I'm sitting with other *Echtran* students tonight. I'm still way too ticked at Mom to sit with my parents.

"It's got to be hard for him," Rigel says. "For both of you, I guess, trying to have any kind of relationship with someone you can't be completely honest with."

"No kidding," I grump. "Not that any of you have to worry about that."

Tristan looks at me in apparent surprise. "Does that mean you guys are actually getting serious with Deb and Bri? I figured you were just having some fun until, y'know, more *Echtran* girls get here in the next launch window."

"Ugh! You sound like Alan." Kira frowns at Tristan. "That's exactly what he accused Sean of doing when we first started going out. I seem to recall you made at least one crack along those lines, too."

A flush creeps up Tristan's neck. "Look, I know I was a real jerk when I first got here. I've tried to make up for it. But even you have to admit there's a big difference between dating outside your *fine* and getting serious with a *Duchas*."

I usually like Tristan, but right now, I have a strong urge to punch him. Sure, Deb's technically a *Duchas*, but he makes it sound like she's a whole other species or something.

"Neither of us planned it that way," I inform him through gritted teeth. "We took Kira up on her suggestion to ask them to the Winter Formal. Then we just…hit it off." Eventually, anyway.

"Yeah, Bri and Deb asked me to nudge you two their way," Kira admits, "though I did check with M before I actually said anything to you and Liam."

I look at Rigel. "The Sovereign *is* fine with us dating the girls, right?"

He shrugs. "She's a little worried that all of you could end up hurt, but she's not mad or anything. If she were, she'd let you know." A corner of his mouth quirks up. "Believe me."

"I'm sure it's hard having to keep such a huge secret from someone you care about." Kira's expression is sympathetic. "I struggled with that myself, when I was still buying into all the crap Sean's Uncle Allister told me. Sean and I nearly broke up over it, before I figured out I was being duped and told Sean everything. Though I guess that's not an option for you or Liam."

"No. Unfortunately," I agree gloomily, though it's nice someone understands. "They made it crystal clear during Orientation how huge the risks are if we don't maintain total secrecy."

She nods. "Believe me, I remember. Since you two were born here on Earth," she adds to Rigel and Tristan, "you probably didn't have the Secrecy Statute shoved down your throats like we did, but it's the very first thing they drilled into us when we got here. And then reminded us of it practically every day."

None of this is helping my mood, even a little. "How many *Duchas do* know about us, besides M's adopted aunt and uncle?" I ask Rigel, suddenly curious. "I guess the Council decided they could be an exception?"

"They didn't have much choice when the President of the United States showed up at M's house and her aunt answered the door," he replies with a chuckle. "Even then, I don't think she'd have believed it if Mrs. O'Gara and Council Leader Kyna hadn't backed M up. Anyway, to answer your question, not many. The President, obviously, and maybe two or three others in his administration. Several foreign leaders, too, because M had to tell them about the Grentl back in September and convince them to take precautions. But I'd say no more than twenty or thirty total?"

My heart sinks even further. I can't imagine Deb or Bri ever becoming need-to-know exceptions to the iron-clad prohibition against revealing our origins.

As though sensing my torment, Kira reaches over and pats my arm. "Hey, don't be so down. Things might still work out."

Though I manage a weak smile of thanks, I sure don't see how. Even if M's right and someday all the *Duchas* will be clued in, it probably won't be for at least a couple of decades. Maybe even centuries. More depressed than ever, I turn away to watch the game and see that Liam's been benched. Again.

Liam does go back in before the end of the game, but only manages a single basket before the final buzzer. Jewel squeaks out a win—barely— though it's no thanks to Liam tonight.

I make it down to the court before our parents do. "I hate to say it, Bro, but that's the worst I've ever seen you play," I tell my brother, careful not to be snarky about it.

"Yeah, no kidding," he grumbles. "I'm surprised I didn't do even worse, considering. Without Bri here, there hardly seemed any point in trying. Not to mention I feel like crap tonight."

I nod, totally in sympathy. "I didn't exactly have a fun evening, either." I really only came at all to support Liam, who's been at least as worried as I have over the past twenty-four hours.

Yesterday, it was totally obvious to both of us that the girls' excuse about some unnamed "friend" having a birthday party was something they made up on the spot. Because they didn't *want* to come to the game tonight. Probably because they're finally fed up with us keeping secrets from them.

Mom and Dad join us courtside then. Both express sympathy for Liam's off game, though I can tell they're secretly pleased. They probably figure it'll help pacify the more critical members of the *Echtran* Council.

On the way home, Mom makes it clear that's not the only thing she's pleased about.

"I noticed your friend Bri wasn't there tonight," she comments cheerfully. "You two haven't had a tiff, have you?"

"No. And you don't have to sound so hopeful, Mom." Liam glowers at her. "She and Deb had to go to a friend's birthday party tonight, that's all."

Except both of us know that's *not* all.

Mom doesn't apologize, but she does give each of us a big slice of carrot cake when we get home. Liam picks at his instead of wolfing it down and asking for another. I don't do much better.

As soon as we're done, Liam and I both excuse ourselves to get ready for bed. Between our "fun" family painting project and tonight's game, he and I haven't had a chance all day to talk without our parents overhearing. So I'm not surprised when he follows me into my room.

"I didn't want to say anything before, but I texted Bri earlier to ask if we're still on for Dream Cream tomorrow," Liam tells me once the door is shut. "She texted back saying she'd let me know…but then added a smiley face. What does that even mean?"

"I don't know. Maybe we'll find out tomorrow."

Liam nods glumly. "Maybe. If they show up."

"Yeah." I have a horrible, sinking feeling that if they do, it'll be to break up with us.

I've sensed a definite difference in Deb these past few days—a subtle withdrawal, more emotional than physical. Ever since she tried to pin me down about how I kept that branch from hitting her and I dodged the question—again. She dropped it, just like I asked her to, but that doesn't mean she stopped thinking about it.

"They both have to be sick of us keeping so many secrets," I tell my brother. "We can't exactly blame them, either. To them, it must look like we're not really invested. Like we don't trust them."

"I totally trust Bri!" Liam protests. "What if…what if we swear them to secrecy? If I tell Bri how important it is to keep everything completely to herself, she will. No question."

I'm sure Deb would, too, but— "That's not our call to make. You know that. Besides, if Mom and Dad ever found out we breached secrecy, I'll bet they really would move us all away from Jewel. Probably far away. I'm not willing to risk that. Are you?"

Liam huffs out a frustrated breath. "The way things are going, I'm afraid I'll lose Bri anyway, if I don't tell her the truth. And I…I honestly don't know if I can survive without Bri. Don't M and Rigel get sick if they're apart from each other too long? I kind of feel like that's happening to me right now."

"I get it. Trust me. I do." The agony in my brother's face perfectly reflects the painful twist in my own gut—like panic, only worse—at the idea of never seeing Deb again. "I *wish* we could tell them everything. Every bit as much as you do. But we can't."

"M acts like she's in our corner about us dating Bri and Deb," Liam says stubbornly. "Maybe she'd be okay with us telling them the truth, too. Why don't we ask her?"

I shake my head, refusing to grasp at such an unlikely straw. "Even if *she* were okay with it, there's no way the Council would ever agree. According to Mom, some of them still don't like her dating Rigel—and they're *graell* bonded. It sounds like Kira and Sean still get a lot of pushback, too, just for being from different *fines*. I'm sure they'd consider this a whole order of magnitude worse. There's a reason they made us memorize the Secrecy Statute during Orientation, you know."

His shoulders slump and he nods, the brief hope in his eyes flickering out. "I know. You're right. It just…sucks."

"No argument from me."

"I guess all I can do is try my best to convince Bri I really do love her. Even if I'm never allowed to give her any of the answers she deserves. If that doesn't work…" He trails off hopelessly.

I swallow, afraid to count on anything working at this point. "I'll do the same with Deb, but it's possible nothing we say—that we're allowed to say—will convince them we really do care about them. If so, we'll just have to live with whatever the girls decide to do. No matter how much it hurts."

31

Process of elimination

Deb

THE NEXT DAY, Bri and I meet before lunch to work out the final details on how we're going to confront M this afternoon.

"From everything I researched on cults," I tell Bri, "the hardest part will be convincing M she's being controlled by these people."

"That's what those videos I watched said, too," she agrees. "We need to somehow make her understand that the O'Garas don't really have her best interests at heart. She'll never believe that about Rigel, though. She really loves him and I think he really loves her, too."

I nod. "I expect he's as deluded as she is, since he was probably indoctrinated years ago. But no matter what, we need to be *super* careful not to paint him as any kind of bad guy in this. That would instantly put M on the defensive."

"Not to mention making her mad at us," Bri says. "If we bring Rigel up at all, it should only be along the lines of also wanting to rescue him. Let's just focus on NuAgra and maybe the O'Garas, especially at first. This still won't be easy. Even the professional deprogrammers I listened to say it's a tricky, long-term process to separate someone from a cult, and only succeeds about half the time. We absolutely *have* to try, though, no matter how pissed M gets."

I frown down at my notes. "It'll be hard to avoid upsetting her. The experts say when someone's belief system is challenged, they first get angry, then depressed when they start losing faith in their cult leader. That's probably Mrs. O'Gara, from what we saw last night."

"If we can convince M we're only doing this out of love, maybe she'll finally open up to us," Bri says hopefully. "I mean, she used to share absolutely *everything* with us, starting with me in kindergarten."

"Yeah, I think that's the best way to approach her," I agree. "If we can just get her to repeat to us some of the things they've been telling her, we can start using logic to show her how off base it all is."

Bri nods vigorously. "Exactly. But the *main* thing we need to do, right from the start, is remind her what good friends we've always been, and that we still really, really care about her."

At one-thirty, armed with our talking points and a lot of determination, Bri and I ride our bikes over to M's house.

Her Aunt Theresa answers when we ring the bell. "Oh, hello, girls. Marsha didn't tell me you'd be coming over today."

"We didn't plan it in advance," Bri tells her. "But we were out on our bikes anyway and decided to stop by to see if she's home."

Mrs. Truitt steps back. "She is. Why don't you come in and I'll let her know you're here. Marsha?" she calls up the stairs. "Some friends are here to see you."

A moment later, M comes down. "Oh, hey, guys. What's up?"

"We, uh, just wanted to talk," I say. "About, um, boys and stuff." Bri insisted that would be the best way to get M alone, since she'd hardly want to talk about boys in front of her aunt and uncle.

M gives us a knowing grin. "Sure! We can go up to my room. Aunt Theresa, can I bring some cookies from the kitchen?"

Her aunt smiles—something she seems to do more often than she used to. "You girls go on and I'll carry up a plate, along with some milk."

We all thank her and M leads us upstairs. When we get to her room, I realize it's been months since I've seen it, though it hasn't changed much. She still has posters of space-related stuff on the walls and those little glow-in-the-dark stars on her ceiling, reminding me of all the sleep-overs we had here over the years.

Bri and I sit cross-legged on her bed, just like old times, while M sits in her desk chair facing us. The two of us exchange a look and Bri nods. She turns to M to deliver the opening we rehearsed, but M speaks first.

"Things seem to be going really well between you two and the Walsh brothers these days."

"Um, yeah, they are," I admit, trying not to let thoughts of Lucas distract me.

Bri nods. "I think Lucas likes Deb as much as Liam seems to like me, though she took a little convincing early on."

"I think so, too," M agrees, winking at me. "So does Rigel. I asked him, since boys sometimes see things a little differently and he knows them both pretty well."

"Really?" I *think* Lucas feels the same way about me I do about him, but hearing it confirmed is nice. "What did—?"

Mrs. Truitt comes in just then with a tray loaded with a big plate of cookies and three glasses of milk. "Here you are, girls. Have a nice chat."

As soon as she's gone, Bri gets up and closes M's door. "Actually," she says, sitting back on the bed, "it wasn't boys we really came here to talk to you about, though I guess they're part of it. M...we're worried about you."

M's eyebrows go up. "About me? Why?"

I lean forward. "Because we care about you, and we've noticed how you've changed over the past year and a half, and...we think we know why.

"You do?" M looks from me to Bri, who nods.

"Yes. We think it involves all these new NuAgra people and what they're really doing out there."

M sits back against her chair, one brow skeptically raised. "You don't still think they're some white supremacist cult, do you? I explained to Deb—"

"Not really, no," I tell her. "But they're definitely up to more than just secret agricultural research. We think they're also doing something to people—at least their own people. You can't deny there's something different about them."

At that, M lets out an exasperated breath. "Just because they're all fairly new to Jewel—"

"It's not just that," Bri interrupts. "Haven't you noticed that *all* our best jocks are associated with NuAgra, one way or another?"

"Rigel's not," M immediately objects. "Neither is Sean."

"Rigel's dad is," I'm forced to point out, though I'd really hoped to keep Rigel's name out of this for now. "Didn't they hire him to set up their internet or something? And Sean's dating Kira, whose parents work there, just like Molly's dating Tristan."

With a transparent attempt at nonchalance, M shrugs. "None of that is particularly surprising, when you think about it. In a town as small as Jewel, most of the locals have known each other forever. So it only makes sense that the newer people would gravitate toward each other."

"Yeah, everyone's noticed how they all stick together," Bri agrees. "Also, how crazy good-looking most of them are. Not just the ones at school, either, but the adults, too. Even my parents have mentioned it. It goes way beyond just being new to Jewel. But what worries us the most is that they've somehow drawn *you* into whatever it is they're doing."

M makes a scoffing sound, but I swear I see some worry in her eyes. "Me? Why do you think that? It's not like *I've* ever been any kind of athlete!"

"You never used to be," Bri agrees. "But I called your Taekwondo school Thursday, and it sounds like you are now. Your teacher says you've become one of his best students, that you've improved amazingly over the past year and a half. In other words, since Rigel got here. That's why we think maybe it's his family that got you involved with whatever NuAgra's doing."

"You called my Taekwondo school? Seriously?" M stares at Bri, who nods sheepishly. "Anyway, this whole idea is crazy! When Rigel and I started dating, neither of us had ever even *heard* of NuAgra. It was a whole year later before they moved their headquarters to Jewel—and Rigel had nothing to do with that."

"Probably not," I admit, "but his parents might have. His dad, at least. What if…what if the Stuarts and the O'Garas were part of some advance group to check things out before NuAgra moved all their people here?"

"They wouldn't necessarily have told Rigel anything about it," Bri says quickly. "He might not have any idea at all of what they're really doing."

Again, M frowns back and forth between us. "He doesn't," she says firmly. "I can absolutely promise you that Rigel doesn't know any more about NuAgra than I do."

"That's probably true," I concede. And it could be, since M herself knows a whole lot more than she's admitting.

"In that case," Bri says, "we should all be worried about him, too. We wouldn't care all that much if they were only experimenting on their *own* people, but you and Rigel have somehow been sucked into it, too, and that's not okay. We don't know why they targeted you, or how they persuaded you to go along with whatever their agenda is—"

"Agenda?" M echoes. "Sorry, but I'm not at all convinced they're doing anything they shouldn't. Just because a few of their kids are good athletes, or better looking than average? That's hardly proof they're up to no good."

Bri and I regard her sadly. We knew this would be tricky, but she's being even more stubborn than we expected.

"I'm sorry," Bri says, "but we're pretty sure they are. Maybe you're in so deep now you can't see it. And we know it'll be hard to get you out… but we love you, M, so we have to try!"

M sighs, sounding as frustrated as we are. "Get me out of *what*, exactly? Why are you so sure I've been…indoctrinated or whatever by NuAgra?"

I decide it's time to stop beating around the bush.

"Because you've been going out there, M, and not just for their tour," I tell her. "I was curious where you and Molly went every Saturday night, so I followed you last weekend. But when I asked you Monday, you and Molly claimed you went shopping in Kokomo that night— which I knew for a fact you hadn't."

"That's when we knew you were definitely hiding something," Bri says. "After that, Deb and I were so worried about you we, um, staked out NuAgra last night. We took binoculars and climbed up on top of that old, abandoned gas station across the street and watched you and Molly and her mom go through the gate. Also Rigel's dad and Mr. Cormac and a few others we didn't recognize. We still don't know what it is you're all doing there, but it's obviously something you didn't want us to know about, or you and Molly wouldn't have lied to Deb about it."

M opens her mouth, then closes it, apparently stuck for an explanation.

Finally, she says, "What about Liam and Lucas? Their parents actually work at NuAgra, unlike the Stuarts or O'Garas. Aren't you worried about them, too? Or at least worried they'll have to break up with you, if you keep digging into company secrets they're not allowed to talk about?"

"Of course we're worried about them, too," Bri says. "We're in love with them, so how can we not be?"

"In love?" M repeats doubtfully. "I know you're always falling in love, Bri, but—"

"No!" Bri cuts in. "This is different. Way different. Now I finally know what love is. Liam is…like a part of me I didn't even know was missing."

I stare at Bri. "You, too? That's *exactly* how I feel with Lucas! He…he says he feels the same way about me." Then I turn back to M. "So yes, we really are in love and absolutely don't want to lose what we have with our guys. But Bri and I talked it over before coming here and decided it's a price we're willing to pay if it means keeping *you* safe, M."

Bri nods fiercely. "You and I have been friends forever, M, and as much as I love Liam, *you* matter even more to me."

"That's…" M pauses, her green eyes bright with the beginnings of tears. "That's really, really sweet of both of you. I appreciate that you care so much, I do, but I swear I'm not in any danger. At all. I *wish* I could convince you of that."

Bri and I exchange a glance.

"Why don't you try?" Bri suggests. "Tell us what they've told you."

"I'm not—" She breaks off, frowning.

"Not allowed to?" I guess. "By who? Mrs. O'Gara?"

"We, ah, saw how the guard at the NuAgra gate bowed to her last night," Bri says, "so we figured she must be their leader, or one of them. I know you like the O'Garas a lot, especially Molly, but…*bowing*? C'mon, M, that's exactly the kind of thing people in a cult would do."

Weirdly, for a second M almost looks like she's about to laugh, but she immediately gets serious again. "It's not a cult. Though…I guess I can see how it would look that way from the outside."

"Cult or not," I say, "they must be giving *something*—radiation or maybe some special serum—to their members to make them stronger. And faster. Maybe even better looking. I'm sure it feels great, but it can't possibly be safe. For any of you. That's why we're so worried."

M shakes her head. "No. They're not giving me drugs or radiating me or anything. I promise. Please don't worry."

"How can we not?" Bri practically shouts. "M, I've known you since we were both five years old, and you've absolutely changed over the past year and a half, starting when Rigel got here. For a long time, I just chalked it up to being in love, but that's not enough to explain everything else. He, or maybe his parents, have definitely been doing *something* to you, maybe without you even knowing. How else do you explain the withdrawal-type symptoms you got when the Stuarts went away Thanksgiving before last? Or how crappy you felt when you and Rigel broke up that first time? I know you're in love with him, but I also think you've developed some kind of…of dependency on whatever he or the others are giving you. *Please*. Let us help you!"

For several long seconds, M doesn't say anything. Her eyes go sort of unfocused, like she's thinking really hard. but then her eyes snap back to us and she nods.

"You're right," she says. "It's time."

32

Alley-oop

Bri

"THIS IS GOING TO TAKE A WHILE," M tells us. "Why don't we all have a cookie while I figure out where to start."

Deb and I share a startled look as we each take a chocolate chip cookie from the plate. Will she actually come right out and tell us the truth? Or are we about to hear some carefully rehearsed speech? I take a bite of one of Mrs. Truitt's excellent cookies and a sip of milk without taking my eyes off of M.

"Okay," she begins. "You're both right—sort of. There *is* something different about all the NuAgra people, but it's nothing to do with a cult, or unethical experiments, or racism or anything like that."

"So what is it?" Deb asks.

M looks back and forth between us, her expression suddenly really serious. "I'll tell you, but you have to swear to keep it *absolutely* secret, okay?"

When we both hesitate, she adds, "Once you know, I think you'll understand why."

"Only if you promise that no one—including you—is in *any* danger because of it. If so, I'm sorry, but no deal, M," I say apologetically. No way am I swearing myself to silence if people are getting hurt!

To my surprise, she grins. "Done. Absolutely no one is in danger because of this secret. Now can you promise to keep it?"

Deb and I exchange another look and silently come to an agreement.

"Okay." I turn my attention back to M. "As long as it's safe, we promise to keep it absolutely secret," I tell her, as curious now as I am worried. "So why *are* all the NuAgra people different?"

She takes a deep breath and says, "They're all—okay, you're totally not going to believe this part—they're all from Mars."

I gasp and cough, choking on my last bit of cookie and milk. "I'm sorry, *WHAT*?" I sputter as soon as I can get words out.

"They're from Mars," she repeats. "They came to Earth last summer. Most of them, anyway. A few were already here, like the O'Garas and the Stuarts—just like you guessed."

Setting down her half-eaten cookie, Deb leans forward. "Is this the cover story they told you to use if someone asks too many questions? So they'll decide you're just crazy and leave you alone? You have to know that won't work on us, M. We've known you too long."

M smiles. "I know it sounds crazy. I didn't believe it either when Rigel first told me. I was sure Trina put him up to it, to make fun of me. You know, because of my Martian Princess phase, back in grade school." She seems calm and *sounds* totally rational, but—

"Just…just stop." I put up a hand. "You can't seriously expect us to believe this? I mean, we *know* you, M. We know *you* can't be from Mars. We grew up together, right here in Jewel. And all the others…" I shake my head. "We know there's something weird going on, but c'mon. *Martians?* Like… there are so many problems with that. We have probes on Mars, so we know there's no way it can support life. And if they're really *aliens* who just got here a few months ago, then no way would they be able to fit in as well as they have."

"They're not aliens. They're human, and they speak English there," M says, still in that bizarrely reasonable tone. "Along with their native Nuathan, which evolved from ancient Gaelic. The original colonists came from what's now Ireland. Which, by the way," she says to Deb, "is why they're not more diverse. They never had a chance to be. But Martians have now been going back and forth to Earth for around five hundred years, so they've had time to become familiar with our language and culture and everything. They still have to take crash courses on how to fit in when they first get here, and I'm sure there are some gaps, but it mostly seems to be working."

I look at Deb and can see that her brain is working as furiously as mine. I'm sure she's thinking about all those little anomalies we've noticed, like Liam and Lucas telling us they'd never seen The Wizard of Oz, that they'd never tried onion rings. The look on Liam's face when we walked into the sleet outside the Lighthouse Cafe—not just surprised, but *shocked,* like he'd never seen or felt such a thing before. Is it possible…?

"No. There has to be another explanation," I insist. "How can people have been coming here from *Mars* for five hundred years without anyone knowing?"

"They're a lot more technologically advanced than we are," M explains. "Their ships are disguised to look like big space rocks and they're really careful about when and where they land, so they won't be noticed. Also, the ones who came here and decided to stay on Earth mostly lived in remote Martian-only communities, where they didn't have to worry so much about fitting in. But now a whole lot more are moving here, so they have to spread out more. It seems to be going pretty well so far, though of course there've been challenges."

By now, my head is spinning. M really, truly seems to believe everything she's saying, which means she must be even more thoroughly brainwashed than we feared.

"M," Deb says gently, "I'm sure Rigel or the O'Garas were very convincing when they told you all this, but it's not true. It can't be. The sooner you can accept that, the sooner you'll be able to—"

Abruptly, M stands up and opens her door. But instead of storming out like I expect, she says, "I can see it's going to take more to convince you." Then she calls down the stairs, "Aunt Theresa? Can you please come up here?"

I don't know what I expected, but it definitely wasn't this! When I look over at Deb, her eyebrows are as close to her hairline as mine must be.

Several seconds later, a puzzled-looking Mrs. Truitt steps into the room. "Do you girls need something else?"

"Yes," M tells her. "Bri and Deb have been noticing a lot of strange things, so I decided it's finally time to let them in on the, um, big secret. Not surprisingly, they're having a hard time believing me. Maybe it will help if you confirm it all for them."

Mrs. Truitt frowns. "Everything? About you and…and all the others?"

M nods. "I haven't had time to tell them much yet. Just that we're all originally from Mars."

Deb and I stare, boggled, as Mrs. Truitt turns to us. "I'm afraid it's all true, girls. It, ah, took me a while to accept it, too, after Marsha told me, but I've...seen enough now that I can't doubt it." Then, to M, "Perhaps you could show them what you showed your uncle? That was fairly convincing."

"Oh, good idea!" M says. "Thanks, Aunt Theresa."

With a last, uncertain smile at us, Mrs. Truitt goes back downstairs.

My mouth is hanging open. I don't know what to think. Mrs. Truitt—straitlaced, prim and proper *Aunt Theresa* just backed up this insane Martian story. Just how deep does this thing go?

Grinning now, M picks up her cellphone. "Honestly, I trust you guys a *whole* lot more than my Uncle Louie not to tell anyone about this. He actually— Well, never mind that. Here. Look."

She touches her phone, then holds it up to her face—I know some of the newer ones use facial recognition. Then a small, lit rectangle suddenly appears in midair.

"What's that?" Deb and I gasp together.

"A holo screen." M reaches out a finger and taps something on the hovering, translucent panel. "This phone is also an omni—a really cool piece of Martian tech that does all sorts of amazing things. I can demonstrate more stuff later but right now, I just want to show you this."

As she speaks, another picture forms in midair, this one stretching halfway across her room. Gaping, we stare at soaring buildings of pink stone or crystal, with futuristic-looking silvery trains zipping past them.

"This is a vid from Thiaraway, the capital city of Nuath, the colony on Mars," M explains. "That's where I actually spent most of last spring and summer, when everyone here thought I was in Ireland."

At first, my brain refuses to comprehend what I'm seeing. Slowly, I force it to work again...and almost start to believe her. If all this is true, it would explain so much. Except...

"But where do *you* come into all this?" I demand. "You can't be one of them. You grew up *here*, remember? In Jewel."

"I did," she agrees. "Mostly. But you know I'm an orphan, and that I never knew who my real parents were. Well...last year I found out they were from Mars. In fact, I was born there. I wasn't brought to Earth until I was about a year old."

This revelation sends me reeling. M, my oldest friend, my bestie, is a *Martian*? I just sit there opening and closing my mouth as a gazillion questions flit through my mind. The first one out of my mouth is, "How do the O'Garas fit into this? Is Mrs. O'Gara the Martian leader or something? The way that guard at the gate bowed to her—"

"Um, he wasn't bowing to her," M tells us with an apologetic little smile. "He was actually bowing…to me."

Deb and I both stare at her. "Huh?" we ask in unison.

"Er, yeah. Believe it or not, *I'm* their leader. Their Sovereign."

I gasp as something suddenly clicks into place. "So…back in second grade, when you pretended you were a Martian Princess—?"

M nods. "Turns out I wasn't pretending after all. I really, truly was a Princess, even if I didn't know it yet. My father was heir to the Martian throne. Except…there was a coup."

She goes on to explain how her parents escaped to Earth with her when she was a baby, then were killed here a year or so later. M herself somehow survived, but everyone on Mars believed she'd died, too. At least until Rigel's family discovered her alive in Jewel.

"That's the whole reason they moved here," she explains, "and why Rigel was so interested in me right from the start—not that he told me the truth right away. But just like you guys, I started noticing things, so I pestered him for answers." She chuckles. "Then, when he finally *did* tell me, I assumed Trina put him up to it, like I said. I don't think I completely believed him until his parents backed up his story, with a lot more details. Even after that, it took a *lot* of getting used to. I still don't feel like much of a leader half the time, though I think I'm getting better at it."

I blink at her for a long moment. It's getting harder and harder to doubt her story when so many details fit things I remember. "This…this is actually true isn't it?" I breathe in amazement.

M smiles gently at me. "It really, truly is."

I shake my head slowly, a stupid grin spreading on my face, and then suddenly I start to giggle, and before I know it I'm laughing uncontrollably. And then so are M and Deb—we're all laughing together until tears are streaming down our faces, all the tension of the past several weeks draining away in an outburst of hilarity.

"OMG, M!" I cry once I can speak again. "You're from *Mars!*" that sets us all off again, but we're able to get ourselves back under control more quickly this time.

"Okay, I have a million and one questions, but back to the O'Garas," I say with a little hiccuping giggle. I take a deep breath to recenter myself. "I assume they also acted friendly from the start because of the

Mars thing, but what was the deal with Sean? Things got super weird between you and Rigel after he got here."

"Oh, yeah. That." M crinkles her nose in a grimace. "It's kind of complicated, but according to Martian tradition, Sean was supposed to be my Consort. In other words, I was expected to basically get engaged to him. As you might imagine, Rigel wasn't real keen on that idea. Neither was I. So things were really awkward for a while, until it was all sorted out."

Deb frowns at her. "So when you and Sean were dating last spring—?"

"It was all for show, because of Martian politics. Rigel and I never *really* broke up, but we had to make it look that way. It sucked big time —especially for poor Rigel. Everything's all good now, though. And Sean's really happy with Kira."

"Oh, they're adorable," I agree. "So she's one of the ones who just came to Earth last summer?"

"Yep. Her and all the other NuAgra students. Oh, except Tristan. He really did move here from Denver, just like he said. He and Rigel were both born on Earth, to Martian parents. I think all the others were born on Mars, though, including Cormac. Er, Mr. Cormac. He's my official bodyguard, as well as Vice Principal."

"No way. *Mr. Cormac* is a Martian too??" I ask in disbelief. That brings up a bunch of other questions, and every answer seems to lead to three more. But M answers them all so calmly and rationally that it's impossible not to believe her. Then, after we've already been talking for two solid hours, she drops yet another bombshell—she and Molly O'Gara are sisters!

"We only found out a couple of months ago," she responds to our amazed exclamations.

"Ew, but doesn't that mean Sean's your brother? And you and he were still supposed to—?"

M laughs. "No, no. Molly's adopted, too. I thought you knew that? She's not actually related to the O'Garas at all. Everyone thought her real parents were farmers back on Mars who died, but...it's kind of a long story."

Deb glances at the clock on M's nightstand and suddenly jumps to her feet. "Can we hear that one later, M? We were supposed to meet Lucas and Liam at Dream Cream at four, and we're going to be late!"

"Oops!" I bounce off the bed, too, suddenly realizing I never texted Liam to confirm we'd be there. *Oh crap*!

"Uh, what should we say to them?" Deb asks M, her hand on the doorknob. "Can we let them know you told us the whole big secret? Or do you need to tell them first?"

M grins. "I'm sure they'd much rather hear it from you. I expect they'll be ecstatic. It's...pretty awful having to lie to people you care about. Believe me, I know. I'm *so* happy I won't have to do that anymore with you two—my oldest, best friends!"

I wait till we're outside to pull out my phone and fire off a quick message to Liam.

"I hope the guys are actually there," I say worriedly as we hustle to our bikes. "Yesterday, when Liam texted asking if we were still on for today, I said I'd let him know, but then I never did."

Mostly because I wasn't sure what my answer should be until we talked to M. Then talking to M ended up taking longer than planned and sweeping every other thought out of my head!

"Dad told me when he got home last night that Liam had a terrible game—and I'm sure it was at least partly my fault," I say guiltily, mounting my bike. "I still can't believe I yelled at him on Friday, right in the middle of the cafeteria!"

"You said you apologized later," Deb reminds me.

"I know. But—" I break off as my phone dings. "Oh, they are there! They're waiting for us. Let's hurry!"

I stuff my phone in my pocket and we take off at top speed.

"I feel like I'm going to wake up any minute and find out our whole time at M's was a dream," Deb comments as we turn from Garnet onto Opal.

"Same here," I admit. "Do you think we're crazy to believe everything she told us today? M's always had a *really* good imagination."

Deb doesn't answer until we're almost to Diamond Street. "It all definitely *seems* crazy. But Mrs. Truitt backed up everything M told us, and those holo-videos she showed us with her phone-thing were awfully convincing. And if it's true, it explains pretty much every weird thing we've noticed since Rigel got here."

"Yeah. I honestly can't think of any other explanation that would make *more* sense, given all the weirdness. And there's no way she could have possibly made all of that up on the spot. She didn't even know we were going to show up today." Reassured, my spirits bubble up. "I can't wait to see the boys' expressions when they find out we're finally in on the huge secret they haven't been able to tell us. We knew it was more than agricultural research, but holy cow! Think how hard that must have been for them, especially when we kept pestering. Poor guys."

"Yeah." Deb grins over at me. "Now I understand why Lucas thought it was safer to let us believe they're racists than to find out they're really aliens from Mars!"

I laugh. "My mom has a book called *Men Are From Mars, Women Are From Venus*…But our boyfriends really *are* from Mars!"

Deb laughs, too, and we both speed up, more eager than ever to see our guys.

33

Celestial mechanics

Lucas

"THEY'RE LATE." Liam glances at the door of Dream Cream for like the tenth time. "Assuming they're coming at all. Bri never did—" His phone chimes in his pocket and he frantically digs it out. "They *are* coming! But..." Frowning, he hands me his phone.

Bri's text reads, *On our way! Don't leave! We need to talk!*

I hand back his phone, a cold lump forming in the pit of my stomach. "She didn't add a smiley face this time," I point out.

Liam looks again at the text. "Yeah. I noticed. Crap. That can't be good."

Taking a deep breath that doesn't actually calm me at all, I nod. "Remember, we agreed last night that we'll abide by whatever decision the girls make. Keeping secrets from them is hard, but *knowing* we're keeping secrets has to be even harder for them."

"Are you sure we can't just—?" Liam starts to ask, his face screwed up in a pained grimace.

"No. Come on. We've been over this. I'd rather risk Deb breaking up with me than never see her again at all. Which could totally happen if we cave and tell them the truth."

Liam huffs out a frustrated breath. "You make it sound like a choice between— Wait! They're here!"

I turn, my heart suddenly pounding, as Deb and Bri come through the door. Liam and I are sitting near the front of the little ice cream shop, so the girls spot us instantly. Deb gives me a tentative smile, and a huge chunk of the stress I've been feeling melts away. Surely that's a good sign?

"Hi, guys!" Bri's smiling, too, but she also looks a little anxious. Uh-oh. "Sorry we're late," she continues. "We have something important to tell you, but—" She glances at a family seated nearby, whose three small children are making a lot of noise.

"How about we go to a quieter table?" Deb suggests. I can tell she's struggling with some strong emotion. Double uh-oh.

Without even letting us answer, the girls head for a booth in the very back corner of the shop. Liam and I scramble to our feet and follow them, exchanging fearful looks behind their backs.

Bri plops down on the bench facing the outer door and scoots in to make room for Liam. Deb does the same across from her. My hopes rise again. Until Bri speaks.

"This is better. What we plan to talk about definitely requires some privacy."

"Wait!" Liam pauses in the act of sitting down, clearly distressed. "First we have something we need to say to you."

I nod, my eyes locking on Deb's as I slowly take my place next to her. "We know it's been hard for you both to accept that we have to keep so many secrets from you. To you, it probably seems like we don't trust you, but I swear that's not it!"

"It's not," Liam agrees, sitting the rest of the way down. Taking both of Bri's hands in his, he stares into her face, his expression anguished. "I trust you with my life, Bri. If it was only my secret, I'd tell you in a heartbeat, I promise."

Snagging Deb's hand, too, I tug her closer to me. "We both would. There's no one in this world I trust more than you, Deb. No one. But the things we're not allowed to talk about, well, they involve a whole lot of people besides just us and our family. More people even than the NuAgra workers here in Jewel. There's a *really* good reason we're not allowed to tell anyone. I...we hope you'll trust us enough to believe that. It doesn't mean we don't care about you. Because we do. I do."

I say it like a vow, gazing into Deb's beautiful blue eyes, pleading for her to understand. To my surprise, the corners of her mouth twitch up in a tiny smile.

"We do believe you." She looks back at me unflinchingly, as though daring me to doubt her sincerity. "You'll know why when you hear what we have to tell you."

"Yes!" Bri exclaims. "You don't have to worry about keeping secrets from us anymore!"

Startled, I frown at Deb. "What…what does she mean? Why not?"

"Because we both know the whole truth." Deb's openly smiling at me now. "Everything you weren't allowed to tell us."

I gape at her, sure I've misunderstood.

"Wait! What?" Liam sounds as confused as I am. "What exactly do you know?"

"Everything," Bri cheerfully repeats. "About…" She looks conspiratorially around the shop and drops her voice to a whisper. "About Mars and all."

Liam and I stare at the girls, absolutely dumbstruck. For a long moment, I can't get my brain to engage—fear and hope are waging a fierce battle inside me. Finally, I manage just one word.

"How?" It comes out in a strangled whisper.

"M told us." Deb's sweet smile makes my frozen insides start to thaw. "Just this afternoon, before we came here. We went to her house and started laying out all the strange things we've been noticing—mostly about her, not you guys—and…she explained everything. It was a *lot* to take in, but she eventually managed to convince us it's all true. I'm sorry we gave you both such a hard time last week about keeping secrets. Now we totally get why you had to."

A relief I'm still half afraid to feel seeps through me.

"M told you? Everything?" I hear Liam asking dazedly.

"Everything she could squeeze into two hours," Bri confirms. "She promised to tell us more later, when we have more time. That's why we were late—we kept asking her more questions."

I look questioningly at Deb and she nods. "What Bri said. At first, we tried really hard to poke holes in M's story. We thought she'd been brainwashed, maybe even drugged, by the Stuarts or the O'Garas or someone else at NuAgra. All the clues pointed to it being a cult, or something even worse. That's why we went to talk to her—to convince her to break free from whatever she'd been sucked into. Instead, she ended up convincing us."

"Wow," I breathe. Gazing into Deb's incredibly, purely honest eyes, the last of my fear gives way to relief, then joy. I lean in and Deb eagerly meets my kiss, our mutual joy seeming to mingle through our lips. Not till I straighten do I notice Bri and Liam are kissing, too.

"This is awesome!" Liam exclaims after a moment, grinning widely. "C'mon, let's all get some hot chocolate, then you girls can tell us the whole story."

The four of us troop to the front counter to order our hot chocolates, then take them back to our booth in the corner where we can talk without being overheard. Fortunately, this late in the afternoon on a wintery Sunday, the ice cream shop is deserted except for the noisy family near the front.

Though I'm cautiously happy, I still can't quite make myself believe that Deb knows. Knows that I came to Earth from Mars, knows that M is our Sovereign, knows…everything. The idea that I can now be totally honest with her is both incredibly freeing and slightly terrifying.

"It's so cool to think you two grew up on a whole different planet," Bri whispers excitedly as we sit back down. "What was it like? M showed us a few videos, but didn't give us a lot of details. There wasn't time. It must have been really different?"

Liam throws an arm around her shoulders and pulls her closer to him. "Different, yeah, but definitely not better. Not in my opinion, anyway." He shoots a glance my way.

I respond with a chuckle. "Earth has definitely grown on me." Deb and I are already sitting close enough that her hip and thigh press lightly against mine, a wonderful feeling. "There are a few things I miss, sure, but what I've found here more than makes up for them." I smile at her to make my meaning clear.

She smiles back. "I'm glad to hear it. But I also want to know what it was like there. M says the whole…colony?…is underground, but the vids she showed us didn't look like that."

"It doesn't feel like that, either," I assure her. "The, um, roof is a mile up and disguised by holos that look just like regular sky. Earth sky."

"Except it never rains or snows, of course," Liam chimes in. "Weather has probably been the hardest thing to get used to here, at least for me. I love everything else." He leans over and gives Bri a quick kiss.

Deb startles me with a chuckle. "Now it makes sense you didn't know what 'break the ice' meant. I guess you never had ice back in… Nuath? I think that's what M called it."

I nod. "Right on both counts. That's what it's called, and no, it never gets cold enough to freeze anything, not naturally. We don't even put ice in drinks, water is so strictly rationed there."

"Wow, I hadn't thought about that part," Deb admits. "But I suppose it would have to be. I guess there aren't any lakes or rivers or anything?"

Liam and I both shake our heads.

"No water baths or showers, either," Liam says. When Bri wrinkles her nose, he quickly adds, "We took ionic showers, instead. A whole lot faster and they get you way cleaner, too. That *is* one of the few things I miss about Nuath."

"Ionic...?" Bri echoes, shaking her head. "Wow, I guess there's still a ton we don't know."

Liam grins. "Yeah, it'll take forever to explain it all, but I don't mind scheduling plenty of time together for that."

"Not just anywhere, though," I caution. "I'm sure M impressed on you both how important it is to keep the truth about us totally secret?"

Both girls nod.

"She said it could be dangerous if too many people found out too quickly," Deb says, "but she didn't get a chance to tell us exactly why. She was too busy answering all our other questions."

"It could definitely be dangerous," I confirm. "Really dangerous. Already, a few *Duchas*—sorry, that's our term for regular Earth humans —have tried to break into NuAgra to spy on it because they think we might be aliens. One even kidnapped M a few days after we got here to try to prove it. She was lucky to get away."

Bri stares at me. "Whoa, she didn't tell us *that*. We won't tell anyone, we swear. And we'll be really careful about where we talk about it between ourselves."

"*Really* careful," Deb reiterates. "We absolutely don't want to risk anything happening to you. To any of you."

The concern in her eyes makes me lean over to kiss her again. "Mmm," I murmur. "You taste like chocolate and whipped cream —delicious."

That makes her blush, though she's also smiling. "Okay, now that we've established how super secret we need to keep all this, tell us more. What made your family decide to come to Earth, and to Jewel? What did it feel like to leave everything you knew? Where did you land and where did you live before you came to Jewel?"

"And how much of what you've told us about yourselves is true and what isn't?" Bri adds. "What was your spaceship like? And did you really only get here last summer?"

Liam and I both chuckle at the torrent of whispered questions, then do our best to answer them, though the girls keep coming up with more. Before we know it, it's a quarter past five and getting dark.

"We should probably head out soon," I say regretfully. "Mom made us promise we'd be home by six, and you girls are on your bikes, right?"

They nod and we all reluctantly get to our feet.

"Can I maybe call you later?" I ask Deb as we take our empty cups back to the counter.

"Of course! But…" She drops her voice to a whisper. "Will it be safe to talk about this sort of thing on the phone?"

I hadn't thought about that. "Actually, I'm not sure," I reply as we all go back outside. "Maybe you should ask M? She's basically the final word on everything to do with us, so if she says it's okay, then it is."

The girls exchange a startled glance.

"It's still so weird to think of M that way," Bri says, shaking her head. "I mean, I've known her since we were five years old and she was always so…*normal*. Like me. Worse than normal, since we were both total losers most of our time growing up."

Liam's brows go up. "A loser? You? No way!"

Bri laughs. "Thanks, but…yeah. All three of us were, weren't we, Deb?"

"She's right. Until Rigel got here and he and M started dating, we were probably the three least popular girls in school."

"True," Bri agrees. "Our only real friends were each other. Maybe it's just as well you didn't meet me back then," she adds to Liam. "No way you'd have asked me to the formal."

As he protests that, I draw Deb aside. "I'm so glad I don't have to keep secrets from you anymore," I tell her softly. "It was killing me that I couldn't be completely honest with you. I wanted to, so much."

"I know." She puts a hand against my cheek and the tingle I've sometimes thought I get from her touch is now unmistakable. "It had to be way harder for you than it was for me. And bizarre as the truth is, it's a whole lot better than most of the things I imagined when I was trying to figure it out on my own."

"So you're not…freaked out that you've been dating an alien?"

She laughs, a delicious sound. "You're not an alien! M was really clear that you're all human, just…more evolved than the rest of us. Are

you sure *you* don't mind dating a primitive—what was the word?
—*Duchas*?"

"Mind?" I lower my lips to hers. "I'm happier than I've ever been in my life."

A few flakes of snow start to drift down as Liam and I walk the girls to their bikes. We snag a few last kisses along the way, before going back to our car to head home.

"What do you think?" Liam asks as I pull away from the curb. "Should we tell Mom and Dad the girls know?"

I frown. "I guarantee Mom won't like it."

My brother snorts. "Maybe not, but what can she say? It was the Sovereign herself who told them, so she can't very well be mad at *us* about it."

He's right…technically. "I guess we'd better tell them before they find out from anyone else. Considering how upset Mom was about—"

"That gossip Alan spread at NuAgra? Yeah," Liam agrees. "You're right. We'd better."

✦

"You're later than you said you'd be," Mom greets us when we come in through the garage door to the kitchen. "You didn't go anywhere other than Dream Cream, did you?"

Liam rolls his eyes. "No, Mom, geez. We were totally in public the whole time. Besides, we're not late. We said we'd be home by six and it's barely a quarter till."

She glances at the clock on the stove. "Very well. I did agree you can occasionally go out with *Duchas* girls, but I can't help worrying you'll become so comfortable with them that you'll forget to be discreet."

We'd planned to wait till after dinner to share our big news, but at that, Liam can't restrain himself.

"You don't have to worry about that anymore, Mom, because Bri already knows all about us. Deb, too."

"What?" Dad slams the refrigerator, a head of lettuce in his hand. "What do you mean, they know?"

I exchange a glance with my brother, then shrug. "Just what Liam said. As of this afternoon, Deb and Bri are both completely in on our big secret. And no, we didn't tell them," I add as Mom sucks in an outraged breath. "The Sovereign did."

That stops them both. For a long moment our parents just look from us to each other and back, before Mom finally finds her voice again.

"But...but why? Why would she do such a thing?"

"They're her oldest friends," I point out. "I imagine she was even more tired of lying to them than we were. Also, they'd apparently noticed a lot of, er, anomalies—about her, I mean, not us, so much. So she finally decided it was safer to tell them the truth than let them make up theories about what's going on."

Mom presses her lips together, frowning, then sighs. "Well. I suppose it's out of our hands, then, though I can't help worrying that the Sovereign is—"

"Eilis," Dad interrupts warningly. "You know how I feel about your criticizing Sovereign Emileia after all she's done for our people. It sounds as though she chose the better of two difficult paths. In any event, it was her decision to make. And now you needn't worry that one of our boys will inadvertently let something slip to their girlfriends."

She flinches slightly at that word, but nods. "I suppose you're right. I just hope nothing...bad will come of it."

"The Sovereign has said all along that eventually, we'll have to let the *Duchas* know about our people," he reminds her. "She no doubt considers these longtime friends of hers among the most trustworthy to begin that process."

"They are! They're totally trustworthy," Liam interjects. "Aren't they, Lucas?"

I nod vigorously. "Definitely. Probably more than a lot of our people are. Please don't worry, Mom. They understand how important it is not to let the truth about us go any further. The Sovereign swore them both to secrecy before she told them."

Both of our parents relax noticeably, though Mom still wears a slight frown. Liam and I offer to help with dinner then, giving us all a chance to talk about something else for a while.

Not until we're carrying our dishes back to the kitchen after dessert does Mom bring up the subject again.

"I do hope you're right that these girls can be trusted with such potentially dangerous knowledge," she says, opening the sterilizer cabinet. "They're still quite young. You all are. Too young, perhaps, to realize how...fallible people can be. Even some *Echtrans*. I'm sure that's even more true of *Duchas*. I only pray we won't all come to regret the Sovereign's decision."

____

34

Elementary

____

Deb

THE SECOND we get back to our houses, before we even put our bikes away, Bri texts M to ask if we can use our phones to talk about what we learned today, with the guys or each other. She responds quickly, but asks us to hold off until she can check with Rigel's dad, since he's apparently their top security expert.

"Bummer," Bri says. "Come over after dinner, then, okay? So we can talk more."

I do, of course, but another hour-plus of discussing our mind-boggling new perspective doesn't come close to exhausting the subject. We pick it back up—discreetly—on the bus the next morning.

"Do you think M will tell all the other NuAgra kids that we know?" Bri quietly wonders as we sit in the back with our heads together. "It might make things a little less awkward."

"Or more awkward," I whisper. "What if they're weirded out to hear we're in on their secret?"

That question is partially answered when our bus pulls up to the school. Lucas and Liam are at the curb as usual, but just behind them are all the other Martians who sit at our lunch table—M, Rigel, Molly, Tristan, Sean, and Kira. As soon as we're off the bus, M motions us off to the side, away from the other students heading into the school.

"Don't be mad, but I went ahead and told these guys that I let you in on the whole shebang yesterday," she tells us in a low voice. "Rigel suggested we all have a quick confab before the bell."

He nods. "We might be able to talk more at lunch but we can't count on it, since someone who doesn't know could sit at our table. My biggest concern," he tells us, looking really serious, "is to keep M safe. As Sovereign, if the truth gets out too quickly, she'll be the one most at risk."

"Why?" I ask. "No one at school is likely to guess that, are they? We didn't, and we know her better than anyone who's not...you know."

"True." M smiles at us. "That's why I decided it was safe to bring you in on everything. But there are others who can't be trusted, who might have heard rumors about me. Like Ginny Farmer."

Bri frowns. "Bryce's little sister? That Trina wannabe on the JV cheer-leading squad?"

"Yes, her. I didn't go into details yesterday, but back in September, their dad kidnapped me after overhearing something my Uncle Louie said. Mr. Farmer was already into alien conspiracies, so he jumped to the conclusion that there was a big alien plot to invade Jewel, and I was the one leading it. He was obviously wrong about the invasion part, but he did get the leader part right."

I look at Lucas. "That's the kidnapping you mentioned yesterday?"

He nods.

"Rigel's mom used something to make Mr. Farmer mostly forget everything," M tells us, "but it was apparently only temporary. We don't know exactly how much he remembers now, or what he's told his kids."

"Enough that Ginny keeps giving poor Adina and Jana a hard time about being NuAgra kids," Molly says. "I've heard her ragging on them in cheerleading practice."

The warning bell makes us all jump.

"I've noticed Adina and Jana try to avoid Ginny in Chorus," Bri comments as we hurry toward the school building. "We will, too. Should we tell Adina and Jana we know?"

"Definitely not during class," Rigel says. "For now, it's probably safest if you pretend you *don't* know, at least at school. Then you'll be less likely to say something that could be overheard."

In the atrium we all split up, though not before I get a quick, delicious kiss from Lucas.

"See you at lunch," he murmurs. "With any luck, we can talk more then."

Luck is with us—though with all ten of us sitting at one table, there's not much room for anyone else. I'm glad, since Bri and I have already thought of a bunch more questions.

"Tell us more about that kidnapping," Bri says to M, the moment we sit down. "I always knew Mr. Farmer was kind of a nut case—and a drunk. But not that he was an alien conspiracy theorist."

"He believes in a lot of conspiracies," Rigel tells us. "That's just one of them."

M nods. "And my uncle made it worse, though not on purpose. I meant it yesterday, when I said I trust you two more than I do him. He was so excited after I told him the truth, he couldn't keep his mouth shut. Fortunately, no one but Mr. Farmer believed him."

She quickly tells us how Mr. Farmer tricked her aunt into bringing M out to his deer ranch, where he locked them both in a meat cooler to keep M from going to that night's football game.

"Bryce had told him Rigel always plays worse when I'm not around, which is mostly true. So Mr. Farmer decided if Rigel had a bad game without me there, it would somehow prove we were both aliens. Luckily, I managed to get word to Rigel, so he played the best he ever had."

"Wait, was that the next game after Homecoming?" Bri asks excitedly. M nods. "So *that's* why Rigel played like a top NFL quarterback that night!" Bri shakes her head wonderingly. "I wondered why you never did that again."

Rigel smiles ruefully. "Yeah, I didn't dare. Some of our, uh, people were pretty upset about me being so conspicuous. That's seriously frowned on."

I look over at Liam. "Is that why your parents—and Lucas—acted upset when you played basketball so well, that first game over break?"

"You get why now, don't you?" Lucas says before Liam can reply. "The Council has threatened to ban *all* our athletes from playing sports if they start attracting too much attention."

"The Council?" I echo.

"The *Echtran* Council," M clarifies in a low voice. "Our top governing body here on Earth—along with me, of course. Mrs. O'Gara is on it. Also Rigel's dad and Tristan's mom. I don't always agree with them, but I try not to oppose them unless it's necessary."

Bri looks at Liam and Sean, then Rigel. "So...none of you are allowed to play your best, even to win games?"

"Nope," Rigel says. "They don't really like us winning all the time, either."

"True," Sean confirms. "They're the reason Rigel had to lose that last football playoff game. If he hadn't, the Council would have yanked us all off the basketball team. Which they might anyway, unless we can bring ourselves to lose a game or two." He glances at Liam, who grimaces.

On the way to class after lunch, Bri looks disgruntled, too.

"What's wrong?" I ask her.

"It's just... It doesn't seem fair that all our best athletes have to pretend to be *worse* than they actually are."

I chuckle quietly. "You say that, but even with them all holding back, you and I still made the connection between them and NuAgra and started drawing conclusions. I imagine a lot more people would get suspicious if they played even better."

She nods glumly. "I suppose. It's just...I was really looking forward to our basketball team going to State again this year."

Now I laugh out loud. "Honestly, Bri, could you *be* any more obsessed with sports? Isn't it enough that the Jewel Jaguars have the best football *and* basketball teams they've ever had in the whole history of the school?"

That gets a smile from her. "You're right, I shouldn't complain. Especially since everything's turned out *so* much better than we ever expected!"

"Exactly!" I agree. "I think we must be two of the luckiest girls on the whole planet!"

+
+ +

We're just setting down our trays at lunch the next day when M suggests Bri and I swing by the original "NuAgra table" with her.

"Rigel and I talked it over and decided I should tell them all that you know about us now," she explains. "If any of them are going to freak out, better they do it when I'm there to talk them down than risk them finding out some other way, who knows where. This way, we avoid possible future awkwardness."

Bri and I both shrug and agree, but glance nervously at each other as we follow M across the cafeteria. Maybe M's right that this will avoid *future* awkwardness, but it's bound to be pretty darned awkward right now! Lucas and Liam, clearly sensing our anxiety, come along.

For their first week or two here, all eight of the new NuAgra kids sat together at this one table. Now, only five do—senior Alan, sophomores Erin and Grady, and freshmen Adina and Jana. That leaves half the table empty, but almost no non-Martians ever sit there.

"Good thing Trina's stopped sitting here," M murmurs as we get close. "Otherwise, this wouldn't work at all, obviously."

"Yeah, I think Alan finally froze her out," Liam says with a chuckle. "Bet the others are relieved."

All five look up as we approach, their expressions more curious than concerned. Until M starts talking.

"Hey, guys," she says so softly I can barely hear her, though I guess all the Martians can, with that extra-sensitive hearing Lucas told me about. "You've met my good friends Bri and Deb, haven't you?"

They all nod, now looking slightly wary.

"Well, I thought you should all know that this past weekend, I decided it was finally time to clue them in on who we all really are. I wanted to tell you upfront myself, so you won't worry if you hear it from someone else later."

Already, Alan's frowning. "Someone else? Who else knows?"

"No other *Duchas*," M quickly assures him. "Not at school. The only other ones in Jewel who know are my adopted aunt and uncle. I mean other *Echtrans*, maybe out at NuAgra. You told your parents, right?" she asks Liam and Lucas, who both nod.

"But why—?" Alan begins, still frowning.

M cuts him off. "Because they're my two oldest friends and I know I can trust them. Completely." There's a note of authority in her voice that I've never heard before.

Alan turns slightly pink and shuts up, but I notice three of the younger kids still look worried. Jana mostly looks irritated.

"You mean we still have to be totally careful around everyone else?" she asks. "We can't tell *our* closest *Duchas* friends?"

"No," M replies, rather sharply. "No one else. Definitely not yet. If you think someone's getting too suspicious, asking too many questions, tell *me*, okay? For now, nothing else changes. Not all *Duchas* can be trusted—as we well know."

Alan gives a sour chuckle. "Guess you won't be telling Trina anytime soon, then?"

"Definitely not." M rolls her eyes. "I don't even want to think how she'd use *that* against me—like she does everything. I'd say she's about the *last* person we can trust with this information."

The others all murmur their agreement. Smirking, Alan nods, too.

"Anyway, that's pretty much it," M says. "It obviously doesn't mean you can talk to them about—you know—where anyone else might hear, but at least you don't have to worry about letting anything slip around them. They both know exactly how secret this needs to stay for now, so no worries there, either. 'Kay? Just wanted you to know."

"Okay, that *was* pretty awkward," Bri tells M as we head back to our table. "But I guess you're right that it was better to get it over with right away."

I agree, but the way they reacted prompts me to ask Lucas how his parents took the news.

"They were a little startled, of course," he replies with a tiny frown. "But once we explained it was M who told you, they were okay with it. Especially Dad. It helps that M's been saying for a while now—in her column and broadcasts and stuff—that eventually we'll have to let all the *Duchas* know. Though maybe not for years. Or decades."

That makes sense, though I imagine some of us might not be ready to hear it even then. "Wait. Did you say broadcasts? And a column?"

He nods. "Yeah, there's a brand new *Echtran* network that airs a daily news show. M and Molly do a half-hour segment on it once a week. And M's been doing a column for the weekly *Echtran Enquirer* for a couple of months now. Mostly about where she stands on various issues, her plans for the future, that kind of thing."

"Huh. Wow." I look over at M, boggled all over again by the secret life she's been leading. It's mind-blowing to think she's been doing all this stuff while still going to school like a regular sixteen-year-old. I feel a surge of sympathy for the amount of stress she must have been—must still be—dealing with.

On Lucas's other side, I hear Bri and Liam also talking about how Mr. and Mrs. Walsh feel about us knowing their secret.

"Mom'll come around," Liam is cheerfully assuring her. "Dad's been working on her. I'm more worried Alan will stir up trouble—again." He glares over at the other table. "It would be just like him."

"What kind of trouble?" Bri asks. She sounds scared now.

Rigel, overhearing, answers before Liam can. "Not all of our people are on the same page when it comes to how we should be integrating into Earth society."

"Among other things," Tristan adds, with a grimace I don't understand. "I don't think either of you needs to worry, though. So far, the only real threats have been to M and Molly."

"And to Rigel, don't forget," M says. Then, to us, "Remember I told you on Sunday that Rigel and me being together goes against long-standing *Echtran* traditions? Some of our people have issues with that. A few have actually tried to *do* something about it, but don't worry. They're in custody now."

Even so, concern lingers in her eyes—yet another source of stress she has to deal with.

⁺⋅⁺

"Poor M," I whisper to Bri on our way to fifth period. "I'm only just starting to realize how hard this past year must have been for her, keeping up with all her school stuff on top of all the responsibilities she has now. Not to mention worrying about crazy, disgruntled people on both sides—theirs and ours, I mean—possibly plotting attacks."

Bri nods, looking thoughtful. "Yeah, it's amazing she hasn't cracked under the pressure. Remember what Liam and Lucas told us she and Rigel did back in September to keep those *real* aliens from messing up our whole planet...on Homecoming night? No wonder M didn't seem totally invested in getting elected Junior Homecoming Princess!"

At that reminder, I have to laugh. "Yeah, here we were getting our feelings hurt because she didn't seem to properly appreciate all the work we did campaigning for her. And all the while, she was worried about saving the Earth from annihilation!" I shake my head disbelievingly.

Bri laughs, too. "And we had absolutely no idea. I guess being a Princess—or Sovereign—isn't necessarily as wonderful a gig as you'd think."

35

Binding energy

Lucas

"CAN we meet in the media center again after school today?" I ask Deb in Art class. "After our first session last week, we talked about making it a standing Tuesday/Thursday thing, but then—"

"But then I begged off on Thursday." She smiles self-consciously. "Because of Chorus. Or mostly because of Chorus."

And also because she and Bri were convinced by then that everyone associated with NuAgra was involved in some nefarious plot.

"Yeah," I agree. "So I didn't want to take anything for granted."

"Good. You shouldn't." Now her smile is teasing. It makes me want to kiss her—not that I dare right here in class. "But yes, I'll be there today."

Like last week, I go straight to the media center after sixth period and snag the same table, off in the corner. I'm guessing this time we'll spend even less time on art and a lot more time talking. The more privacy, the better.

A couple minutes after the final bell, some organized group shows up, but fortunately they gather on the opposite side of the big room for their meeting or whatever. They're already making a fair bit of noise when Deb joins me.

"Oh, I didn't know the Euchre Club was meeting here today," she says, glancing over at them. "Should we go somewhere else?"

I shrug. "This is probably as good a place as any if we want to talk about, y'know, stuff. They're providing us plenty of cover."

"True. Though maybe we should at least *pretend* this is an art lesson?" Sitting down next to me, she sets out drawing materials, then shoots me a sly smile.

I take advantage of the librarian's attempt to quiet the card players to steal that kiss I denied myself earlier, though it has to be a quick one. "I'm guessing you've thought of more questions?"

She nods. "Lots. Of course. For example, I'm dying to hear more about where you grew up. But first, can you tell me exactly what it was M and Rigel did back in September to save the planet? You and Liam mentioned it on Sunday but didn't really give us any details."

"Oh, I guess we didn't, we were trying to answer so many questions at once. I'm not sure they ever told us the entire story, but here's what I know…

"We'd just finished up our Orientation in Dun Cloch, Montana and were nearly to Jewel when our bus driver was told to stop in Chicago and check us all into a hotel until further notice. None of us had any idea what was going on until the next day, when there was an announcement from the Sovereign—M. According to her, aliens—the same non-human aliens that created Nuath thousands of years ago and hadn't been seen since—were in orbit around Earth. She said they were planning to release a massive electromagnetic pulse that would disrupt all the power grids and electronics on the planet. It would have been…really, really bad. But she and Rigel managed to stop them by— I don't know how much she's told you about their bond?"

"She said they can read each other's thoughts, which is pretty freaky. And that they…enhance each other, make each other stronger and faster and I don't know what all else."

I hesitate for a moment, then decide M shouldn't mind me filling Deb in. She probably plans to do it herself anyway, when she has time.

"Right. Well, they can also apparently generate an impressive amount of electricity together, though I don't know exactly how much. Rigel told me they used it to boost a positron beam that somehow turned the aliens' EMP back on itself. Maybe you saw the light show that produced?"

Deb gasps. "Yes! The paper said it was from an intense solar storm, an extra-strong Aurora Borealis. *M and Rigel* did that?"

"Yep. After we got here, I pestered them both for more details, since the official reports were kind of vague. One bit most people don't know is that our Scientists didn't expect M or Rigel to survive the attempt, even if they succeeded. They obviously did, though. Fortunately."

"Wow," Deb breathes, then shakes her head. "Now I feel even more guilty about the way Bri and I nagged M to take her Junior Princess campaign more seriously, when the whole time she was expecting to *die* on Homecoming night!"

She looks so distressed, I put an arm around her. "Don't feel bad. You didn't know, and she couldn't tell you," I remind her. "I'm sure she never blamed you. At all."

"Thanks." She manages a small smile. "I guess you're right." Pulling herself together, she takes a deep breath. "So… Tell me about growing up on Mars. What was your school like?"

I spend the next hour sharing details about Monaru, the industrial center and largest city in Nuath, and the school Liam and I attended there.

"It must have been hard to leave all your friends, huh?" she asks sympathetically.

"A little," I admit. "But M was right that a whole lot of us will need to relocate to Earth, and soon. It's the only way to make Nuath's power last longer. Even so, unless something changes, it's expected to run out in just a little more than fifty years."

Deb's eyes get wide. "M told us that was why you all came here, but not how urgent it was. Earth's energy crisis is nothing compared to yours! Oh, is that what your project is about, the one you were working on over winter break?"

"You're quick." I grin at her. "Yes, I'm hoping to find a way to reduce the power our gravity-antigravity generators use—which is a lot. And… I think I'm making progress."

I've barely started describing my project to her when the late bell rings and we have to gather up our untouched art supplies.

"I can't claim I'll understand much," Deb says as we leave the media center, "but I'd love to hear more about your project. As much as you're willing to tell, anyway."

"The trick will be getting me to shut up, once I start talking about it," I tell her with a grin.

She slants a teasing glance up at me. "You? But you're the quiet one!"

Laughing, I put my arm around her waist and pull her closer. "It's always the quiet ones you have to watch out for," I reply with a wink.

That gets a giggle out of her, so of course I have to kiss her again.

⁘

Once outside, I spot Liam and Bri a short distance from the two late buses. Kissing, of course. Not that I'm one to criticize these days. When they see Deb and me approaching, they break apart with obvious reluctance.

"Hi, guys," Bri greets us, looking only the slightest bit self-conscious. "I went to watch Liam's basketball practice. It's funny how noticeable it is that he, Sean and Alan are all holding back, now that I know they have to. It'll make watching tomorrow night's game even more interesting." She shoots a flirty glance at Liam.

He smiles back. "And now I won't feel like I'm letting you down when I don't play full out, since you'll know why. Man, it's *great* not having to keep secrets anymore!"

"I agree, but we still have to be careful around everyone but Bri and Deb," I remind him. "We can't let this new freedom make us careless."

Liam shakes his head. "You always have to be the sober voice of reason, don't you? I *do* know that. Duh. If—" He breaks off when one of the bus drivers honks the horn. "Guess we'd better go."

It's a bummer that even though Jewel High only has two activity buses, Liam and I are on a different one from the girls. Deb and I at least manage one last, excellent kiss before parting.

"See you tomorrow," I murmur as I let her go.

"Can't wait." She smiles up at me, the affection in her blue eyes warming me straight through.

I really have to hurry, then. Liam and I are the very last to board our bus, barely a second before it pulls away. We brace ourselves on the other seats as we make our way to an empty one near the back.

"Life is pretty good these days, isn't it?" Liam comments as we sit down.

"Better than I ever thought it could be," I admit.

He cocks an eyebrow at me. "So, no regrets now about moving here?"

I'm in a good enough mood after my time with Deb this afternoon that I don't mind giving my brother his "I told you so" moment.

"Not a one," I tell him, answering his grin with one of my own.

After dinner, Mom sets out a rhubarb pie she made for dessert. "At work today, I discovered I'm not the only one who feels it could be dangerous for teenaged *Duchas* to know about us," she says almost offhandedly. Her studied nonchalance tells me she's been holding that in ever since getting home from NuAgra.

"Who have you been talking to?" Liam demands before I can.

She frowns at his tone. "A friend or two at NuAgra. Why?"

He frowns back. "Well, M only today decided to tell the other *Echtran* students at school that Bri and Deb know, so you probably should have cleared it with her before telling anyone else."

Mom blinks, then gives a little shrug. "I don't see why it should matter. It's obviously far riskier for those girls to know our secret, than for any of *our* people to know that they know."

"Deb and Bri don't pose any risk," I protest. "They won't tell anyone. They've promised both M and us." At lunch, I wondered if Alan might try to stir up trouble again by spreading that news around at NuAgra, but I didn't expect our mother would.

"Yes, yes, so you said before," Mom replies with a sniff. "Still, promise or not, they are young enough that they might easily speak without thinking, only to regret it later. It's one thing for the Sovereign to tell her *Duchas* guardians, who are adults. But teenagers..." She trails off, shaking her head.

"It's no riskier for them to know than for *us* to know," Liam tells her. "We're teenagers, too, in case you hadn't noticed."

She raises a brow at him. "Of course I have. But you, at least, went through Orientation and know, or should, how very vital it is to maintain secrecy at present. Though based on how often we've had to speak to you about overdoing things when you play basketball, I don't know how well the message sank in. Teenaged *Duchas*, on the other hand—"

"You make it sound like they're just random teens that M decided to tell," I interrupt. "She's known Bri and Deb most of her life, so I think we can trust *her* judgment that telling them was safe. Even if you don't trust mine or Liam's. And Liam's right—you shouldn't have mentioned it to anyone until the Sovereign said it was okay."

"Oh, heavens." She actually rolls her eyes. "It's not as though I broadcast it to everyone at NuAgra, I merely discussed it briefly with a few friends. What possible harm can that do?"

Her dismissive question gives me an ominous feeling, like she's tempting fate. I shove back from the table, my pie forgotten.

"Hopefully none."

The next morning, I do my best to shake off the weird premonition I felt last night. The few minutes I get to spend with Deb before school help. More strongly than ever, I feel my built-up tension release the moment we touch. A week ago, that worried me. Not now.

"See you at lunch?" I ask in the atrium, reluctant to let her go.

She laughs. "Of course! And in Art class. And after school?"

I regretfully shake my head. "Because of Liam's game tonight, Mom's insisting—again—that we both stay at NuAgra till she and Dad leave." Liam and I both hoped she'd stop trying to keep us away from the girls now that they know the truth, but so far that doesn't seem to be the case.

"At the game, then, for sure. It's at Elwood, right?"

I do my best to match her upbeat mood. "I think that's what Liam said. And yes, I'll definitely see you there! Meanwhile…" I lean in for a kiss to sustain me until lunchtime.

Rather than give into my lingering misgivings over the next hour or two, I try to focus on how well my relationship with Deb is progressing. With the whole secrecy thing behind us, we get along great now. I've also noticed the pleasant tingle I feel when we touch is stronger than ever.

Theories about what that could mean have been teasing me off and on ever since I first kissed Deb at Donner's Farm. The one I'm leaning toward still seems unlikely. But on the way to third-period Chemistry, I decide to ask the only people who might have an answer.

M and Rigel are already at their shared lab table when I reach the classroom. Before I can change my mind, I walk over to them and blurt out my question—quietly.

"Do either of you think it's possible for one of us to bond with a *Duchas*?" I whisper.

They're both clearly startled, but then Rigel starts to grin. "Go on," he says to M. "Tell him what Shim told you."

M's smiling now, too. "You probably realize a lot of our people still don't believe in *graell* bonds at all," she reminds me softly. "But last week I started noticing certain recent, ah, improvements in Bri and Deb, so I made some inquiries."

"Improvements?" I blink. "How could Deb be improved on when she's already perfect?"

"Liam would probably say the same thing about Bri." M's grin widens. "Though I suppose as someone who's known them for years, and who isn't blinded by love, some things might be a little more obvious to me than to you. Anyway, I asked Regent Shim, back on Mars, and he—"

The bell rings, cutting her off.

"After class, I'll tell you what he said," she promises.

Frustrated, I nod and hurry to my lab table, where Amber's flirting is even more irritating than usual. By now, she *has* to realize I'm dating Deb. I ignore her.

The instant class is over, I grab my backpack and catch up with M and Rigel as they go out the door. Liam, clearly curious about my hurry, joins us a second later. Which is fine. He may as well hear this, too.

"So," I say, too quietly for any nearby *Duchas* students to hear. "You were going to tell me what Regent Shim had to say about my, um, question?"

M nods, looking amused again. "You might not know this, but Shim has studied *Echtran* genetics, and the *graell*, more than anyone alive. So he's the person most likely to know whether a bond could potentially form between an *Echtran* and a *Duchas*. His response was really interesting."

"Whoa!" Liam looks at me, brows raised. "You've been wondering that, too?" Then, to M. "Tell us!"

The four of us slow down, letting our classmates pass us, as M continues.

"Apparently Shim started coming up with theories about the *graell* several decades ago, but once Rigel and I bonded, he started digging into archives and doing more research on it. He now believes that what causes the, ah, enhancements when a couple bonds is actually a more extreme form of the way all Martians affect each other. It's not obvious in Nuath, but here it was noticed centuries ago that we develop more of the positive traits that differentiate us from the *Duchas* when we live around other *Echtrans*. It's one reason so many still live in *Echtran* communities like Dun Cloch and Bailerealta.

"Shim says that sort of proximity switches on our beneficial genes and switches off detrimental ones, making us stronger, smarter, et cetera. He believes *all* humans share the same basic genetic potential. *Echtrans* just maximize it better than most Earth humans, probably thanks to something the Grentl did to us, way back when."

I try to recall my early Nuathan history from school. "When they first created Nuath, you mean? As a sort of…lab?"

M nods. "We've known for a long time that the aliens who brought us to Mars performed some sort of genetic experiments on our ancestors, but we never knew exactly what. Shim thinks—and his research supports it—they somehow came up with a way to activate our good genes and suppress bad ones. Eventually, that became self-perpetuating and continued even after they abandoned the colony. He says it's totally possible that the same way *Echtrans* are, um, better, when they're around other *Echtrans*, we could have a similar positive genetic effect on *Duchas* over time, too. Especially if we happen to be *closely* associated with them." She winks at Liam and me.

"As for bonding, if everything else Shim says is true, why not that? Sure, there'll be plenty of doubters, but Rigel and I are living proof that the *graell* is real. So we're the last ones who'd tell you it's impossible."

Which is all the answer I need. For now, anyway.

36

Cliffhanger

Deb

I'VE ALWAYS PRIDED myself on being observant. In fact, both my mother and sister sometimes tell me I'm too observant for my own good—it's why they were never able to pull off surprises for me. But prior to this week, there were plenty of things I *never* noticed that now seem glaringly obvious.

Like the way M and Rigel sometimes go quiet at lunch, their eyes unfocused—which means they're talking telepathically to each other. Or how some of the others occasionally whisper so quietly I can't hear them, even when I'm close enough I should be able to.

At tonight's away game, Bri points out something else I never noticed before—how often Sean, Alan and Liam pass the ball to one of their other teammates when it would be easier for one of the Martian guys to make a basket. Now she nudges me every time it happens.

Sean hands the ball off to Pete instead of scoring and Bri and I exchange yet another secret smile. Because now we know *why*.

"Liam seems to be in a way better mood than at the last game I went to," I comment to Lucas at one point.

"He is. I think he's enjoying this game more than any he's ever played," he replies, his voice sending the same delicious shiver down my back it always does. "Even though he still has to hold back, now he knows he's not disappointing Bri by doing it. That used to bother him a lot."

I nod sympathetically. "I can see that. Poor guy. I'm so glad neither of you has to pretend around us anymore."

"Me, too." He takes advantage of the crowd cheering another basket to give me a quick kiss.

"Hey, no fair," Bri protests teasingly from my other side. "If I have to wait till later, you guys should have to, too."

We just laugh.

When the halftime buzzer sounds, Bri jumps up, as always. Lucas and I follow her down to the court, where she hurries over to talk to Liam before he has to follow the team to the locker room. Once he does, she comes back over to us.

"I'm gonna hit the restroom real quick," she says. "You want to come with, Deb?"

I shrug and nod even though I don't need to. I also don't want to leave Lucas for even a few minutes, but accompanying each other to the bathroom is an unwritten part of the girlfriend code.

"Want me to get you a water?" Lucas asks as we part in the hall just outside Elwood's gym.

"Sure, that would be great." We snag another quick kiss, since his parents are nowhere in sight, earning another mock frown from Bri.

Grinning, I follow her to the ladies' room. "See? There *are* perks to dating someone who doesn't play sports."

That makes her laugh. "I guess it does mean you get more time to spend together during the season, especially during games. Not that I'd ever want to trade boyfriends."

Following the signs to the restrooms, we round a corner and see a long line for the ladies' room—no surprise.

"Guys never have to wait," Bri grumbles. "Want to see if we can find a different one? I don't want to risk missing the start of the second half."

Since I also don't want to miss any more of my precious time with Lucas than I can help, I'm in favor of that plan. "I don't know this school very well, but we're bound to find one faster than we'd get through that line."

We continue down the hallway until it tees, then look left and right. No other bathroom is in sight, but the right-hand way dead-ends after a few dozen yards, so we turn left, quickening our pace. After two more turns, we finally see a pair of restrooms up ahead.

"Finally!" Bri exclaims. "I'd have given up if I didn't really need to go."

As we hurry forward, I hear footsteps behind us and glance back to see three adults, two women and a man. A little young for parents, so probably teachers.

Uh-oh, are we not supposed to be here? Then I notice they're just chatting between themselves, not even looking at us. Bri's already pushing open the door to the girls' bathroom, so I don't bother mentioning my momentary worry.

Following her into the empty restroom, I step into the stall next to hers. Might as well take this opportunity, even if I don't really need to go. I'm quick enough that we both flush at the same time and come out together to hurriedly wash our hands.

"I hope we can find our way back to the gym," I joke, reaching for a paper towel. "This was more—"

Suddenly, the bathroom lights go out, pitching us into darkness and stopping me mid-sentence.

"Oh, crap. Power outage," Bri says in the dark. "That'll make it harder!"

"I don't think it's the whole school," I reassure her—and myself. "There's light showing under the door, so the hallway must still be lit. Come on."

I've barely taken two steps toward the comforting strip of bluish-white along the floor when something soft and pungent unexpectedly covers my mouth and nose.

"Mmph! Dn't!" I protest, wondering what stupid game Bri is playing. But then I hear her making similar noises from a few feet away.

Even as I twist away from the muffling cloth, trying to figure out in the dark who it can be, a wave of dizziness hits me. My knees start to buckle, but a strong pair of hands grab my upper arms to keep me upright, the cloth now gone from my face.

"Don't give her too much," my captor cautions in a fierce whisper. "We don't want to have to carry them."

"Good point," comes another whisper from Bri's direction. "Now, if you two girls don't want to be hurt or worse, you'll stay quiet and come with us."

I'm propelled forward, too disoriented to do more than put one foot in front of the other.

The bathroom door opens into the brightly lit hallway and our attackers are revealed as the two women I saw behind us a few minutes ago. The man is waiting in the hall.

"Got them?" he asks, like that's not obvious. "Did you remember to search them?"

"Not yet," the woman holding me answers.

I'm vaguely aware of her digging into my pockets. Then the man holds me while she ducks back into the bathroom for a moment.

"Okay, let's go," the man says when she returns. "This way."

Our three abductors hustle us down the hall in the opposite direction we came from, away from the gym and anyone who might help us. I look dazedly over at Bri in time to see her panicked face looking back at me.

"Deb, what's—?" she starts to ask when the woman holding her slaps a white cloth over her mouth.

"None of that," she mutters. "Guess you need a little more."

My captor does the same to me, making my head swim again, my vision going foggy.

I'm not sure how much time passes—maybe only minutes?—before we're hauled through a side door into the parking lot. It's cold without my coat, but I gulp gratefully at the fresh air, hoping to clear whatever drug they've given me from my system so I can think—and maybe scream.

Unfortunately, though the parking lot is still full of cars, no one's around. Our kidnappers, apparently less worried now about being seen or heard, half-drag us to a nearby van. The man opens the back hatch, then hurries to the driver's side door.

"Get them in and shut the back. Let's go before anyone shows up."

The two women bodily lift us into the rear of the van with such apparent ease that, even in my confused state, I realize they must be Martians. The back hatch slams shut and the engine roars to life, but before I can even try to guess why Bri and I have been taken, the cloth is back over my nose and mouth and everything fades to black.

When I come to, I'm lying on a loveseat in a totally normal-looking living room, my hands and feet bound by what feel like thick zip ties. Craning my neck, I see Bri, similarly restrained on a nearby sofa, just starting to stir. Shutting my eyes again, I pretend I'm still out while peering through my lashes to locate our captors. I don't see them, but nearby voices tell me they're close enough to hear if we say anything out loud or try to escape. So instead, I start listening.

"—early," I hear a male voice complaining. "The plan was for you to grab them after the game was over. Fergus isn't even here yet."

"The stupid girls gave us an opportunity we couldn't pass up," a female voice responds—one of the women who abducted us, I think. "They went off on their own at halftime, so we followed them. Nobody saw us. It would have been much harder to nab them after the game without anyone noticing, with the parking lot full of people leaving."

A different male voice chimes in. "She's right. We already knew it would be tough to separate them from all the other *Duchas* before they could drive off. This was both easier and more discreet. With luck, no one will notice they're missing for at least another hour."

"Now that we've got them," the second woman says, "what do we plan to do with them? Did Fergus decide?"

"It should be a joint decision, shouldn't it?" The first woman sounds irritated. "Why are we letting Fergus call the shots? If we're not careful, this could become much more dangerous for us than two *Duchas* teens knowing our secret. If you ask me—"

The other woman cuts her off. "We didn't. Fergus was right—this situation was far too risky to let stand. At least now these girls are in no position to tell all their little friends about us. Imagine what would happen if they stir up a mob."

"I agree," the first male voice declares. "Fergus may not be thinking completely clearly right now, but he made an excellent point. Once he gets here, we can all discuss what— Ah! That must be him now."

I look over at Bri again and see her staring at me, fully awake now. Her mouth opens and I quickly shake my head to tell her to stay quiet. Even as she responds with a tiny nod, I have to stifle an urge to cry out myself from the near-blinding headache that suddenly hits. Maybe shaking my head wasn't such a great idea.

From the other room, I hear the four already here greeting the newest arrival, Fergus, and telling him they already have the "dangerous *Duchas*" at their mercy. Dangerous? Us? Really?

"Good work." His voice is slightly higher and more nasal than those of the other two men, and more unpleasant. "If we hurry, we should be able to dispose of them before anyone comes looking."

Footsteps come our way. I risk another quick look at Bri, then exaggeratedly close my eyes, hoping she'll take the hint and do the same.

"Still out, I see," Fergus says approvingly. "Excellent. That will make this even easier. I assume you made sure they can't be traced here?"

"Yes, we left their cellphones back at the school and we definitely weren't followed," one of the women tells him.

"When you say 'dispose of,' what exactly do you have in mind?" the other woman asks sharply. "Do you actually propose…killing them?"

I hear a snort. "Of course. How else can we be certain they won't spread the word?"

"Perhaps we can have their memories modified?" the same woman suggests. "They're only children, after all. Killing them would make us little better than Faxon."

"Modify their memories?" Fergus sounds disbelieving. "Do you happen to have a Healer friend nearby with the equipment necessary to do that? No. I didn't think so."

One of the other men finally speaks up. "Sharra has a point, Fergus. Our people are supposed to have evolved beyond killing. These girls haven't even committed a crime. It's their *Echtran* boyfriends who violated secrecy."

"Does it matter?" Fergus's frustration and mounting anger are clear in his voice. "We all agreed that their knowing poses far too great a danger to our people. What are two lives—mere *Duchas* lives, at that— compared to putting our entire race and culture at risk?"

The third man in the room speaks up. "Er, no offense, Fergus, but we'd rather not all end up like Noreen."

"My wife should never have been hauled off to Dun Cloch!" Fergus shouts. "She killed that *Duchas* woman completely by accident. Even the investigators agreed about that. If her original plan had succeeded, she'd have been hailed as a hero."

"By some," one of the women concedes. "Or she might have brought the full wrath of the Sovereign and the Council down on all of us. She may yet, if—"

Fergus makes a sound almost like a roar. "Fine! If none of you have the courage to do what must be done here, I'll do it myself. Keep an eye on them. I'll be right back."

I hear him stomping out of the room, presumably to bring back something that will be lethal to Bri and me. Playing possum no longer seems like our best strategy. We need to do *something* to stop them, to get away!

But what?

37

Chain reaction

Lucas

BY TWO MINUTES into the second half of the basketball game, I'm starting to get worried. What could be taking Deb and Bri so long? I know women's restrooms usually have longer lines than the men's, but surely not *that* long?

I try to force myself to relax, to just watch the game and be patient, but as another few minutes tick past, my certainty that something is wrong is too strong to ignore. M and Rigel aren't here tonight, but I spot Kira sitting a short distance away. Tamping down my growing panic, I make my way over to her.

"Kira," I whisper, "would you be willing to go check the girls' bathroom? Deb and Bri went right at the start of halftime and still haven't come back. I'm afraid one of them might be sick or something."

Though she looks startled, she nods. "Sure, no problem."

Too anxious to sit here and wait, I accompany her down the bleachers and out of the gym, then down the hall toward the restrooms. There's definitely no line. In fact, no one else is even around.

"Wait here, I'll go have a look," Kira tells me, pushing open the door to the girls' bathroom. She reappears a moment later. "Nope, empty. Have you tried messaging Deb?"

"Oh! No." I feel stupid that never occurred to me. Since getting to

Jewel, the only people I've texted or called have been Liam and my parents.

Pulling out my phone, I bring up Deb's contact. *Everything okay? I quickly type. Where are you?*

Kira and I wait, but seconds stretch into minutes with no reply. I try calling. It rings several times. Then I hear Deb's voice, surprisingly perky.

"Hi, this is Deb. I can't answer my phone right now, but—"

My brief hope dashed, I disconnect, shaking my head. "Went to voicemail."

"Maybe she left her phone in her coat pocket," Kira suggests.

Though I inwardly curse at the delay while Deb might be in trouble, I follow Kira back to the gym and up to my seat, where I hurriedly go through the pockets of Deb's coat, then Bri's. No phones.

A glance at the scoreboard shows there are only six minutes left in the game, which means Deb and Bri have been gone for well over half an hour now. Something is *definitely* wrong.

"Should we try calling M?" I whisper to Kira, unable to think of anything else.

"Do you have her contact?"

I shake my head, deflated, but Kira holds up her phone. "I do. Just a sec."

She taps out a message and sends it. "I think she and Molly might be recording a broadcast tonight, but she should see it when she's done. Do you think one of the girls got an emergency call from home and had to leave in a hurry?"

"Without their coats? Anyway, I think Bri's dad drove them tonight and he's still here, so they wouldn't have a car."

"Then they must still be here in the school," Kira says.

She's right—unless… No, I won't assume the worst. Not yet. "You're right. I'm going to go look for them."

I'm grateful when Kira offers to come along, since she's the one M will call when she gets her message. When we pass the girls' bathroom, she peeks inside again but it's still empty.

"Maybe they went to another one if the line was too long?" she suggests. "Let's check them all."

Together, we jog down one hallway, then another, until we spot another restroom. Like before, Kira goes in to check. Meanwhile, I try calling Deb again, mostly because it's better than doing nothing at all. To my surprise, I hear ringing…from inside the bathroom. Could M be calling Kira back?

But a minute later, Kira comes out holding two phones, one still ringing. I recognize it as Deb's just as her voicemail picks up again.

"They were in the trash," Kira tells me. "I wouldn't have thought to look there if you hadn't called again."

Sudden fear grabs me by the throat. "You realize what this means, don't you? Someone must have kidnapped them. But who?"

Kira frowns. "I'm guessing one of our people. Rigel was right that there are *Echtrans* who can't be trusted, especially outside of Jewel. If word got around that Bri and Deb learned our secret… Fear can make people do awful things. I'm going to— Oh! M just messaged me back. I'll call her."

She does. After quickly explaining the situation to M, she hands the phone to me.

"Exactly how long have they been missing?" M asks before I can say anything.

"Since halftime, and the game must be about over," I tell her. "I don't know what to do. They could have been taken anywhere by now!"

There's a second's pause, then she says, "Let me get hold of Rigel. Together, we may be able to help you find them. What's your number, so I can call you back directly?"

I give it to her and she clicks off.

"Let's go back to the gym," I say to Kira. "Liam will want to know about this, too."

"So will Sean," Kira agrees. "This has the potential to blow up into a major incident none of us want. If it gets out to the local media that two girls have been kidnapped—"

I shake my head. "No. We'll find and rescue them before that can happen. Come on."

The game has just ended when we reach the gym, the floor crowded with fans congratulating our players. Kira heads for Sean as I shoulder my way through the throng around Liam and pull him aside. He starts to protest, then takes a good look at my face.

"What's going on? Where's Bri? She's usually the first one to—"

"She's disappeared. Deb, too. We think someone snatched them during halftime. Kira found their phones in the trash."

Liam goes pale. "Snatched them? Who? Why?"

"We don't know yet, but it can't be good. M said she and Rigel would try to locate them—I don't know how. Maybe it's one of their *graell* abilities. I hope so."

"So do I. But what if— Oh, hi, Mom. Hi, Dad."

Our parents look curiously from Liam to me.

"Is something wrong?" Dad asks.

We both nod.

"Deb and Bri disappeared during halftime. They went to the restroom and never came back," I tell them. "We think they were taken by somebody. Kidnapped."

Mom raises a skeptical brow. "Oh, come now. It's far more likely they simply remembered some other commitment and left, and forgot to tell you."

"No, Mom," I tell her. "Their cellphones were ditched in a bathroom. They never would have done that themselves. M promised me she'd try to find them, but I'm worried it could already be too late."

Our mother's eyes go wide. "You involved the Sovereign?" she asks me in a strangled whisper.

"They're her best friends," I snap. I can't believe she isn't taking this seriously! "Come on, let's get out of this crowd."

"Good idea," Dad agrees. He, at least, looks concerned.

When Mom tries to get Liam to go shower, he blows up at her.

"Are you kidding? Every *second* could make a difference! Don't you get that, Mom? I'll grab my coat, but then we need to *go*."

I quickly retrieve both girls' coats, too. Liam rejoins us outside the gym a minute later and we all head outside. I frantically scan the parking lot. No sign of the girls, but I spot Deb's mom's car.

"Look!" I point. "That means Deb drove them tonight, not Bri's dad like I thought. So he probably won't realize they're missing."

Liam glances back toward the high school. "Is that a good thing or a bad thing?"

"Not sure. But if Kira's right and they were nabbed by *Echtrans*, it gives us a little more time to find them before it turns into an even bigger problem."

"Don't be ridiculous," Mom scoffs. "*Echtrans* would never do such a thing."

I just give her a withering look and turn back to Liam. "Maybe we should—" My phone rings, cutting me off.

It's M. "Lucas, I think Rigel and I have located them. They're definitely still in Elwood, but I'm not sure how to give you directions so you can find them. Are you still at the school?"

"In the parking lot," I tell her. "How—?"

"Never mind that," she says. "Just a moment. I'm going to try to pinpoint you, then Bri again, to get an idea of how far apart you are."

For several nerve-wracking seconds I wait, the phone at my ear, before she speaks again.

"Okay, it looks like they're not too far, maybe a mile and a half from your position. Due west. Head that way for a mile or so, then call me back so we can triangulate again."

"Got it." I stick my phone back in my pocket and turn to my parents. "Let's go. The *Sovereign*—" I stress the word to Mom— "says we need to drive west. Now."

Dad nods and we hurry to our car and get in. "West, you say?" he says.

"Yes."

It takes a few minutes to get out of the parking lot, what with all the other cars leaving at the same time, but then Dad turns left—the opposite direction from home.

"Is this due west?" I ask.

Dad shrugs. "Not sure, but it's definitely not east."

"I'll bring up the map on my phone," Liam says, leaning forward as though that will make Dad drive faster. "Okay, we're going sort of northwest. Turn left if you get a chance and we'll do our best to dead-reckon it."

I expect another argument from Mom, but she remains silent. I'm glad I invoked the Sovereign's name.

After a few hundred yards, Dad turns left. Then, at Liam's direction, he turns right.

"Okay, now we're going due west," Liam says, staring at his phone. "How far are we going?" he asks me.

"I'm supposed to call M back once we've gone a mile."

Nodding, he keeps watching his phone. "That's about a mile," he says a few moments later. "Give her a call." The anxiety in his voice matches what I'm feeling.

I hit the button to return the last call and M picks up immediately.

"Good job," she says. "You're less than half a mile from them now. Keep heading in the same direction and I'll stay on the phone."

I relay the message to Dad, who speeds up. "How far now?" I ask M several seconds later.

"Not far at all. Can you turn slightly south?"

Peering ahead through the windshield, I see we're approaching what looks like a residential area. "Dad, take that next left, okay?"

He does.

"Where now?" I ask M.

"Slow down. You're really close."

Guided by her directions, we make a right turn and proceed past four or five more houses before M tells us to stop.

"You should be right next to wherever they are now. Why don't you get out and look around? I'll hang up now so Rigel can focus better on his driving. We're on our way to meet you, in case you need help."

I step out of the car and glance around at the nearest houses in what seems to be a fairly nice neighborhood. Liam gets out, too, but our parents stay in the car.

"What are you going to do?" Mom whispers through the passenger window. "You can't just start knocking on doors."

"We will if that's what it takes," I snap, making her blink. "Don't you get it? Deb's in danger. Nothing else matters as much as that."

Turning away, I stride toward the closest house but come to my senses enough to pause just before reaching the door to listen first. Over the past week or so, I've thought my hearing might be getting better. Now I'm sure of it. As soon as I focus, I can clearly hear a TV set blaring, some comedy show.

"I don't think it's this one." I grab Liam's arm before he can pound on the door. "Let's try across the street."

We both sprint to the house opposite and I again stop to listen. This time, I hear people arguing inside. Sharpening my hearing even more, I begin to make out words.

"—dangerous," a female voice is saying. "What if their bodies are found?"

Bodies?? Liam and I exchange a horrified glance.

"They won't be," a harsh male voice replies. "I'll make sure of that. But the longer we wait, the bigger the risk people will start looking for them before we finish. Enough of this dithering. It's time."

That's all we need to hear. As one, Liam and I rush the door, shoulders lowered. With a resounding crash, it slams open, askew on its hinges. Recovering our momentum, we barrel forward into a large living room where five adults are gathered around Deb and Bri, who are laid out on couches with their eyes closed.

Unconscious? Or…?

As the people in the room wheel to face us, a feral snarl rips from my throat and I launch myself at the man who was just leaning over Deb. Taken by surprise, he goes down with a grunt. Liam almost simultaneously slams into the man nearest Bri. Two down.

But only for a moment.

Already the two men we tackled are struggling to their feet as the two women and the third man converge on us menacingly. One of the women is brandishing a cloth and even from several feet away, I smell a pungent aroma from it.

"Don't let her touch you with that," I yell to Liam. "And watch that guy!" I add as the man he knocked down reaches into his pocket.

Nodding, Liam gives the man a kick in the chest that lands him back on the floor.

Now we're really in the thick of it, our element of surprise gone. One woman, the one without the cloth, hangs back but the other three converge—four, when the man Liam just took out again scrambles back up. Not that I care about the odds when Deb's life is on the line. Or being any kind of gentleman.

When the woman with the cloth lunges toward my face, I don't hesitate to block her—hard—with a forearm to the side of her head. That sends her flying backward to slam into the arm of the couch Bri's on with an *oof.*

But now the man who wasn't hit grabs my other arm, yanking me toward him as he tries to wrap his other arm around my neck. I drop nearly to my knees to escape a choke hold, then drive the top of my head into his stomach, dimly aware of Liam trying to fend off the other two men. Already, the woman I shoved is coming toward me again. At least I made her drop the cloth.

I draw back my right fist, ready to punch her right in the face when she gets close enough. The sight of Deb, bound and helpless, maybe even dead, does away with any inhibitions I might have had against hurting other *Echtrans*. These people deserve to die.

Unfortunately, we're still outnumbered five to two, and Liam's now partly incapacitated, one man holding his arms behind him while the other fumbles for something to tie him up with—or worse. Plus, the woman who initially hung back is now entering the fray, handing something that might be a weapon to the man I just head-butted. Crap.

The first woman leaps out of the way of my punch at the last second, practically landing on top of Deb. Liam is struggling mightily but slowly being overpowered by the two men who have him. The third man points the silver thing in his hand at me and fires, just barely missing. A black hole appears in the wall above Bri.

I lunge toward Deb, determined to keep her safe at all costs if it's not too late. I'll shield her with my body if I have to. The woman who fell against her manages to get upright before I reach her…but then goes down again with a gasp. That's when I notice Deb's eyes are open. She actually managed to kick the woman in the back with her bound legs!

"Way to go!" I grin at Deb despite the trouble we're all in, I'm so relieved she's alive and conscious.

Then I have to dodge another shot from that energy weapon that makes my hair stand on end, it passes so close. Since that guy's clearly the most immediate threat to all of us, I grab the woman next to Deb by the arm and sling her at him. Startled, he drops his weapon but doesn't go down.

Liam's now been forced to his knees, one man trying to bind his hands behind his back while the other holds him down—not easy, the way my brother's slinging his upper body back and forth, trying to shake them off. That's when I notice Bri's awake, too.

When Liam's thrashing has the guy behind him off balance, Bri suddenly pitches her whole body off the couch into the man, knocking him over. That lets Liam twist away from the hands on his shoulders and surge to his feet.

But now, the woman who hasn't fought yet has picked up her cloth and is cautiously moving toward the girls, probably to knock them back out. And the guy who shot at me is already retrieving his weapon. It's all looking pretty hopeless for us good guys when I hear more footsteps approaching. Reinforcements? For us or for them?

"What's going on here?" my dad demands loudly. "What are you doing to my sons? And to those girls?"

That distracts the bad guys long enough for Liam to land a solid punch to the face of one of his assailants as the other turns to face our father. He looks both flabbergasted and furious. Mom's behind him in the front hallway, both hands over her mouth.

"I'm calling *Echtran* security," Dad announces, sweeping the room with an outraged glance. "You people are way out of line."

Next to me, the guy with the weapon brings it up to fire at my dad, but I'm quicker. Like lightning, I grab his wrist and give it a ferocious twist. I hear a snap. With a howl of anguish, the man drops the thing again and falls to his knees, cradling his broken arm.

That seems to take some of the fight out of them—that and my dad speaking quickly into his phone. The four uninjured kidnappers bunch together, all looking nervous but defiant. Then one of the women spots our mother just outside the room.

"You!" she exclaims contemptuously. "You must be their mother, Eilis Walsh. My sister told me about you. You should be ashamed!"

Clearly startled, Mom takes a step back, staring at her. "What?"

"Letting your sons consort with these *Duchas* girls." The woman practically spits the word. "It's disgusting. They're practically animals. And then letting them breach secrecy! *You're* the ones who should be exiled to Dun Cloch!"

With that, both she and the man next to her rush at Dad. Liam and I move to intercept them and the fight breaks out again, but with better odds now. Three against four.

Dad actually gets in one impressive blow, and Bri, on the floor, manages to trip one of the women. But we're barely into it when another voice cuts across the room.

"Stop! All of you!" It's M.

Suddenly, I can't move at all. Apparently, no one else can, either. I've heard of "Royal push," but this is the first time I've experienced it. *Definitely* a real thing.

"Rigel, take these five into the next room and immobilize them," M continues as I slowly unfreeze.

He steps forward, a tiny weapon of his own at the ready, and motions them all ahead of him. They comply without question, the man with the broken wrist still moaning.

Then M turns to me. "Wow, well done, all of you! Now, can you tell me exactly what happened?"

38

Narrow escape

Deb

I STARE at M from my position on the couch, awed by the authority that radiates from her. She did tell us, and the boys confirmed, that she's the Martian Sovereign, but this is the first time I've seen her act like one. I'm beyond impressed.

Haltingly, Lucas describes bursting into the house and engaging our captors.

"We didn't realize there'd be five of them, or we might have tried for some kind of plan instead of just barging in. But from what we heard them saying, there wasn't any time to lose." He looks at me, emotion written strong on his face. "I swear, my heart almost stopped when I saw you lying there, Deb. I thought you might be dead!"

"I think we both would have been if you hadn't come in when you did." I gaze gratefully up at him, then say to M, "Lucas was amazing! He and Liam both were."

"Seriously!" Bri agrees from her position on the floor, though by now she's managed to scootch into a semi-sitting position against the couch. "They literally saved our lives, M. They should get medals or something."

M smiles at her, then at me. "I'll do my best to make sure they're properly rewarded." Glancing quickly at Mr. and Mrs. Walsh, who have both backed respectfully into the hallway, she leans over so only Bri and I can hear her, and whispers, "I'll bet you two will, too."

Maybe it's just the aftermath of the stress of the past hour, but I find myself giggling uncontrollably. After a second, Bri joins in. M's lips twitch, too, but she quickly masters herself. That Sovereign thing, I guess.

"I have cause to be grateful to you all." Her gaze takes in the four of us, then Mr. and Mrs. Walsh, hovering behind her. "All of our people do. Though I know it wasn't intentional, you've exposed a dangerous cell of malcontents here in Elwood. This close to Jewel, they likely would have posed a serious threat sooner or later. Now they won't have a chance. I assume they were upset about you guys dating?"

"Mostly that we learned your big secret," Bri tells her, "though they obviously didn't like the dating thing, either."

M's eyebrows go up. "How did they hear I'd told you about us?"

At that, Mrs. Walsh tremblingly steps forward. "I...I think it might have been my fault, Excellency. I, ah, may have voiced my concerns about the issue to a friend or two at NuAgra yesterday. One of the women here mentioned hearing about my boys from her sister..."

"Hm." M frowns. "We'll find out who that sister is and how she's connected to these others. It sounds like we need to take a closer look at some of those working at NuAgra."

Mrs. Walsh bobs her head, clearly abashed, then sends an apologetic look Bri's way. "I...I'm sorry I've been so unsupportive of your relationship with Liam. I realize now—"

"That you were nearly as prejudiced as those people in there?" Liam interrupts accusingly.

His mother nods, her eyes now downcast.

"Good." There's no compromise in Liam's tone. "Now, does somebody have a knife or something so we can cut the girls loose?" He plops down on the floor next to Bri and starts stroking her hair.

Mr. Walsh hurries into the kitchen and comes back with a sturdy pair of scissors. Lucas grabs them and quickly snips the plastic ties binding my wrists and ankles, then hands them to Liam, who does the same for Bri.

"The security detail has arrived," Mr. Walsh tells M as I rub my wrists, sore from when I tried to twist my way out of the zip ties earlier. "I think they're about to take away those...people." He grimaces with distaste. "Clearly, not all *Echtrans* are as morally superior as we'd like to believe."

Mrs. Walsh is clearly still distressed, too. "No. I never imagined any of our own people could behave like that, kidnapping these innocent girls, threatening to—" She breaks off, shaking her head, practically in tears.

"They did more than threaten, Mom." Lucas's voice is as harsh and uncompromising as Liam's was a moment ago. "If we'd been any later getting here, they would absolutely have killed Deb and Bri, based on what I overheard. So no. Just being *Echtran* definitely doesn't make someone a paragon of virtue, no matter what you wanted to believe."

"True," M agrees. "I've seen far too many examples of the atrocities some of our people have been willing to commit. Sometime I'll share a few stories with you. Right now, though, we'd better get Bri and Deb home before their parents start worrying. Explaining why they're late could get awkward in a hurry."

.⋆.

Because time is so tight, Bri and I barely get to say goodbye to our saviors before Rigel drives us back to Elwood High and my mom's car.

There's so much I want to say to Lucas, to ask him, but I guess it'll have to wait till tomorrow. At least I have my phone back. Losing it would have been harder to explain to my mom than being late. Though it's pretty minor compared to saving our lives, I'm grateful Lucas found our phones and brought them along.

"I can tell you're still a little rattled, Deb," M says as I unlock my mom's car in Elwood's now-deserted parking lot. "Why don't you follow Rigel and me back to Jewel? I know you know the way, but…it might help."

It does. With everything that happened tonight replaying endlessly in my thoughts, I'm sure I'd have trouble focusing on the road in front of me without Rigel's taillights as a guide.

Bri and I cling to each other for a moment when we hug goodbye in my driveway. We came way too close tonight to never having the chance again.

Mom is clearly not happy I'm so much later than I said I'd be, but she grudgingly accepts my excuse that we got talking to people after the game and lost track of time. Bri and I agreed that was the most plausible explanation we could give.

"I'm glad I insisted you finish your homework before leaving for the game," she says. "Now you have no reason not to go straight to bed. Try to get a good night's sleep. You look like you could use it."

I'll bet I do.

"Thanks, Mom. I will."

Though I expect to have nightmares, I sleep like the dead all night—no pun intended. When I wake up the next morning, it actually takes me a minute to realize why I'm so sore. Then, when I do remember, I'm half convinced I dreamed the whole thing. It sure *seemed* like something from one of those mystery thrillers I'm always reading…

It takes a glance at my still-chafed wrists to prove beyond all doubt that Bri and I really were almost killed last night. So were Lucas and Liam, when they broke in to rescue us. Will they decide these relationships are too risky after all? For all of us? Can we blame them if they do?

I voice that concern to Bri at the bus stop and she admits the same thing occurred to her.

"I know Mrs. Walsh apologized," she says, "but what happened could totally convince her she was right all along that her sons dating regular Earth girls is a terrible idea. Do you…do you think she might decide to move their family away from Jewel after all?"

"I sure hope not." Like the last time that possibility was mentioned, I grow cold at the thought. The fact that it's still January has nothing to do with it.

Bri and I don't talk much on the bus, both lost in our own anxious thoughts. I suspect we're also still a little shell-shocked over our experience. I'm massively relieved when I see Lucas and Liam waiting in front of the school, just like yesterday morning.

Any doubts I had about Lucas still wanting to be with me are banished when he practically snatches me off the bottom step of the bus. The kiss he gives me, before we even say a word to each other, is further proof of how he feels.

"I swear, I had nightmares all night," he says when he finally, reluctantly lets me go. "I kept reliving that moment when I saw you lying there and didn't know if you were dead or alive. I was never so scared in my life, Deb! It's still hard for me to believe you're okay."

"I'm fine. Really," I reassure him. "I didn't even have nightmares. In fact, I'm not sure I dreamed at all—I slept like a rock. Maybe an aftereffect of that stuff they gave us? Or just the release of all the tension from everything that happened."

He throws an arm around my shoulders, pulling me against his side for the too-short walk into the school building. "Glad to hear it. Now that I've seen you again—safe—I'm sure I'll sleep a whole lot better tonight."

We have to hurry to our classes then, since we spent more time kissing than usual. Liam gets to Pre-Cal right as the late bell rings, so I assume the same was true for him and Bri, though I didn't notice.

At lunch, we don't talk much about what happened the night before, but we're all still a little clingier than usual—Lucas with me, and Bri with Liam. The four of us are taking our trays to the drop afterward when Alan comes over to us, wearing a hangdog expression.

"Look, I...I want to apologize for any trouble I might have caused any of you by talking out of turn at NuAgra," he mutters, so no one else can hear. "Sean told me what happened last night because of stuff that was said there and, well, I guess I've been a little misguided. About our people being so superior and all. I realize now they're not, at least not all of them. Anyway, sorry." He gives an embarrassed little nod and hurries off.

I turn to Lucas, wide-eyed. "Wow, I guess your mom's not the only one who's had an epiphany because of what happened."

"Guess not." His lips are twitching.

Liam outright laughs. "Sorry." He quickly sobers when we all stare at him. "It's just...Alan's been such a pain, hearing him grovel was really satisfying. I'll do my best not to gloat, though."

"Yeah, don't," Lucas cautions him. "Let's see if it lasts first. Come on, or we'll all be late to class."

Though I was hoping to spend time with Lucas in the media center after school today, Bri reminds me as we're leaving fifth period that everyone in the show choir has to stay after to rehearse.

"Ugh." I grimace. "Not just the soloists?"

"Ms. Thurmond said everyone," Bri confirms. "The choreography still needs a lot of work."

Still grumbling to myself, I head to Art to give Lucas the bad news.

"I'm sorry, I totally forgot I had this stupid Chorus thing today."

He's clearly disappointed, but not mad. "After last night, I wouldn't blame you for forgetting your own name. We'll manage some private time soon, I promise. Should we plan on this weekend? It's not like school's the best place for what I have in mind, anyway."

The wink that accompanies his whispered words sends a delightful shiver through me.

"This weekend sounds perfect. Maybe Donner's Farm again?" Those grounds will always feel special as the place Lucas first kissed me—a huge turning point in our relationship.

"Sounds perfect. Or maybe a real evening date? We're about due for one, I think."

"Either sounds wonderful to me," I tell him.

We have to stop whispering and get to work then, but I'm no longer insecure about Lucas's feelings toward me, like I was before getting to school this morning.

That's even more true when we leave class later and he pulls me into a tiny alcove between two banks of lockers to give me an even-better-than-usual goodbye kiss. Because I have to get to Chorus, it's still not nearly as long as I'd like.

"I wish you didn't have to hurry off," he says, echoing my thought. "Tomorrow morning seems like such a long time from now."

"It does," I wistfully agree. "I wish…" I trail off, not sure how to express everything I'm wishing for. Then the bell rings. "Oops. I'd better run."

He gives me one more quick kiss, then I have to hustle.

I'm not nearly as out of breath when I reach the Chorus room as I ought to be, but Bri still raises a brow at me.

"I was afraid you were going to ditch after all. Hard time saying goodbye?"

I nod. "You?"

"Yeah. Liam talked about getting together this weekend, but I'm afraid his mom will come up with some other project to put the kibosh on that."

I hadn't even considered that possibility when Lucas suggested a Saturday date. Now, though, it seems all too likely.

Running our show and focusing on getting my stupid feet to cooperate takes my mind off of things for a while, but when I check my phone as I'm leaving the room, there's a message from Lucas. My heart sinks.

"Crap. I'll bet you were right," I mutter to Bri as I open it. To my astonishment, instead of canceling for Saturday, it's an invite to the Walshes' house for dinner—tonight!

"Did you—?" I start to ask Bri, who's staring at her own phone.

"Dinner? Tonight?" She sounds as amazed as I am. "And Liam says it's his *mom's* idea!"

As we head for our late bus, we both text back that we'll check with our parents and let them know ASAP.

"So," Bri says, once we're on the way home. "Why do you think Mrs. Walsh wants us to come over tonight?" Her nervousness is now evident. "I mean, it's nice of her and all, but…"

"But you're afraid she's going to lay out new, stricter ground rules for what the boys are allowed to do…with us?" So am I.

Bri nods. "Or even break the news to us that they're moving away. She *has* made it pretty obvious she's not a fan of them dating, y'know, non-Martian girls."

After last night, that's bound to be even more true—both of her sons could have been killed by those crazy *Echtrans*. And *we* were the only reason they were in such deadly danger.

"Maybe she's just being nice?" I suggest, though I don't really believe that.

Bri obviously doesn't, either. "I guess we'll find out."

———————————————

39

Swish

———————————————

Bri

STANDING WITH DEB OUTSIDE THE WALSHES' front door that evening, I try to swallow my anxiety.

Whether it's because I'm biracial or just because I'm a regular Earth girl, Mrs. Walsh has implied all along that I'm not good enough for her son. Ever since he first introduced us. Worse, deep down, where I try not to look, I can't fully believe I'll ever be good enough for Liam, either.

"Here goes," Deb says shakily. She looks as nervous as I am to discover what this evening's really be about.

The door opens and suddenly there's Liam, grinning at me in a way that makes a big chunk of my uneasiness melt away. Heedless of Lucas right behind him, he sweeps me into a crushing bear-hug that takes my breath away in more ways than one.

"Hey, I need those ribs!" I laugh.

He relaxes his embrace with a laugh of his own. "Sorry—I still can't believe how lucky I am that I didn't lose you forever. Makes me want to hold you close and never let you go."

Beside me, Deb's been pulled into Lucas's arms, too. Their parents must be nearby, so the boys can only give us brief kisses, but even that goes a long way toward fortifying me and setting me even more at ease.

Weirdly, I can swear I feel an actual…tingle?…when Liam touches me. Sort of like an energy boost, making everything sharper, clearer.

Better. I thought I just imagined it before, but now… Whatever it is, I could definitely get used to it!

At the sound of approaching footsteps, Liam disentangles himself from me. Then his parents come around the corner and I'm startled by the warmest, most open smile I've ever seen on Mrs. Walsh's face.

"Welcome, girls! I'm so glad you could make it on such short notice."

"Thank you so much for the invitation," Deb replies while I'm still trying to figure out what to say.

"Please come in. Dinner's already on the table," Mr. Walsh says with a smile just as friendly as his wife's.

We follow them into the dining room, Liam touching but not quite holding my hand. As he pulls out a chair for me, I'm blown away by the feast they've prepared for us. Nearly a dozen different delicious-smelling dishes are steaming on the table between lit candles and a beautiful floral arrangement.

"Wow, this looks amazing!" I exclaim without thinking.

Mrs. Walsh gives me another sincere-looking smile. "Thank you. I wasn't sure what you girls like, or whether you have any dietary restrictions, so we might have gone a bit overboard."

"Though preparing a meal like this isn't quite as much work for us as it might be for a, ah, typical Earth family," Mr. Walsh confides to us with a wink. "We have a few handy gadgets in the kitchen that make it fairly easy."

"Omigod, do you have, like, Star Trek replicators in your *house*?" I blurt out, unable to conceal my excitement, then immediately feel my ears warm with embarrassment.

Mr. Walsh chuckles. "Not quite. After dinner, maybe the boys can show you a few of the, ah, upgrades we've added since moving here."

The brothers look at Deb and me and nod, grinning. I guess they've been looking forward to that, now they're allowed to. I can't wait!

We dig into the food then, which is every bit as delicious as it smells. Liam and I keep nudging each other's knees under the table and sneaking secret smiles at each other, which makes the meal even more fun.

While eating, we have a lively conversation about life on Mars and the ways it's different from life in Jewel—and how it's the same. It feels totally surreal. Here we are, having a normal dinner in a seemingly-normal home, while calmly discussing *life on Mars* like it's no big deal. I still can't quite wrap my head around it.

The whole time, I keep being boggled by how *nice* Mrs. Walsh is toward us tonight. Like she actually enjoys having us here.

"Thank you so much for this wonderful meal," I say as I finish the amazing pear tart she served for dessert. "It was…I mean, we, uh, really appreciate you inviting us tonight." I hesitate, not sure how to put my mixture of gratitude and apprehension into words.

Mrs. Walsh puts her fork down and looks at me with a pleading, anguished expression. "I owe you an apology, Bri. And you too, Deb. I've been unforgivably prejudiced toward you both. I see that now. Too many *Echtrans*, myself included, like to believe we're not only physically, but morally better than the *Duchas*. That we're above such petty things as the bigotry that still plagues Earth. But last night I realized that belief is simply another form of bigotry, and we're no better after all. Those people who kidnapped you demonstrated that. So did I, with my superior attitude."

She pauses as though she's having difficulty getting the words out. "When I think about what those *Echtrans* meant to do to you two innocent girls, and how their justification was so similar to certain thoughts I've had myself, I— Honestly, I've never been more ashamed." She seems to be on the verge of tears. "You don't owe me your forgiveness, but I'll try to earn it by doing better from now on," she finishes, holding my gaze, then Deb's, with a look that's almost fond.

Too stunned to speak, I just sit there for a moment. Whatever I expected to happen this evening, *this* wasn't it!

Deb finds her voice before I do. "Thank you, Mrs. Walsh." Her voice sounds thick.

I nod. "Yes," I manage. "What you said…means a lot."

"So, does this mean you're going to stop giving us crap about spending time together?" Liam asks, taking my hand. "Even being a couple?" His voice has a slight edge to it, but mostly the question is filled with hope.

"Yes. That's exactly what it means," his mother answers firmly, smiling now. "I owe you boys an apology, too."

Across the table, Lucas lets out a breath like he's been holding it. "About time!" he says, both joy and exasperation in his voice.

Then, to my amazement, Lucas takes both of Deb's hands, leans over, and kisses her *right at the dinner table*. I turn to Liam, wondering if he'll do likewise, but Mr. Walsh loudly clears his throat.

"Now look, you two." Both Walshes are staring at Lucas with a mixture of shock and bemusement. "You have our blessing to go steady or whatever, but that doesn't mean we're comfortable with—what did you call them? PDAs?—right in front of us!"

Deb goes red as a tomato. I have to stifle a laugh, despite my sudden embarrassment.

"Oh, it's almost eight o'clock—time for the weekly broadcast!" Mrs. Walsh exclaims, breaking the tension. "Let's get these dishes cleared quickly so we can all watch together."

Deb and I grab our plates and a serving dish each and follow the Walshes into the kitchen. I'm super confused when, instead of putting their dirty dishes in the sink, Mrs. Walsh opens the cabinet next to it and they all load their used plates right into it. Liam and Lucas turn to Deb and me with twin mischievous grins.

"Um…won't that get all your clean dishes dirty?" I ask uncertainly.

"One way to find out!" Liam answers, daring me.

Even more baffled, I also stick my plate into the rack in the cabinet, as does Deb. Mr. Walsh closes the cabinet, then pushes a button hidden underneath it, waits a moment, and opens it again.

I gasp. The dishes are all sparkling clean! "What—? How—? What —?" I stammer, incredulous.

"It's an ionic sterilizer," Liam tells me with irrepressible glee. "Dunno how the *Duchas* live without them, honestly. We did dishes by hand for two whole weeks before it was our turn to have one installed— it was miserable."

I shake my head in bemusement. "Wow, can you hook me up with one? Because I definitely need one of these in my life! Seriously, how cool is that?"

Everyone laughs.

Then Mrs. Walsh looks at the clock on the oven and gasps. "One minute to eight! Let's get to the living room."

Now I'm confused again. "Is this like…your favorite show?" I ask Liam as he leads me to the couch. It seems weird that they're so intent on watching it even though they have guests over.

Mr. Walsh stops suddenly and looks at Deb and me with a concerned frown creasing his forehead. "Oh, I hadn't thought. Maybe…"

"There's no reason the girls can't watch it with us, is there?" his wife asks. "Now that they know everything?"

He shrugs, looking slightly sheepish. "No, I suppose not. Sorry, girls."

Deb and I exchange a curious glance as we snuggle up to our boys on the couch. Weekly broadcast? I guess it's some Martian thing we normally wouldn't be allowed to know about.

Everyone but Mr. Walsh sits down while he sets what looks like his cellphone into a stand. But it must really be an "omni" like M's, because a holographic screen pops up. He types in what looks like a really long password, then crouches down and puts his face close to the screen.

"Retinal scan," he explains in answer to Deb's and my confused expressions. "I imagine the Sovereign—and our sons—explained how seriously we take security?"

We nod.

He taps another key, and the holographic image solidifies into a logo vaguely like a yin-yang mandala in red and blue, with the words *Echtran News Network* curved underneath. I'm still puzzling over that when M suddenly appears, like she's sitting right here in the room with us!

"Good evening, everyone," she says. "In a few minutes, we'll get to our scheduled interview with the new *Echtran* Minister of Culture. But first, there's an important, possibly time-sensitive topic I'd like to address.

"By now, I hope those of you who settled in *Duchas* towns and cities after arriving during the most recent launch window have had time to become relatively comfortable with your new communities. Though many still primarily socialize with other *Echtrans,* I know some have reached out to become acquainted with, and even make friends with, their *Duchas* neighbors.

"As those friendships develop, some of you may find maintaining the necessary secrecy about our people's origins a bit awkward. We've begun putting together additional materials to help you navigate such situations, as *Echtran-Duchas* friendships will likely become more and more commonplace over time. I very much look forward to the day when we will no longer need to keep our true identities secret from our closest *Duchas* friends. To achieve that end, however, a few interim steps will be necessary.

"I've now taken one of those steps myself by revealing the truth to *my* two closest *Duchas* friends. I've known both of these girls since we were children and believe them to be thoroughly trustworthy. I am joined in that belief by two *Echtran* boys who settled here in Jewel after coming to Earth last summer, and who have since become romantically involved with my friends.

"I realize some of you hearing this may find the idea rather shocking, but honestly, this sort of thing was inevitable once our people began living, working, and learning side by side with *Duchas*. We are all human, one species, and a social species at that. As humans, part of our nature is to connect with other humans, even those with different origins from our own.

"Both personally and as your Sovereign, I very much hope my *Duchas* friends and their fledgling romances will pave the way for a deeper understanding between our two peoples. Only through understanding can we one day achieve true integration of all humans on Earth, regardless of where they were born or to whom."

As Deb and I stare at M's image, stunned, she looks off to the side and nods.

"And now," M says, "we'll continue with our originally scheduled broadcast, which Princess Malena and I recorded earlier. Please join us in welcoming *Echtran* Minister of Culture Fianna Murphy."

The picture switches to a different set where a woman sits on a small couch with M and Molly seated in matching chairs on either side of her. After initial greetings, they begin asking her questions and she answers. I have a hard time paying attention.

Not only is most of what they're talking about totally foreign to me, but I'm still staggered by what M just told…all the Martians on Earth? How many are there? What if others are as crazy as the people who abducted us last night? Was it really a good idea for her to tell everyone about us? These thoughts are still chasing each other around in my head, driving me crazy, when the half-hour broadcast ends.

Liam, as though sensing my anxiety, squeezes my hand. "When do you have to be home? I know it's a school night."

"My mom said 9:30," I answer, and Deb nods in agreement.

"Then we've got time to go for a walk before you need to go—if you want to, that is?" Liam raises his eyebrows at me.

Despite my worries, my heart soars at the thought of being truly alone with him for a little while. "Of course!"

Mr. Walsh gives us a resigned look. "All right. But be back by nine, so the girls have plenty of time to get home before their curfew."

Not needing any more encouragement, all four of us bound off of the couch and start putting our coats on. Once outside, we walk to the end of the driveway together. Then, by unspoken agreement, we head off in opposite directions. Hey, their parents didn't say we all had to stick together!

For a few moments, Liam and I walk in silence, enjoying the feel of our clasped, ungloved hands and this rare opportunity to be together, just the two of us. Being with him sets me enough at ease that I'm mostly able to forget the fears sparked by M's broadcast. I'd planned to mention my worries to Liam, but now decide against it. He might do something boneheaded like suggest that we break up so I'll be safer—and that's the *last* thing I want!

We reach the end of the Walshes' cul-de-sac, where there's an acre or so of undeveloped woods. Instead of following the sidewalk back around, Liam pulls me into the shadow of the trees with a mischievous grin.

I return it with one of my own and launch myself at him, pushing him back against a tree. He gives a little "oof!" of surprise, then laughs and pulls me to him. And then we're finally kissing for real, something we haven't had a chance to do since last Sunday in the car, before the playoff game.

The heady sensation of his lips on mine seems like a reaffirmation of our relationship, a way to tell each other in more than words how thankful we are to still be alive and together. My scalp tingles with a warm, golden sensation that slowly spreads through my whole body until I don't even notice the chill of the winter night.

We finally break apart, gulping in lungfuls of cold, fresh air. I rest my forehead against Liam's neck, breathing in the wonderful scent of him.

"Thanks. I needed that," I sigh.

Under my cheek, I feel the low rumble of a chuckle in his chest. "So did I. I hope we'll get a lot more opportunities from now on."

"We should, right? Now that your parents aren't so opposed to us being together? That was really great of your mom, apologizing for being kind of a pain before. Do you…do you think her change of heart will last?"

"I think so? But whether it does or not, *my* heart has never changed. I don't think it ever will. So it honestly doesn't matter a bit to me what my mom thinks. What matters is what I think and what you think…and how I feel about you."

He gently takes my shoulders and pulls back a little so he can look into my eyes. What I see in his makes my heart turn over.

Still holding my gaze, he takes a deep breath, like he's gathering his courage. "I love you, Bri. I don't know why I haven't said it before, because I've known for a while now. Last night…" He swallows. "Last night, I was *terrified* we were too late. And that I'd never get the chance to tell you." His voice is shaking a little, like he's having trouble keeping his emotions under control.

I feel an answering lump in my own throat as tears prickle behind my eyelids—the happy kind.

"I love you, too, Liam. I think maybe I didn't trust myself to tell you sooner because I've imagined I was in love a few times before, and it always ended up just being some stupid crush. But this…this isn't like *anything* I've ever felt before. It's like—" I grope for words adequate to describe the vastness of what I feel for him. "—like I'm at the mercy of the ocean, being pulled out to sea by an unstoppable undertow. No, wait, that makes it sound like a bad thing. It's a wonderful thing! But also… kind of scary? Like my heart might explode right out of my chest sometimes, like my body isn't big enough to contain everything I'm feeling. Ugh, that doesn't sound right either."

Liam laughs and I can't help but laugh with him. "I know! I know!" he chuckles. "I feel exactly the same way. It's crazy. And terrifying. And the most amazing thing I've ever experienced in my whole life."

He cradles my face with both hands and slowly lowers his lips to mine for an exquisitely tender, sweet kiss. I can *feel* the truth of his words in that kiss. When we finally part, I rest my forehead against his with a sigh.

"So, do you really think an Earth girl—a *Duchas* girl—can be good enough for you?" I try to make the question sound playful, to disguise my lingering insecurity about that.

Slipping a finger under my chin, he tilts my face up to look into his eyes. There's no trace of laughter in his expression now.

"How can you even ask that, Bri? Listen to me, please. You are So. Much. More. Than good enough. Sure, some of my people are prejudiced idiots, but I know *exactly* how lucky I am to have found you. To have you in my life."

And then he's kissing me again, and I'm maybe finally crying a little. Because I'm totally overwhelmed with joy and relief. To have survived the terror of last night, to be alive to experience this amazing moment, and that Liam—again!—somehow knew *exactly* what I needed to hear to set all my fears to rest.

40

Stress-strain curve

Lucas

I'M STILL in an excellent mood when I get to school the next morning. And not just because Mom finally relented about letting Liam and me spend time with our girlfriends. That walk Deb and I took after dinner was our first chance to be truly alone since she learned the truth. Since Donner's Farm, really. Making out in the back seat with Liam and Bri up front wasn't quite the same.

We used the opportunity for plenty of kissing, of course, but also to talk without anyone else overhearing. I never quite got up my nerve to tell her I love her, but we reached a new level of understanding where I think she knows.

When I greet Deb with a morning kiss as she gets off her bus, I try to make my feelings for her even clearer, though without the actual words. After a euphoric minute or so, I raise my head and smile down at her.

"So, Liam and I had an idea," I say, putting my arm around her for the brief walk into the school. "Instead of choosing between Donner's Farm and the Lighthouse tomorrow, how about we do both, and spend practically all day together?"

She positively lights up. "Really? That sounds wonderful!"

"Liam thought of it first," I admit. "He asked our parents after you left last night, and they both said it would be okay. We were thinking

Donner's Farm tomorrow afternoon, then the Lighthouse Cafe in the evening?"

"I can't think of a better way to spend a Saturday." Her winsome smile requires another kiss before we part in the atrium.

I don't mention that Liam and I suspect Mom only agreed because she still feels guilty about her earlier prejudice against the *Duchas*, including Deb and Bri. Between what happened Wednesday and the Sovereign's broadcast last night, she seems to have done a complete turnaround—for now, anyway. Liam's probably right that we should take advantage of it while we can.

Though I haven't said anything about it to Liam—or Deb—I've been dealing with a tiny bit of recurring guilt myself. Because I doubt the girls would ever have been in danger if we'd never gone out with them. Worse, it was my own inept attempts to disguise the truth that aroused Deb's suspicions in the first place—my stupid lie about why Liam broke up with Bri, then my bumbling non-explanation for what I did to that branch at Donner's Farm.

Otherwise, I doubt the girls would have become so curious that M felt like she had to tell them the truth—which is what nearly got them killed. They obviously can't be un-told, but I worry continuing to date us might still put them at risk.

That worry increases at lunch, when M sits down with the four of us, her expression serious.

"I need to apologize to you guys for not giving you fair warning before, um, outing you last night. Did the boys tell you?" she asks Bri and Deb.

"We actually saw it," Deb tells her. "We were at the Walshes' house for dinner, so they let us watch with them."

Bri nods. "We had no idea you were doing stuff like that. We were super impressed!"

M smiles at her. "I hope you all didn't feel too blindsided?"

"Um, maybe a little?" I admit. "At least you didn't name names."

M's smile looks slightly strained now. "Yes, at least I didn't do that. I realized afterward I might have jumped the gun a little, being so public about it so quickly. I was still kind of emotional about how close I came to losing my two oldest friends." She gives first Bri, then Deb, a quick, sideways hug. "I figured it would be better to get out in front of any rumors that might start circulating, but maybe I should have spent more time planning exactly what to say."

"I thought what you said was really good," Liam tells her. "I think Mom, especially, was kind of relieved, since it took the pressure off our family. And she's totally fine now with us dating." He grins over at Bri.

"That's good to hear," M says. "Still, I should warn you all that in the short term, it could—possibly—cause some unpleasantness. Hopefully not, but you should be prepared, just in case."

"What sort of unpleasantness?" I ask, though I'm afraid I know.

M lifts a shoulder in a half-shrug. "Even though I left names out of it, pretty much everyone in Jewel—*Echtrans*, I mean—likely knows who I meant. And most of them have friends elsewhere, both on Earth and on Mars. So it probably won't be long before the news spreads and everyone else knows, too. I wish I could say we've now rounded up *all* the radicals. Unfortunately, we know there are more out there—though hopefully not as close as Elwood."

Exactly what I was afraid of. A glance at Deb shows her looking a little scared, so I immediately put a protective arm around her.

"Does that mean Deb and Bri might still be in danger? Maybe even more danger?" I can't quite keep all trace of accusation out of my voice.

M's wince shows she heard it. "I really, really hope not. I don't want that any more than you do, believe me! But odds are you'll all be fine. We have tons of security set up all over Jewel—probably why they waited till Bri and Deb were in Elwood to try anything. Do let me know if you notice anything that worries you, though."

We all nod, though I'm still frowning.

"In the long run," M adds, getting up, "shifting people's attitudes will make everyone safer, *Echtran* and *Duchas*. The more progress we can make before the next few launch windows, the better. So any little unpleasantness that *might* happen over the next few weeks or months is a small price to pay for a better future for all of us. Right?"

"Right," the others echo, but I don't reply.

Maybe it's because I can't think like a Sovereign, but the idea of *any* risk to Deb feels like way too high a price to pay for…anything. And now I'm more sure than ever that I'm one of the things increasing that risk.

✦

At home that evening, I share my worries with Liam—and this time he doesn't dismiss them.

"Yeah, I've been thinking about that a lot after what M told us today. It would destroy me if something happened to Bri. Especially if it was partly my fault!"

"My thoughts exactly. Any ideas on what we can do to make sure that doesn't happen?"

Liam looks at me apprehensively. "Other than break up with them, you mean? Because I think that might destroy me, too."

"I know. I feel the same way. But...what if that's the only way to keep them safe? If people don't see us hanging out with them anymore, they'll be a lot less likely to assume Deb and Bri are the *Duchas* girls the Sovereign was talking about."

Liam's still groping for an answer when his phone beeps, distracting him.

"It's Bri," he tells me after glancing at the screen. "She and Deb want to know if we can meet them at Dream Cream. She says Deb can't use her mom's car, but they're willing to bike there."

A spike of alarm goes through me. "No! They shouldn't be out alone at night, not now."

"No, you're right," Liam agrees, looking even more miserable. "We could offer to pick them up, but Mom and Dad are about to leave for that thing at the Sullivans' so we won't have a car either. Crap."

"Tell Bri we can't tonight, but we'll see them at Donner's Farm tomorrow. But before then, you and I need to decide what we'll say to them."

Liam nods glumly and texts Bri back. After a second he gets her reply.

"She sounds disappointed but not mad," he tells me. "But I bet she will be tomorrow, if I say I want to break things off for her own good."

I sigh, depression settling over me like a cold blanket. "Deb will be, too. But if making them mad, even making them hate us, is the price of keeping them safe, isn't that what we should do?"

Though Liam doesn't answer, his expression makes it clear he agrees —and doesn't like it any more than I do.

Just this morning, I was looking forward to spending tons of time with Deb in the future. And tomorrow was shaping up to be a totally fabulous day.

Now I have a sick certainty that it might turn into the worst day of my life.

41

Denouement

Deb

"THIS IS GOING to be the best day ever!" Bri exclaims when we meet in my driveway after lunch to drive out to Donner's farm to meet our boyfriends.

"It will," I agree. "Let's go and get it started right away." I unlock the doors and jump behind the steering wheel.

Unlike the last time we went out there, the weather today is perfect. No ice, only a few lingering traces of snow from last week, and several degrees warmer than it's been lately. Better yet, today we should have several uninterrupted hours with our guys, first now, then again tonight. Sheer bliss.

"I'm still pinching myself," Bri says once we're on our way. "It seems so incredible that a guy as perfect as Liam could be in love with a dork like me."

With a gasp, I glance over at her. "Ooh, did he really say the L-word?"

She nods happily. "Thursday night, when we went for that walk. I was never so happy in my life."

I try not to be jealous. I *think* Lucas probably loves me, too, but he hasn't said the actual words yet. Neither have I. Tempted as I've been a few times, the thought of saying it and him *not* saying it back was too scary. Maybe today? Or tonight…?

This time there are three other cars in the gravel lot in front of the store when we reach Donner's Farm, probably because it's such a nice day for the tag-end of January.

"Looks like we won't have the place to ourselves this time," Bri observes. "But there's plenty of room to wander, so we should still be able to— Uh-oh."

At her sudden change in tone, I sharpen my gaze and see Lucas and Liam standing at the edge of the lot, wearing twin expressions of gloom.

"Uh-oh," I echo, as I park and cut the engine. "That doesn't look good. Maybe Mrs. Walsh changed her mind and laid down new rules after all, like we expected to hear Thursday night. Or worse."

We get out of the car and walk over to the boys, more apprehensive now than eager.

"Hi, guys," Bri greets them when we get close. "Um, what's wrong?"

"We, uh, need to talk," Lucas tells us, as though that's not obvious. "Let's find a spot that's a little more private."

With a strong sense of foreboding, Bri and I follow the boys down one of the paths leading away from the parking lot toward the currently-brown berry fields. I'm dying to at least hold Lucas's hand, but he doesn't offer, so I don't quite dare. I notice Liam and Bri aren't touching, either. This looks *really* bad.

Once we're well out of earshot of anyone who could possibly hear us, the boys turn to face us. Something about the way they stand almost shoulder to shoulder brings to mind the phrase "united front."

"Okay, spill." My forceful tone belies the trembling in my stomach. "Whatever bad news you have for us, spit it out."

They exchange an agonized glance with each other, then Lucas gives a little nod.

"You know how yesterday M warned us that those people who kidnapped you aren't the only ones out there who could be a threat? She's right that hearing you two know the truth about us probably scared some people, and scared people can be dangerous. Anyway, Liam and I talked it over last night and decided that the best thing we can do to keep you both safe is to..." He swallows. "To break up with you."

Bri and I just stand there for a moment, stunned. This is even worse than we expected!

Then Bri takes two quick steps to get in Liam's face. "Like hell you will," she tells him. "After you told me just the night before last that you love me? And I *know* you meant it. If this is some self-sacrificing macho crap, forget it. I won't go along with it."

Both boys look startled.

Before either can respond, I jump in. "Bri's right. We're not about to let you guys make some one-sided grand gesture that will make us all miserable, supposedly for our own good. Not a chance. Anyway," I continue when Liam starts to protest, "we're the ones who put *you* two in danger the other night, not the other way around. Those people didn't kidnap us because of *you*, but because M told us the truth about where you all came from. You guys breaking up with us won't undo that. It probably also won't do anything to make us safer."

"Of course," Bri adds with a touch of snark, "if you're worried being with us is putting *you* in danger, I guess we can't stop you from putting your own safety first."

Both boys stare at her, openmouthed.

"What? No!" Liam protests. "That's not it at all! Lucas, tell them!"

"We're only thinking of *your* safety," Lucas insists, the agony in his eyes now tempered with what might be a glimmer of hope. "We know we can't undo what M did by telling you the truth, but staying away from you might confuse any potential enemies. If that can keep you even a little bit safer—"

"I don't see why it should," I interrupt. "If we're really still targets for Martian bad guys, won't we be safer with two big, strong, Martian bodyguards? Unless you don't *want* to protect us from the next attempt...."

I hold my breath, watching Lucas's face as he struggles with conflicting emotions, weighing the logic of Bri's and my arguments. Finally, he meets my eyes, entreaty in his own.

"You don't think the risk—?"

"No. I don't." There's no compromise in my tone.

"Neither do I," Bri says just as firmly. "How can we possibly be safer *without* you than *with* you?" She reaches a tentative hand toward Liam.

He darts forward and grabs it. "Are you sure?" There's no mistaking the hope in *his* expression.

"We both are," I confirm, now holding Lucas's gaze.

The anguish in his eyes abruptly gives way to relief and he closes the distance between us, seizing both of my hands in his. At his touch, an echoing relief washes through me along with the pleasurable tingle I always get from him now.

"We thought—" he starts to say, but I go up on my toes to silence him with a quick kiss.

"I know," I tell him then. "And it was sweet of you to be willing to make yourselves miserable to protect us, but—"

"But really boneheaded." Bri finishes my sentence.

We all laugh at that, suddenly giddy at the release of tension.

"Now," I say after a moment, "how about we get started on spending our day together? I've really been looking forward to it."

Still chuckling, Lucas pulls me against his side. "You've got it. Come on."

The two of us split off from Bri and Liam to head in the opposite direction like we did Thursday night—and for the same reason. After a few minutes, Lucas and I reach a clump of trees where we're well screened from any onlookers. He gathers me into his arms and I tilt my face up to his.

For the next twenty minutes, absolutely nothing matters but Lucas. Being with Lucas. Kissing Lucas. Loving Lucas. Though we still haven't said the word, his lips make perfectly clear how he feels about me. I try my best to communicate the same to him. Words are overrated, anyway.

Finally, after an eternity that isn't nearly long enough, he raises his head with a happy sigh. "How do you manage to be so…perfect?"

Startled, I giggle. "Perfect? Hardly. Though since being with you, I feel like I might be getting a little closer. You seem to bring out the best in me."

He stares at me, suddenly thoughtful. "I could say the same about you—and it might not be just our imagination. Deb, I…I think we might be forming a bond with each other. Maybe not quite like the one M and Rigel have, but—"

"Really?" I stare back. "I've wondered about that once or twice but figured it was impossible, since I'm not even, you know, Martian."

"According to M—well, to Regent Shim, who knows a lot about this stuff—it might not be. Impossible, I mean. Though I guess time will tell, huh? Especially since I plan to spend a whole lot of it with you, for as long as you'll let me. I love you, Deb. I've been wanting to tell you for ages but never got up the nerve until now."

My breath catches in my throat, my heart feeling like it might burst from happiness. "I love you, too, Lucas. And, um, ditto."

And then we're kissing again.

After a blissful two hours wandering the grounds together, we meet back up with Bri and Liam for hot cider and crullers, just like last time. And even more than last time, we're all positively glowing with happiness.

This time when I offer to drop the boys home, they accept—then invite us inside once we get there. Mr. and Mrs. Walsh seem genuinely happy to see us, so the boys must not have shared their stupid breakup plan with their parents. I'm glad.

After another half hour or so, we leave…because Bri and I need to get home to primp for tonight's date!

⁜

In dramatic contrast to our first double date, tonight I have zero misgivings when I walk into the Lighthouse Cafe on Lucas's arm. The fact that it's not sleeting helps, but not nearly as much as the assurance that Lucas loves me, really loves me! I've never looked forward to a date this much in my life.

"You look amazing tonight," he tells me—again—when he helps me off with my coat. "That shade of blue is perfect for you. It matches your eyes."

I grin up at him. "You're looking pretty fine yourself, sir."

And he is. Almost impossibly fine, in his collared white shirt and jeans. How on Earth—or Mars, for that matter—did I ever get so lucky?

"Are you two going to sit down or what?" Liam asks from his spot at our table. "I want to order some onion rings."

That gets a laugh from all of us. Earlier today, the boys reminisced about some of their recent Earth epiphanies, including root beer and onion rings. Thanks to Bri and me.

We've munched our way through more than half of the onion rings when the band starts playing—a slow song. Lucas looks questioningly at me.

"Dance with me?"

Surprised but even more pleased, I nod and let him lead me to the tiny dance floor. "I thought you didn't much like to dance," I say as he puts his arms around me.

"I never used to. In fact, I almost never had before the Winter Formal. And both there and our last time here, dancing with you was way too frustrating for me to really enjoy it. Because I didn't dare do what I was dying to do both evenings—pull you close. Like this."

296

He demonstrates by pressing me tight against him. Needless to say, I don't resist.

"At the time," he continues, "I was convinced giving in to what I wanted so much would be a very bad idea. But now it seems like the absolute best idea ever. I love you, Deb."

Hearing it again is almost as wonderful as hearing it for the first time this afternoon. "I love you, too, Lucas. Now and forever."

"Now and forever," he repeats. "I like the sound of that."

Pulling me even closer, he lowers his head to kiss me, right on the dance floor. Though I've felt insignificant much of my life, right at this moment I feel like the most important person in the world. Because to Lucas, I know that I am.

A Brief History of Nuath
AN INTRODUCTION TO NUATHAN HISTORY,
85TH EDITION

(BASIC CURRICULUM TEXT—USE IN PLACE OF PREVIOUS
EDITIONS)

Overview

Nuath's true origins have been lost in the mists of time. However, it is
generally believed that nearly three thousand years ago, a technologically advanced alien race created the underground cavern on Mars with
its Earth-like environment. The aliens then transplanted the inhabitants
of a small Earth village to this cavern, in order to conduct genetic and
social experiments on their captives. As the human population increased
from a few hundred to many thousands, the habitat was gradually
expanded to its present size. Then, approximately one thousand years
after establishing this underground Martian laboratory, the aliens
departed for reasons unknown, leaving no record of their nature or their
future plans.

Without their alien overlords, the abandoned community, by then
known as Nuath, continued to evolve on its own. By necessity, a system
of government emerged, the earliest leaders chosen from among the
most gifted colonists. This led to the formation of the first *fine,* or bloodline, which divided a few generations later into the Royal and Science
fines. Most of Nuath's governing body is still drawn from those two
groups. Meanwhile, increasing specialization of various skill-sets led to

the rise of numerous other *fines*. There are currently no fewer than ten major *fines*, most further divided into several sub-*fines*.

As the colonists learned to use and adapt technology left behind by their alien abductors, they were able to advance scientifically to the point of building and launching spacecraft of their own. 523 years ago, under Sovereign Arturo, Nuathans first visited their nearest neighbor, Earth, and discovered it was their planet of origin. More expeditions followed, with small groups of Nuathans occasionally emigrating to Earth despite the harsher conditions found there. Those earliest *Echtrans*, or expatriate Martians, are believed to have sparked Earth's Renaissance period. To facilitate communication, Nuath eventually adopted the calendar and measurement system of Earth's Ireland, home of the first real *Echtran* outpost. Because the planet remained socially and technologically backward by Nuathan standards, it was early decided to keep emigrants' origins and abilities secret from their Earth (or *Duchas*) neighbors.

Safely concealed on Mars, Nuath remained peaceful and prosperous, if not perfect, until fifteen years ago, when the ambitious upstart Faxon began sowing discord, stirring up resentment in the less-prestigious *fines* against the Royals and Scientists. Over a two-year period, Faxon gathered enough support to stage a coup, deposing and then assassinating Sovereign Leontine and his wife. A general purge of the Royal bloodline followed, though some survived Faxon's depredations by fleeing to Earth. Among those were Leontine's son, Mikal, with his wife and infant daughter.

The majority of Nuathans, even those who had helped Faxon rise to power, were horrified by his excesses. As his support waned, Faxon resorted to intimidation and repression to maintain control. Fearing Mikal and his family could become a rallying point for the fledgling Resistance movement, Faxon sent a few still-loyal adherents to Earth with orders to eliminate them. When word came back that the last of the Sovereign line had been killed, most Nuathans were thrown into despair. Rebellion having been largely bred out of the early colonists, the Resistance faltered and would have failed but for the efforts of a few Royals, most notably the O'Gara family, who obscured their origins to remain on Mars and rally their people's spirits, restoring to them a measure of hope.

This hope was greatly bolstered when Nuathans learned that the last of Sovereign Leontine's line had not, in fact, perished. The news that his granddaughter, Princess Emileia, had been discovered alive on Earth galvanized the Resistance, allowing them to finally cast off the yoke of Faxon's oppression and remove him from power.

Afterward, Nuathan society began to rebuild itself, striving for an eventual return to its former prosperity and security. This was helped along by the return of the Princess, shortly thereafter Acclaimed Sovereign Emileia. Nuath's recovery now continues under Regent Shim, only slightly hampered by the recent discovery of the colony's near-depleted power reserves.

Though Nuath's Scientists are currently working to extend the power supply, the situation has necessitated accelerated emigration of the colony's populace to Earth, to conserve resources. To encourage voluntary emigration, Sovereign Emileia herself has returned to Earth, where she and the *Echtran* Council are overseeing the resettlement of those who heeded the call to relocate for the good of Nuath.

It must be noted that shortly after the Sovereign's return to Earth, our original alien founders returned to this solar system, with the apparent intent of disabling all of Earth's technology. Thankfully, that catastrophe was averted by a heroic collaboration between *Echtran* Scientists and Sovereign Emileia. It is hoped no further interference by those aliens, now known as the Grentl, will hamper the progress Nuath's people are now making, both on Mars and on Earth.

A Martian Glossary

Acclamation: Nuathan electoral process whereby citizens indicate approval or disapproval of a proposed Sovereign.

agoid (AH-gyoyd): organized protest; opposition.

aitlean (ayt-lee-AN): airplane; primitive aircraft used extensively by Duchas; Earth's primary means of intercontinental travel.

Arregaith (ah-ree-GAYTH) (pop. 1,413): town in southeastern Nuath containing spaceport and supporting industries.

ateamh rioga (ah-TEV ree-OH-gah): a persuasive ability shared by some of Royal blood.

athshondis (ath-SHON-dis): resonance.

Bailerealta (BAY-luh-ree-AL-tuh) (pop. 412): village on the western coast of Ireland, est. circa 1575, populated entirely by Echtrans.

Ballytadhg (BAH-lee-teeg) (pop. 1,106): east-central Nuathan village known for Arts fine and industry.

beidan (BID-den): gossip; scandal.

brath: Martian "vibe" detectable by other Martians.

breag fionn (brag fin): discovery of a lie; detection of falsehood.

caidpel (KAYD-pel): predominant sport in Nuath combining elements of the Irish sports of hurling and Gaelic football.

camastall (KAM-uh-stahl): deception; deceit; falsification.

cannarc (KAN-ark): rebellion; mutiny; resistance.

chabhil (KAB-vil): negotiation; debate; (occ.) ultimatum.

chas pell (CHASS-pel): a ball game played by Nuathan children, nearly identical to the Earth sport of basketball.

Cheile Rioga (KEE-luh ree-OH-gah): Royal Consort.

chomhaerle (KOM-ahr-lee): advice; counsel.

Chomseireach (kom-SAY-rik): Handmaid; lady's maid, chaperone and companion to Princess or (female) Sovereign.

Cinnwund Rioga (KIN-wund ree-OH-gah): Royal Destiny.

cloigh (kloy): to overpower or overthrow; defeat; subdue.

comhriteach (KOM-ree-teek): compromise.

cosc damaste (kosk DAHM-uh-stay): damage control.

coslacht (ko-SLACT): appearance; impression; influence.

Costanta (ko-STAHN-tuh): Bodyguard assigned to protect the Sovereign or other members of the Royal family.

dabhal (DOB-uhl) (*slang*): damn, damned.

dhualgis cumann (doo-AHL-gus koo-MAHN): benevolent duty; royal obligation.

dilsacht (DIL-sok): loyalty; allegiance.

doolegar (DOO-luh-gahr): despondency; depression.

Duchas (doo-kas): normal Earth humans.

Dun Cloch (Dun Klok) (pop. 1,247+): largest *Echtran* compound on Earth, founded 1933 in north-central Montana. Main production hub for Martian technology.

ealu (AY-loo): to break free, escape, or elope.

Echtran (ek-tran): person of Martian birth or descent living on Earth; expatriate.

Echtran Council: governing body for expatriate Martians living on Earth.

Echtran Enquirer: unofficial news source for expatriate Martians on Earth. Tends toward the sensationalistic.

edhmiu (FEY-mew): implementation; application.

efrin (EF-rin): Hell; used as a mild curse.

Emileia (em-i-LAY-ah): current *Thiarna* (Sovereign), granddaughter to Sovereign Leontine; sole heir to the Nuathan monarchy.

fasneis (FAHSH-ness): information; intelligence.

fine (feen): genetically related subsets of the Martian population, each with certain attributes.

flach (flok) (*slang*): socially unacceptable swear word.

foare rioga (fair ree-OH-gah): ancient, traditional syringe used for blood draw to verify Sovereign lineage.

gaiscigh (GAH-sheeg): heroism; act of extreme bravery.

giola uresal (gee-OH-la OO-ree-sal): menial servant.

Glenamuir (GLEN-uh-mer) (pop. 898): largely Agricultural village in northwest Nuath; longtime home of O'Gara family during Faxon's reign.

graell (grayl): intense emotional and physical bond believed mythical by most Martians.

grechain (gree-SHAYN): Nuathan information network, both personal and mass-media; news channels within the greater *grechain*.

Grentl (GREN-tuhl): advanced non-human alien race from an unknown part of the galaxy; likely founders of underground human colony on Mars.

hiarmarti (hee-ehr-MAHR-tee): consequences; results; price to be paid.

Hollydoon (HOL-ly doon) (pop. 1,677): largely Agricultural village in northwest Nuath; suffered particularly harsh ravages by Faxon's forces.

Horizon: one of four Nuathan transport ships traveling between Mars and Earth during biennial launch windows.

Insealbau (in-SALL-baw): Installation, as of Nuathan Sovereign.

Installation: Nuathan ceremony signifying a new Sovereign's ascension to power.

Jewel (pop. 5,013): town in north-central Indiana noted for corn, artisan jewelry and annual Jewel Jewelry Festival.

Launch window: period occurring approximately every 26 Earth months and lasting approximately four months, when the distance between Earth and Mars is small enough to allow travel between the two planets.

MARSTAR: official channel for communication from Echtran Council to expatriate Martians living on Earth, generally in the form of MARSTAR Bulletins.

Miochan (mee-OH-kan): healing; curing; a major fine.

moill (mahl): delay; postponement.

naesc geaniteach (nesh gan-it-EEK) genetic affinity.

nimhic (NIV-ik): antidote; cure.

Nuath (NOO-ath): underground human colony on Mars.

omni: a small, multifunctional device developed on Mars.

orinacht (OR-in-ott): propriety; seemliness.

pleanal (plenn-UHL): advance planning; scheming.

Populists: a minority movement among Nuathans advocating equal rights and representation for all fines. (Sometimes referred to as "Anti-Royals.")

probalreith (pro-BAHL-reth): opinion poll; public opinion.
probleid (pruh-BLAYD): privilege; status.
Quintessence (kwin-TESS-ens): one of four passenger vessels used to transport Nuathans between Earth and Mars.
Rigel (RY-jel): a blue supergiant star, approximately 860 light years from Earth, located in the constellation Orion; 7th brightest star visible from Earth, its brightness (or apparent magnitude) making it an important navigational star; Rigel Stuart, son of Ariel and Van Stuart.
rundacht (ROON-dahct): extreme secrecy; classified information.
scar a cheila (scar ah KAY-lah): separated; torn asunder; ripped apart.
Scriosath: memory erasure, the most complete being the tabula rasa or "blank slate," the highest form of official punishment.
Sean O'Gara (shawn oh-GAYR-uh): son of Quinn and Lily O'Gara; destined Cheile Rioga (Royal Consort) to Princess Emileia.
shilcloas (shil-CLO-ahs): hearing another's thoughts; telepathy.
sochar (SO-kar): Nuathan credits, used to purchase anything beyond provided necessities.
spiare (spee-AH-ray): spy; snoop.
stochail (sto-KAYL): preparation, as for a battle or journey.
streach suas (stretch SOO-ahs): resist oppression; underground resistance.
taghal ardus (TAHG-ul ar-DOOS): first touch causing a "tingle" between opposite sex teens, rarely repeated on second touch.
taigde (TAG-duh): research; records.
Teachneaglis (TAK-nee-glish): small minority of Nuathans and Echtrans who prefer to do without most modern advancements, primarily found in the villages of Bailerealta on Earth, and Keary and Eriu on Mars.
teachneoc (TEEK-nee-ok): technology; gadgetry.
teachtok (TEEK-tok) (*slang*): non-omni phone.
threoirach (TRO-rok): instruction; orientation; guidance.
tinneas (TIN-es): physical illness. Rare among Martians except in the very elderly.
toachai (TO-uh-kay): future; destiny.
triail (tree-AYL): test or audition; ordeal by trial.
Tullymayne (TULL-ee-mayn) (pop. 1,993): town in southeastern Nuath containing main transportation hub and supporting industries.
twilly: obnoxious person; jerk.
udaris thusmithoir (oo-DARE-is thoos-MITH-er): parental authority.
unbaen: dictator

Acknowledgments

Several people helped to make this book much better than it would otherwise be: my wonderful team of Beta Readers (you know who you are!); my local author critique group—Leigh Court, Rita Boehm and Shirley Jones; Aubrey, who shared valuable insights into Bri's character and concerns as a biracial teen growing up in the American midwest; Mary Strand and Douglas Metcalf, who helped with the basketball details; and most especially my daughter, Bethany Barber, who has long been my "Alpha Reader." Now Bethany joins me as a co-author, as she wrote Bri's chapters for this book and had a hand in my final revisions. Every one of you played an important role in helping *Unraveling the Stars* become the best book I'm currently capable of writing. Thank you!

About the Author

A New York Times and USA Today bestselling author, Brenda writes novels of sparkling romantic adventure spanning Regency England, Americana, contemporary teen science fiction and more. Which ever you pick up, you'll find excitement, romance and, always, an uplifting happy ending. In addition to writing, Brenda is passionate about embracing life to the fullest. She enjoys scuba diving (she has over 60 dives to her credit), Taekwondo (where she's currently working toward her 4th degree black belt), hiking, traveling…and reading, of course!

For a free Starstruck short story and the earliest news about Brenda Hiatt's books, subscribe to her newsletter at: brendahiatt.com/subscribe

Connect with Brenda at:
brendahiatt.com